INNOCENCE PROVES NOTHING

As SHE LED the way towards the glow in the distance, Keira felt her senses expanding as they always did on a hunt, taking in every detail of her surroundings. This section of the ship was clearly little used, the scent of dust and decay in her nostrils enough to tell her that, even if the dilapidated state of the walls and the malfunctioning luminators hadn't already made it perfectly obvious.

People definitely came through here though, and in considerable numbers, there could be little doubt of that: the layer of dust and grime underfoot had been disturbed in the middle of the corridor, drifting more thickly along the edges and in the corners. Too many feet had passed for her to be able to estimate numbers and frequency, the prints overlapping and obliterating one another, but two parallel lines were still visible on the top layer, where the cart she pursued had passed mere moments before.

She smiled eagerly, anticipating the bloodshed to come. The grace of the Emperor still glowed within her, the deaths of the sinners she'd just sent to His judgement a sacrament she burned to repeat.

More Sandy Mitchell from the Black Library

• DARK HERESY •

SCOURGE THE HERETIC

• CIAPHAS CAIN •

HERO OF THE IMPERIUM
(Contains the first three Ciaphas Cain novels –
For the Emperor, Caves of Ice and
The Traitor's Hand)
Book 4 – DEATH OR GLORY
Book 5 – DUTY CALLS
Book 6 – CAIN'S LAST STAND

A WARHAMMER 40,000 NOVEL

Dark Heresy

INNOCENCE PROVES NOTHING

Sandy Mitchell

For Tony, for use of the office.

A BLACK LIBRARY PUBLICATION

First published in Great Britain in 2009 by
BL Publishing,
Games Workshop Ltd.,
Willow Road, Nottingham,
NG7 2WS, UK.

10 9 8 7 6 5 4 3 2

Cover illustration by Clint Langley.
Calixis Sector map by Andy Law.

A CIP record for this book is available from the British Library.

US ISBN 13: 978 1 84416 676 3

Distributed in the US by Simon & Schuster
1230 Avenue of the Americas, New York, NY 10020, US.

See the Black Library on the Internet at
www.blacklibrary.com

Find out more about Games Workshop
and the world of Warhammer 40,000 at
www.games-workshop.com

Printed and bound in the US.

IT IS THE 41st millennium. For more than a hundred centuries the Emperor has sat immobile on the Golden Throne of Earth. He is the master of mankind by the will of the gods, and master of a million worlds by the might of his inexhaustible armies. He is a rotting carcass writhing invisibly with power from the Dark Age of Technology. He is the Carrion Lord of the Imperium for whom a thousand souls are sacrificed every day, so that he may never truly die.

YET EVEN IN his deathless state, the Emperor continues his eternal vigilance. Mighty battlefleets cross the daemon-infested miasma of the warp, the only route between distant stars, their way lit by the Astronomican, the psychic manifestation of the Emperor's will. Vast armies give battle in His name on uncounted worlds. Greatest amongst his soldiers are the Adeptus Astartes, the Space Marines, bioengineered super-warriors. Their comrades in arms are legion: the Imperial Guard and countless planetary defence forces, the ever-vigilant Inquisition and the tech-priests of the Adeptus Mechanicus to name only a few. But for all their multitudes, they are barely enough to hold off the ever-present threat from aliens, heretics, mutants – and worse.

TO BE A man in such times is to be one amongst untold billions. It is to live in the cruellest and most bloody regime imaginable. These are the tales of those times. Forget the power of technology and science, for so much has been forgotten, never to be relearned. Forget the promise of progress and understanding, for in the grim dark future there is only war. There is no peace amongst the stars, only an eternity of carnage and slaughter, and the laughter of thirsting gods.

THE HALO STARS

DRUSUS MARCHES

Sentinel

Pulsara

Settlement 228

The Lathes

Landunder

Obol Quill

MALFI

Dusk

MALFEAN SUB-SECTOR

Sinophia AG 218

TRANCH

VAXANIDE

SEPHERIS SECUNDUS

THE PERIPHERY

Gauf Magna

Naif

Meridian Saturn

1968

Fides non fferus. Accuum, Peneticus

Kuinward

Morior in Suus muneris est scio eternus bita

PROLOGUE

The Gorgonid Mine, Sepheris Secundus, Calixis Sector
107.993.M41

DESPERATE MEN TAKE risks, and there are few people in the galaxy more desperate than those fleeing the wrath of the Inquisition. Meres Tancred ran, not daring to look behind him, heedless of the unforgiving stones wreaking irreparable havoc on boots which had cost him as much as the annual upkeep of a dozen serfs. The breath rasped in his throat, and he suppressed the urge to cough as the wind shifted, bringing with it the stench of smoke from the burning mansion in the distance.

'What happened?' one of his companions asked plaintively, and Tancred shook his head, almost grateful that his lack of fitness had rendered him virtually incapable of speech. The trouble with being a seer, apart from the constant fear of discovery, was that the handful of people privy to your secret expected you to have all the answers.

'Inquisition,' he gasped out after a moment, slowing a little as the three of them began to approach the main workings of the mine. That much was obvious, even to someone without his gift; the shuttles which had swooped over their heads as they'd approached Adrin's mansion, fortuitously late for the gathering he'd called, had been devoid of insignia, but could have come from nowhere else. The Adeptus Arbites garrison at the Isolarium relied on tracked, armoured behemoths to get around, on the rare occasions civil unrest provoked their direct intervention by becoming severe enough to threaten the smooth flow of tithes to the Imperium, and the Royal Scourges had neither the training nor the resources to mount an airborne assault. That left the survivors of the Inquisition facility in the Forest of Sorrows, which the allies of the group Tancred served had so recently raided, rescuing untold numbers of innocent victims from the terror of the Black Ships in the process.

The psyker's jaw clenched angrily as he considered that. He'd hoped the off-world mercenaries had wiped them out completely, but in his heart of hearts had always known that was unlikely. The agents of the Throne were formidable warriors, and even the exotic weaponry the Faxlignae had somehow been able to scavenge from alien sources wouldn't even the odds to that extent.

'What do we do now?' his interlocutor asked, a shrill edge of panic beginning to enter his voice, and Tancred forced himself to sound confident.

'We escape,' he answered briefly, raising his voice to be heard over the scream of an ore shuttle dusting off from one of the pads scattered around the perimeter of the vast pit. They arrived and departed every few minutes, feeding the insatiable maws of the ore barges which hung in orbit above Sepheris Secundus like flies around carrion, and as his eyes turned to follow it, he felt the first faint stirrings of hope. 'On one of those.'

'Escape where?' the third man asked, speaking for the first time; Tancred didn't know him well, but remembered his name was Vogen, and that he was a pyrokine, like the majority of psykers in the coven. 'They'll know who we are as soon as they begin interrogating the others. Nowhere on Sepheris Secundus will be safe.'

'Then we'll have to go off-world,' Tancred said, trying not to let the flicker of apprehension he felt at the idea show on his face. He glanced up involuntarily, as if the constellation of ore barges hanging above their heads would somehow become visible through the constant covering of wind-blown cloud.

'Off-world?' Drusus, the first of the group to have spoken, clearly wasn't happy at the prospect of being uprooted from everything he knew. 'But we can't! Who knows what's out there?'

'I know what's back there,' Tancred said, with a brief glance at the crimson glow behind them. 'And I'd rather leave on an ore barge than a Black Ship.'

'Me too,' Vogen agreed. If Drusus still felt disposed to argue the point he kept his opinion to himself, and trotted in the wake of his companions without another word. 'Which way now?'

'Follow the road,' Tancred replied, raising his voice a little to carry over the clamour of the traffic. Even at this hour heavily laden lorries still rumbled along the hard-packed surface, the beams of their headlights wavering randomly with every jolt, the Waymakers perched precariously on their ramshackle platforms atop the cab roofs warning of their approach with trumpets and drums. The drivers seemed too intent on keeping their promethium-farting charges under control to pay any attention to the trio of fugitives hurrying along the fringe of the carriageway, but Tancred kept a wary eye out for any signs of interest among the scattering of serfs on foot. To his relief none of them seemed willing to meet his eye, their innate deference to anyone clearly of noble status enough to blunt their curiosity; and he would have bet a considerable sum of money that most were on clandestine business of their own in any case, this long after nightfall.

His advice turned out to be sound, to his own vague surprise, and he breathed silent thanks to whichever of the Powers was guiding his footsteps. After less than a kilometre they came across a landing pad, little more than a patch of roughly levelled ground surrounded by heaps of ore, where teams of sweating serfs shovelled lumps of rock onto a rattling conveyor belt by the light of a portable luminator. The other end terminated in the hold of a grounded shuttle, which looked almost full by the faint gleam of citylight falling from the metropolis above, and the flickering drumfires which marked the perimeter of the cleared zone.

'How do we get aboard?' Vogen asked, as they slunk into the welcoming shadows between the ore heaps.

Tancred considered the matter. They might be able to board the conveyor unseen outside the narrow cone of arclight, but that would be chancy at best, and he didn't much care for the prospect of being tipped onto a heap of jagged rocks at the other end in any case. The lip of the loading hatch was too high to scramble up, and even if it wasn't, attempting to do so was bound to attract attention. Cautiously, he reached out with his mind, feeling the faint echo of consciousness on the other side of the looming vessel, then narrowed his focus, skimming surface thoughts like a chef lifting fat from the top of a stockpot.

Swiving cold. Miserable mudball. No place for a voider…

Tancred smiled, and led the way round the vast bulk of the heavy lifter. It was bigger than he'd realised, the size of a small building, and he found it difficult to believe something that huge could ever fly, let alone bear them to a starship in safety. But the Powers provided, if you trusted their guidance.

'What do you want?' a voice asked from the darkness. It was surly, devoid of the deference a lifetime of privilege had conditioned Tancred to expect, and he felt a surge of irrational resentment. The tip of a lho-stick glowed red in the gloom, and after a moment he began to discern a blacker silhouette behind it. The man's mind became sharper, boredom and irritation giving way to sullen hostility.

'We need transport,' Drusus blurted out. 'Right away. We can pay…'

'I'm sure you can,' the pilot said, his thoughts becoming clearer by the second. *Arrogant little nosewipe. Typical mudball aristo, thinks the galaxy revolves around his arse.* The lho-stick fell, and was ground underfoot. 'Now swive off, I'm busy.'

Tancred wasn't sure where the surge of anger came from initially; the shock of a peasant refusing to do what was required of him, irritation with Drusus for provoking the man unnecessarily, or perhaps it was a gift from the Powers. Whatever its origin, it swept through his mind like a riptide, focusing his will into a white-hot dagger, which he drove into the diffuse consciousness ahead of him. The pilot staggered, with an inarticulate cry, then straightened slowly.

'What did you do?' Vogen asked warily.

'What I had to,' Tancred answered brusquely, his attention focused almost entirely on maintaining his connection with the pilot's mind. *Fly us out of here. Find us a starship.*

He wasn't sure how long he could keep this up; the strain was incredible, and he could feel his victim's consciousness roiling like a thundercloud, dissipating slowly with the effort of trying to disentangle itself from his own. If he didn't break the connection soon, one of them would die, he could feel it. Maybe even both of them.

But desperate men take risks, and there are few people in the galaxy more desperate than a man on the run from the Inquisition. He held on to the squirming mind in front of him, and began to climb the boarding ramp in the wake of his unwilling puppet, hoping he'd have enough time to complete what he'd so precipitately begun.

ONE

Icenholm, Sepheris Secundus
108.993.M41

'ANY IDEA WHAT it is yet?' Drake asked, pausing on his way to the breakfast table to converse briefly with Vex. The former Guardsman was ravenously hungry, a circumstance which had driven him from his bed shortly after dawn, and he'd been vaguely surprised to find any of the other Angelae up and about at this hour. Nevertheless, the techpriest was sitting in his usual corner of the villa's living room, gazing thoughtfully at the sliver of strange, ivory-like material he and Horst had recovered from the depths of the Fathomsound mine. Perhaps, Drake thought, he hadn't been to bed at all: acolytes of the Adeptus Mechanicus tended not to bother with mere human weaknesses like sleep, if they could wire themselves up to avoid them.

'None at all,' Vex replied politely, his tone so even that Drake wasn't sure if he appreciated the courtesy of being spoken to, or resented the interruption. 'If it's as ancient as it appears, however, it's quite likely to predate any archives on Sepheris Secundus.'

'Perhaps you'll have better luck on Scintilla, then,' Drake said, hoping he'd managed to sound sufficiently matter-of-fact about the disturbing notion that he'd shortly be treading the soil of another world. Well, that was what he'd joined the Imperial Guard for, he reminded himself, to get off the planet of his birth and carve a new destiny among the stars, untrammelled by the petty snobberies and rigid social hierarchy of his home world. He was undoubtedly doing that, though hardly in the manner he'd expected when he'd thumbprinted the enlistment papers.

'Perhaps.' Vex nodded thoughtfully. 'The archives at the Tricorn are an unrivalled depository of arcane informa-tion, at least within the Calixis Sector. Not to mention the Adeptus Mechanicus shrines in the main hives, which also boast extensive technotheological libraries.'

'Best of luck, then,' Drake said, moving on to the side table. Despite the hour, the servants had done their job with their usual unobtrusive efficiency, and an array of chafing dishes was already laid out, leaking appetising aromas. He lifted a couple of lids, his mouth flooding with saliva, and considered their contents. 'Would you care for some breakfast?'

'Just a little recaf,' Vex said, 'if you'd be so kind.'

Drake suspected the tech-priest had simply accepted the offer out of politeness, but poured the bitter drink anyway, then a second one for himself. The sun wasn't visible yet, glowing wanly through the perpetually over-cast skies, but the reflectors in the surrounding mountain range were already concentrating what little radiance they could collect onto the glittering city of glass sus-pended between the peaks. The effect was breathtaking, like a spider's web encrusted with frost, enlarged and folded over on itself as intricately as the steel of a master-crafted swordblade, and Drake moved towards the terrace, determined to enjoy the sights of his home world while he still had the chance. For a moment, moved by idle curiosity, he glanced down towards the squalor of the Gorgonid mine, kilometres below, hoping to catch a glimpse of the orange glow which marked the site of the mansion he and the others had raided a few hours before, but could see no sign of it; either the conflagration had burned itself out by now, which hardly seemed likely, or the bulk of the city's superstructure hid the smouldering ruins from view.

'Couldn't sleep either?' A fresh voice broke into his reverie, feminine, and uncharacteristically cheerful. Keira joined him on the terrace, her yellow silk robe clinging tightly to her well-muscled body as the wind pressed the fabric against her, as oblivious to the early morning chill as the native Secundan. Her purple hair was untidy, still swept back from her forehead with the scarlet bandana she'd worn the previous night.

For a moment Drake considered reminding her that the servants would be scandalised to see her wearing red, the colour reserved for royalty on Sepheris Secundus, then decided against it. She'd undoubtedly take offence, and annoying her wasn't a particularly safe thing to do. Besides, the sight of a cheerful Keira was an unexpected novelty, and one he felt like enjoying for a while longer. So he shook his head instead.

'Still a bit keyed up after last night, I suppose.'

'That's the grace of the Emperor,' Keira said, her face preternaturally flushed, and a faraway look in her eye. 'We're still suffused with it, after sending so many heretics to His judgement.'

Drake nodded slowly, and sipped at his recaf. It sounded more like the residual adrenaline sloshing around their systems to him, but he'd gathered that Keira's Redemptionist faith was important to her, and that slaughtering the Emperor's enemies played a large part in her devotions. Another reason not to give the young assassin a reason to dislike him: if she took it into her head that he was just another sinner to be purged, even his status as a provisional member of the Angelae Carolus might not be enough to deflect her wrath. 'That must be why I'm so hungry,' he said, regretting the remark as soon as he'd said it.

Keira seemed to think the point a reasonable one, though, as she simply nodded, joining Drake at a small table in a corner of the terrace, out of the prevailing wind, its surface inlaid with a mosaic of coloured glass forming the crest of the minor noble house from which the villa had been rented. She nodded at the former Guardsman's heaped plate. 'If you've got any favourite local dishes, you'd better enjoy them while you can.'

'We're leaving soon, then,' Drake said, trying to ignore the shiver of apprehension which accompanied the thought.

The young assassin nodded. 'This evening. No point in letting the trail grow cold.'

'Quite,' Drake agreed, trying to hide his unease at the sudden realisation that he'd be transiting the warp before nightfall, and he might never see the city of his birth again. 'If Vos and Elyra need backup when they get to Scintilla...'

'They'll have it,' Keira told him, with quiet assurance. 'The inquisitor will be there well before their ship arrives, and he'll make all the necessary arrangements. They'll be as safe as if the Emperor Himself was walking beside them.'

'That's reassuring,' Drake said. Keira knew their patron far better than he did, and her confidence in him was heartening, but his best friend and the sanctioned psyker he was guarding had a long way to go before they arrived in the Scintilla System, and a lot could still go wrong before they made it somewhere Inquisitor Finurbi could provide some discreet assistance if they ran into trouble. 'When do we leave?'

'You'll have time to pack, if that's what's worrying you,' Keira said. 'Our ship won't be leaving orbit for hours yet.'

'That seems a long time to wait,' Drake said, warming his hands round the recaf mug. 'If we're going to beat the *Ursus Innare* to Scintilla, shouldn't we leave as soon as possible?'

'Don't worry, we will,' a new voice chimed in. Drake turned in his seat to see Mordechai Horst, the leader of the Angelae cell, leaning against the doorframe. As ever, it seemed, only Drake, who had grown up in Icenholm, and Keira, born and raised on the belly of Ambulon, the fabled walking city on Scintilla, were completely comfortable out here on the terrace, so close to the vertiginous drop on the other side of the balustrade. 'It's just an ore scow, so they'll need to drop back into real space more often than we will to correct their course. And every time they do that, they'll lose a little more of their lead.'

Keira glanced up, colouring slightly as she registered Horst's presence, before relaxing into an elaborately casual pose, while Horst fixed his gaze about a centimetre above her left shoulder. So, they were both still trying to pretend they didn't feel the way they obviously did about one another; Drake suppressed a wry smile, and did his best to keep his mind on the business at hand, instead of the unintended entertainment.

Keira nodded in agreement. 'Charter vessels take far fewer hops, so we'll be there in half the time.'

'Something of an exaggeration,' Vex put in, glancing up from the sheaf of handwritten papers he'd recovered from the heretic cell they'd raided the previous night. The recaf he'd requested was cooling untouched beside him, Drake noticed, which hardly came as a surprise. 'But we should still arrive ahead of them, if the warp currents are favourable.'

'You've booked us on a Chartist ship?' Drake asked, his apprehension growing by the minute. There was only one such vessel in orbit he knew about, its arrival heralded by rumour and gossip as always.

Horst nodded. 'The *Misericord*.' He glanced at Drake, visibly surprised by the Guardsman's reaction. 'Is something the matter?'

'It's a jinx ship,' Drake said. 'Brings bad luck wherever she goes.'

Horst and Keira glanced at one another, finally making eye contact, then turned back to Drake with almost identical expressions of tolerant amusement.

'It's just a ship,' Keira said.

'It's more than that,' Drake insisted. 'The last time she put in here we had the serf riots, and the time before that there was the mirepox outbreak, and back in 989 two ore barges collided in low orbit just after she came out of warp; they both went down, and one of them took out a whole village when it hit. The *Misericord's* a jinx all right.'

'And bad stuff never happens when she's not in-system, does it?' Keira asked, sceptically.

Drake shook his head. 'Of course it does. But it's always worse when she's here. Look what happened this time, daemons and everything.'

'He might just have a point,' Keira said slowly, her assurance beginning to waver a little.

Horst shrugged. 'Even if he does, we're still boarding her. It's our duty.' He smiled, a little thinly. 'Besides, we're on a mission for the Emperor. I can't see Him letting a bit of bad luck get in our way.'

'No, of course not,' Keira agreed, looking a great deal happier.

Drake took another slug of his recaf, which had begun to grow tepid, and wished he could share her confidence.

The *Ursus Innare*, the Warp, Date and Time Meaningless

VOS KYRLOCK STIRRED, and woke in hell. Quite literally, he thought fleetingly; beyond the walls of the cargo hold lay the realm of daemons and worse, the Dark Gods themselves, with nothing but the psychic shields and the sigils of warding etched into the battered hull to protect the fragile bubble of reality which cocooned them all. Every now and again the metal groaned, responding to the subtle stresses of the engines and the megatonnes of ore contained within the storage bins; every time it did so he started involuntarily, picturing some malign horror scrabbling at the hull, intent on devouring the souls inside.

'You'll drive yourself mad, thinking like that,' Elyra said, her pale face and blonde hair tinted orange by the flickering fires which lit the vast, shadowed space of the hold they occupied, supplementing the wan and erratic glow of the handful of luminators suspended from the ceiling, between the mouths of the chutes down which the ore had been dumped from the hangar bays above. At least the group of fugitives they'd joined had been allowed to disembark before the hatches in the floors of the shuttles had been opened, pitching their contents down into the darkness below; knowing the kind of people behind the smuggling racket, Kyrlock wouldn't have been all that surprised if their human cargoes had been dispatched the same way. Beneath each chute the surrounding rock rose in ragged hillocks, obscuring the metal horizon of the bulkhead walls, but he could still see around a dozen other fires from here, each one marking the location of a different group of ragged and desperate refugees, united by little more than a greater distrust of all the rest. It was like a miniature version of the Tumble, the lawless sprawl of slag heaps where the underworlds of Icenholm and the Gorgonid transacted their business, he thought, gangers and all, just scooped up and swallowed whole by the starship.

Then the import of Elyra's words hit him, and he felt a shiver of pure dread rattle his bones. Elyra was a firestarter, not a telepath: if she could suddenly read his mind, the influence of the warp must be leaking in here somehow, changing her, changing them all...

Elyra grinned, although in a manner Kyrlock found far from reassuring. 'All I'm reading is your body language,' she said, a faint air of disdain suffusing the words. The persona she'd assumed in order to infiltrate the Shadow Franchise's people-smuggling ring, and the rogue psyker underground which was using it for purposes of their own, was that of a self-centred sociopath; after years of service to the Inquisition, she wasn't about to break that cover now with an inappropriate show of concern for someone else. This was the best she could do, given their chances of being overheard, and Kyrlock appreciated the subtle gesture. 'I've seen it before in first-time warp hoppers, fretting about where they are and what's out there.' She picked up a lump of shale, and threw it with sudden vigour, and surprising accuracy; its trajectory terminated with a rattle and a rodentine squeal, followed by panic-stricken scurrying in the surrounding darkness. 'This is solid, and this is real, Vos. You'd do better worrying about the rockrats snacking on your toes while you're asleep.'

'Ew. Thanks for that cheerful thought.' Zusen, one of the trio of juvie wyrds travelling with them, sat up, and huddled her bedroll a little more tightly around herself. As usual she'd settled down to sleep close to Kyrlock, seeming to find his presence reassuring, and, as usual, the Guardsman tried to hide his unease at her proximity with a friendly smile. Elyra had made it perfectly clear that they needed to keep on the right side of the juvies to follow them through the next link in the chain, and find out who was offering rogue psykers a refuge; not just on Sepheris Secundus, but, potentially, across the entire sector.

'You're welcome,' Elyra said flatly.

'It's good advice,' Kyrlock said, grateful to have something else to focus on, even if it was just the skinny little wyrd who followed him around like a lost puppy. Not that he wouldn't normally have enjoyed a young woman paying him so much attention, even if he did prefer them with a bit more meat on their bones; but he couldn't shake the knowledge of what she was, even for a moment, and she flat out gave him the creeps. Elyra was a psyker too, of course, but she was sanctioned, her powers in the service of the Emperor, and he'd learned to trust her during the earlier stages of their mission together. 'Better make sure you sleep with your boots on; although that won't help against a pack of them. If you get swarmed, they can strip you to the bone in a matter of minutes.' He threw another chip of greasy shale on the fire, watching carefully until the heat sweated the pitch out, and it ignited, hissing gently. The fire was their lifeline. If it ever went out, the rockrats would move in, and he didn't want to think about what that would mean.

'I'm keeping my boots on anyway,' Zusen told him, appearing like a wan little ghost in the flickering half-light. 'Put anything down around here and it'll grow legs.' She turned her head, scanning the other fires suspiciously. A fight had just broken out near one of them, terminating abruptly as one of the participants grabbed a rock seconds before the other did, felling his opponent with a single blow. No one else in the group reacted at all as the victor resumed his place next to the flames, after a cursory rummage through his enemy's pockets.

'Very likely,' Elyra agreed, ostentatiously ignoring the spectacle. 'Which is why Vos and I never sleep at the same time, and I keep my little friend here handy.' She lifted her backpack, which was resting on her lap, just enough to reveal a glimpse of the laspistol inside, ready to be drawn in a heartbeat.

'Me too,' Kyrlock agreed, with a nod towards the chainaxe and shotgun lying next to his own pack, which he'd been using as a pillow. He didn't think any of the other refugees would dare attempt to rob them, after seeing how well armed and proficient at violence both he and Elyra were, but it would be foolish to take that for granted. Desperation could drive people to pretty much anything, in his experience.

'Then I'll turn in for a while,' Elyra said, unrolling her own blanket. Trosk and Ven, the other two members of their party, were still snoring faintly, to Kyrlock's unspoken relief; it was bad enough having to look after one of the wyrds on his own, never mind all three of them. 'Wake me if anything interesting happens.'

'You can count on it,' Kyrlock assured her. After a while the psyker's breathing became more regular.

'Vos,' Zusen said quietly, moving a little closer, 'it's all right to be scared. Everyone is. Even her.' The young wyrd stared at Elyra, her expression unreadable. 'She just hides it well, like you do.'

'I'll just have to take your word for that,' Kyrlock said. Zusen was an empath, able to sense people's emotions. He forced himself to smile, fighting the impulse to move as far away from her as possible. 'But I don't think you need your gift to know how I feel about being here.'

'You'd be surprised.' A faint, fleeting smile appeared on the girl's face, then vanished like clearing mist. 'You hide how you're feeling very well.' Then, to Kyrlock's heartfelt relief, she turned away, and began rummaging in her rucksack for a compressed protein bar. 'We're getting short of these.'

'Then we'll have to eat less.' Kyrlock took a length of twine from his pocket, and began to knot it deftly. 'Unless I get lucky with this.'

'What is it?' Zusen asked, tilting her head for a better view.

'A snare.' Kyrlock turned his head a little, pinpointing the nearest source of scrabbling in the rocks surrounding them. It was growing louder even as they spoke. 'Rockrats'll be out in droves soon.'

'You can't eat rats,' Zusen said, smiling shyly, then her face twisted with revulsion as she realised he was perfectly serious. 'That's disgusting!'

'So's starving,' Kyrlock said. 'I've tried both, and believe me, rat stew's preferable.' He stood, before honesty compelled him to add, 'Just about.'

'What do you mean they'll be out soon?' Zusen asked after a moment, and Kyrlock shrugged, glancing at the motionless body in the distance.

'They'll be after the bait,' he said, not waiting to hear her reaction to that.

TWO

High Orbit, Sepheris Secundus
109.993.M41

DESPITE HIS AMUSEMENT at Drake's obvious disquiet on the short hop to the *Misericord's* parking orbit, Horst found himself staring out of the shuttle's viewport at the approaching leviathan with a faint sense of foreboding, which he tried hard to convince himself was merely the onset of the void sickness which plagued him almost every time he was forced to travel outside an atmosphere. It was easy to see why the vessel had acquired so sinister a reputation; at first sight it looked more like a collection of scrap than a functioning starship, a misshapen assemblage of smaller hulls, jammed and fused together to no discernible pattern. It looked diseased, Horst thought, the bulges of airlocks and auspex arrays speckling the surface like pustules, or fungal growths. There even seemed to be a small asteroid or two embedded somewhere among the mess. The sheer size of it had been a shock too; even the bulk ore carriers keeping apprehensive station with it in the crowded skies above Sepheris

Secundus were dwarfed in comparison, vessels the size of battleships seeming no larger than the shuttle they rode in.

He was no stranger to warp travel, but in all his years of errantry on behalf of the Inquisition, and the Adeptus Arbites before that, he'd never seen a spacecraft so huge, or so ramshackle in appearance.

'Fascinating,' Vex said, craning his head a little to gain a better view of the looming monstrosity over his colleague's intervening shoulder. 'That section looks like part of a Swallow-class courier boat, although the drive assemblies are clearly from a much larger vessel. The originals appear to be mounted on that pylon over there, although I'd have expected them to shear off by now; Omnissiah alone knows how they compensate for the lateral stresses.'

'They probably don't,' Drake said gloomily. 'Bits fall off it all the time. Ask Barda if you don't believe me.'

As if on cue, the young pilot's voice was suddenly audible over the comm-bead in Horst's ear. 'Sorry to be taking the long way round, but I'm trying to avoid the debris cloud,' he said. Once again, Horst noted, he dispensed with the elaborate honorific most Secundan hirelings would have found as natural as breathing; clearly his active involvement in last night's heretic hunt had left him feeling more like a full member of the team than a mere employee.

'Debris field?' Keira asked, a faint note of concern in her voice, and Horst felt a brief flare of irritation. It was hardly Drake's fault that the young assassin had seemed unusually distracted of late, but his comments about the so-called jinx ship this morning hadn't exactly been helpful in getting her focused again. She was dressed in her cameleoline bodyglove, which she tended to favour whenever she was expecting trouble, and had slipped a kirtle over the skintight garment to conceal her sword and collection of throwing knives. She'd chosen a muted green, which echoed the colour of her eyes, and the bodyglove was mimicking it precisely, imparting an air of sober respectability to her ensemble, which was undercut somewhat by the crimson bandana she insisted on sporting as a visible sign of her faith. Horst knew she'd found the Secundan prohibition on red clothing particularly irksome, and had resumed wearing the colour of the Redemption openly at the earliest opportunity.

'It's no problem,' Barda assured her, his voice suffused with confidence. 'Just bits of garbage and other detritus drifting in the wake of the ship. Most of the really large ones have a collection like this following them around. Some of it's been here for centuries, probably.'

'Will it prevent us from docking?' Drake asked, trying a little too hard not to sound hopeful.

'Of course not,' Barda replied, an edge of amusement creeping into his voice. 'I just need to angle the vectors right.'

'Thanks for telling us,' Horst said, as the shuttle banked a few degrees to avoid a lump of frozen organic matter the size of a groundcar, presumably flushed from the sanitary tanks decades before. A few score metres away he caught a glimpse of something metallic, then what looked uncomfortably like a desiccated corpse, and returned his attention to the interior of the tiny utility craft, seeking some distraction from his rising nausea. He turned to Vex. 'If this stuff really is that old, it must have followed the vessel through the warp,' he said thoughtfully.

'Well, of course,' the tech-priest replied, as evenly as ever. 'The theology of interstellar travel isn't exactly my area of expertise, but the Geller field of a vessel this size must extend for quite some considerable distance. Anything in the immediate vicinity would be carried into the warp along with it, and regurgitated back into existence at the other end.'

'Bits falling off,' Drake said gloomily. 'Just like I said.'

* * *

'LET ME GET this straight,' Barda said, glancing up briefly from the controls to meet the reflection of Horst's eyes in the armourcrys in front of him. He hadn't been too surprised to see the leader of the Angelae team enter the narrow flight deck a few moments before: like any member of the Cloudwalkers' Guild, the young pilot was used to clients butting in, wanting to see what was going on, or to be reassured that their lives and property were in safe hands. What had astonished the young pilot was the nature of Horst's errand. 'When you say you want to extend my contract, you mean you want me to come to Scintilla with you?'

'I realise it's a lot to ask,' Horst said. 'If you come with us, you'll be cutting yourself off from everyone and everything you've ever known. Even if you do return here one day, nothing will ever be the same again.' His eyes regarded the pilot seriously from beneath his fringe of dark hair, his sober mien at odds with the brightly coloured clothing he'd put on in order to better look the part of a Scintillan merchant returning home after concluding whatever business had brought him to Sepheris Secundus. His turquoise cravat contrasted vividly with his orange silk shirt, and the magenta brocade jacket covering it, which, Barda suspected, concealed his bolt pistol.

'Why would I want to?' Barda asked, with honest astonishment. He was well aware that his restricted upbringing among the guild had left him ill-equipped for any kind of life outside the limited confines of his birth caste, something which, like most Secundans, he'd never thought to question; until fate, or the hand of the Emperor, had led Inquisitor Finurbi to requisition his services. Now, the safe, settled tenor of his existence had been disturbed, beyond any hope of righting, and he found himself eager to seize the new possibilities his association with the Angelae were opening up. 'The guild will still want a formal enquiry into the loss of my

Aquila, and if I'm found culpable, that's a bond debt I'll never be able to repay.'

'It's hardly your fault we got shot down by heretics,' Horst said. 'You were in the service of the Inquisition at the time, and our people on Sepheris Secundus can testify to that. Captain Malakai will make sure you've got nothing to worry about from that quarter, I can assure you.' He shrugged. 'If you'd rather stay here, I can vox your guildmaster before we break orbit, and tell him to consider your services retained by the Inquisition indefinitely. Other teams will be active on Sepheris Secundus from time to time, and they'll be as grateful as we are for the services of such an exceptional pilot.'

For a moment Barda found himself tempted to accept the offer, and return home secure in the protection afforded by Inquisitorial patronage, but by now he'd seen too much of life beyond the limited horizons of his birth guild to settle for so little any more. Besides, protected or not, he'd always be known as a jonah, a pilot who'd lost his ship, shunned by the other Cloudwalkers for the rest of his days.

'It's a kind offer,' he said, after pausing just long enough to seem as though he was thinking it over, 'but, everything considered, I'd rather tag along to Scintilla.' He returned his attention to the controls. 'Now, if you'll excuse me, I need to concentrate for the next few minutes.'

They were close enough to the vast vessel by now for the encrustation of spires, auspex arrays, hatches and other ironmongery which clung to the surface of the *Misericord* to have become more visible, making it look uncannily like a vast misshapen log, coated in metallic bark. Barda fed power to one of the manoeuvring thrusters, rolling the tiny vessel neatly around the last piece of debris; Horst's reflection ahead of him flinched, looking mildly nauseous, but there was no time to wonder about that: the vast hatch of the main hangar bay was hauling itself over the metal horizon, and it was time to line up his final approach.

The vox chimed. 'Approaching shuttle, you are not authorised for this flight lane. Break off at once.'

'Sorry about that.' Barda glanced up at Horst. 'I should have warned you. *Misericord* flight control has a reputation for being difficult. They'll probably keep us in a holding pattern for hours before they allocate us a landing slot, just because they can.'

'No they won't,' Horst said, taking a couple of paces into the flight deck to activate the vox himself. 'This is Inquisition shuttle *Righteous Indignation* demanding immediate clearance, authorisation code transmitting now.' He keyed a complex set of digits on the cogitator pad. 'Put us somewhere out of the way of the rest of the passengers, and have someone in authority waiting to meet us. Is that clear?'

'Yes, sir.' The response was immediate, and, Barda was sure, tinged with apprehension. 'Proceed at your earliest convenience.'

As he banked the shuttle slowly towards the growing maw of the docking bay, Barda found himself grinning. It seemed his new vocation had quite a lot going for it.

KEIRA WASN'T EXACTLY sure what she'd expected to find aboard the *Misericord*, but the reality felt strangely anticlimactic. Although she wouldn't care to admit it, Drake's words back at the villa had disturbed her; she was firmly of the opinion that the Emperor made luck, good or ill, as a sign of His favour, or, more frequently, displeasure, but there was no denying that some places and individuals attracted misfortune to an unusual degree. Given the great age of the Chartist vessel, and its close connection to the warp, it would hardly be surprising if it was indeed tainted in some way, but it wasn't that thought which left her so uneasy; by the logic of her beliefs, the miasma of ill-fortune which Drake seemed so convinced clung to the vessel could only be the result of some deep-rooted sinfulness endemic to it.

As always, the contemplation of sin, in any of its manifold forms, made her pulse quicken, the righteous anger swelling in her chest, along with the desire to extirpate it by shedding the blood of the unworthy. Not that she'd be able to give way to the impulse here, she thought regretfully, even if she did find any evidence of moral laxity; she'd been an Inquisition operative for too long to lose sight of the bigger picture, and breaking the psyker underground took priority over everything else she could envisage. On the other hand, if His Divine Majesty thought her worthy enough to dispatch a few more sinners to His judgement, and arranged things so that they crossed her path in any case, she wouldn't exactly object.

Mordechai caught her eye. 'Are you all right?' he asked, and she nodded, trying to ignore the peculiar sensation of pressure in the pit of her stomach which seemed to appear out of nowhere whenever she became the object of his attention. 'You seemed a little distracted there for a second.'

'I'm fine.' She glanced around, trying to get a sense of the ship they'd so recently boarded. The hangar bay didn't seem all that different to those she'd passed through before, on previous voyages through the warp on the Emperor's business. 'Just trying to get our bearings, that's all.'

The high ceiling overhead was vaulted, throwing back the din of the seething activity around them, and chased with devotional murals, obscured almost to opacity by generations of accumulated grime. Narrowing her eyes a little, Keira could just about make out the figure of the Emperor Himself, apparently shrivelling things with too many eyes, tentacles, and teeth to ashes with a single gesture.

'An invocation of His protection against the denizens of the warp,' Vex said, following the direction of her gaze for a moment. 'Quite a common image aboard vessels of this kind.'

'That makes sense,' Keira agreed. Despite knowing how irrational the impulse was, she found herself looking for anything which looked like the daemon they'd encountered in Adrin's mansion, but if there was a representation of the tentacled monstrosity which had fought them there, it was too thickly covered to find.

'I can't see any other passengers,' Drake said, glancing around suspiciously as he descended the shuttle's boarding ramp to join them. The other utility craft they could see were all cargo lifters, the contents of their holds being removed by deckhands in particoloured livery, who were conversing and complaining in some shipboard patois which seemed to intersect with Imperial Gothic at roughly one word in ten as they sweated boxes and bundles onto wheeled pallets. Here and there, Keira caught a glimpse of the looming bulk of heavy lift servitors, too far away to see in much detail, but the general impression she got was of long use and decrepitude, their lurching gait betraying worn components and necrotising flesh.

'They'll be coming aboard on the main reception decks,' Horst explained. 'As we need to keep a low profile, I instructed the crew to direct us to one of the secondary cargo bays.'

Keira nodded, acknowledging the wisdom of this. Their shuttle had no obvious indication of its ownership, beyond the crimson and grey livery which marked it as the property of the Inquisition to anyone familiar with the organisation they served, and the chances of anyone aboard being aware of what that signified was extremely remote. On the other hand, after the raid on Adrin's mansion the previous night, rumour and gossip would be sweeping all levels of Secundan society, and it was just possible that someone about to take passage on the *Misericord* would have heard enough to register something suspicious about their arrival if they were seen.

Her pulse quickened. It was even possible that a few heretics had slipped through the net, and were hoping to find refuge here. She hoped so; a blood hunt would help to while away the tedium of the voyage.

'This is just a secondary bay?' Drake asked, his tone incredulous, and Keira nodded.

'By the standards of this ship, yes.' Remembering he'd never been off-world before, she tried not to sound too patronising. 'Most of the Chartist vessels are big, but this one's huge even compared to them.'

'Quite so,' Vex confirmed, consulting his data-slate. 'The *Misericord's* unique; there's no other vessel like it in the sector, if not the entire Imperium.'

'Thank the Throne for that,' Drake muttered, glancing around at the bustle surrounding them as though expecting ruin and misfortune to suddenly appear behind him.

'That must be our reception committee,' Horst said, and Keira turned her head to follow the direction of his gaze. A small group of people were trotting towards them, their status in the shipboard hierarchy immediately apparent from the speed with which the bustling deckhands hurried out of their way, and the armed escort accompanying the new arrivals.

'About sinning time,' she said sourly. Horst had invoked the authority of the Inquisition, demanding the presence of someone senior among the crew to meet them, and so far as she was concerned, that meant the delegation of shipfolk should have been waiting on their arrival, not the other way around. 'Don't they realise who they're dealing with?'

'I imagine that was the reason for the delay,' Horst said, apparently finding something amusing about her irritation. 'They probably felt there was safety in numbers.'

'Well, they got that wrong,' Keira said, with quiet satisfaction. If the Angelae found any irregularities aboard the

Misericord worth reporting to the Tricorn, the entire crew could be purged if necessary.

'Quite,' Horst said, taking a couple of steps towards their new hosts, and holding up his rosette where it could clearly be seen. It was a pointless gesture, the identification code he'd transmitted on their approach having established their *bona fides* beyond all reasonable doubt, but the effect was gratifying all the same. As the blood-red letter I caught the light from the overhead luminators, it flared threateningly, and the little party of shipboard dignitaries quailed visibly.

From habit, Keira devoted a little more of her attention to the armsmen escorting them; if, against all rational expectation, the approaching group were bent on treachery, they would be her most pressing concern. Though not much of one, she suspected; there were only a dozen of them, armed and armoured in a fashion she found most curious. All carried semi-automatic shotguns, which looked well cared for and functional, but their clothing looked as though it would have been more at home on a feral world somewhere. All wore archaic sallet helms and brightly polished breastplates over shirts of mail, which would undoubtedly offer some protection against conventional melee weapons, but very little against the Angelae's guns, and none at all against the monomolecular edges of her own blades.

The most senior member of the detail was easy to pick out, his gleaming armour covered with a bright azure cape, and his helmet crested with a long crimson feather, which she found a reassuring sight; for a moment she wondered if he shared her faith, before reason reasserted itself. Red was hardly a colour exclusive to the Redemption. He'd clearly noticed her scrutiny, and returned it, bright blue eyes lingering on her for a moment before moving on to take in the rest of the Inquisition party. A moment later his attention was back on her, and he nodded a coolly professional greeting.

Keira returned it, quietly impressed. The fellow had recognised her as the most immediately dangerous member of the group, rather than Drake or Horst, as most people would have assumed, which spoke highly of his professional abilities. If they needed to fight their way out of here, he'd be the one to watch.

'Why's the one in the middle wearing a mask?' Drake asked, and Keira's attention switched to the most conspicuous of the shipboard dignitaries surrounded by the cluster of armsmen.

'Evidently a local custom,' Vex said, consulting the data-slate again. 'The shipboard officers wear masks at all times when on duty, revealing their true faces only to members of their own caste.' He paused, paging down the document on the miniature display screen. 'At least that was the case when this account was written; it's only seven hundred years old, so I don't suppose things will have changed much in the interim.'

'They have a caste system here too?' Drake asked, apparently relieved to find something about the *Misericord* he was able to understand.

Vex nodded. 'At least as rigid as the one on Sepheris Secundus, if not more so. All with their own customs and practices, which make little sense to outsiders.'

Horst nodded too, trying to sound reassuring. 'Don't worry about it. All the Chartist vessels have their own traditions, particularly when it comes to interacting with their passengers.'

That was true, Keira thought. The stewards aboard the *Splendour Empyrian*, which they'd travelled on to reach Sepheris Secundus, had spoken entirely in rhyme; even a simple request for an evening meal had provoked the recitation of a menu couched in the form of a villanelle. At least their counterparts aboard the *Misericord* could hardly be that annoying.

'She looks pretty senior, at any rate,' Drake said, glowering suspiciously at the woman in the mask. The blank visage turned slightly, as if aware of his scrutiny. 'Judging by all that ornamentation.'

That didn't mean much, Keira thought; in some places she'd been, the more elaborate the clothing the lower the status of the wearer, but in this instance she thought the former Guardsman was probably right. The midnight-blue of the woman's mask was encrusted with embroidery in gold thread, depicting the swirl of the galaxy, angled so that Holy Terra itself was centred in the middle of her forehead. The cloth it was composed of must have been of a particularly fine weave, since she could evidently see where she was going despite the film of fabric across her eyes. In contrast to the elaborate mask, the robes she wore were plain, the blue fabric gathered at the waist with a simple knotted belt, from which a small cloth bag hung, embroidered with a stylised sun and moon.

'Greetings, in the name of our captains, and the lives they command.' The woman curtseyed, her back straight, addressing Horst directly. The archaically armoured troopers fanned out, flanking the boarding ramp of the Inquisition shuttle with every sign of being no more than an honour guard, although Keira had little doubt that they could turn out to be far more than that with no more warning than a barely perceptible gesture from the woman in the mask. The guard commander and another man she'd barely noticed stepped forwards to flank her. 'Who might your leader be?'

'It might be me,' Horst responded, with a hint of amusement probably only Keira knew him well enough to recognise. 'So let's assume it is, and get down to business. Who are you?'

'Selene Tweendecker, Magistratrix of Hospitality to the Beyonders Exalted, of the Lords, Siblings and Officers of the *Misericord*.' She curtseyed again.

'Mordechai Horst. You already know who I work for.' The leader of the Angelae nodded once, curtly. It was a

technique Keira had seen him use before: the more elaborate or effusive an official greeting, the less impressed
he was going to seem by it. It emphasised that however
important his interlocutors thought they were, that
meant nothing to the Inquisition.

'Of course.' The mask made Selene Tweendecker's
expression unreadable, but Keira could tell from her
body language that Horst's bluntness had rattled her. The
woman's posture radiated nervous tension, however well
she was able to modulate her voice. 'May I introduce
Captain Raymer of the Merciful, and Provider Prescut of
the Minions of Stewardship?'

'You may,' Horst said, while the two men accompanying her bowed formally. He gestured to his own
companions. 'That's Vex, Drake, and Milady Sythree.' He
glanced at Keira as he made the final introduction, presumably to see if she'd noticed the little joke at her
expense; she'd impersonated a minor aristocrat on
Sepheris Secundus in order to infiltrate Adrin's cabal of
heretics, and her success in so doing still seemed to
amuse him. She inclined her head a millimetre or two in
acknowledgement, despite her instinctive disapproval of
levity at a time like this. They were about the Emperor's
business, after all.

'We are honoured by your presence.' Despite her even
tone, Tweendecker's attitude made it abundantly clear
that she would have preferred the honour to have fallen
to someone else, preferably on a different ship. Her head
tilted back slightly, as she glanced up the cargo ramp.
'Will your pilot be joining us?'

'No.' Horst shook his head. 'He'll remain aboard the
shuttle for the duration of the voyage. Once our luggage
is unloaded, the hatches will be sealed, and none of your
people will enter this hangar until we reach Scintilla. Is
that understood?'

'Perfectly, Exalted Guest.' Raymer nodded, the crimson
plume in his helmet bobbing respectfully. 'I can post

sentries outside, if that be your wish.' He looked at Horst appraisingly, gauging his reaction.

'That won't be necessary,' Horst said, and Raymer nodded, clearly having expected nothing less. Accepting the offer would have implied that the Inquisitorial team felt vulnerable, something no agent of the Throne would ever admit. Not to mention the fact that an armed guard outside would be bound to excite curiosity among the crew. 'Our own precautions will be more than adequate.' He didn't elaborate: the Inquisition's reputation for ruthless efficiency would be all the deterrent required to ensure Barda's solitude for the foreseeable future.

'That won't be a problem for us,' Tweendecker assured him. 'Once these cargoes have been removed, there won't be any need to disturb your hireling in any case.'

'I'm sure our colleague will be pleased to hear that,' Horst said, implying that Barda was an acolyte, with the full authority of the Tricorn behind him, without actually saying so. Keira appreciated the subtlety. Mordechai could be an insufferable prig sometimes, it was true, but he was able to use words as cleanly and precisely as she could the blades she carried.

Tweendecker had clearly taken his meaning, as her back stiffened even more than before, and she nodded with only the barest pretence of affability. 'Then we're most gratified,' she said.

'Good,' Horst said, favouring her with a wintry smile. 'I'm glad we understand one another.'

'That being so,' Tweendecker said, 'I withdraw to convey your greetings to the bridge. Have you tidings for me to carry to the captain of the day?'

'I'll summon him myself if we need to speak to him,' Horst said.

'Your servant, as are we all,' Tweendecker said, curtseying again, and withdrawing behind the protective line of her archaically armoured escort as quickly as she decently could. With a crisp salute, Raymer followed, and the whole detachment moved away as rapidly as decorum allowed, disrupting the routine of unloading as comprehensively as their arrival had done.

Only Prescut, the chief steward, remained, standing at the bottom of the ramp as if waiting for orders, as patiently as one of the servitors in the distance.

THE MAN LOOKED back at Horst, returning his scrutiny with the carefully maintained detachment of the well-trained servant. Of indeterminate age, he had the pallid skin so common to the void-born, his grey clothes cut in a style which had been conservative a millennium ago. The only splash of colour about him was an ornate silk sash around his waist, bright threads tracing a design of intricate abstraction which made Horst's eyes ache and lose focus if he tried to make out the details; despite his obvious immediate suspicion, he soon came to the conclusion that this was a natural consequence of the design rather than a subtle indication of warpcraft. A large collection of keys hung from it, most of them too pitted with rust to have any possible real function any more, unless it was as some signifier of rank, next to a chalk-smeared slate and a small cloth bag bearing the same design as the one Tweendecker had carried.

After a moment the man bowed deeply, nodded to each member of the group in turn and led the way across the echoing hangar bay.

'Just a minute,' Horst snapped, and the man stopped, almost in mid-stride, before turning back with an air of world-weary patience which managed to convey, without actually saying so, that this happened a lot. 'I have a few questions to ask.'

By way of a reply, the man reached into his left sleeve, and produced a slip of parchment, which he handed to Horst with a theatrical flourish, like a street entertainer completing a conjuring trick.

'What does it say?' Keira asked, most of her attention still on the departing delegation. The bustle surrounding them was less now than it had been, the majority of the parked shuttles emptied of their cargo, and she had to raise her voice a little against the increasing roar of engines as they began to depart.

'It says he can't speak,' Horst said.

'Oh, great,' Keira said. 'Can't they find us one who can?'

The grey-clad steward shook his head, grabbed the slate hanging from his sash, and began scribbling on it with a stub of chalk from the bag at his waist.

Horst glanced at the message. 'Apparently, the Minions of Stewardship are forbidden to converse with the passengers,' he said, unable to keep an undercurrent of incredulity from his voice. Prescut shook his head, and scribbled a short, emphatic phrase, before holding the slate up once more. 'Sorry, with anyone.'

'That must make their jobs a little difficult,' Drake commented, looking about as baffled as Horst felt.

'Oh, wonderful. We had stewards who wouldn't shut up all the way out here, and we're going to be stuck with ones in a perpetual sulk all the way back,' Keira said with feeling.

'It's a curious custom,' Vex agreed, 'but hardly unprecedented. No doubt they'll be capable of dealing with any requests we might make.'

Prescut shrugged eloquently, and wiped the slate with a sleeve which, now Horst's attention had been drawn to it, was quite clearly ingrained with chalk dust. *To the best of our ability,* he wrote.

'That's comforting,' Horst said. He fought the impulse to shrug in return. 'We have some luggage to shift. Can you see to that?'

Prescut nodded, then, without warning, stuck two fingers in his mouth and emitted a piercing whistle, which echoed around the vast chamber, even managing to make itself heard over the rumble of the departing shuttles. The nearest group of deckhands waved in response, and began to amble over, pushing a cart ahead of them.

Drake flinched at the unexpected sound, his hand flickering for a moment in the direction of his Scalptaker, before he stilled the motion, and smiled apologetically at Horst. 'Sorry,' he said. 'Took me by surprise.'

'Me too,' Horst said, making light of it, but troubled all the same. Drake had been jumpy ever since he'd first heard they were boarding this vessel, and if he didn't get a grip soon, he was going to turn into a liability. Perhaps it would be safest to leave him aboard the shuttle with Barda. 'If this place is getting to you...'

'I'm fine,' Drake said. 'I'll get used to it.'

There was no time to argue the point, so Horst let it go for now. Prescut was instructing the trio of cargo handlers, in a rapid display of hand-waving which presumably everyone was familiar with, and they began to trot up the shuttle's boarding ramp with an air of evident purpose.

'That's far enough.' Barda appeared at the top of the metal incline, his hand resting ostentatiously on the laspistol Elyra had given him, which he was wearing holstered openly on his hip. Horst sighed inwardly; despite the young pilot's assurance that he'd been practising with the weapon, he was probably more of a danger to himself than to anyone else if he drew the thing. Nevertheless, he certainly looked the part, Horst had to give him that, his neat grey flight suit blending into the shadows at the top of the ramp to impart an air of subtle menace even Keira might have envied.

. The leading deckhand stepped back a pace. 'Naya rushabout, skyborne. Toldus shiftabox, thassit, no underhand.' He shot an anxious glance at the mute steward, and the small group of acolytes accompanying him. 'Thassalgood, ritenuff?'

'It's fine,' Horst assured him, and turned his attention to Barda. 'You know what we'll need while we're here. Make sure they find it. And nothing else.'

'He's keen, anyway,' Drake said, his evident amusement at the young pilot's enthusiasm for his new role overriding his uneasiness, at least for the moment.

'No bad thing, if it's properly directed,' Horst said, watching as the deckhands descended the ramp again, laden with boxes and bags.

Vex winced as the largest and most muscular of the trio hefted the metal-banded trunk containing his precious demountable cogitator onto the handcart with an audible thud, and muttered a brief prayer to the Omnissiah for its preservation. Noticing his agitation, Keira smiled encouragingly. 'It'll be fine,' she said, without much conviction.

'I hope so.' Vex didn't seem very convinced of that either. 'It took me days to realign the cogwheels and resanctify the vacuum tubes after we got to Icenholm.' His voice dropped. 'And the manuscript's in there. It was the safest place I could think of.'

Horst nodded. The handwritten instructions for operating Adrin's infernal device were heretical in the extreme, and the sooner they were safely lodged in the Ordo Hereticus library at the Tricorn the better. 'Good idea,' he said. The cogwheel device of the Adeptus Mechanicus was prominent on the lid, and he doubted that anyone but a tech-priest would dare to open it for fear of drawing down the wrath of the Machine-God. Not to mention the subtle traps Vex had built into the case as a precaution against the rare exceptions whose curiosity or cupidity might overcome their fear; anyone attempting to force the lock would receive a jolt of energy sufficient to incapacitate them for hours, if it didn't kill them outright.

'Careful,' Drake said, stepping forwards to supervise the loading process, apparently relieved to have found some distracting makework. Content to let him draw the shipfolk's attention, Horst withdrew up the boarding ramp, to have a quiet word with Barda.

'I've given orders to keep this hangar secured,' he said, 'but I'd advise against going for a stroll too often. If you see anyone in here at all, vox us at once, and under no circumstances allow anyone else to board.'

Barda nodded, and patted the grip of his laspistol. 'No problem there,' he assured Horst, with what the team leader hoped wasn't misplaced confidence. 'The minute you're gone I'm raising the ramp, and I'm keeping everything sealed tighter than a voider's purse until I see you walking across the dock out there again.'

'Good man.' Horst nodded his approval, and the young pilot's chest swelled visibly. He glanced around the cramped confines of the passenger compartment. 'But you'll be in here a long time. Are you sure you won't find it a bit claustrophobic?'

Barda shook his head. 'I've made solo supply runs to the outer void stations, a month or more at a stretch. And this is roomy compared to my old bird.' A hint of sorrow flickered across his face at the thought of his lost Aquila. 'I'll be fine.'

'I'm sure you will,' Horst said. 'Besides, I've a job that ought to keep you from getting too bored.' He turned and led the way into the cockpit, indicating the sensorium suite and the vox-caster. 'How well are those going to work in here?'

'It depends what you're wanting to do with them,' Barda said. 'They won't pick up much beyond the hull, unless Savant Vex can encourage the machine-spirits somehow. But I'll be able to keep in touch with you and the others.'

'That's good.' Horst nodded. 'How about any other signals traffic?'

'Not a problem,' the young pilot assured him. 'I can monitor pretty much any frequency you like.' A faint smile played across his face. 'This is an Inquisition vessel, after all. The scanning systems and message filters are far more sophisticated than anything in civilian service.'

'Then I'd like you to keep an ear out for anything unusual,' Horst said.

'Will do.' The young pilot nodded, an element of doubt entering his voice for the first time. 'The thing is, we're aboard the *Misericord*. Pretty much everything here's unusual.'

'So I've heard,' Horst said dryly. Evidently Barda was as impressed by the stories about the vessel as Drake had been. 'You'll just have to use your best judgement.'

'I'll do my best,' Barda promised, and Horst went to rejoin the others.

'Oh, there you are,' Keira said, a faintly waspish tone creeping into her voice. Evidently the delay was beginning to irk her. The cargo lifter on the adjacent pad, the last shuttle left in the hangar apart from their own, was powering up to depart, gusts of air from its manoeuvring thrusters elbowing their way past the surrounding sound baffles to tug at her hair and kirtle. 'I was beginning to think you'd got lost.'

'Sorry to disappoint you,' Horst said, the tart response almost reflexive; it seemed that despite their recent attempts to get along, they were slipping back into their old adversarial relationship, the habit too hard to break. He turned to Prescut, who had been waiting patiently beside the ramp; as he stepped off it, the metal slope began to rise, retracting back into the belly of the shuttle. 'Where to now?'

The question had evidently been asked before, while he'd been talking to Barda, because the mute steward held up the chalkboard at once. *The Beyonder's Hostelry*, he read, little wiser than before.

'Lead on, then,' he said, setting out across the echoing metal plain, which had been humming with industrious activity so short a time before. Now the small group of

Angelae, the steward and the trio of porters were the only people left in sight, and he felt uncomfortably exposed. After a moment he glanced back at their shuttle, where Barda was still visible in the cockpit, and dismissed the fleeting impulse to wave a farewell.

After a moment Prescut stopped beside a bulkhead door, which cranked slowly open with a squeal of protesting metal as he tapped a numeric code into a data-pad on the wall nearby, and the cavalcade passed through into a wide corridor walled with verdigrised metal, lit at intervals by luminators set into the ceiling. One of the Merciful from the escort detail was waiting there, failing to conceal his bored impatience, and sealed the hatch behind them under Horst's watchful eye before hurrying off about his duties. A few other shipfolk were passing by on errands of their own, but having little idea of what their liveries and symbols of office denoted, Horst had no clue as to what those might be. No other passengers being visible, they drew a few curious glances, but no one seemed all that interested in either the Angelae or their business.

'One problem taken care of,' Drake muttered, looking a little happier.

Horst nodded. 'One less thing to worry about,' he agreed, making slightly more of an effort than he'd expected to need to sound carefree.

Drake shook his head. 'I wouldn't say that, exactly,' he demurred.

Horst shot him another look, hoping the former Guardsman wasn't about to fall prey to more introspective doom-mongering, but never got the chance to reply. Prescut was opening another hatch, and a moment later they stepped through into pandemonium.

THREE

The *Misericord*, Secundus System
109.993.M41

'WHERE THE HELL are we?' Drake asked, his senses suddenly overwhelmed by a barrage of noise and movement. Instincts honed on the battlefield kicked in, and he moved without thinking, taking shelter in the lee of the doorway, already reaching for the rugged revolver in his shoulder rig before his conscious mind took over and registered that they weren't in any immediate danger. Keira glanced at him, but instead of the expression of sardonic amusement he'd expected, her face was merely reflecting an astonishment as great as his own.

'The main reception deck, I assume,' Vex said, glancing at his data-slate again. 'It matches the description here in most significant particulars.'

'Throne on Earth,' Keira said, rounding on Prescut as the heavy utility door thudded closed behind them, 'what part of "low profile" do you people fail to comprehend?'

'I don't think there's any harm done,' Horst said, as the steward circled the words *Beyonder's Hostelry* on his chalkboard, added an arrow beside it, and scribbled *Quickest* with an air of bewildered innocence. 'No one's going to notice us in a crowd like this.'

'I suppose not,' Drake agreed. The deck was vast, two or three times the size of the hangar bay they'd landed in, huge marble columns rising to support a ceiling covered in decorative frescoes. Nothing like the one they'd seen before, he noted cynically, not here, where graphic depictions of the terrors of the warp might alarm the passengers; instead, the ceiling had been split into three roughly equal segments, each one given over to stylised representations of the worlds between which the *Misericord* perpetually moved. Sepheris Secundus was roughly overhead from where Drake was standing, cheerful and preternaturally healthy-looking serfs wresting chunks of ore from the ground, while benevolent barons patted them on the shoulders with expressions of solicitous concern, or made obeisance to a royal personage of uncertain gender who was laying a lump of rock on an altar to the Emperor.

'That one's Scintilla,' Keira said, pointing to the most distant mural, where a tower the size of a city rose from a storm-flecked ocean, over which the clouds were parting to allow the hand of the Emperor to descend protectively above it. 'The Lucid Palace.'

'Does it really look like that?' Drake asked, staring in awestruck wonder at the building where the Sector Governor lived, and from which the entire Calixis Sector was governed.

'More or less,' Horst said. 'Fewer angels flapping about the last time I saw it.' Keira shot him a sharp glance, no doubt doing her best to ignore the casual impiety.

'So that must be Iocanthos,' Drake said, craning his neck to look up at the third great painting, where noble warriors clashed amid the garish ghostfire blooms. It seemed a remarkably bloodless battle to him, most of the casualties falling unmarked, as though they were about to get up again, like children playing at orks and Guardsmen.

'Yes, it must,' Keira said. Then she grinned ferally. 'Wouldn't give those pretty boys much of a chance against the real thing, though.'

Intrigued, Drake was about to ask if that meant that she'd been there, met, perhaps even fought, the perpetually feuding warriors who ruled the place, but there was little time for conversation. After only a couple of steps into the echoing concourse, it was all he could do to keep track of his companions among the throng of people surging through it.

Everywhere he looked there was movement, passengers drifting from the great bronze doors leading to the main docking bays towards the far end of the huge arena, breaking and eddying around the marble columns, while shipfolk moved through and around them in a complex dance. Many were stewards like Prescut, expertly herding their charges like ovinehounds, while pretending to defer to them, while others carried the baggage of the new arrivals, arguing loudly the whole time in the same patois as the deckhands Prescut had pressed into their service.

All levels of Secundan society seemed to be represented here, Drake thought, even the serfs, although he was surprised to see so many of those. Most of the nobles had brought servants with them, of course, in some cases entire retinues, but a large group of peasants was visible wandering through the hall, apparently unsupervised, gazing at their surroundings with awestruck apprehension.

'Who are they?' he asked, and Prescut shrugged, scribbling for a moment on his slate.

Cargo, Drake read. His incomprehension must have shown on his face, because Horst elaborated before he could ask the obvious question.

'New thralls,' he explained. 'For the DeVayne Incorporation.'

Drake nodded. The Incorporation was one of the sector-wide Great Houses, its fortune founded on the manpower it provided wherever the Imperium needed it, and its agents were constantly buying the labour contracts of serfs from the royal family and the noble houses of Sepheris Secundus. Uncounted numbers were dispatched off-world every year, to Emperor knew where, but there were always more where they came from, and for many of the serfs toiling in the mines the dream of being selected by the men in grey was the closest they could ever hope to come to the idea of escape from the burdensome lives they led. Of course things weren't likely to be any better wherever they ended up, but they could hardly be worse, and at least they would be different.

Drake watched, as they were herded out of sight by a group of the Merciful, in a different direction to the general drift of passengers.

'Warp charms, only twenty thrones, get 'em while I've got 'em,' a hawker chanted, weaving his way though the crush with one eye perpetually cocked for a flash of approaching armour. 'Protect your soul in transit, guaranteed to repel any daemon, or your money back.' He stopped in front of Keira, and dangled a cheap medallion with a picture of the Emperor on one side and a crudely engraved prayer on the other in front of her face. 'How about you, pretty lady?'

'Sin off, before I feed you your fingers,' Keira said, grabbing his wrist and squeezing the pressure point. The vendor gasped, and went white; after a moment she let him go, and he scuttled off into the crowd without a backward glance.

'Very subtle,' Horst said sarcastically. 'That'll keep us from attracting any attention.'

Keira's jaw tightened as she bit back an equally tart response, and Drake tried to hide his amusement. It seemed they were still trying to deny their mutual attraction by bickering with one another. 'I'm supposed to be your bodyguard, remember?' she pointed out.

'Are you?' Drake asked, ingenuously. 'I thought that was me, and you were the amanuensis.' Their hastily arranged cover story, for the benefit of the other passengers and most of the crew, was that of a Scintillan merchant and his entourage, although the only member of the group who obviously looked his part was Horst, who had dressed that morning in the most ostentatiously expensive bad taste he could contrive. Vex could never pass for anything other than what he was, but it wasn't unheard of for junior members of the Adeptus Mechanicus to be engaged as advisors to a mercantile house, so his presence among the party wouldn't excite too much comment.

'Well, I'm the bodyguard now,' Keira said, with undeniable satisfaction, and Drake shrugged. She was certainly better suited to the role, and his charcoal-grey shirt and trousers were certainly nondescript enough for him to pass as a glorified clerk.

'I'd better practise my calligraphy, then,' he said. To his relief Keira and Horst both smiled, and the tension between them dissipated as suddenly as it had blown up.

'What's happening to our luggage?' Vex asked suddenly, and Drake turned. The trio of porters they'd requisitioned had abandoned the cart, backing away from it with undeniable expressions of apprehension, while a quartet of other shipfolk surrounded it possessively. They didn't seem particularly formidable opponents for the heavily muscled porters, and for a moment Drake was at a loss to explain their sudden retreat, until he saw a glint of metal in the hand of the woman leading the group. A knife, held by someone who knew how to use it.

'It's being stolen!' Drake shouted, trying to force his way through the crowd to intervene, but the crush of bodies was too dense. By the time he'd ducked and

danced around a couple of highborn Secundan matri-
archs discussing the dress sense of a mutual friend with
finely tuned malice, and their comet tail of maids and
attendants, the cart had disappeared.

'Which way?' Horst demanded, grabbing the nearest
porter.

'Thatwise.' The man pointed. 'They's Receivers, edged
up withall.' He shrugged, as though he expected that to
be the end of the matter.

'I don't give a heretic's prayer who they are,' Horst
snapped. He tapped the comm-bead in his ear. 'Keira,
Iocanthos side.'

'Intercepting,' the young assassin replied coolly, and
Drake turned to look back. While he and Horst had
plunged impulsively into the crowd, she'd remained
where she was, watching out for their quarry with the dispassionate eye of a raptor hovering over a thicket full of
game. Vex hadn't moved either, still fiddling with his
data-slate, as though he expected to find an entry on baggage snatchers and how to deal with them.

Without another word Keira turned, and slipped
through the crowd in the direction Horst had directed, as
smoothly as a swimmer cutting water. Comparing her
progress with his own lumbering attempt to force passage through the hindering bodies, Drake set out after
her.

'Follow the thralls,' Vex advised, and Horst changed
direction, Drake pacing him as best he could as he
dodged around a baggage cart trundling in the wake of a
bickering couple, a squalling child and a harassed-
looking nanny. 'Our felons appear to be heading for the
same exit.'

'Acknowledged,' Horst said, apparently happy to take
his word for that, although Drake hadn't a clue how the
tech-priest could possibly know. There was no time to
ask, however, as their quarry was in sight at last, the two
most muscular of the felons propelling the cart at a pace

which would probably have menaced life and limb if their two confederates hadn't been clearing the way for them, expertly placing themselves to divert or check wandering passengers without appearing to do so deliberately. In spite of himself, Drake was impressed; the gangers' rapport and effortless teamwork must surely mean this was a practised routine, and that the quartet were professional thieves. Well known to the Misericordians, too; the shipfolk who observed their approach stepped carefully aside with deliberate casualness, affecting not to notice the careering trolley. Drake glanced around, but, as he'd expected, the only Merciful he could see were too far away to notice the fracas, or intervene effectively if they did. The thieves had timed their strike well, which only served to reinforce his impression of professionalism.

'I see them,' Keira voxed, her eagerness to shed blood thickening her voice. Hearing it, Drake shivered, seeing again in his mind's eye the spectre of death incarnate he'd first encountered in the blizzards of his home world, where she'd come within a heartbeat of killing him and Vos just to prove some kind of point. If Inquisitor Finurbi hadn't been there to call her off she might well have done, without a second's hesitation or remorse. 'I can take them easily.'

'Wait,' Horst replied. 'Let them get somewhere less public first.'

There was a flicker of movement in Drake's peripheral vision, and Keira was suddenly there, nodding in reluctant agreement. 'Good point,' she conceded, to both men's unspoken relief. A public display of her lethal talents would effectively end any chance the team had of remaining undercover. A tight smile played across her face. 'At least we won't have to wait long.'

That much seemed to be true. The woman leading the thieves had reached a portal in the wall, big enough to have driven a Chimera through, and was tapping out a code on another datapad welded to the jamb. It began to creak open, splitting down the middle to retract into the bulkhead on either side.

'Hurry,' Horst said, as their quarry slipped through, and the twin doors began to grind closed again. Drake redoubled his efforts, but the faster he tried to go, the more he became mired among the ever-shifting bodies surrounding him. Keira slipped easily though the narrowing portal, and a moment later Horst broke free of the entangling crowds to follow her. Cursing, Drake lengthened his stride, and felt himself falling as his shin caught against the outstretched leg of an overdressed young man in the colours of a minor Scintillan noble house, who had turned to converse with his cronies, heedless of anyone else who might be in the way.

'Have a care, there, fellow,' the nobleman drawled, while his friends sniggered in sympathy. 'You'll wrinkle my hose.'

'Rut your hose, and the drab who bore you,' Drake snapped, rolling to his feet and making a running dive for the closing door. For a moment he thought he'd left it too late, and condemned himself to an agonising death as the constricting slabs of metal met, crushing him between them, but Horst was there, grabbing his arm and dragging him to safety just as they met with a resonant *clang*, cutting off the indignant babbling of the affronted parasites behind him.

'Which way?' Keira asked urgently, and Drake looked around, trying to get his bearings. They were in a corridor similar to the one Prescut had guided them along on the other side of the reception hall, its metal walls bare and corroded with age. Deep pits of shadow lay between the wall-mounted luminators, several of which were flickering in a fashion he found subtly unnerving, and which Vex would no doubt have found an affront to the Omnissiah had his attention been drawn to them. It stretched away in both directions, its ends lost in the gloom, and several side corridors could be seen branching from it whichever way he looked. Right in front of them a wide staircase descended into the bowels of the ship; Drake could see nothing of where it went, but judging by the clamour echoing upwards, that was the direction the thralls had taken.

'Left,' Vex replied confidently, his voice echoing faintly in Drake's comm-bead. The Guardsman didn't have a clue how the tech-priest could know this, but the other Angelae seemed to trust him, and pelted off in the direction he'd indicated without hesitation. Drake followed, drawing his pistol, now that they were out of the public areas, the weight in his hand a reassuring presence.

'Stop where you are!' a voice yelled, and he glanced down the corridor ahead of them. A pair of Merciful, on a routine patrol judging by the casual way they were holding their shotguns, had just emerged from a side passage, and were staring at the oncoming Angelae in wrathful astonishment. 'Back beyonderside, you swive-brained maggots!'

They might have been able to talk their way past, Drake reflected later, if it hadn't been for the gun in his hand. As it was, the pair of comic opera troopers noticed it almost simultaneously, and began to bring their own weapons to bear. Cursing, Drake levelled the Scalptaker, hoping he'd be able to bring them down without killing them, but he never got the chance. Ululating gleefully, Keira leapt into the attack, drawing her sword in a single fluid motion.

Her first strike took the leading Merciful's right hand off at the wrist, and sheared through the stock of the shotgun as though it was no more substantial than paper; even before the severed limb hit the floor, she'd spun the weapon to lead with the pommel, smashing it into the narrow strip of the forehead of the second man visible between the bridge of his nose and the lip of his helmet. He went down hard, hitting the deck with a clangour of metal against metal, and she whirled again, poised to dispatch the first with a thrust through the heart.

'Stop!' Horst yelled, in the nick of time, and she checked the motion with palpable reluctance. 'The manuscript!' He hurdled the fallen trooper, and kept running. With a 'moue of disappointment, Keira turned to keep pace with him. 'They're out of our way, that's enough.'

Drake hesitated for a second as he passed the fallen men, but the injured Merciful was already scrabbling a pocket vox from the sabretache at his belt; reasonably certain that aid would be with them before he bled out, and mindful of Horst's injunction to keep their minds on the objective, he followed his colleagues without a second thought.

'I thought you were only supposed to kill sinners,' he panted, catching up with Horst and Keira.

The girl looked at him as though he was stupid. 'Everyone's guilty of something,' she said.

'Oh.' Drake was completely taken aback. 'I guess that simplifies things, then.'

'Generally.' If she recognised the sarcasm in his tone, she was refusing to rise to it.

'They've turned right,' Vex said in his ear, and he seized on the distraction gratefully. 'About thirty metres ahead of your current position.'

'I see it,' Horst responded, angling towards a cross corridor, from which a flickering orange light could be seen. It struck Drake as somehow sinister, but he couldn't quite put his finger on why.

'They've slowed,' Vex added, a moment later. 'You should be closing the distance now.'

'Thanks, Hybris,' Horst said. He glanced at Drake. 'I guess they must be tiring, with the weight of the cart.'

Keira was drawing ahead of both men again, like a hunting hound let off the leash, and disappeared into the shadowed passageway several seconds before they reached it. 'I think they're about to get a lot slower,' Drake said.

Despite the urgency of their errand, he found himself moving more cautiously as they reached the new corridor. The air currents wafting from it smelled of dust and decay, and most of the luminators along its length were broken, working only fitfully, if at all. The orange glow came from somewhere in the depths of it, and Drake tightened his grip on the comforting weight of the Scalptaker.

A single, choked-off scream echoed through the air around them, and both men plunged unhesitatingly into the gloom.

'Two heretics down,' Keira reported, an unmistakable edge of satisfaction in her voice even through the attenuating effect of their comm-beads. 'Pursuing the others.'

'Wait for us,' Horst said. 'We don't know what's in here.'

'Nothing but dead heretics,' Keira said, a hint of the same exultation Drake had noticed back at the villa suffusing her tone. 'Some of them are still moving at the moment, that's all.'

'There could be other crewmembers around,' Horst said, 'and we don't want any more unfortunate incidents if we can avoid them. Don't engage anyone else unless you're certain they're hostile.'

'These ones definitely were,' Keira said, glancing up as they approached her. She was standing on the edge of the pool of light cast by one of the functional luminators, although she'd discarded her kirtle, becoming barely visible in the shadows surrounding them as the cameleoline of her bodyglove had adjusted to the new environment. She shuffled her feet, moving the soles of her boots fastidiously away from the spreading slick of blood on the deck plating.

Two of the bandits had evidently attempted to ambush her from the shadows, a mistake they'd paid for in a brief flurry of sword strokes. The woman who'd led the gang had been neatly sliced into three sections, her torso, legs and head scattered around the passageway, the knife she carried still gripped in one flaccid palm, while the man who'd helped her clear the way for the cart in the crowded reception hall lay a few paces beyond, bisected by a single diagonal strike as he attempted to flee. Drake was no stranger to death and destruction, and had inflicted enough of it himself in his earlier life as a Royal Scourge and an Imperial Guardsman, but the casual precision of the kill still chilled his blood. Or perhaps it was the smell.

'Any sign of the others?' Horst asked, and Keira shrugged.

'They must have come this way, and known we were after them. Why else would these two be trying to mount an ambush?' she pointed out.

'Makes sense to me,' Drake agreed. 'They must have been counting on their local knowledge to take you by surprise.'

'Well, the surprise was all theirs,' Keira said, with vindictive satisfaction. She shook the blood off her sword with deft precision, and slipped it into her scabbard. Then she turned towards the orange glow. 'Coming? Or shall we just wait for them to die of old age?'

As SHE LED the way towards the glow in the distance, Keira felt her senses expanding as they always did on a hunt, taking in every detail of her surroundings. This section of the ship was clearly little used, the scent of dust and decay in her nostrils enough to tell her that, even if the dilapidated state of the walls and the malfunctioning luminators hadn't already made it perfectly obvious.

People definitely came through here though, and in considerable numbers, there could be little doubt of that: the layer of dust and grime underfoot had been disturbed in the middle of the corridor, drifting more thickly along the edges and in the corners. Too many feet had passed for her to be able to estimate numbers and frequency, the prints overlapping and obliterating one another, but two parallel lines were still visible on the top layer, where the cart she pursued had passed mere moments before.

She smiled eagerly, anticipating the bloodshed to come. The grace of the Emperor still glowed within her, the deaths of the sinners she'd just sent to His judgement a sacrament she burned to repeat.

She took a deep breath, and murmured one of the calming litanies the Collegium Assassinorum had taught her. The holy zeal of Redemption would help her to visit the Emperor's wrath on the unworthy, but could lead her into error in the more measured phase of the hunt. Her instructors had shown her how to refine that fire, and shape it into a more subtle instrument of His divine will, and she exulted in that knowledge now, as it made her a more effective servant of Him on Earth.

She listened carefully, tuning out the most easily identifiable sounds from her consciousness one by one: the almost inaudible padding of her own footsteps, far softer than the footfalls of either of the men hurrying behind her, the susurration of her breath and the thudding of her heart. That left others: the drip and trickle of water, betraying a corroded pipe somewhere in the darkness ahead of her, and a gentle regular splashing sound. That, though subtle, was enough to mask any other noises unless she concentrated hard, trying to pierce the auditory barrier they erected across her synapses.

There. A faint murmur, which might have been voices, and a booming rattle, perhaps made by the cart.

'You're closing the distance,' Vex said, his voice as level as ever in her comm-bead, and her smile widened, sure now that the Emperor was with her. She could picture the tech-priest, still standing among the whirling crowd in the embarkation hall, oblivious to his surroundings, his head bent over his data-slate, following their progress on the tiny screen as he tracked the signal of their earpiece transmitters.

'Good,' Horst said. 'Any idea what we're getting into?'

'None at all,' Vex replied. 'The section you're in is off the map appended to my travel guide. Hardly surprising, as they wouldn't expect passengers to be there. I've asked Barda to use the auspexes in the shuttle to obtain a rough idea of the topography, but the recalibration required is complex, and he has yet to complete the necessary rituals.'

'Good idea, anyway,' Horst said. 'Tell him to keep trying.'

'Watch your feet,' Keira said. 'The floor's uneven here.' A small step, little more than a centimetre in depth, ran across the corridor from side to side, disrupting the smooth run of plating underfoot, and she crossed the discontinuity without breaking stride. It seemed to be canted, a millimetre or two higher at one end than the other, and the floor appeared different on the other side as well. 'Cross corridor. Which way?'

'Right,' Vex said, and she turned to follow the direction he'd indicated, Drake and Horst hard on her heels. Like the passageway they'd just left, the luminators here were wall-mounted, although for some reason they were only on one side this time. The shape of it was different too, higher than it was wide, and the floor, ceiling and right-hand wall were all textured the same: only the wall opposite the luminators was distinctive, panelled in a metal lattice like the one they'd been walking on a few moments before.

Struck by a sudden thought, she glanced back at the tunnel they'd just emerged from. The corridor mouth was raggedly cut, by a plasma torch or some similar tool, confirming her guess. 'I think we're in a different hull,' she said. 'Remember the cluster of derelicts we saw on the way in?'

'It's getting lighter too,' Drake added, his voice taking on a tinge of unease. He hefted his handgun warily, his eyes probing the shadows for signs of ambush. 'That could mean people.'

'Probably,' Keira agreed cheerfully. More people meant more sinners to dispatch to the Golden Throne.

'Then let's move quietly,' Horst said, 'and try not to attract too much attention.'

'You're no fun,' Keira said, vaguely surprised to find herself joking at a time like this, and returned her mind to the business at hand. Before she had time to consider the implications, she led the way down the corridor in the direction Vex had indicated.

A heavy bulkhead door was ahead of them, although it had clearly not been closed in scores of generations, its upper half propped open by thick I beams. The ridge running across the floor, where its twin had once retracted into the opposite wall, had been bridged by a welded ramp of deck plating, about half a metre high, into which a groove had been worn by centuries of passing feet. Keira could see nothing of the chamber beyond, although Drake had been right, the fitful orange glow seemed brighter there.

Well, there was only one way to find out what lay inside. Picking up her pace, she trotted forwards, and up to the top of the slope.

'What's there?' Horst asked, and the young assassin moved aside a little to give him a better view as he joined her.

'Water,' she said. The doorway was halfway up the wall of the rotated room beyond, and a balcony had been constructed there, thrusting out into the open space on strongly welded girders. Like the corridor they'd entered by, the chamber was far higher than it was wide or long, the ceiling, in which another portal, closed this time, could just be discerned, about twenty metres above their heads. Clear fluid was seeping from corroded joints in a pipe run on the wall which had evidently once been the ceiling, trickling down in a constant stream, and the walls were wet with condensation, which left the air dank and chill.

As they made their way onto the echoing deck, Keira glanced down, unsurprised to see the glint of black water only a metre or so below them. Orange highlights danced and glittered, reflecting the guttering torches stuck into sconces welded to the wall, and she nodded, with sudden understanding. With half the deck flooded, the luminators wouldn't work, their machine-spirits affronted by the dampness.

'People must come here a lot,' Drake said, indicating the hissing flames.

'Often,' Horst agreed, from the far end of the platform. A line of ropes dangled down into the water next to where he was standing; puzzled, Keira moved to join him. The former arbitrator reached out and hauled on the nearest; after a moment, a rusting bucket broke the surface. 'Thought so.' He opened his hand again, and the bucket sank out of sight.

'It's a dead end,' Drake said, gazing around them in angry frustration. 'There's nowhere they could have gone!'

'Apart from over there,' Keira said, pointing to a portal identical to the one they'd entered the flooded hold by, on the far wall. A single rusting chain connected the platform they stood on to a similar one beneath it.

'Oh right.' Drake snorted with derision. 'They carried the cart and our luggage across that, like acrobats in the carnivora.'

'They might have done,' Horst agreed, with a trace of amusement, 'but they're more likely to have used the raft.' He pointed to the platform on the opposite shore, where a dark shape lay close to the pilings, almost invisible among the shadows.

'Oh.' Drake shrugged, looking faintly abashed. 'I hadn't noticed that.'

'It's easy to miss,' Horst assured him, more to spare the Guardsman's feelings than because it was true, Keira thought. There was no doubt about it: however annoying he could be, Mordechai was good with people.

'Then let's get it over on this side,' she put in impatiently, and raised a hand to the chain. It moved easily, to her surprise, the end disappearing through a hole in the decking with a faint rattle and a splash, squeaking a little as it ran over a rusting pulley. After a moment she felt the weight of the raft come on as the chain tautened, and heaved, leaning back and hauling on the wet, flaking links, drawing them in hand over hand. The smell of damp rust reminded her of blood, and she smiled, taking that as a sign of the Emperor's favour.

'Let me give you a hand,' Horst said, joining her at the chain. 'Danuld, keep watch.' He began to pull too, adding his own strength to hers, the heavy raft moving easily through the water towards them. Without words, they slipped into an easy rhythm, moving together without conscious thought.

A few moments later the dock shook, a resonant clang announcing the arrival of the raft, and Keira turned, assessing it critically. Like most things they'd seen since leaving the passenger areas, it was constructed of metal, its crude form belying the obvious care with which it had been made. An underhiver by birth, Keira was intimately familiar with the patched-together contrivances common to such regions, and she could tell at a glance that this had been made by someone who knew what they were doing, and how to use their tools. The welds were neat and regular, and the joints robust.

'Is it safe?' Drake asked, a hint of uncertainty crossing his face, and she nodded.

'It won't sink, if that's what you're worried about.' She shrugged, unable to resist teasing him a little. 'Not unless someone starts shooting at us. Puncture the buoyancy tanks and she'll go down like a stone.'

'If that happens we'll be dead before we get a chance to drown,' he returned, his intonation leaving her unsure of whether he was seriously considering the matter, or merely replying in kind. 'We'll be sitting waterfowl bobbing about on that thing.'

'We haven't seen any sign of guns so far,' Horst reminded them, as humourless as ever, and Keira shrugged again.

'You don't need a gun to shoot people. Plenty around here you could make a bow out of.'

'Then let's not wait around to find out,' Horst replied practically, and strode onto the raft, adjusting his balance slightly as it wallowed under his weight. 'I had enough of this sort of thing in the Fathomsound.'

Keira followed, with Drake reluctantly taking up the rear. The raft settled a little deeper into the water as each of the Angelae boarded it, but remained stable, as she'd expected. A metal mesh deck, probably made from scavenged floor plates, was welded to a frame of girders, which in turn had been fastened above a pair of cylindrical buoyancy tanks. She reached up and grabbed the chain. 'Let's get moving,' she suggested.

This time, to her vague disappointment, it was Drake who joined her, leaving Horst to watch the far shore suspiciously, his bolt pistol at the ready. The rapport they'd shared before had felt good, right somehow, and although Drake hauled on the chain with a will, their efforts simply didn't synergise in quite the same way. They made good progress though, she had to admit that, the former Guardsman making up in sheer nervous energy what he lacked in finesse, and it made more sense for Horst to be watching their backs, the explosive tips of his pistol bolts able to do far more damage to an attacker than the simple slugs of Drake's revolver.

To her mingled surprise and relief they made it to the far shore without incident, although she'd been mildly concerned by the appearance of a party of shipfolk on the jetty they'd just left, a few minutes into their journey. They'd shown no interest in either the raft or its occupants, however, merely busying themselves with drawing water, which they decanted into a tank on wheels; by the time the Angelae had gained the far bank, the foraging party had vanished again, trundling their liquid booty off to Emperor knew where.

'Hybris, I need a direction,' Horst voxed, as the team of acolytes disembarked, their boot-heels clattering on the welded metal plate of the jetty. Keira winced, certain that the noise would have alerted every heretic for hundreds of metres around, but there was no help for it; silent stalking simply wasn't an option with her friends along.

'Straight ahead of you,' Vex responded. 'They've opened up the distance a little, but they're not hurrying any more. They must think they're safe from pursuit.'

'Or waiting for their friends to catch up,' Keira said, allowing herself to savour the memory of the kills again. This was something she understood, a welcome distraction from the doubts and uncertainty which had begun to plague her.

'Well, life's full of little disappointments,' Horst said, and she nodded, appreciating the implied compliment.

'How does he know where they are?' Drake asked, as they began to move out again, along a corridor almost identical to the one they'd been following on the far side of the lake. 'Some kind of technosorcery?'

'There's a tracker in the cogitator's case,' Horst told him. 'Among other things. The Mechanicus are cautious when it comes to looking after their toys.'

'Could you make a bit more noise, please?' Keira asked irritably. 'They might not be able to hear us coming yet.'

'Good point. Sorry,' Horst said, leaving her feeling surprised and gratified. They picked up their pace, running in silence, or, in the case of her companions, as quietly as they could, which still sounded cacophonous to her Collegium-trained ears, but at least it was a marginal improvement.

To her surprise, the flickering orange torchlight wasn't confined to the lake chamber, as she'd expected, but appeared to be coming from somewhere up ahead as well. She began to move a little faster, drawing ahead of her colleagues, but Horst made no move to call her back; this was what she excelled at, and she knew he'd let her get on with it without interference, unless he saw very good reason to intervene. Another canted doorway was a few metres ahead, and she loped up the ramp without hesitation.

'Holy Throne!' she breathed, unable to contain her astonishment. She'd expected another platform, like the ones in the flooded hold, but this was something more, a narrow bridge jutting out and across a deep shaft, which descended further than she could see, its bottom lost in the shadows beneath her feet. Doorways and cross corridors could be discerned, pockmarking the walls of the abyss at regular intervals, the flickering light of torches or fires wherever they led to mingling with the attenuated glow of still-functioning luminators. This had obviously been a main corridor once, when the vessel had been a ship in its own right rather than a mere component of the *Misericord*; she glanced up, finding that, as she'd expected, it receded into the distance above her head beyond the range of her vision. A couple of faint lines might have been bridges like the one she stood on, but there was no way to be sure, and speculation was fruitless in any case. Only one thing mattered: her quarry was in sight at last.

Halfway across the bridge, two men were pushing the familiar handcart, still laden with their luggage, too absorbed in conversation to have noticed her arrival. The metal-banded chest containing Vex's cogitator, and the all-important manuscript, was still visible at the bottom of the heap, and she drew her sword, with a faint sigh of relief, as her companions finally caught up.

'Halt in the name of the Throne!' Horst shouted, levelling his bolt pistol. The two men turned, one diving for cover behind the cart, while the other drew a shock maul from beneath his coat and began to run back towards them.

'Mine!' Keira said, advancing onto the bridge and taking up a guard position with her blade. The man hesitated for a second, then came on, no doubt confident that his power weapon would be more than a match for a sword, especially one wielded by a mere slip of a girl.

The crack of a heavy-calibre pistol echoed round the chamber, followed instantly by the whine of a ricochet, and sparks flew from the ramp where Horst and Drake were standing. It seemed one of the bandits had a gun after all.

Both men dropped and returned fire, Drake's revolver slugs striking more sparks from the metal plating of the bridge. The gunman hunkered down behind the solid bulk of the cart and fired again, with no more accuracy than before; he clearly wasn't used to opponents who shot back, and had probably relied on the weapon merely to intimidate up until now.

'I can't get a clear shot,' Drake grumbled, steadying his hand against his forearm.

'I don't need one,' Horst said, levelling his bolt pistol and squeezing the trigger.

Keira's opponent charged in without finesse, and swung the shock maul, clearly intending to batter the sword out of the way, and fell her with the backswing. She evaded the strike easily, and kicked out, taking him in the stomach; she could have gutted him on the spot, but so crude a stroke would have been unworthy of her. Sending heretics to judgement was a sacrament, to be done with elegance and refinement wherever possible, and there was plenty of time to dispatch this one in a more aesthetically pleasing manner.

He must have been an experienced brawler: instead of folding, as she'd expected, he pulled back at the last minute, absorbing most of the impact, and pivoting to drive in a blow against her knee. Surprised, Keira blocked the strike at the last possible second, shearing the tip off the shock maul, and feeling a jolt even through the insulating gloves of her synsuit as the capacitors discharged. She stumbled, the molecule-thick edge of her blade slicing an ugly gash through the decking at her feet before she could recover her balance. Her opponent was falling, his muscles spasming as he absorbed the full charge of his own weapon; he was probably dead before he hit the mesh, but she struck upwards anyway, severing his head neatly from his body as he met the rising blade on his way down. A good, clean kill to honour the Emperor.

Horst's pistol bolt hit the wheel of the cart and detonated, turning the fine wire of the spokes into instant flechettes. The gunman screamed, flailing backwards, and fell into view, where Drake took him at once with a shot to the head. Horst fired again too, at almost the same instant, and the bolt detonated against the metalwork of the bridge, just missing the gunman as his body jerked with the impact of the bullet.

Keira felt the weakened structure shudder below her bootsoles with an ominous groaning sound, and turned to leap for the portal. The whole bridge began to fall away beneath her as she pushed off, the metal shearing where her sword had gashed the deck plates, and for a heart-stopping moment she thought she wasn't going to make it; then Horst's hand closed around her arm.

'Hang on, I've got you,' he said, pivoting on the very brink of the abyss, as her toes scrabbled for purchase on the sloping metal, drawing her back to safety. His arms closed around her, and she returned the pressure instinctively as they staggered back onto a firmer footing, their hearts hammering in unison.

'Thanks.' She exhaled slowly, curiously reluctant to break away from the inadvertent embrace; then a grinding, tearing sound, as though the ship itself was clearing its throat, snatched her attention back to the here and now. She turned, watching in fascinated horror as the entire bridge toppled into the abyss, taking the cart, its contents, and the bodies of the thieves down with it. A carillon of overlapping echoes rose from the depths, as the plummeting debris bounced and ricocheted from innumerable obstructions, managing to muffle the sound of the final impact so effectively that she couldn't even begin to estimate its depth.

Drake was the first one to speak, after the clangour had diminished enough for his words to be heard at last. 'Nads,' he said, feelingly.

'My thoughts exactly.' Horst reholstered his bolt pistol, and turned away, without a second glance.

'The tracer's no longer transmitting,' Vex said, cutting into their comm-beads again. 'Have you managed to recover the manuscript?'

'No,' Keira said flatly. 'We've lost it. Along with everything else.'

Drake scowled at the abyss, as if he suspected it of deliberately mocking them. 'What did I tell you?' he said sourly. 'The ship's cursed.'

'I don't care if it's crewed by daemons,' Horst said, a determined set to his jaw, as he began to lead the group back the way they'd come. 'We'll just have to recover the document.'

'Right,' Keira agreed, taking heart from his obvious determination. 'So what's our first move?'

Horst shrugged. 'I haven't the faintest idea,' he admitted.

FOUR

High Orbit, Scintilla, Calixis Sector
235.993.M41

'Daemons.' Inquisitor Grynner frowned, so immersed in the reports his aide had obtained for him that he remained unaware of having verbalised the thought, and immune from the flicker of irritation he would normally have felt at the lack of mental discipline the involuntary reaction betrayed. Jorge Grynner's mind was the sharpest weapon in the arsenal of his unending war against the enemies of the Emperor, and he took a quiet pride in its keenness. Only rarely did he allow himself to feel surprised, and confusion was something he generally regarded as happening to other people. 'Merciful Throne, what have they stumbled into?'

A polite knock on the door broke into his reverie, and Grynner found himself welcoming the interruption. Perhaps discussing matters with his most promising pupil would help to order them in his mind. He raised his voice a degree or two above the conversational, just sufficient to penetrate the barrier between them. 'Pieter. Come in.'

'Inquisitor.' The young interrogator entered the inquisitor's private study, clearly attempting to gauge his patron's mood. He'd taken it upon himself to acquire the transcripts Grynner had been reading, a display of initiative which could either help or hinder his future career, depending on its eventual outcome. 'I hope the files were helpful?'

'To some extent,' Grynner said, gesturing his protégé to one of the padded chairs ranged around the room. As was his habit, however, he remained behind the desk. 'I take it you read them yourself?'

'I skimmed through them,' Pieter Quillem admitted, unabashed, despite the clear breach of protocol which perusing a report intended for a superior represented. As such things went, though, Grynner felt, it was a minor enough transgression, and probably augured well for his promotion to fully-fledged inquisitorial status, where overmuch respect for the niceties could be more of a handicap than a help. Heretics didn't play by the rules, and neither did those charged with rooting them out. 'Just to make sure they were worth a little of your time before I brought them to your attention.'

'Commendably efficient, as always,' Grynner commented, noting a subtle change in Quillem's body language which betrayed the young man's carefully concealed relief. 'Even if they do seem to raise more questions than they answer.'

'I'm a little confused too,' Quillem said, clearly taking the remark as nothing more than a habitual part of the mask of unworldliness his patron presented to the world. 'If there's any clue about what happened to Inquisitor Finurbi, I've not been able to spot it.' His voice took on a slightly hesitant tone, as if wary of implying some criticism of a superior. 'To be honest, if you hadn't told me he was a friend of yours, I wouldn't have placed much credence in any of these reports. So much sounds like the wildest exaggeration, I'm not too sure how much trust we ought to place in these operatives of his.'

'More than you might think, Pieter,' Grynner replied, allowing a tone of mild reproof to enter his voice. 'Carolus does have a tendency to co-opt anyone he feels might be useful more or less on impulse, like these Imperial Guard troopers Kyrlock and Drake, but his judgement is invariably sound. As evidenced by their actions in these reports.'

'If you believe these reports,' Quillem reminded him. He'd been Grynner's protégé long enough to know when his mentor felt the need of a dissenting voice to test the strength of the conclusions he'd been forming. 'You've only got their own word for what they've been up to.' He shrugged. 'And you have to admit, all this stuff about daemons is pretty hard to swallow.'

'Possibly,' Grynner allowed, with a faint inclination of his head. 'Never having met any myself, I couldn't really comment on that.' Quillem had never encountered one either, of course, and acknowledged the fact with a nod of his own, before Grynner continued. 'Perhaps I should ask Karnaki what he thinks; it's really more his area of expertise than mine. Nevertheless, this man Horst is a former member of the Adeptus Arbites, and in my experience such servants of the Emperor are seldom given to flights of fancy.'

'Not as a rule,' Quillem agreed, nodding again. 'So is there anything in what he says here which strikes you as useful?'

'Oh, most assuredly,' Grynner said. 'For one thing, these reports convince me I was right to approach Carolus for aid with our own investigation.'

'The psykers, you mean,' Quillem said, to show that he was keeping up.

'The psykers. Precisely.' Grynner nodded, the connection growing more concrete in his mind as he spoke. 'The mercenaries who attacked the Black Ship containment facility on Sepheris Secundus were equipped with xenos technology. The only heretic group in the sector with access to that much of the stuff is the Faxlignae, and we found clear traces of the presence of wyrds aboard the freighter they'd been using.' To be more accurate, on boarding the crippled hulk, they'd found traces of the activities of wyrds, which had consisted largely of slaughtering the crew and absconding with the xenos artefact the ship had been smuggling.

'That still bothers me,' Quillem said, returning to a point he'd made often. 'The Faxlignae are scavengers, collecting xenos blasphemies in pursuit of Emperor knows what agenda; they've never shown the slightest interest in psykers before, and they've been active for nearly three hundred years. Why would they go to so much trouble to liberate dozens of them on Sepheris Secundus now, and why would they have some aboard one of their smuggling vessels?'

'Two very good questions,' Grynner admitted, 'to which I wish I had equally good answers.' He hesitated a moment before going on. 'A rather disturbing possibility is that whatever they've been planning for the last few centuries is entering a new, and perhaps final, phase.'

'Which would explain the wraithbone,' Quillem conceded. The ill-fated freighter, the *Eddia Stabilis*, had been carrying a fragment of the enigmatic eldar substance, according to their most reliable information, although the Librarian attached to the Deathwatch kill team Grynner had dispatched to search the vessel had assured them there wasn't a trace of the stuff aboard by the time the *Emperor's Justice* had intercepted it. That had been good enough for Grynner: nothing so tainted by the energies of the warp could have escaped the preternatural senses of a Space Marine sanctionite.

'Indeed it would,' the inquisitor agreed. 'Which raises the further question of why, if they were allies, the psykers acted as they did.'

'No mystery there,' Quillem said, with rather too much assurance for his mentor's peace of mind. Promising as he was, the boy still had a regrettable tendency to jump to conclusions. 'Just a good old-fashioned double-cross. Heretics are treacherous by nature, and psykers are usually insane to boot. They just wanted the wraithbone more than the Faxlignae did, and grabbed it as soon as they got the chance.'

'Perhaps.' Grynner suppressed a sigh, and cleaned the lenses of his spectacles on the end of his neck cloth, a practised affectation which, like the rest of the façade of absentmindedness behind which he preferred to mask his intellect, had long since become a habit so ingrained he barely noticed it. 'Which rather begs the question of what they wanted it for. Not to mention the somewhat pressing matter of where it is now.'

'I wish I could offer an opinion on that,' Quillem said. 'But I really have no idea.'

'Of course not,' Grynner said, replacing the spectacles on the bridge of his nose. He had no real need of them, the periodic juvenat treatments which maintained his physical age at around a quarter of his actual one keeping his eyesight as keen as his mind, but they were an essential part of the vague persona he liked to project, like the neat grey robes he habitually dressed in. He'd lost count of the number of heretics over the years who'd discounted the faintly absurd little man with the air of a minor Administratum functionary as any threat to their interests until it was far too late. 'But perhaps Carolus can help us make sense of it, if he resurfaces in time.'

'Perhaps,' Quillem said cautiously. He laid a new dataslate on his patron's desk. 'At least these agents of his ought to be arriving in-system soon. I thought you might like to review the arrangements you asked me to make concerning them.'

'Of course,' Grynner said, picking up the slate and paging through it. After a moment he nodded. 'Well done, Pieter. I think this will do admirably.'

'Thank you, inquisitor.' His protégé nodded, unable to completely conceal his satisfaction. 'Then, if you'll excuse me, I'll return to our own lines of enquiry.'

'By all means,' Grynner said, dismissing the young man with a nod. But he remained thoughtful long after the door had closed behind him.

The *Misericord*, the Warp, Date and Time Meaningless

IT WAS AN article of faith among the acolytes of the Omnissiah that emotions were a weakness of the flesh, to be overcome by pure reason and the judicious application of augmetic enhancements, but in spite of the meditational subroutines he was running in the background of his thought processes, Vex felt perturbed. His initial shock on hearing of the disaster at the bridge had subsided, but the full ramifications had still to be processed, likely outcomes calculated and assigned numerical probabilities, and the worst-case contingencies planned for.

He had already begun the task when the other Angelae rejoined him in the concourse, their mood subdued, and he'd had little attention to spare for his surroundings as Prescut had ushered them out of the echoing hall, towards the passenger accommodation. It was all very much as the account of an earlier voyage he'd been reading on his data-slate described in any case; perhaps to ease any psychological discomfort the passengers might be suffering from, the public areas of the vessel had been decorated in a fashion intended to resemble a planetary environment. For reasons known only to the ship crew, however, if any of them could still recall what they were, the style was that of a feral world, where the blessings of the Omnissiah had barely advanced beyond hammered iron and gunpowder. Corridors were flagged with stone, concealing the deck plates beneath, while tapestries hung from every wall, the gaps between them veneered with wooden panelling, intended to obscure the pure, clean lines of the metal from which the vessel had been constructed, and which he would have found far more congenial to contemplate.

At length, the mute steward had conducted them to a suite of rooms and left them to their own devices, no doubt with a sense of relief scarcely less acute than Vex's own.

'Can we talk?' Horst asked, as soon as the polished wooden door had closed behind him, and Vex nodded, after a quick recitation of the ritual of seclusion, with the aid of a pocket auspex calibrated to detect any vox-transmitters in the vicinity. At last, sure that the battered but comfortable furnishings in the cramped common area concealed no eavesdropping devices, he stowed the auspex in a pocket of his robes, next to his precious data-slate.

With everyone present, the small room felt crowded. Even so, it was far larger than the cabins and the tiny balnerea radiating from it; each was scarcely large enough for a single person to occupy at any one time, and Vex felt a barely acknowledged sense of relief that the latter was one facility he wouldn't have to bother taking his turn at more than a few times during the voyage. Like the corridors outside, the metalwork of the walls had been covered with tapestries depicting scenes from Saint Drusus's crusade, although rather than stone the floor in here had been covered with wood, in rough-sawn planks, over which a couple of rugs had been thrown, apparently at random.

'You'd think they'd have cleaned up in here a bit,' Keira grumbled, patting the arm of the padded chair she'd taken and raising a small cloud of dust. 'They're charging us enough for the passage.'

'We've got a lot more to worry about than a bit of dirt,' Horst told her, leading Vex to anticipate an equally tart response from the assassin; to his vague surprise, however, she held her tongue, merely nodding in agreement. The differences which had bedevilled them on Sepheris Secundus appeared to have been resolved, at least partially, for which the tech-priest was quietly grateful. The incipient tension between Keira and Horst had disturbed him, threatening as it had done to disrupt the smooth functioning of the team, not least because the reasons for it continued to elude him. The former arbitrator turned to Vex. 'Have you still got the artefact?'

'I have.' Vex nodded, and produced the sliver of ivory-like material for everyone's inspection. As usual, they all seemed reluctant to take it from him, or examine it too closely, and he returned it to an inner pocket of his robe after ensuring that everyone had seen it. 'Although without the manuscript, I'm far from confident of being able to deduce its origin or purpose.'

'Then recovering it should be our highest priority,' Drake said, eliciting nods of agreement from the rest of the group.

'Easier said than done, though,' Keira demurred. 'It's a labyrinth down there. Throne alone knows how we get to the bottom of the shaft, or what we'll find when we do.'

'We could ask for a guide,' Drake suggested. 'The senior crew know we're Inquisition. They won't dare refuse a direct appeal for help.'

Horst shook his head. 'But it won't stop them gossiping about what we're looking for. Even if we don't tell them, it'll only take one person to notice, and word of the manuscript gets out.'

'They're hardly likely to tell any of the passengers,' Vex put in, and Horst nodded again.

'Of course not,' he agreed. 'But there are thousands of shipfolk aboard, and heresy spreads like the pox in a bordello.' Keira flushed at the metaphor, and Horst cleared his throat hastily. 'Better to keep all knowledge of it to ourselves, if we can.'

'If we take a guide with us, they don't have to come back,' Keira pointed out reasonably, and with impeccable logic.

Horst shook his head. 'I'd rather not expend any more of the shipfolk if we can avoid it. We're going to be aboard a long time, and if we upset them too much they can make life extremely awkward. We've enough bad feeling to smooth over as it is.'

'How long are we going to be here, exactly?' Drake asked uneasily, and Vex turned to look in his direction, happy to supply the information he wanted.

'It's hard to be precise,' he said. 'Time within the warp has little meaning in the conventional sense. We should emerge in the Scintilla System around two weeks after we entered it, as such things are measured in the materium, but our subjective experience may seem considerably longer or shorter than that.'

'I see.' Drake clearly didn't, but nodded anyway. 'That's a big help. Thanks.'

'You're welcome,' Vex said, wondering for a moment if the Guardsman was being sarcastic, but even if he was, devotees of the Machine-God ought to be above responding to petty slights of that nature.

Horst tapped his comm-bead. 'Barda. Have you finished recalibrating the auspexes yet?'

'Just about,' the young pilot confirmed. 'The returns are fuzzy, but I'm getting what looks like an image of the hull metal. Anything that doesn't read solid is a gap of some kind.' He paused for a moment. 'I'm sending it through now.'

'Receiving,' Vex said, attuning his data-slate to the vox frequency the shuttle used for remote telemetry. A faintly diffuse image began to appear on the screen, dark lines coiling around and through it like the veins and arteries of a diseased heart. There was too much information to fit on the tiny pict receiver, even at maximum reduction, and he tracked and zoomed the image, searching for the

section he wanted. After a moment he identified the
Beyonder's Hostelry, pinpointing their suite by the echo of
everyone's earpieces, and from there was able to back-
track to the reception deck. He angled the device so that
his companions could see the display, although he pri-
vately doubted that anyone else would be able to make
much sense of the image.

'It's a labyrinth!' Drake said, obviously trying to pick
out the location of the shaft, and failing completely.

'I'll refine the image before we attempt to enter it,' Vex
assured him.

'Will that take long?' Keira asked, and Vex suppressed
the faintest of sighs. The lost cogitator would have made
short work of the task, but the comparatively limited
data-slate would just have to do.

'Several hours at least,' he said.

'That's the last of it,' Barda said, then hesitated. 'You
know you asked me to listen out for anything unusual?'

'Yes,' Horst said. 'What have you got?'

'I'm not sure how significant it is,' Barda admitted, 'but
according to the internal vox traffic, the bridge lost contact with one of their damage control teams about twenty
minutes ago. They don't seem too worried about it yet.'

'Hardly surprising,' Vex said. 'There's so much metal in
the hull, any short-range vox-casters would be unreliable
at best.'

'Thank you for bringing it to our attention, though,'
Horst added.

'Why have they got damage control parties assigned
while we're in the warp?' Keira asked, intrigued.

'There was a minor collision early this morning,'
Barda said. 'A piece of junk from the debris field
impacted just aft of the primary heat exchangers. They
didn't have time to repair the hull damage before getting under way, so they sealed off the section, and sent
teams in to check the adjacent ones for any signs of
structural stress.'

'Isn't that dangerous?' Drake asked, clearly picturing daemons swarming in though a hole in the hull plating, and Vex shook his head reassuringly.

'No. The Geller field extends for some distance beyond the hull, so the warp itself is repelled far beyond any weaknesses in the outer structure.'

'Which is how come the junk follows the ship about in the first place,' Keira added helpfully.

'Quite.' Horst reactivated his comm-bead. 'Barda, can you try and find out exactly where the impact was? If there's any damage near the shaft we lost the manuscript down, we might have to plan a way around the sealed section.'

'Will do,' Barda promised, and cut the link.

'So.' Keira leaned forwards, eager to be active again. 'What's our next move?'

'Talk to Raymer,' Horst said. 'Those thieves were professionals. If he doesn't know who they were, he's no good at his job.'

'That makes sense,' the assassin agreed. 'What about me?'

'What you're best at,' Horst said, and the girl smiled.

'Who do you want killed?'

Horst stared at her for a moment, then evidently realised she was joking. His shoulders lost a little tension, and the corners of his own mouth widened a little. 'I meant the other thing you're best at. Scout around, blend in, get the feel of the place.'

Keira nodded, and stood. 'No problem.'

As she reached the door, Horst called her back. 'If you do have to kill anyone,' he added as an afterthought, 'for Throne's sake make it look like an accident.'

The *Ursus Innare*, the Warp, Date and Time Meaningless

'SOMEONE'S AT THE door,' Ven said, his eyes unfocused, a faint tremor shaking his body. Elyra looked at him, masking her concern, still conscious of the part she was playing. If warp travel was hard on most people, it was far more so on psykers; even shielded as she was by the rituals of sanctioning, she could feel the taint of the unclean realm beyond the freighter's Geller field scratching at her mind, taunting and insidious, like the breath of a ravening animal on the back of her neck. The juvies must be feeling it too, she knew, even more strongly, as they were unprotected by the blessing of the Emperor, and Ven worst of all. The lad was a nascent seer, his gift still undeveloped, and, like most of his kind, seemed to have trouble distinguishing between objective reality and the constant barrage of outside impressions echoing through his head.

'About rutting time,' Kyrlock agreed, cocking his head to listen to a scraping of metal somewhere in the distance. 'It's been Throne knows how long since the last drop.' He prodded Trosk with the toe of his boot, and the shaven-headed youngster rose to his feet, with his habitual air of detachment. 'Better come on, if you want to eat something other than rat for a change.'

With a growing sense of relief, Elyra heard the booming echo of the bulkhead hatch, somewhere beyond the tumbled heaps of ore surrounding them. It seemed Ven had been speaking no more than the literal truth for once, although, given his propensity for vagueness and misdirection, it was equally likely that he'd been feeling the presence of some warp entity scrabbling at the ship's defences.

'You heard the man,' she agreed, and glanced round at the makeshift camp. Ven would be a liability on the supply run, but she didn't like the idea of splitting the group now. The brief spasm of violence they'd witnessed a few days before was an early warning sign, she was sure, and anyone left on their own would be all too vulnerable to the predators beginning to emerge among the refugees. 'Zu, can you bring Ven?'

'Sure,' Zusen said, moving away from Kyrlock with palpable reluctance. Ever since the Guardsman had rescued her from a would-be violator on Sepheris Secundus, she'd practically glued herself to him, seeming to find his presence reassuring; at least Elyra hoped that was all it was. For a moment she found herself wondering if Keira had managed to work through her manifest infatuation with Horst yet, or was still in denial about her feelings, but such speculation was fruitless, so she let it go. There was more than enough to be concerned with here and now.

'I can manage,' Ven said, his expression truculent, and Elyra breathed a faint sigh of relief. If he was entering one of his lucid phases, that would be one less thing to worry about.

'Good,' she said. 'Then come on.' She led the way over the treacherous surface of shifting shale, avoiding the spots which seemed to fluoresce in the all-pervading gloom, not looking back. Kyrlock would be right behind her, she knew, and the juvies would follow: the person she was pretending to be wouldn't show the slightest concern for anyone else, so neither should she.

'You heard the lady,' Kyrlock said, right on cue. He shouldered his chainaxe, the supporting harness rigged for a fast, one-handed draw if he should need it, and hefted his shotgun meaningfully. 'Bring the packs and bedrolls.' They'd be returning to the same spot, and the fire which kept the rats at bay, but leaving property unattended here would be tantamount to throwing it away.

'Right you are,' Trosk agreed, a faintly mocking tone in his voice as always, and shouldered Elyra's pack along with his own. That was good, she'd left it there to see if anyone would bring it along for her without being instructed to; the fact that the most recalcitrant of her unwanted charges had done so meant that her *de facto* leadership of the group was going unchallenged, at least for the moment. There was nothing in it she particularly needed in any case, her laspistol was already tucked into the waistband of her trousers, a visible deterrent to anyone prepared to make trouble.

A few moments of slipping and sliding brought the little group to the main entrance to the hold, where a trio of Shadow Franchise goons were standing, shotguns of their own held ready for use. They were accompanied by a pair of the ship's crew, easily distinguished from the franchisemen by the patches on their jackets depicting a stylised bear astride some cylindrical object surrounded by water, who were carrying a large crate between them.

'Room service,' one of the franchisemen said, as the voiders set the heavy box down with a faint grinding of stone against stone. The others laughed, mocking and humourless, while Elyra and her charges joined the growing crowd of refugees hovering around the group. 'Fair shares all round, and remember to play nice.' They began to retreat back towards the portal, the crewmen first, and then the gangers, who kept the crowd covered with casual disdain.

'They're nervous,' Zusen whispered. 'Trying not to look afraid.'

Elyra nodded, eyeing the tableau narrowly. That much was obvious, even without the little wyrd's dubious gift of empathy. 'Afraid we'll make a break for the rest of the ship,' she replied softly. Well, she could hardly blame them for that; conditions here were pretty bad, and without the threat of firearms she had no doubt that a few of their fellow travellers would have been desperate enough to try it.

After a moment the hatch boomed closed again, and the crowd surged forwards.

'Back!' someone shouted, his face partially obscured by the shadow of some structural girder high above their heads, blocking one of the fitfully working glowglobes. As he turned, casually punching one of the other refugees to the deck, his visage was revealed; to Elyra's complete lack of surprise, it was the victor of the brief, brutal fight she'd witnessed before. He was flanked by the rest of his party, most of whom were bearing makeshift weapons of one kind or another, mainly mining tools. 'This is ours, and we're keeping it!'

'It's supposed to be for everyone!' one of the women shouted, and the man laughed.

'Take it then,' he suggested, to the evident amusement of his cronies. The sharpened shovels and pickaxes in their hands made it all too evident that they'd been planning this since the last supply drop, correctly divining that controlling the food supply meant power over the ragged groups of refugees. The faction the woman belonged to, mainly families with children, milled uncertainly. 'Or perhaps you'd like to do something for me in exchange.' His tone made it pretty obvious what he had in mind.

'You can't talk to my wife like that!' A thickset fellow, who looked more than capable of taking care of himself under most circumstances, strode forwards aggressively.

'I'll talk to the bitch any way I want to.' The ringleader swung the handle of his pickaxe, taking the fellow in the face: he fell heavily, the woman screamed, and most of the children in the group started crying.

'Rut this,' Kyrlock said loudly. The would-be bandit king turned in astonishment, wondering who else would dare to challenge him, and began to look uncertain for the first time. The former Guardsman grinned ferally, and cocked his shotgun, with a *clack* which echoed loudly in the cavernous space. 'You and your sumprats are going to go away now. While you still can. Because if I can still see or smell you ten seconds from now you'll be dead. Understand?'

'You're bluffing,' the man said, trying and failing to sound confident.

'Am I?' Kyrlock said evenly. 'I know some of you saw what happened to the last piece of bootscrape I found picking on a woman. Seven seconds.'

Little ripples of alarm began to flicker around the gang, which intensified as Elyra drew her laspistol. She caught the muttered phrase 'shot him in the nads and left him to bleed to death,' and summoned up a grin as vindictive as Kyrlock's own. 'Happy to repeat the trick,' she said, 'even with a smaller target.'

'Four seconds,' Kyrlock added, conversationally.

That was enough: even if their leader was stupid enough to hold his ground, his cohorts were beginning to sidle away, and he started to follow them. 'This isn't over,' he blustered, moving away from the box at last.

'Then you're an even bigger fool than you look,' Elyra said, striding forwards to take possession of it. She heaved the lid open with her free hand, not wanting to risk relinquishing the laspistol for a while yet, and pulled out a greasy block of reconstituted protein. 'Families with children first, then everyone else. One pack each.'

'Thank you!' The habwife was gazing at Kyrlock as if he was Saint Angevin reborn, while her husband climbed groggily to his feet. He bowed in Kyrlock's direction, swaying a little as he did so.

'In your debt, noble sir,' he said, as though the Guardsman was a minor aristocrat rather than a petty criminal who'd come into the service of the Inquisition by a series of bizarre coincidences. But then deference was practically hard-wired into the DNA of a Secundan serf.

Kyrlock shrugged, looking a little uncomfortable. 'Don't mention it,' he said.

'Vos, you were amazing!' Zusen said, mercifully deflecting attention from Elyra, and she began to sigh with relief.

'Growing a conscience?' Trosk asked quietly at her elbow. 'I'd have thought you'd be wanting to keep it all for yourself now, not give it away.' He was staring at her appraisingly again, his tone faintly mocking as always, and once more Elyra began to feel uneasy.

'What, and pass up the chance to keep the sheep happy?' She shrugged dismissively. 'Now they're too grateful to ask any awkward questions, and they're less likely to turn me in if the bounty warrant on my head's made it as far as Scintilla.'

'How very pragmatic,' Trosk said dryly, handing a ration pack to the nearest refugee. 'Are we leaving anything for those charming fellows who tried to take it all?'

Elyra made a show of considering the matter. 'Might as well,' she conceded at length. 'They'll only steal some if we don't.'

'Maybe you should have killed them while you had the chance, then,' Trosk suggested casually.

'Maybe,' Elyra said, feeling as though she was being tested in some way. 'But Vos would never have pulled the trigger so close to the crowd. Shotguns spread, and he might have hit one of the sheep by mistake.'

'So he's the one with the conscience, eh?' The idea seemed to amuse Trosk greatly. 'Who'd have thought it?'

The *Misericord*, the Warp, Date and Time Meaningless.

'THEY WERE RECEIVERS of Bounty,' Raymer said. Despite the archaic armour he wore, his office was efficiently functional, to Horst's carefully concealed relief. Apart from the banner depicting the *Misericord* gripped in a mailed fist hanging from the wall above the captain's desk, where he would normally have expected to see the Imperial aquila, he might have been in any provincial precinct house. Here, on the crew side of the armoured bulkheads separating the shipfolk from their passengers, there was no attempt to conceal the metalwork of the walls, which Horst appreciated; he'd been an investigator for far too long to feel comfortable with that degree of artifice. It smacked of deception, which, in his experience, meant that the deceiver had something to hide.

'I'm sorry.' Horst shrugged. 'The name means nothing to me.'

'I don't suppose it does,' Raymer said, his tight smile failing to disguise his antipathy. Which was hardly surprising under the circumstances, Horst thought; practically the first thing the Angelae had done after coming aboard was to maim two of his men. The Merciful officer hadn't mentioned the incident, and Horst felt that it would be tactless to raise the matter himself, so the subject had been avoided so far, increasing the gently simmering undercurrent of resentment he'd felt permeating the air since his arrival.

'Are they one of the shipboard castes?' Drake asked, from his seat on Horst's left. After some deliberation, the arbitrator had elected to bring him along; Vex would need peace and solitude to refine the resolution of the map to something usable, and Drake was far too keyed up to sleep. Keira too, probably. He found himself wondering where she was, and forced the thought away; she was perfectly able to take care of herself.

'They're one of the oldest,' Raymer said, looking faintly uncomfortable for the first time. 'But many of the members in the outhulls don't conform to their original purpose.'

'Which was?' Horst asked.

'Which was, and is, to scavenge reusable materials for the Company of Fabricators, the Followers of the Wire, and anyone else who needs them.' Raymer shrugged. 'There's a considerable element, however, which interprets that remit in the widest possible way.'

'Stealing from the passengers,' Drake said.

'Mainly the passengers,' Raymer said. 'Which means the majority of our people don't much care what the Receivers do.' He smiled coldly. 'With the Merciful being the obvious exception.'

'Obviously,' Horst said, with a careful lack of inflection. Let Raymer interpret that how he liked. 'Where do we find them?'

'The outhulls, mostly,' Raymer said. His expression hardened. 'You've already found your way into the fringes of those without too much trouble, I hear.'

'I hope your men are recovering,' Horst said, relieved to have the source of the tension out in the open at last.

'The Suterers tell me they're stable,' Raymer said coldly. 'No thanks to you.'

'They were obstructing Inquisition agents in the pursuit of heretics,' Drake said. 'They should consider themselves lucky to be alive.'

'Of course.' Raymer inclined his head a few millimetres in a parody of respect. 'I'm sure Kalum thinks the loss of his hand a small price to pay for the recovery of your underwear.'

'What we may have lost or recovered is no concern of yours,' Horst said, with a quick glance at Drake to forestall an angry reply.

'You said they were mostly in the outhulls,' Drake said, changing the subject with a surprising display of tact. 'Where else would we find Receivers?'

'In the Gallery of Sin,' Raymer said after a moment. 'Some of them come in from time to time to sell whatever they've salvaged.' He put just enough stress on the final word to imbue it with palpable cynicism.

'If you know they're congregating in the outhulls, why don't you just take a squad or two down there and arrest them?' Drake asked.

'Because it can't be done,' Raymer replied, with a hint of impatience, 'even if I was prepared to try suppressing an entire guild without the consent of the captains. You've seen the fringes; imagine that, stretching for kilometres in every direction.'

Having seen several underhives in the course of his life, Horst was able to do so with little difficulty. He nodded. 'I take your point,' he said. 'What's down there, exactly?'

'Pretty much everything,' Raymer told him curtly. 'Beyonderside takes up less than five per cent of the

Misericord. Next to that you've got the bridge, officers' quarters and the holdings of the castes who deal directly with the passengers. Then you're out to the fringes, where the main cargo holds, the engines, the Renderers' farms and the other support stuff is. Outhull's hardly used at all, unless we get more cargo than usual.' He hesitated, looking uneasy. 'Outhull's best avoided, even for the shipborn. Although with your attack bitch along, you'll probably be safe enough.' He didn't look altogether convinced of that, although he clearly didn't care too much one way or the other.

'That's reassuring,' Horst said blandly. 'I'll tell Keira you were appreciative of her skills.'

'You can tell her whatever you like,' Raymer said. 'So long as you keep her on a leash around my people.'

'Don't worry,' Horst said, relieved he'd had the foresight not to bring the young assassin to the meeting; if he had, the conversation would probably have ended in bloodshed by now. 'We're just as keen as you are to avoid any further unfortunate incidents.'

'I'm pleased to hear it,' Raymer said. 'And if you could avoid slaughtering too many of the passengers between here and Scintilla, I'd appreciate that too.'

'We'll do our best,' Horst assured him, standing to leave.

FIVE

Scintil VIII Void Station, Scintilla System
240.993.M41

MUON'S BAR WAS halfway along the void station's
Esplanade, at the confluence of two of the most heavily
travelled corridors. One led to the primary docking bays,
the other to the commercial zone, where the cargo brokers were based, and pretty much anything could be
bought or sold. Its location made it the perfect spot for
brokers and ships' crews to meet and haggle, and its
owner overheard a lot. Which made him one of
Quillem's most useful assets.

'Mr Quillem,' Muon said as he walked through the
door, a non-physical barrier of multicoloured smoke
kept swirling in place by an arcane system of air jets; like
most such establishments on the station, Muon's never
closed. 'This is an unexpected pleasure.' He put down the
glass he was polishing, and poured a careful measure of
a thick blue liqueur into it, while Quillem stepped over a
recumbent patron halfway between the door and the bar.
His pockets had been expertly turned out, although by

the staff or his erstwhile companions, Quillem couldn't be bothered to guess. 'Your usual?'

The code was simple enough; the colour of the drink meant *we can talk freely.* Or at least as freely as possible in a public space. Quillem nodded, took a cautious sip in case any of the handful of patrons occupying seats in a few of the booths happened to be glancing in their direction, and found to his relief that it was actually quite palatable.

He settled on a bar stool, and leaned over the counter, contriving to look as if he'd had quite a lot to drink already. *Au fait* with the routine, Muon adopted the distantly polite expression of bar staff everywhere listening to rambling recitations of misfortune or personal aggrandisement. If any of the earnest whisperers in the shadows were to look up from their dealing now, all they'd see was a maudlin drunk boring the bartender, although if Quillem was any judge, none of them were likely to. Letting your attention wander in a place like Scintil VIII was liable to cost you plenty, and you'd be lucky if money was all you lost.

'The *Eddia Stabilis* was a dead end, Muon,' Quillem murmured, toying with the drink. No one else was at the bar, but he couldn't be certain that was going to last; better to get straight to the point.

'I'm sorry to hear that,' Muon replied, plying his cloth over the pristine surface of the counter top. It was thinly veined marble, of out-system origin, and imparted an air of elegance to the establishment which its regular clientele found reassuring. The tables were wrought iron, with a thin patina of gilt, worn thin enough in places to show the duller glint of the underlying metal; the regulars found that reassuring too. It meant Muon's had been here a long time, a rare point of stability in a constantly shifting milieu of quasi-legal entrepreneurship. On his stroll down the Esplanade to get here, Quillem had spotted over a dozen new businesses which had sprung up since his last visit, flourishing like fungus on the corpses of the less successful. 'I hope you're not going to ask for a refund.'

'The Emperor will step down from the throne before that,' Quillem reassured him, referring to a popular superstition that His Divine Majesty would resume His corporeal form at the turn of the millennium. He didn't believe it, of course, any more than Muon probably did; the expression had become a colloquial reference to something that would almost certainly never happen. Like Muon relinquishing any money that had come into his hands. 'Your information was sound. Things just didn't work out at our end, that's all.'

'I see.' The bartender's inflection was cautiously neutral. Muon had only a vague idea of who Quillem represented, the interrogator had made sure of that, but he undoubtedly had his suspicions. After all, the Scintilla System was widely known to house the headquarters of the Calixian Conclave, and the kind of information Quillem bought and bartered could only be of interest to a few groups other than them.

'I'd really like to know how you heard about it,' Quillem said quietly. 'Not to mention what was on board.'

'Xenos stuff, that's all I heard,' Muon said. 'Just like I told you the last time.' He was a short man, florid of complexion, and tilted his head back a little to look Quillem full in the face, the better to give the impression of earnest sincerity. 'One of the crew was getting a little drunk in that booth over there, and said something about xenos, then everyone else shut him up.' Quillem glanced at the booth in question, currently unoccupied. It was angled so that very little of it could be seen from the bar. Muon's voice took on an aggrieved tone. 'They weren't subtle about it either. Took me ages to get the stains out.'

'Who were the voiders talking to?' Quillem asked.

'I've no idea,' Muon said, probably truthfully. If he had anything to offer, he'd have tried to sell it by now. 'Stationers for sure, I could tell by their accents, but that doesn't narrow it down much.'

'Well, that's something,' Quillem said, knocking back the drink. Most of the major brokers, not to mention the minor ones, were owned and run by families native to the void station, but that tiny snippet of information would eliminate a few. As for the rest, they'd just have to do it the hard way, trawling through innumerable data records in the hope of finding out which brokerage had arranged to shift cargo aboard the doomed freighter. Not that it would necessarily help, even then: there was no guarantee that this hadn't been a private arrangement negotiated by a handful of crewmen, to the fatal ignorance of their shipmates.

'I might take a guess, though,' Muon said thoughtfully, refilling Quillem's glass, just as he was about to stand.

'Based on what?' Quillem asked.

'Not much, really,' the bartender admitted. 'But when I cleaned up after they left, I found a transport pass in the pocket of the one they'd left behind.' He looked momentarily aggrieved. 'They'd helped themselves to his money, the thieving skags, but at least I got a couple of creds for the clothes. And a few more for the body, of course.'

'Of course,' Quillem echoed. Pointless asking who the buyer had been; it could have been anyone, from an unsanctified tech dabbler wanting spare parts for a malfunctioning servitor, to the owner of one of the bushmeat stalls scattered around the Esplanade, or any one of a dozen even less savoury explanations.

'Anyhow,' Muon went on, 'the pass was still good for a return trip to the lower docking arm. So I'm guessing that's where the ship was.'

'Seems likely,' Quillem agreed, taking another sip of his drink. 'Which helps me how?'

Muon looked at him as though there was drool on his chin. 'The dregs down there see a lot, don't they? Maybe one of them knows who set up the deal, or saw who the crew was talking to. If you really get lucky, you might even find the one who carried the boxes aboard.'

Quillem nodded. It was a long shot, but he'd taken wilder ones in his time. 'Worth a try,' he conceded. Leaning across the counter, he palmed a high-denomination scrip, and let it flutter to the floor beside the bartender's foot. 'Oh look, you've dropped something.'

'So I have.' Muon scooped it up, and came level with the bar again. 'Will there be anything else?'

'I don't think so,' Quillem said. A few more patrons had drifted into the establishment while they'd been talking, laying claim to unoccupied booths, where Muon's underlings scurried to take their orders, but a couple of them were taking up stations at the bar, including an underdressed and over made-up joygirl of indeterminate age. From Muon's apparent indifference, it was clear that she paid some kind of rent for running her business from his.

'Well, remember to drop by any time you're passing,' Muon said, and began to polish another piece of glassware.

The *Misericord*, the Warp, Date and Time Meaningless

DRAKE HADN'T BEEN entirely sure what he expected the Gallery of Sin to be like, but his first impression of it was a curious mixture of surprise and vague disappointment. It seemed to have been a cargo hold originally, but a few generations ago someone had started to build a town inside it: the corridor they'd entered the Gallery by had suddenly opened out into an alleyway between two buildings, *faux* feral in style, like pretty much everything else he'd seen since coming aboard. That, in turn, opened out into a square, choked with people and market stalls.

He glanced around, trying to get his bearings. 'Nothing particularly sinful here that I can see,' he said, trying not to sound as though he felt cheated.

'Sinfulness is everywhere,' Keira replied, ever the Redemptionist; moved by curiosity, he'd once asked Horst what her creed involved, and, after a short conversation, felt very relieved that he hadn't actually made a pass at her that night in the villa. He couldn't quite quash a faint stirring of envy when he considered the girl's obvious infatuation with the team leader, but all things considered, he was well out of that one. Good luck to Mordechai if he ever tried to do anything about it.

'Perhaps we should split up,' Vex suggested. 'This deck is quite extensive, and we ought to be able to cover it more efficiently if we go our separate ways.'

'No.' Horst shook his head. 'I don't trust anything on this ship. No one goes off alone.' He nodded at the assassin. 'Apart from Keira, if we need to use her talents.' Thanks to her formidable scouting ability, they already had a reasonably detailed picture of the parts of the ship immediately adjoining the *Beyonder's Hostelry*, to supplement the map Vex was painstakingly building up from Barda's auspex readings.

'I agree,' Drake said, 'but Hybris does have a point. Maybe if we pair off?'

'Sounds reasonable,' Horst conceded. 'You two head that way, Keira and I will take the other. We should meet up again somewhere on the opposite side.'

'A reasonable compromise,' Vex agreed.

'Right.' Drake nodded, and turned to follow the techpriest, who was already striding towards an alleyway on the opposite side of the square. For a moment he lost sight of him through the press of the crowd, then, to his relief, caught a glimpse of a white robe, and picked up his pace.

'Good morrow, honoured traveller,' a voice cried out, and a slim fellow in a leotard dyed in patches of violently clashing colour cartwheeled in front of him. 'Welcome to the Gallery of Sin, where jocularity reigns, and spirits are light.'

'Not now,' Drake said, trying to step round him. 'I'm in a hurry.' Vex had already disappeared down the mouth of the alley.

'How can you be in a hurry in a place where time flows backwards?' the entertainer asked, pulling a face of exaggerated puzzlement.

'I just am.' Drake suppressed the urge to plant his fist in the middle of that infuriating grin. Horst wouldn't be pleased if he drew attention to himself, he knew, and his soldier's instincts hadn't deserted him, even here; out of the corner of his eye he caught a glimpse of burnished metal. A Merciful patrol, making sure that whatever passed for law and order here was being maintained. If he started a brawl now, he'd probably get his kneecaps shot off before he could identify himself. Come to think of it, judging by Raymer's attitude, if they did recognise him they'd probably be glad of the excuse. Instead, he reached into a pocket and pulled out a couple of coins. 'Can you do conjuring tricks?'

'But of course.' The entertainer bowed deeply. 'I'm a journeyman of the Company of Imbeciles, which means I can prestidigitate with the best of them. Not to mention tumble, juggle, recite a lay, sing you a ballad, mum, mime, or…'

'Then vanish,' Drake interrupted, flicking the coins in the man's general direction. They were snatched out of the air by reflexes almost as acute as Keira's. 'Swive off and entertain someone else.'

Getting past the man at last, he sprinted for the mouth of the alley down which Vex had disappeared, and swore under his breath. The tech-priest had vanished completely.

* * *

Scintil VIII Void Station, Scintilla System
240.993.M41

THE LOWER DOCKING arm was well away from the main
body of the station, at the end of one of the booms pro-
jecting from the main superstructure like questing roots
from a tuber. Once the primary point of access to the
whole structure, the hangar bays and anchor points out
here had declined in importance as the station grew, and
larger, better appointed facilities had been built around
the central hub, which had been enlarged and extended
so much over the intervening millennia that now the
original Scintil VIII was little more than a blister on the
hull of its own distended senescence. These days, the
lower arm's relatively isolated position made it the perfect place for ships to dock if the business which brought
them here was better carried on away from official
scrutiny.

Quillem had taken the local transport system to get
there, since the walk was long, and the luckless crewman
Muon had told him about had ridden on it at least once;
Inquisitor Grynner had impressed upon him repeatedly
over the course of their association that even the smallest
detail could be significant, and there was no telling what
might be unearthed by following in the footsteps of one
of the conspirators. In fact, nothing had been, beyond a
reminder of how uncomfortable the contraption was to
ride in, and why he generally preferred to avoid it.

Quillem clambered down from the rattling cart, lined
with benches, which had slowly emptied as the con-
veyance trundled further and further from the more
densely populated heart of the station. As he, and a
handful of other passengers, stepped off the slowly moving vehicle onto the platform beside the track, the
brakewoman eased her weight off the heavy lever currently pressing pads against the wheels, allowing the cart
to pick up speed again. It clattered into the conduit

between the decks reserved for it, and its many equally uncomfortable fellows, dragged along by the piston in the pneumatic tube between the guide rails, and vanished.

Quillem dawdled away from the platform, content to let the tide of drifting humanity carry him along, observing his surroundings. As if conscious of its heritage, the station looked older here, the metal of its corridors duller, passageways a little darker and narrower, the votive shrines to the Emperor unkempt, and the offerings they held meagre. The people seemed shrunken too, at least those he took for local residents, the crews of the docked starships wandering among them generally at least a head taller.

Despite its relative isolation, though, the community here seemed to be thriving. Just a few metres from the conduit platform, Quillem found a miniature replica of the Esplanade, complete with bars, shops, street hawkers and a few more dubious enterprises aimed at parting visiting crewmen from their coin.

Interesting, but unhelpful. Sidestepping a local joygirl who seemed to regard him as a potential client, and ignoring the subsequent gesture implying that he preferred the company of his own gender, Quillem started down a side passage. Hostelries catering to the ship crews wouldn't be much use to him; he needed somewhere the locals hung out.

He found the ideal place without too much difficulty, guided as much by his nose as by his eyes, a small shanty jammed into an angle between two buttresses supporting an overhead walkway. Like those surrounding it, the ramshackle building sprawled out from its supports to annex as much of the passageway as its proprietor thought he could get away with without blocking the passing traffic entirely. The smell of cooking wafted towards him, and he found himself unexpectedly salivating; it had been a long time since his last meal.

As the curtain across the entrance fell into place behind him, every pair of eyes in the place swivelled momentarily in his direction, then away again, with elaborate displays of uninterest. Just as he'd expected. Round here, a strange face would mean one of two things: trouble for its owner, or trouble for someone else. Either way, no one would feel like drawing attention to themselves until they were sure which way the equation was going to operate.

The main item on the menu, chalked up on the wall behind the counter, appeared to be fine-ground offal stuffed into lengths of animal intestine, served with pulped tubers. None of the locals eating here seemed to have been poisoned yet, and it certainly smelled appetising enough, so Quillem ordered a plateful, and glanced round for somewhere to sit. Perfect. There was a gap in one of the communal benches lining the walls, between two heavily muscled men who quite clearly worked the docks here. He squeezed himself into the space, with an affable nod, just sufficient to apologise for the inconvenience, and began to eat.

'Are you sure you're in the right place?' the man on the left asked, after a moment, just conversationally enough to mute the incipient challenge if Quillem turned out not to be the one in trouble here.

The interrogator chewed, swallowed, and nodded. The food was better than he'd expected; quite palatable, in fact. 'I'm hungry, they've got food. I'd say so.'

'It's just that we don't get many shipfolk in here,' his interlocutor persisted.

Quillem ate another mouthful, and shrugged. 'That explains it. I'm not one.' Out of the corner of his eye, he could see the men surrounding him evaluating this fresh and unexpected piece of information. If he wasn't off one of the ships in dock, he must have come from the main body of the station. People didn't do that without a very good reason. Add in the fact of his easy self-confidence, and he came down heavily on the Trouble for Someone Else side of the balance. Suddenly he had incrementally more elbow room, despite the crowded nature of the benches. He smiled easily. 'I'm looking for anyone who might have helped load a freighter called the *Eddia Stabilis*, Stobart-class freight hauler, came through here about four months back.'

'What do you want know for?' the man on the other side asked, a little too casually, before poking another forkful of food through a minuscule gap in his beard.

Quillem ate another mouthful or two, then glanced pointedly around the crowded chop house, packed with people pretending not to eavesdrop. 'That's my business.' He stressed the word 'business' just enough to make it clear that he was prepared to pay for the information he wanted, and noted the sudden quickening of interest among his immediate neighbours with wry amusement. 'I want to know which broker handled her cargo, and if anyone who helped shift it noticed anything unusual.'

'What sort of unusual?'

Quillem shrugged. 'The sort they'd have noticed if it was there, believe me.'

'I see.' His interlocutor went quiet, and chewed his food thoughtfully.

'You want Downunder Reach,' the first man said after a moment. 'Lot of dregs down there might know something. Lucky for you, we're going that way. We can show you, if you like.'

'Very kind,' Quillem said dryly. He finished his meal at a leisurely pace, and stood. 'Whenever you're ready?'

The *Misericord*, the Warp, Date and Time Meaningless

LIKE MOST MEN of his calling, Hybris Vex wasn't very comfortable with people. Long familiarity with the other Angelae enabled him to predict their responses under most circumstances with a fair degree of accuracy, but, on the whole, people baffled him. They were capricious, and irrational, and he much preferred the orderly dictates of dispassionate logic. That was why he'd become an acolyte of the Machine-God in the first place.

Ironic, then, that he'd become a foot soldier for the Inquisition, a calling which, despite his distaste for it, kept inflicting human contact on him regardless. On the other hand, being a member of the Angelae also enabled him to further his understanding of the Omnissiah in ways forever denied to most of his brethren. The psychic booster which Tonis, the rene-gade tech-priest, had built, for instance, was a complete perversion of all the Machine-God stood for, and yet there were elements of its construction which had been quite breathtaking in their elegance. The loss of the manuscript had been a grave blow indeed; there was no telling what further secrets a prolonged study of it might have revealed.

'Mind the way, there, sir!' a cheerful voice cried, break-ing his reverie, and Vex stepped back a pace, just in time to avoid a collision with a man in a floppy green hat, pushing a handcart loaded with small, ripe fruits. 'Tempt you to a punnet of hayberries, straight from the agridecks?'

'Thank you, no.' Vex glanced round, wondering why Drake wasn't dealing with this, then realised for the first time that his colleague wasn't with him. That was dis-turbing, though no real cause for alarm. The crowds were so thick in this street, it would have been easy to become separated without noticing.

Well, finding the Guardsman again should be a simple matter of logic. Vex recalled the way he'd come with a fair degree of accuracy, and this peculiar mock village would undoubtedly be laid out to some underlying street plan. If he retraced his steps to the previous corner, he would probably see Drake taking the same route he had.

'Suit yourself, sir,' the street peddler said, and moved off, pushing the cart ahead of him like a battering ram, scattering passers-by with cheerful indifference. Most of the ones inconvenienced were passengers, Vex noted dispassionately, those whose distinctive garb and void-born pallor marked them out as native Misericordians stepping nimbly out of the way without breaking stride. 'Haaaaayberries! Get your haaaaayberries! I won't be round tomorrow! The donkey's…' The voice cut off as he turned a corner, subsumed into the general babble surrounding him.

Vex reached the end of the street, and glanced both ways, vaguely surprised to see no sign of Drake in either direction. The buildings were pressing in a little closer than he remembered, their tile roofs overhanging the narrow thoroughfare, and he dismissed a sudden flicker of unease. The luminators in the metal sky above cast the shadowless light of perpetual noon, offering no clue as to orientation, but logical deduction should suffice. If he just kept going in the same direction, he'd eventually reach the edge of this urban masquerade, and then it would simply be a matter of skirting it until he found the way back to the *Beyonder's Hostelry*.

He raised a reflexive hand to the comm-bead in his ear, before remembering that, like Drake's, it was back in their quarters; the miniature voxes were rare and expensive enough to excite unwelcome comment if anyone noticed their presence, and they'd been reluctantly relinquished in the interests of anonymity. *How much we take the Omnissiah's gifts for granted*, he thought ruefully, *until we no longer have them.*

Picking out the nearest alley mouth on the other side of the street, between a shop selling boots and a patisserie, neither of which interested him particularly, he started down it, fighting an irrational urge to run. At least there were fewer people down here, he thought, with some relief.

* * *

The *Ursus Innare*, the Warp, Date and Time Meaningless

'I'M NOT SURE it was wise to intervene,' Elyra said quietly. The three wyrds were asleep, so far as she could tell, rolled in their blankets on the other side of the firepit, where lumps of oily shale flickered and flared fitfully. 'We're supposed to be trying to blend in.'

'No we're not. We're supposed to be the hardest bastards on the ship,' Kyrlock replied, his voice equally low. 'We made a big impression when we took Kantris down; even if most of the people around us didn't see what happened, they heard about it, believe me. If I hadn't challenged that cocky little arsewipe we'd have made ourselves look weak, and a few of them would start to wonder why.'

'I see.' Elyra nodded thoughtfully. She was playing the part of a former bodyguard to a minor Secundan aristocrat, fleeing a bounty warrant with a pack full of her former employer's jewellery, which had explained her proficiency with a laspistol to the satisfaction of the Shadow Franchise operatives who'd arranged their passage on the ore scow. Behind the carefully constructed façade of sociopathic detachment, however, she was out of her depth in this dog-eat-dog environment. Kyrlock, on the other hand, had grown up in it, so she was inclined to trust his judgement.

Kyrlock shrugged. 'Tumble rules, basically. We slapped him down, so we're top canids again. Until the next time.'

'The next time?' Elyra asked.

Kyrlock shrugged again. 'There's always a next time.' He looked pointedly at the distant flickering of the bandits' fire. At the moment none of the men around it seemed intent on causing trouble, just sitting sullenly, exchanging remarks in an undertone, but Elyra could almost see the tension hanging in the air above them. 'We shook his leadership; he'll have to do something to keep his followers in line.'

'Come after us, you mean?' Elyra asked.

Kyrlock nodded. 'If he's stupid enough. Even if he isn't, we've made ourselves the ones to take down if you want to be king of the spoil heap. Someone else might grow a pair before we get where we're going.'

'I see.' Elyra considered it. Despite her distaste at the idea, it seemed to make a brutal kind of sense. She'd seen enough of life on Iocanthos to know that you could even run a planet like that, if you really wanted to, or simply didn't care enough to change things. 'So we sleep lightly from now on.'

'When don't we?' Kyrlock asked rhetorically. 'Do you want this watch, or shall I take it?'

'You might as well sleep,' Elyra said. 'I'm not that tired.' Which wasn't entirely true, but her mind was too busy to rest. She strained her ears, listening for sounds of stealthy movement in the shadows around them, but heard nothing beyond the familiar scrabbling of the rockrats.

Nevertheless, she slipped her hand inside her pack, and took hold of the laspistol, her thumb resting lightly against the safety catch.

SIX

The *Misericord*, the Warp, Date and Time
Meaningless

DESPITE THE SUSPICION she couldn't quite shake, that the
Gallery's appellation was somehow merited in a subtle
fashion she was failing to discern, Keira was beginning
to enjoy herself. The cheerful bustle around her was a
welcome contrast to the cramped confines of the *Beyonder's Hostelry*, and for once she had Mordechai's
undivided attention. That was undeniably pleasant,
even though she still couldn't quite bring herself to
acknowledge why.

She glanced at Horst, wondering if he was secretly
pleased to be spending time alone with her, but his attention was all on the shops and market stalls surrounding
them, scanning their contents for any sign of their missing property. Inspired by his dedication, she resolved to
keep her mind on the business at hand as well.

'Seen anything you like yet?' Horst asked, and she
followed the direction of his gaze; he'd stopped in
front of a store selling women's apparel. Surprised, she

halted her own progress, and assessed the goods on display critically. 'That one's definitely your colour.' he said.

'It seems quite practical,' she agreed. The blouse and trousers were loose-fitting, so she'd be able to conceal her weapons easily, and the crimson material appealed to her Redemptionist sensibilities. There was no denying that she needed some fresh clothes, either; she'd been wearing the bodyglove and kirtle since she'd come on board, and they were both getting a little ripe by now. She took a step towards the shop. 'It wouldn't hurt to try it on, would it?'

'Wait a minute,' Horst said, looking at the window a little more intently. A white garment was on display towards the back of the emporium, and although it was half-obscured by the intervening racks, they both recognised it instantly. The robe of a tech-priest.

'Can I help you, honoured travellers?' The proprietress, a short woman in a jewelled turban and a purple floor-length gown which didn't quite match it, glanced up as the two Angelae entered her shop.

'I hope so.' Horst smiled, in an open and friendly manner. 'We were just passing, and noticed that white robe over there.'

'You have excellent taste,' the woman observed, nodding judiciously. 'That's an Iocanthan wedding dress, although it would make a perfectly good informal gown…'

'Actually, it's the vestment of a tech-priest,' Keira cut in, keeping her voice conversational, but with just enough of an edge to convey that she wasn't in the mood for any vapid sales patter. 'Quite a restricted market for that, I'd have thought.'

'How lucky that we happen to be travelling with one,' Horst added, 'who lost his luggage when we boarded.' He regarded the woman narrowly. 'He'll be so pleased that we managed to find a replacement.'

'I wouldn't know anything about that,' the shopkeeper said airily. 'I bought it in good faith, and that's how I'm selling it.'

'I'm sure you did,' Keira said, smiling easily as she suppressed the impulse to get the information she wanted the direct and simple way. 'But I'd like to know where you found it. They may have more.'

'Just the one I could see,' the woman said, letting the sentence hang.

'Which would be where, exactly?' Horst asked.

The shopkeeper shrugged. 'I've a business to run. Sometimes the details get a little blurred. I'm sure you understand.'

'Of course I do,' Keira said, removing the robe from the rack. 'But I'm sure our friend will be pleased to get this one, anyway.' She turned, and plucked the red suit from the window display. 'And I really can't leave without this. It's just my colour.' She let the smile harden. 'Or we could take our custom elsewhere.'

'Fifty thrones,' the shopkeeper said. Horst glanced pointedly at the price tags, which totalled considerably less, and dug some currency out of his pocket. 'Oh yes, it's coming back to me. Cuddy in the lower market. He has a lot of second-hand items, if you get my drift. All bought in good faith, of course.'

'Of course,' Horst said, handing her the money.

The shopkeeper smiled. 'I'll just put those in a bag for you, shall I?'

THE LOWER MARKET turned out to be a maze of stalls, jammed into the confluence of three main thoroughfares apparently entirely at random, funnelling visitors and shipfolk alike through a quincunx of commerce. Cuddy's was bigger than most, and had a large sign above it proclaiming ownership, so Horst was able to spot it quite easily; but actually reaching it through the dense and eddying crowd had proven frustratingly difficult. If Keira hadn't been with him he might never have got to it at all, but she slipped between the obstructing bodies with a stream of ingenuous apologies, and the judicious use of elbow and knee, to clear a path for him.

'There.' Keira pointed to a shirt Horst recognised as one of Drake's favourites, and reached out a hand to grab it. A few moments later they'd managed to recover half a dozen items, far fewer than they'd originally lost, and none of them of any particular significance, but Horst felt his spirits rising as he handed a fistful of coins to the stallholder. They were clearly on the right track.

'You've a good eye, young madam, that you have,' Cuddy said, as the currency disappeared. 'Was there anything else you'd be wanting?'

'That all depends on what else you've got,' Keira replied, managing to look pleased at the compliment and slightly slow-witted, which clearly disarmed the stallholder. 'We're travelling with a tech-priest who lost his luggage, and we heard you might know a Receiver who could help him recover it.'

'Sorry.' Cuddy shook his head dolefully, as though his inability to help was a mortal wound to his self-esteem. 'I did have one of their robes in a while back, but it's already gone, and there wasn't anything else in the batch with a cogwheel on it.' His expression grew faintly suspicious as realisation belatedly dawned. 'You've just bought everything else that came in with it.'

'Some of our property got mislaid at the same time,' Horst said blandly. 'But I don't see why you should be left out of pocket. I'm sure you paid for everything in good faith.'

'Just so,' the merchant agreed, with a sidelong glance at a Merciful patrol forging through the crowd nearby, articulating apologies and profanity in roughly equal measure. 'Legitimate salvage, he said.'

'Our friend's very anxious to recover one item in particular,' Keira said. 'A metal-bound box, about so big.' She spread her hands to indicate the size of the cogitator case. 'Mechanicus sigils all over it, so it'd be hard to miss. He's offering a substantial reward.'

'I can pass the word along,' Cuddy said, a spark of cupidity kindling in his eyes, 'but he shouldn't get his hopes up. Anything like that I'd have been offered; not many here can shift that kind of merchandise.' He shrugged, and pointed to a nearby tavern. 'You could try talking to Verren anyhow, he'll be over in the Dancing Ambull I should think. At least if he's still got some money left.'

'Thank you,' Keira said, with a dazzling smile, which the storeholder reciprocated in a faintly sheepish fashion. 'You've been very helpful.' To Horst's surprise she remained cheerful as they began making their way towards the hostelry, and he found himself wishing she could be like that a little more often. She glanced at him, clearly elated by the progress they'd made. 'Do you think Hybris and Danuld are having this much luck?'

DRAKE PAUSED AT the intersection of two alleyways, and glanced in both directions. Neither looked particularly promising, but at least the crowds had thinned out here, so he was able to make better time. He was certain that Vex would have realised they'd got separated by now, and would probably be retracing his steps, but the maze of twisting alleyways made any attempt to find him problematic at best.

As he looked around, hoping to find some kind of clue where to go, he caught sight of movement in the distance. A small group of passengers, their clothes unmistakably of Secundan cut, were striding along an intersecting alley; if he hadn't happened to be looking in that direction he would have missed them entirely, as they disappeared behind the corner of a building in a matter of seconds.

For a moment he thought nothing of it, then a belated sense of realisation kicked in. The group was moving confidently, with evident purpose, the first passengers he'd seen who looked at home here. Of course they might just have taken passage on the *Misericord* before, and knew their way around because of that, but it was also possible they were up to something illicit. Either way, following them would at least feel more purposeful than wandering around the warren of alleyways at random, attracting the amused attention of the shipfolk.

Easing the Scalptaker loose in its shoulder rig, Drake set out after his quarry.

VEX WAS BEGINNING to feel considerably discommoded. Despite the rigorous application of logic, he was still lost, and beginning to suspect that, contrary to all reasonable expectation, the Gallery of Sin conformed to no underlying principle of design. Suppressing a sigh of irritation, he turned down another alleyway which looked as though it was going in the right direction, but which, like so many others, veered off on a different heading entirely about halfway along its length. Then his spirits rose. A trio of fellow passengers were walking towards him, the first people other than shipfolk he'd seen for some time. Perhaps they'd be able to give him directions that actually made sense. Heartened at last, he began to pick up his pace.

'It's him!' The leader of the group raised a hand, and pointed. 'The tech-priest! He's carrying it!'

A lifetime of devotion to dispassionate logic had done nothing to quell Vex's innate survival instincts: indeed, his years of service to the Inquisition had honed them to a degree most of his colleagues would have found astonishing. By the time the other two men in the little group had broken into a run he was already moving, diving for the meagre cover afforded by an odiferous metal bin overflowing with rubbish. As he landed behind the fortuitous refuge, trying not to wonder what the small objects which had squashed under his weight were, a blizzard of razor-edged ice shards clattered from the galvanised plate.

Psykers! A visceral loathing for the warp spawn flooded through him, and he drew his autopistol, mouthing the prayer of accuracy as he pulled the trigger.

The round impacted on the wall, millimetres from the head of the leader, who twisted aside at the last possible second; Vex had been certain that his aim was true, and expressed his displeasure with another couple of rounds. Again, the fellow evaded both shots, something which should have been impossible.

There was only one logical explanation: he was a wyrd too, a seer of some kind, able to predict where the bullets would impact.

That made two out of three, which meant that the third man was probably warp-touched too; a hypothesis confirmed a moment later as a ball of flame erupted into existence and hurtled down the alleyway towards him. Vex ducked back behind the bin, feeling a burst of heat as the fireball impacted against the metal, his nostrils choked with the sudden stench of burning garbage.

Popping up again he fired, not bothering to waste any more ammunition on the precog, and saw the pyrokine stagger, before another blizzard of ice crystals sent him diving for cover once more. His position wasn't good, he had to admit; he'd managed to wound one assailant, but the other two were still very much in the game.

THE DANCING AMBULL was crowded, and clearly catered for passengers as well as shipfolk; glancing around as they entered, Keira noticed almost as many Secundan fashions as Misericordian guild liveries among the clientele. Like the rest of the Gallery of Sin, it tried to maintain the illusion of being part of a planetside village somewhere, although if anywhere like this had ever existed on

Scintilla it had done so before millennia of industrialisation had expunged every trace of the bucolic from the globe. Keira found the whole thing curiously soulless, like the make-up on the faces of the joygirls circulating among the customers with varying degrees of hopefulness or resignation, obscuring the real person beneath with a false smile and a painted complexion.

'Sorry.' One of them bumped into her and moved on, her deadened eyes resting on Horst for a moment before registering that he appeared to be with Keira, and the young assassin felt an unexpected pang of pity for the girl, instead of the fierce contempt she usually reserved for sinners.

To hide her confusion, she spoke. 'Don't mention it.' The girl turned back, clearly surprised to be treated with any kind of courtesy, especially by a passenger, most of whom probably regarded her as little more than a commodity, and Keira smiled in the open, friendly fashion which had proved so effective with the stallholder. 'Perhaps you can help me. I'm looking for a man named Verren; I gather he's something of a regular here.'

'The booth in the corner,' the girl said, indicating a nook on the far side of the taproom. She shrugged. 'You won't get much sense out of him, though. Not after the amount he's had.'

'Nevertheless,' Horst said, 'we'd like to try.'

'Suit yourself.' The girl shrugged, and began to turn away; then, for no reason Keira could see, she swung back towards them. 'What the hell, I'll introduce you. It might help if he sees a familiar face.'

'That's very kind of you,' Keira said, searching the girl's face for any sign of deceit, but the mask didn't slip for a second. Perhaps she was just hoping to be paid for her assistance.

'That's me,' the girl agreed flatly. 'All heart.' She began to weave her way through the crowd of patrons, several of whom turned to watch her progress with obvious signs of appreciation.

Keira frowned, disapproving on principle of Lustful Thoughts, which many of the Redemptionist tracts she'd memorised as a child warned were the first step towards bringing down the wrath of the Emperor, but she had to concede that the girl's attire was probably as much to blame as the men in question were. Her skirt was short, reaching down no further than mid-thigh, and clinging tightly to the curve of her buttocks, while her blouse was low-cut and diaphanous, revealing and accentuating the better part of her breasts. Well, if the aim was to attract customers, it seemed to be working.

'Mind on the job,' Horst murmured, and Keira nodded, grateful to him for keeping her focused. Since entering the service of the Inquisition she'd learned to ignore the small sins when that was the price of doing the Emperor's work, but it wasn't always easy; luckily, Horst knew her well enough by now to have a fair idea of when her Redemptionist instincts were stirring. She began to recite a calming litany, forcing her thoughts back onto the stony path of duty.

'Verren?' The joygirl leaned over a small man slumped into the angle of bench and wall, and after a moment his eyes opened, focusing blearily on her cleavage.

'Jenie? Whatja want?' His breath would have felled a grox, even from where Keira was standing.

Jenie flinched visibly, and stood upright again, her glossy black hair swirling around her face. 'These beyonders want a word with you.'

'What about?' Verren hauled himself upright, and Keira got her first good look at him. He was short and wiry, with thinning hair, his face blotched with broken veins. His clothes were old and shabby, and smelled almost as badly as he did. He was very drunk, in the superficially lucid fashion of the confirmed alcoholic, and she began to wonder if this was going to be a complete waste of time. It was hard to imagine getting anything useful out of this sorry specimen of humanity, beyond spare parts for servitors.

'About your last scavenging trip,' Horst said, slipping into the bench opposite. He began to lay a few of the items they'd recovered from Cuddy's stall on the tabletop between them. 'Where you found these.'

'Did I?' Verren asked, peering at them sullenly. 'I can't rightly remember.'

'I'm sure I could help jog your memory,' Keira said, taking a step forwards, but Horst held up a hand to forestall her.

'That's a shame. I thought a quiet chat over a glass or two of amasec might be to everyone's advantage.' He nodded to Keira. 'Could you get some drinks please?'

'Of course.' Keira smiled tightly, trying not to resent being sent on so menial an errand, and slipped away through the crush. By the time she returned, with four tumblers of the clear golden liquid, the prospect of free alcohol had loosened Verren's tongue at least as effectively as the more direct methods she'd been contemplating, and, she had to admit, a great deal more discreetly.

'Whatja want to know?' Verren asked, seizing the glass eagerly, and draining it in a couple of swallows.

'A friend of ours lost something recently,' Horst said. 'Along with these items. He's prepared to pay a great deal for its recovery.'

The harlot Jenie was still hovering near the table, which tended to confirm Keira's suspicion that she was hoping to be rewarded in some way for helping them, and she handed her one of the drinks.

'Thank you.' The girl took it and sipped, her surprise apparently genuine; it was clear from her expression that she didn't really like the liquor, but was making a show of drinking it out of politeness.

'What's he looking for?' Verren asked, casting covetous eyes at Horst's drink, and Keira placed her own on the table in front of him. She didn't care for spirits in any case, her Redemptionist upbringing leading her to consider alcohol as little more than sin in liquid form, although she'd developed rather more of a liking for wines than she was comfortable with in the course of a number of undercover assignments where she'd been obliged to drink the stuff to blend in. She'd thought appearing to order the same thing for herself would put Verren at his ease, though, and the small subterfuge seemed to have worked.

'A box, with metal bands, about so big.' Horst went through the same pantomime Keira had with Cuddy, and the Receiver shook his head.

'Din't see nothing like that.' He shrugged, and took a swallow of Keira's offering, a little more slowly as the quality registered; she'd bought the most expensive stuff in the bar, as a subtle indication that they were prepared to be generous in return for the right kind of help. Relaxing a little as the glow of the liquor spread, he opened his arms expansively. 'The stuff I did find was well scattered, mind. Cases burst open, and that.'

Picturing the kilometres-deep shaft down which the handcart had plunged, Keira could well believe it. The cogitator case could have ended up anywhere.

'Could you show us the way down there?' Horst asked, and Verren shook his head.

'Beyonders stay beyonderside. That's how it's always been.'

'I think we can arrange an exception,' Horst said, and an expression of apprehension began to curdle on Verren's face.

'You're them, aren't you?' he asked hoarsely. 'The inquisitors. I heard you was aboard.'

Keira exchanged a quick glance with Horst. It seemed that word of their presence was seeping through the crew rather more quickly than they'd hoped. 'We're not inquisitors,' she said. 'But we work for one. And we'd like you to guide us through the outhulls.'

'I'm not going back down there,' Verren said, gulping the rest of Keira's drink and reaching out for Horst's. 'I barely got out the last time, and that's the truth.'

'I don't think you quite grasp who you're dealing with,' Keira began, but Horst shook his head, and she subsided, glowering in her most intimidating manner.

'What do you mean, barely got out?' he asked evenly.

Verren shook his head. 'I could hear 'em in the dark. They come after me, see? But I know the passages, and I shook 'em. I'm not going back, and you can't make me.' He glared at Horst with alcoholic belligerence.

'Who came after you?' he asked.

Verren shook his head emphatically. 'I dunno, and I'm not about to find out. But they're the ones as got Rikko, you can bet on it.'

'Who's Rikko?' Keira asked.

'Best scavver in the outhulls, Rikko,' Verren said. 'Nothing he couldn't find. But something found him on his last trip down, no question. He never come back, see? And he's not the only one.'

Horst and Keira exchanged glances again, remembering the transmission Barda had intercepted.

'Who else has gone missing?' she asked.

'Couldn't give you their names,' Verren said, casting a covetous glance at the almost untouched drink in Jenie's hand. To Keira's surprise, the harlot handed it to him without prompting. 'Couple of other Receivers, though, and a party of Riggers, I heard. Maybe some others.'

'Thank you,' Horst said, standing slowly. 'You've been very helpful. Enjoy your drink.' He turned and left the bar, Keira falling in at his shoulder as they regained the bustling street.

'That's it?' she asked incredulously. 'You're not going to make him show us where he found the stuff?'

Horst shook his head. 'What would be the point?' he replied quietly. 'As soon as he sobers up, the shakes'll set in, and he'll be about as much use as a heretic's oath.

And even if we do herd him into the tunnels, he'll make a run for it the first chance he gets. We'll be better off relying on Hybris's map.'

Keira nodded, acknowledging the truth of his assessment. 'You're right,' she conceded grudgingly. 'He's obviously more scared of his bogeymen than he is of us. More fool him.'

'I can show you the way.' Jenie tugged at Horst's elbow, and both Angelae turned to look at her; the harlot's pose of self-confidence wavered a little under their combined scrutiny, but she rallied quickly, and continued. 'My sire was a Rigger, worked the outhulls most of his life. Took me down, too, when he could. I know my way around all right.' An expression of cunning crossed her face, which Keira had seen often on people who thought they had some kind of advantage in negotiations when they didn't really understand the kind of people they were dealing with. 'Besides, I know who you are. I was there when you told Verren, remember?'

'That's right, you were,' Horst said. He smiled at her, in a manner designed to put her at her ease. 'So I suppose you'd better consider yourself hired.'

'She'll need some more suitable clothes,' Keira said. 'She can't go grubbing around in the outhulls dressed like that.'

'A good point,' Horst agreed, palming some coins, and handing them to Jenie. 'Go and find something appropriate.' He waited until the girl had trotted off to a nearby stall, and was comfortably out of earshot. 'Unfortunately, Verren's discretion can't be so readily relied on.'

'I'll take care of it,' Keira assured him. 'A man as drunk as that's bound to have an accident on the way home.'

DRAKE HAD BEEN hanging back, in case the little group he'd been following were looking out for any attempt to keep them under surveillance, but as it turned out he needn't have bothered. They kept moving purposefully, as if knowing where they were going, although a couple of times they'd hesitate, looking to the man who was obviously the leader. Not that his clothing gave any indication of his authority: all three were dressed in the multi-hued jackets and trousers favoured by minor Secundan aristocracy, and those sufficiently wealthy to imitate the fad, but the other two clearly deferred to him. After a moment's thought, the leader would point confidently down a nearby alleyway, and the trio would resume their purposeful advance.

They'd just done this for the third or fourth time since he started following them, disappearing down an intersecting cleft between two buildings, when Drake heard the unmistakable sound of gunfire. All thought of caution evaporated: drawing the Scalptaker, he sprinted after them, apprehension gnawing at his gut. He was familiar enough with firearms to have recognised the timbre of an autopistol, the kind of weapon Vex carried; which didn't mean the tech-priest was at the centre of the disturbance, of course, but had he been a betting man, that would be where he placed his money.

As Drake rounded the corner of the intersection, he felt a brief flicker of satisfaction that his instinct had been right. The tech-priest was crouched behind an overflowing garbage bin, holding his gun, while the three men he'd been following fanned out, raising their hands. At first he was puzzled, wondering why they didn't take cover: then a fireball erupted from the hands of the man on the left, conjured into existence just as Elyra had done, and with a sudden shock of horrified realisation he knew them for what they were. Wyrds, like the ones who'd escaped from the Citadel of the Forsaken; at the memory of the witches they'd encountered in the snow-shrouded forest, and the power wielded by the deranged leader of the heretic cult they'd raided in the depths of the Gorgonid, Drake shuddered.

His shock was only momentary, however; even as Vex fired, wounding the pyrokine, he was bringing up the Scalptaker, taking careful aim at the group leader. That was simple common sense, pick him off and the others would be thrown into a state of confusion, easy prey for the two Angelae.

To Drake's uncomfortable surprise, however, it didn't prove as easy as that: somehow the shot missed, the leader moving at the last possible second, turning to look in his direction with a lazy grin. 'Another Throne agent,' he called to his friends. 'Kill him too!'

The third psyker turned, raising his hand, but Drake was faster, his years of military service sharpening his reflexes; he fired twice, the rugged revolver kicking against his hand and coming back on aim for the second shot just after the first bullet hit the mark, as he'd known it would. He'd gone for the chest the first time, concentrating on the biggest and easiest target, and as the man folded, his head dropped to meet the second bullet. Blood, bone and brain spattered the wall, and the wyrd hit the cobbles hard. He wouldn't be getting back up, either, and Drake switched his aim, going for the wounded pyrokine, who seemed to be trying to summon another fireball.

'Danuld!' Vex called, his voice echoing flatly in the narrow thoroughfare. 'The other one!'

For a fraction of a second Drake hesitated, but he trusted the tech-priest's judgement, and switched his aim, sending two more rounds at the leader. Which left only one in the chamber before he had to reload…

As he'd half-suspected, the leader moved again, at exactly the right moment, a fluke of circumstance so unlikely it had to have been the result of some warp-spawned power, and Drake felt his muscles cramping with frustration. Vex fired too, at almost exactly the same instant, emptying his magazine, and looking vaguely put out as the man evaded the storm of bullets with the same casual ease. The blizzard of rounds ripped into the corner of the alleyway, raising a cloud of pulverised plaster and brick, through which Drake could just see the Secundan disappearing.

'Interesting,' Vex remarked conversationally, snapping a fresh clip into his weapon, and taking a few steps in pursuit. 'He can predict the attacks of more than one assailant at a time. Not many wyrds can do that.'

'Lucky for us,' Drake said, raising his pistol to dispatch the pyrokine, who was clutching at a nearby wall for support, his face grey. Before he could pull the trigger, though, he was interrupted.

'Drop the skagging gun, rutface, or I'll cut you off at the knees!' a new voice bellowed, accompanied by the sound of running feet.

Drake looked round, to see several sets of brightly polished armour converging on their position. He smiled. 'And they say there's never an enforcer around when you need one,' he said.

'I said drop it!' the leader of the Merciful squad shouted, snapping a round into the chamber of her shotgun, clearly in no mood for levity.

'I think we should comply,' Vex said calmly, allowing his autopistol to fall to the cobbles. Drake nodded, and followed his lead. 'It would be somewhat ironic to be killed by the forces of law and order, having just seen off a gaggle of heretics.'

'What about him?' Drake asked, pointing to the wounded pyrokine. The psyker's greying face had taken on the unmistakable expression of a man who felt he had nothing left to lose.

'I'll ask the skagging questions!' The Merciful sergeant was close enough now to prod him in the chest with the barrel of her shotgun, tiny globules of spittle spattering his face as she bellowed at him from a few centimetres away. 'And I just might shoot first!'

'Armsmistress,' one of the troopers accompanying her ventured, with a sidelong glance at the wounded pyrokine. 'Something's wrong here…'

'Of course it's wrong!' the Merciful leader snapped, her ire momentarily directed towards her subordinate. 'Murder always is!'

'I think you'll find that the execution of wyrds and heretics doesn't constitute murder under most interpretations of the appropriate statutes,' Vex put in helpfully.

'Shut up, cogboy!' The sergeant glared at him, her face framed by a tangle of chestnut curls escaping from under her ridiculous archaic helmet. 'The law's my business, not yours!'

'Uhm, Armsmistress…' the trooper persisted, 'that man's smoking…'

'I could do with a lho myself about now,' the sergeant said, her mood abruptly switching from belligerent to the merely testy. She glanced at the pyrokine, and her eyes widened in shock. 'Emperor's gona–'

The pyrokine exploded, in a gout of superheated air and charred viscera, which sent everyone reeling. Drake's face stung from the sudden burst of searing heat, which reminded him momentarily of the forest fire which had erupted after the shuttle crash he and Kyrlock had gone to investigate, only to find themselves sucked into a greater, more complicated battle than he'd ever dreamed possible as a simple Guardsman. A moment later the air around them had returned to the relatively comfortable temperature he'd grown used to aboard the *Misericord*, only the stench of burned flesh and the staining on the cobbles remaining to bear witness to the gruesome miracle he'd just witnessed.

'What the hell just happened?' the Merciful sergeant demanded. She began to bring her shotgun up to cover Drake again. 'What did you do to him?'

'We didn't do anything,' Drake said. 'We were never here.' Ignoring the threat of the weapon pointing at him, he reached into his coat pocket, and pulled out the thin disc of metal Horst had given him back on Sepheris Secundus. The rosette gleamed gold under the shadow-less light spilling from the metal sky above, the stylised letter I in the middle of it glistening like freshly shed blood. The little group of Merciful shuffled back an involuntary pace, glancing at one another in sudden apprehension, as they recognised the sigil of the Inquisition. 'Which means there's nothing for you to report. Understand?'

'Of course, inquisitor,' the sergeant said, lowering her gun, and suddenly becoming a model of polite cooperation. It seemed that at least the rumours of their presence had filtered down to the rank and file of the Merciful, and none of them were keen to emulate the last patrol to have got in their way. She hesitated. 'What should we do about the bodies?'

For the first time since he'd joined the Angelae, Drake began to fully appreciate the power he was able to wield, even as so lowly a functionary of the holy ordos. It could get addictive, he thought, finding the notion an uncomfortable one. There didn't seem much point in correcting the sergeant's misapprehension about his status within the organisation, so he let that go without comment.

'These two killed each other,' he said. 'Probably over money, or the favours of a joygirl. I'm sure your investigation will find a plausible reason.'

'I'd recommend disposing of the corpses as rapidly as possible,' Vex added. 'Even a dead psyker can sometimes be an attractive host to a warp entity.'

'They'll be over the side before you leave the Gallery,' the sergeant said, her tone sober.

The trooper who'd spoken before shrugged. 'Lucky that one committed suicide so thoroughly,' he added.

'Maybe he didn't,' Vex said, once the Angelae had moved out of earshot. 'He probably just lost control of his curse while attempting to use it against us.'

'It saves us a problem, anyway,' Drake said. 'Although it would have been nice to interrogate him first.' He looked at the tech-priest narrowly. 'He might have told us why they were after you in the first place.'

'To recover this, I imagine,' Vex replied, pulling the sliver of ivory from a pocket in his robe, and returning it after a moment's puzzled examination, much to Drake's relief. 'The seer seemed able to sense its presence.'

'Oh,' Drake said, scanning the crowds around them with renewed vigilance, although the third psyker seemed to have vanished into the maze of narrow streets as thoroughly as if the warp itself had reached out to swallow him. None of the other passers-by seemed tainted by the realm of Chaos, or particularly interested in a couple of passengers making their way back to the *Beyonder's Hostelry*; nevertheless, he found himself wishing he'd reloaded the Scalptaker while he'd had the chance. 'Then let's hope we've scared him off for good.' Or at least until Keira could track him down and send him to the Emperor's judgement.

'Indeed,' Vex agreed, although it was clear from the care with which he spoke, and his watchful demeanour, that he didn't believe that any more than Drake did.

SEVEN

The *Ursus Innare*, the Warp, Date and Time Meaningless

THE BANDITS MADE their move while Kyrlock was on watch, which was their first mistake; after a lifetime of expecting unpleasant surprises from the wildlife in the forest where he'd foraged for timber, and the scarcely less savage denizens of the Tumble, he could hear what they undoubtedly thought of as a stealthy approach long before they realised they were in earshot.

'Elyra.' He spoke quietly, nudging the psyker with his foot, as he pretended to do nothing more than throw another piece of fuel on the fire. The luminators in the ceiling of the cargo hold were as fitful as ever, still throwing the rubble-choked space below into perpetual twilight, and he wanted the wanly flickering flames as bright as he could make them before their assailants arrived. 'Company's coming.' At first that would work to their attackers' advantage, the light from the fire dulling the defenders' night vision, while making them more visible from outside the circle of firelight; but once the brigands moved into the attack they'd be dazzled for a moment as their eyes adjusted, giving him and Elyra the edge.

'How many? Where?' Elyra asked, waking at once, her voice so low that Kyrlock found himself straining to hear her. Her hand moved slowly under her blanket, flicking off the safety catch of the laspistol she'd been grasping even in her sleep.

'Half a dozen, maybe. Two groups, trying to flank us. Ten and four o'clock, from where I'm sitting.' He flicked the safety of his shotgun off as he spoke, his hand curling round the butt, concealed, he hoped, by the angle of his body.

'Most of them are to your ten,' Zusen whispered, surprising him. He'd thought the juvies were asleep. 'I can feel their anger, feeding off one another. There's less emotion the other way.'

'Thanks,' he whispered back, grateful for the extra information despite its source. 'Now keep your head down.'

'I didn't know you cared,' she replied, the feeble attempt at levity undermined by the trembling of her voice, and, moved by an unexpected flare of compassion, Kyrlock squeezed her arm reassuringly with his free hand.

'It'll be all right,' he told her, hoping that would turn out to be true, and she nodded, barely perceptibly in the darkness.

'They're coming! Death in the dark!' Ven sat up suddenly, his face blank, the echoes of his voice splintering from the jagged piles of rock surrounding them. Kyrlock swore colourfully and brought up the shotgun, all hope of luring the bandits inside the circle of firelight, where the odds would be evened again, gone.

'There!' Zusen pointed, and he discharged the weapon along the line of her arm, hearing a scream among the enveloping shadows.

'Thanks, juve, I owe you one,' he said, pulling the trigger again. The larger group had evidently scattered, though, as he failed to hit any more of them: instead the rockpiles echoed to the sound of hurrying feet as the startled bandits scrabbled for cover.

'I'm not a…' the young psyker began indignantly, then fell, a stone the size of his fist smacking into her forehead. More of the improvised missiles began to whistle through the air around them, and Kyrlock dropped to the shale beside the girl, sending two more hailstorms of shot in the direction they'd come from.

'Slingshots?' Elyra asked, and Kyrlock nodded, surprised for a moment, before remembering that his brother had shown her one of the makeshift weapons while they'd been hiding out with him in the Tumble.

'Must be,' he agreed. Normally they wouldn't be all that effective against firearms, but it would only take another lucky shot or two to neutralise the advantage their superior weapons gave them. He fired again. 'We need to even the odds a bit. I can't see well enough to pick them off.'

'Who needs to see them?' Trosk asked, sounding a little more animated than he usually did. The pose of sardonic detachment had slipped, allowing a harsh, cold edge to enter his voice, and Kyrlock shivered in spite of himself.

'What do you mean?' Elyra asked warily, cracking off a couple of pistol shots, which seemed equally ineffectual; at any rate, the rain of stones continued unabated.

'This.' Trosk stood, apparently unconcerned about the possibility of being struck down, and raised his hand as if waving an oncoming groundcar to a halt. 'This is your only warning,' he called into the surrounding shadows. 'Leave now or die!'

A hail of derision and profanity was his only answer, along with another barrage of rocks, none of which touched him.

Although he couldn't have said why, Kyrlock felt the hairs rising on the back of his neck. He glanced at Elyra, who was staring at the young wyrd, an expression of stunned surprise on her face.

'Trosk, no!' she shouted, but he was either too intent on whatever he was doing to hear her, or simply didn't care. His face had taken on an expression of grim concentration, completely oblivious to anything happening around him.

Abruptly, Kyrlock's attention was snatched by the sound of running feet crunching on the shale around them, and he rolled to his feet, bringing up the shotgun. Two men were closing in on him, taking advantage of the distraction the hail of stones had afforded, one of them the leader of the bandits he'd challenged over the crate of food. The other he didn't recognise, but he knew the type: physically strong but not overly bright, always willing to follow the lead of someone a little cleverer and more charismatic, so long as the easy scores kept coming. When they didn't, he'd look for someone else to do the thinking for him. Clearly this attack was the leader's last-ditch attempt to keep control of his followers.

Kyrlock squeezed the trigger, blasting the fellow's chest to bloody ruin, expecting to see the leader felled by a las-bolt from Elyra's pistol as he did so. By the time he realised that her attention was still on Trosk, running towards the young wyrd in a desperate attempt to prevent him from unleashing whatever power he had against their attackers, it was too late: the bandit chief was too close for him to bring the shotgun round and fire again.

Screaming with inchoate rage, the bandit struck at him with the edge of a sharpened spade, which Kyrlock dodged by millimetres. Dropping the shotgun, he unslung the chainaxe from across his shoulders, powering up the weapon as he aimed a blow with the butt end at his opponent's head. The bandit ducked, slashing for his belly with the end of his improvised weapon, but Kyrlock was too quick, and brought the whining polearm round in a wide arc, stepping back to open up the distance enough to bring the rapidly rotating adamantium teeth into play. Sparks flew as they hit the metal of the blade, and the bandit retreated a little, looking for an opening.

'You can still end this,' Kyrlock said, with an apprehensive sideways glance at Trosk; Elyra had closed half the distance between them, and he became abruptly aware that only a handful of seconds could have elapsed since the duel began. 'Walk away now, while you can.' Before Trosk did anything to reveal what he was...

'You're afraid of me.' To Kyrlock's amazement, the man was grinning, completely misunderstanding why he wanted to end the confrontation as quickly as he could. 'Well you should be, you grox-rutting son of a mutant.'

He charged in again, a berserk, bar brawler's attack, completely devoid of finesse, and Kyrlock evaded him easily, striking out at his leg with the chainaxe. The whirling teeth bit deep, in a spray of blood and macerated tissue, and the man howled, falling heavily to the ground.

'Big mistake,' Kyrlock said, preparing to finish him. Before he could administer the *coup de grace*, however, he felt a faint trembling in the kilotonnes of rock surrounding them. The bandit chief's eyes widened in shock, and Kyrlock turned, just in time to see the largest heap of shale sliding inexorably downwards, engulfing the patch of shadow the volley of stones had emerged from. A few faint screams, abruptly terminated, echoed for a moment over the rumbling of the landslide, then silence descended, wrapped in a cloud of choking dust.

'Merciful Throne! You're all witches!' The bandit chief soiled himself, and scrabbled backwards, stark terror etched on his face.

'Not all of us,' Elyra said, turning to face him. She brought up the laspistol. 'Vos there's perfectly normal. Whatever that is.'

'I won't tell anyone! I swear!' the bandit babbled, still trying to back away.

'No, you won't,' Elyra said, and shot him through the head at point-blank range, reducing his expression to a charred, bloody mask in an instant. Only Kyrlock knew her well enough to see the momentary hesitation before she pulled the trigger.

'You had no choice,' he said. 'But if you'd waited a second or two, I'd have done the job for you.'

'I know.' Elyra smiled thinly, grateful for the gesture of sympathy. 'But sometimes you have to make the hard decisions yourself.'

'What was so hard about it?' Trosk asked, looking at her curiously. 'They were scum. They deserved to die.'

Elyra sighed, the mask of detachment already back in place. 'No argument there, hotshot. But using your talent like that was dumb. What if one of them got away, or someone else saw what happened here?'

Trosk shrugged. 'We'd kill them too, I guess. Who cares about a couple more sheep one way or the other?'

'You just don't get it, do you?' Elyra said, her anger more genuine than feigned if Kyrlock was any judge. 'You can't just kill everyone you come across in the hope of covering your tracks. Sooner or later someone's going to realise that bodies are turning up wherever you go, and start to wonder why. Next thing you know, you'll be on the first Black Ship out of the system. I've survived as long as I have by only using my gift when it's absolutely necessary.'

'Right.' Kyrlock nodded. 'We could have handled a few dregs without you dropping an ore heap on their heads.' He cocked his head quizzically. 'How did you manage that, anyway?'

'He's a geist,' Elyra said.

Trosk nodded. 'I prefer the term telekine, though,' he said.

'Like I give a rut what you prefer,' Elyra said, her assumed persona now fully in place again. 'Any more grandstanding, and you and the other juvies can find your way to wherever you're going on your own. Clear?'

'Pellucid,' Trosk assured her. 'And speaking of the others...' He gestured towards them. Ven was curled up in a foetal position, whimpering quietly, his mind overwhelmed by the sheer volume of sensory and extra-sensory input flooding through it, while Zusen was still stretched out on the shale, groaning quietly as consciousness began to return.

'Go and help Ven,' Elyra ordered; after a moment, to Kyrlock's quiet relief, Trosk complied, which meant that her leadership of the group was still going unchallenged, in spite of any reservations the shaven-headed wyrd might have. She glanced down at Kyrlock, who was squatting beside the prostrate girl. 'How is she?'

'She'll live,' Kyrlock said, probing the mat of blood-soaked hair around the wound cautiously, eliciting a faint whimper of pain as he did so. 'No sign of a fracture, thank the Emperor, but she's going to have a hell of a headache for a while.' As if to confirm the fact, Zusen stirred, groaning as she tried to move her head. 'Luckily she's a tough little runt.'

'If that's your idea of a compliment, no wonder you haven't got a girlfriend,' Zusen said, trying to sit up. After a moment she gave up the attempt, and slumped back again.

Kyrlock caught her before her head could hit the stones, despite the deep unease he always felt in close proximity to her. She felt surprisingly light in his arms. 'How do you know I don't just prefer boys?' he asked, trying to sound unconcerned.

Zusen started to laugh, then stopped abruptly, wincing. 'I'd know,' she said, with complete assurance.

She probably would at that, Kyrlock thought.

Elyra glanced at Kyrlock, and smiled without humour. 'Looks like we're still kings of the spoil heap,' she said.

'For the time being,' Kyrlock agreed, retrieving his weapons.

The *Misericord*, the Warp, Date and Time Meaningless

'CAN WE TRUST her?' Drake asked, with a glance towards the balnerea, where Jenie was changing into the clothes she'd bought in the market. He'd been more than a little surprised when Horst returned to their quarters accompanied by a common joygirl, but he supposed the team leader knew what he was doing.

'I think so,' Horst said, keeping his voice too low to be heard through the intervening door. 'She seems sincere enough about wanting to help. Keira thinks she's after the reward money we dangled in front of the Receiver who found some of our stuff.'

'Sounds reasonable,' Drake said. 'Whatever we run into down there, it can't be any worse than the usual way she makes a living.'

'Verren seemed pretty scared,' Horst said, 'but I don't think we should take that too seriously. The state he was in, he'd have run from his own shadow.' He was wearing a comm-bead again, and broke off suddenly, apparently listening to something in his earpiece.

Drake slipped his own into place, just in time to hear Barda responding to an earlier enquiry.

'The Riggers are still missing,' the young pilot confirmed. 'The bridge issued an edict about two hours ago, requiring the Receivers of Bounty to keep an eye out for them, and render any assistance they might require. No one seems worried enough to dispatch a search party yet, though.'

'Any other disappearances been reported?' Drake asked.

'Not as such,' Barda replied. 'There are rumours on some of the internal channels, but no one in authority seems to be concerned. Receivers tend to wander off on their own anyway.'

'Could the psykers Danuld and Hybris ran into have anything to do with it?' Horst asked.

'I suppose it's possible,' Barda said, after a momentary pause for thought. 'But nothing's been said about wyrds and witches, and I'd expect that sort of story to spread fast.'

'That's true,' Drake agreed. 'Anyone flinging fire and ice around is kind of hard to miss.'

'Which brings us back to our assailants,' Vex put in. He took the sliver of bone from his pocket, and gazed at it speculatively. 'I'm sure this was what they were after.'

Drake nodded. 'The seer seemed able to divine its presence,' he agreed. 'He seemed to know exactly where you were the whole time I was following them.'

'Which implies he knows what it is,' Horst said.

'Why wouldn't he?' Vex asked rhetorically. 'The most logical inference is that they were members of Adrin's coven, fleeing from the purge on Sepheris Secundus. It's quite likely that they had their abilities boosted by Tonis's infernal machine.'

'Perhaps we'll know more when Raymer and his toy soldiers have finally got round to identifying them,' Drake said. He'd given the Merciful instructions to trawl through the passenger manifest for anyone matching the descriptions of the three wyrds, a job Vex could have done in a fraction of the time if they hadn't lost his cogitator, and was chafing at the delay. 'A search of their quarters should turn something up.'

'Like the one that got away?' Horst said, and Drake fought down a flash of resentment at the implied criticism.

'If he remains beyonderside, it should only be a matter of time before the Merciful find him for us,' Vex said reasonably. 'It's a relatively confined area, and Danuld and I were able to furnish them with a detailed description.'

'It's the "if" that worries me,' Horst replied. 'This ship's the size of a small hive. Anyone making it to the outhulls could stay hidden indefinitely.'

'Like the Malcontents,' Jenie said, emerging from the balnerea. The three Angelae turned to look at her. She was dressed in practical coveralls, and stout boots, and seemed a great deal more comfortable in them than in her working clothes, which she carried balled up under one arm. She'd scrubbed the heavy make-up from her face as well, the residual dampness of her ablutions lending the dark brown skin of her cheeks a glow of vitality that had been missing from her features before. Somehow, Drake thought, she seemed far more attractive now than she had done in the revealing attire she'd just discarded.

'Who are they?' Horst asked.

Jenie shrugged. 'Anyone who doesn't like the caste they were born into, or who asks too many questions about the rules. The captains and the Obeyers call that treason against the ship.'

'Treason's usually regarded as a capital offence,' Vex remarked, and the girl nodded grimly.

'Here too. So if you step out of line, your only chance is to head for the outhulls before they catch you.' She shrugged. 'Not many do, and even fewer make it, but the stories persist. Some say there's a whole guild of Malcontents down there, but I doubt it.'

'That does seem unlikely,' Vex agreed. 'Even on a vessel this size, resources are limited. If there are indeed outlaws at large in the far reaches of the ship, they must be quite few in number.' He glanced up as Keira entered the cramped common area, nodding to Horst as she pushed the door closed.

'I took care of that thing we discussed,' she said.

'Thanks.' Horst echoed the gesture. 'Better grab some food and rest while you can.'

'Sounds like we're pulling out soon,' Keira said, an edge of eagerness entering her voice.

'I've managed to refine my image of the area around the shaft,' Vex said, 'and plot a conjectural route, which ought to get us to our destination reasonably expeditiously.' He handed his data-slate to Jenie, who took it awkwardly, and peered at the map with what looked to Drake like vague bafflement. 'We're here, and this is the section of outhull we're interested in.'

'Oh yes, I get that now,' Jenie said. She shrugged, and dropped the bundle of clothing on a nearby chair, raising a faint cloud of dust. 'It looks kind of different on the screen.'

'Do we need to work our way around the damaged section?' Drake asked, and Vex shook his head.

'Not according to Barda. The impact site was nearby, but none of the passageways we need have been sealed.' He looked at Jenie for confirmation. 'Does this route seem plausible to you?'

'Good as any,' the joygirl agreed. 'No telling until we get down there, really.' She smiled, a little uncertainly, at the assembled Angelae. 'It'll be fine. Trust me.'

The *Emperor's Justice*, Scintilla System 242.993.M41

'This man Voyle.' Inquisitor Grynner inclined his head, and glanced at the data-slate in front of him. 'You're certain he was the shipping agent who dealt with the *Eddia Stabilis* the last time she was in dock?'

Quillem nodded. 'I spoke to a couple of the men he hired to shift the cargo. None of them noticed anything out of the ordinary, although they were certain the ship was smuggling something.'

'Were they indeed.' Grynner permitted a faint trace of interest to enter his voice. 'Why so, if nothing was out of the ordinary?'

'Because it's the lower arm,' Quillem said. 'It would be more unusual if a vessel docking there didn't have something to hide.' He gestured towards the data-slate. 'Besides, Voyle's on the fringe of the Franchise. Not a full member, but a confirmed associate of several known gangers.'

'A connection I'm sure he finds useful in his legitimate business dealings,' Grynner said dryly.

'Quite.' Quillem nodded confirmation. 'In return for which, he does the Franchise an occasional favour, like holding cargo for them.'

'Which he seems to be doing at the moment, according to these informants of yours.' Grynner read on in silence for another minute or two. 'Were they at all forthcoming about what he's taking care of so diligently?'

'They have no idea,' Quillem told him. 'The ship departed again a little over two hours after docking, and Voyle didn't hire any casual labour to handle the heavy lifting.'

'Hardly surprising, under the circumstances,' Grynner said, glancing up from his reading again. 'A bulk freighter would normally take several days to unload, not just a couple of hours. Whatever it delivered wasn't part of its regular cargo.'

'Just what I thought,' Quillem said. 'Another xenos artefact for the Faxlignae, perhaps?'

'It's possible,' Grynner agreed. 'Voyle may have over-seen the transfer of the wraithbone to the *Eddia Stabilis* on their behalf as well; even if he didn't do so directly, someone close to him probably did.'

'Then perhaps,' Quillem said speculatively, 'we should pay Mister Voyle a little visit.'

'Perhaps you should,' Inquisitor Grynner agreed, with a barely perceptible nod of the head.

The *Misericord*, the Warp, Date and Time Meaningless

'JUST THROUGH HERE,' Jenie said, standing in front of the doorway in the shadow of the now deserted reception hall, through which the Angelae had pursued the thieves on the evening of their arrival. She seemed a little tense, which was hardly surprising under the circumstances; every now and again Horst noticed her staring at Drake's Guard-issue lasgun in horrified fascination. They'd stopped off at the shuttle for some extra equipment on the way, and being reunited with the weapon seemed to have improved the Guardsman's spirits considerably. 'I don't have the access codes, though.' She made the admission nervously, as if fearful of the reaction it might provoke.

'That shouldn't prove a problem,' Vex assured her, commencing some ritual with the aid of his data-slate and a small device he'd produced from a pocket in his robe.

'I don't like this,' Keira said quietly. 'We're too exposed.' She glanced around the vast expanse of the hall, which echoed eerily without the throng of passengers passing through it. The luminators had been dimmed, intensifying the shadows, and the columns supporting the roof loomed threateningly. It was easy to imagine unseen assailants crouched behind them, taking careful aim...

'It won't be for long,' Horst assured her, hoping he was right. A moment or two later his patience was rewarded, as Vex muttered a final incantation, consulted the screen of his data-slate, and punched a sequence of numbers into the lock. The doors began to grind open.

Drake was through first, his lasgun levelled, and Horst heard a startled yelp from the corridor beyond; hurrying through after the Guardsman, he found him covering a thin fellow in grey overalls, accompanied by a hulking servitor festooned with bundles of wires, springs, small cages and bags of rotting food. The man's eyes were wide with shock.

'Identify yourself!' Drake snapped, and the fellow nodded eagerly.

'Norvik Cotto, journeyman dispatcher of the Communion of Ratters. I've got a docket...' He held up a piece of tattered flimsy, on which scrawled words could be faintly discerned among the stains. 'There's a nest around here, see? Don't want 'em getting beyonderside, and alarming the ladies, do we?' His lips stretched, in what he probably hoped was an ingratiating smile.

'That seems in order,' Drake said, after a cursory glance, as if he knew what he was looking at. He lowered the lasgun, to the ratter's evident relief.

'So get lost,' Jenie said, staring at him in a belligerent fashion. 'You've never seen Merciful in plain clothes before?'

'Don't think so,' Cotto said. 'But then how would I know?' Now the gun wasn't pointing at him, he seemed intrigued rather than frightened. With a gesture to the servitor, which lurched into motion behind him, he wandered off down the corridor, whistling a tune Horst vaguely remembered had been popular on Scintilla a generation ago. The words were vulgar in the extreme, concerning a joygirl and an ecclesiarch, and he glanced at Keira, but fortunately she didn't seem to recognise it.

'Would you like me to deal with that too?' she asked quietly, and Horst shook his head.

'Thanks, but I don't think it'll be necessary this time.' He turned to Jenie, raising his voice to a normal conversational level. 'That was quick thinking.'

The joygirl shrugged. 'Ratters are all a bit simple. Small caste, heavily inbred. He'll have forgotten all about us by this evening, and even if he hasn't, he'll believe what I told him.'

'Good.' Horst turned to Drake. 'Try to remember there are a lot of shipfolk around on the upper levels. You can't shoot them all.'

'Right. Sorry.' Drake slung the lasgun across his shoulder. 'I didn't think, just went straight into the standard drill.' He looked a little crestfallen, and Horst patted him on the shoulder, next to the strap of the lasgun.

'Good. We'll need those Guardsman's reflexes of yours further down. Just try and keep them under control until we do.'

'No problem,' Drake assured him, looking a good deal happier. He glanced at Jenie. 'Which way from here?'

'The stairs.' She indicated the staircase opposite the portal, where Vex was standing, consulting the data-slate. 'They're the fastest way down, at least to begin with.'

'That's my conclusion too,' Vex said, and the girl relaxed, barely perceptibly.

'Then let's go,' she said. Despite the confident ring of her voice, she held back a little, waiting until Keira and Drake had taken point before commencing her descent after them.

The staircase was wide and well lit to begin with, and they made good time, descending a score of levels in as many minutes. At first the landings and branching corridors were bright and well used, and they caught sight of a number of crew members going about their business, mostly, to Horst's relief, from a distance. Many of their liveries and accoutrements were unfamiliar, no doubt denoting membership of castes essential to the running of the ship rather than the welfare of the passengers, although he caught a few glimpses of blue-clad officers, their faces masked as Tweendecker's had been. On the few occasions they passed shipfolk more closely they drew the odd curious glance, but little else, before the Misericordians' attention returned to their own affairs.

The first time this happened Keira's hand dropped to the hilt of her sword, but it soon became evident that they weren't to be challenged, and even she began to relax a little. 'Don't they care who we are?' she asked, a tone of mild incredulity suffusing her voice.

'Of course they don't,' Jenie said. 'We're not part of their caste, or doing anything that impinges on their work. The only ones who'd even notice us are the

Merciful, and they hardly ever come this deep unless they're summoned.'

'Is it just me, or is it getting darker down here?' Drake asked, and Vex nodded sagely.

'Ambient illumination has decreased by twenty-seven per cent over the last twelve levels. We appear to be transiting a region consisting mainly of storage areas, where little activity would be expected during a voyage, so it would be reasonable to reduce energy usage wherever possible.'

'So we can expect no light at all lower down,' Keira said, with little enthusiasm.

Recalling the darkness of the shaft down which their luggage had vanished, Horst nodded. 'Looks that way,' he agreed.

'Lucky we brought the luminators, then,' Drake said.

'They should prove sufficient,' Vex agreed. He'd checked them all personally before leaving the shuttle. 'All are fully charged.'

'Well then,' Drake said, with a reassuring smile at their guide, 'we should be fine.'

'We appear to have reached the lowest level in this section,' Vex said. Drake and Keira left the bottom of the staircase, looking in opposite directions along the passageway it opened onto, as they had done at every intermediate flight. Drake still had his lasgun slung, but his left hand eased the strap from his shoulder, and he kept his right ready to take the weight of the butt. Keira had her miniature crossbow strung, ready for use, strapped to her right thigh next to a quiver full of quarrels, but her hand still hovered over the hilt of her sword, which didn't surprise Horst at all; she'd always preferred her bloodshed up close and personal.

'We have,' Drake confirmed, after a cursory glance at the blank metal wall where the next flight of steps should have been. 'So what now?' He spoke to Jenie, but it was Vex who replied, the green glow of his data-slate display reflecting eerily from his white robe in the deepening gloom.

'There seems to be a navigable shaft on the other side of this hold,' he said, indicating a stout metal door ahead of them.

Horst approached it. As he'd expected, another keypad controlled access, and he stood aside wordlessly to let Vex commune with the mechanism as he had before. After a moment the portal began to grind open, releasing a blast of warm, foetid air which made him gag.

'Sinning hell,' Keira said. 'It smells like something died in there.'

'Well, you'd know,' Horst said, hoping to lighten the mood a little, and began to draw his bolt pistol. Pale illumination was visible beyond the opening door, and he could hear movement, and the murmur of voices.

'Have we arrived, noble sir?' a voice asked, and a man in the cheap utility clothing of a Secundan peasant peered hopefully round the widening gap.

'Not yet,' Horst said, removing his hand from the weapon as the scene in front of him became clear for the first time. The cargo hold stretched into the distance, packed with milling humanity, seeming almost as crowded as the reception hall had been; evidently the thralls they'd seen there had just been the latest arrivals. The air stank of unwashed bodies, greasy cooking smoke and the sharp, bitter reek of human waste. 'I'm afraid we need to disturb you for a few minutes, that's all.'

'That doorway over there,' Vex said, pointing, and Horst nodded, just able to make out the distant portal through the maelstrom of humanity. Breathing as lightly as he could, he began to forge a way through the press of bodies.

Within seconds he'd lost sight of all his companions, and began to feel an irrational surge of panic rising within him. He turned his head, his attention fixated on the doorway in the distance, convinced that if he lost sight of it he'd never be able to find it again, and would remain trapped in this hellish place for eternity. The faster he tried to get to it, the further away it seemed, and he found himself fighting the temptation to draw the bolt pistol after all, and clear the way with a few well-placed shots. If it hadn't been for the instinctive way the Secundans moved aside for an evident social superior, without ever coming into physical contact with him, the claustrophobia might have overwhelmed him completely.

'Mordechai?' Keira appeared at his elbow, regarding his floundering progress with evident amusement, and the sensation of panic ebbed away, replaced at once by relief. 'What is it with you and crowds?'

Suddenly they were making progress, just as they had in the marketplace, and he reached the cold metal door to find Vex already at work on the locking mechanism. He leaned his back against it, looking around for Drake and Jenie.

'There's Danuld,' Keira said, pointing, and Horst caught sight of the former Guardsman at last, forging through the crush with grim determination. Jenie was with him, clinging to the strap of his lasgun as though she feared that to let go would invite catastrophe.

'I have the code,' Vex said, and the door began to squeal open, dislodging a shower of rust, which pattered uncomfortably down the back of Horst's jacket. 'Interesting. This section is apparently little used.'

Something of an understatement, Horst thought, stepping into the darkness beyond. The air here felt dry and musty, tickling the back of his throat, and as he kindled his pocket luminator he wasn't surprised to find the deck plating underfoot drifted with dust.

'The maid's day off, do you think?' Drake said, with heavy-handed humour, as Vex pressed the runeplate to close the door behind them. The stench and the babble of voices were abruptly cut off as the thick slabs of metal clanged together, and he unslung the lasgun with a palpable air of relief, snapping his own luminator onto the bayonet lugs.

'What was your first clue?' Keira asked, then turned to Jenie, whose face appeared to have acquired a greyish tinge, a hint of concern entering her voice. 'Are you all right?'

'I will be,' the girl said, with a transparent attempt to make light of the matter. 'Who were those poor people?'

'DeVayne thralls, on their way to Scintilla,' Horst told her.

'Oh.' She considered this. 'I thought all the beyonders stayed in the hostelry.'

'All the ones that aren't classified as cargo,' Horst said. 'It's a pretty rough galaxy out there.'

'Right.' Apparently recovered now, Jenie straightened up, and glanced at Vex. 'Shouldn't you be locking that behind us?'

'What's the point?' Vex asked, a hint of surprise entering his voice. 'Where would they go?'

'Oh,' she said again.

'Better keep moving,' Horst reminded everyone. 'We're still a long way from where we need to be.'

'We are indeed,' Vex agreed. 'And the going will be considerably more difficult from now on.' He consulted the data-slate again. 'This way, I think.' He glanced at Jenie. 'Do you concur?'

'Yes, I suppose so.' The girl roused herself from her reverie with an obvious effort, and Horst watched her carefully as she walked over to join the tech-priest. The encounter with the thralls had obviously affected her more deeply than she was willing to acknowledge, and, for the first time, he began to wonder if their guide was going to be more of a liability than an asset.

EIGHT

The *Misericord*, the Warp, Date and Time Meaningless

DESPITE THE DOUBTS he'd initially felt about leaving his home world to roam the void with the Angelae, Barda was quite enjoying the trip. It certainly didn't hurt that he had the entire shuttle to himself, and was able to luxuriate in the unfamiliar experience of solitude. The guildhouse of the Cloudwalkers had always been crowded, and flying solo was the only time he'd ever had to be alone with his thoughts. Even then he'd had to stay alert, watching his instruments, apart from the rare occasions he'd taken a supply shuttle to one of the outlying void stations, and had been able to simply coast for hours at a time.

This was even better: parked in the deserted hangar bay, he didn't need to make the periodic course corrections that a long journey in free flight would have required, although he conscientiously ran the periodic systems checks he would normally have been doing in any case. The habit was too ingrained to break, and, like any member of his guild, it was a matter of personal pride to ensure that his vessel would be ready for use the instant his clients required it.

He continued to monitor the *Misericord's* internal communications too, as Horst had instructed, but so far had gleaned nothing else worth passing on. Vex had set up some complex filtering system to record anything which seemed significant, so all he had to do was skim through the summary it provided every hour or so to see if the tireless machine-spirit had spotted something it thought worth bringing to his attention, but every now and again he would pick one of the dozens of vox-channels at random and listen to it in person for a while. He was curious about the strange enclosed world of the ship he rode on, and enjoyed the small glimpses his eavesdropping gave him of the way it functioned.

He'd hardly expected to receive a message himself.

'Inquisition shuttle, this is Captain Raymer of the Merciful. Is anyone there?'

'*Righteous Indignation* responding,' Barda replied, allowing the strict vox protocols of his profession to mask his surprise.

'Good.' Raymer wasn't happy about something, that much was clear from the tone of his voice. 'I need to talk to Horst, but he's not responding to his vox.'

That was hardly surprising, Barda thought. According to the last auspex echo he'd had, the Angelae were so deep in the bowels of the ship that their short-range comm-beads would be effectively shielded by the bulk of the metal surrounding them. Even the powerful transmitter aboard the shuttle would have difficulty getting through by now. 'I'll relay a message,' he said diplomatically, 'as soon as he becomes available.'

'Becomes available?' Raymer snarled. 'Who the hell does he think he is, the Lord Shipwright?'

'He thinks he's a representative of the Inquisition,' Barda said, enjoying the novelty of being able to talk back to someone in a position of power and authority without fear of the consequences. 'What do you want to tell him?'

'Fine, have it your way,' Raymer said, reining in his temper with an audible effort. 'Tell him we've finished our check of the manifest, and the men who attacked your colleagues weren't registered as passengers.'

'You mean they were members of the crew?' Barda asked.

'Of course they weren't,' Raymer snapped back. 'You think I wouldn't know if we had wyrds aboard?'

'It's not for me to speculate,' Barda replied, hoping he was managing to mask his amusement. 'No doubt Acolyte Horst will discuss the matter with you at his convenience, if he needs more information. Was that all?'

'Yes, that's all,' Raymer said, and cut the link abruptly.

Barda turned to the main vox transmitter, and relayed the information as crisply as he could, hoping the Angelae were still able to receive it; then, despite knowing a reply was impossible, he sat listening to the static on the channel they were using for several minutes.

'DID YOU GET that?' Keira asked, glancing back at Horst. Barda's voice in her comm-bead had been tenuous, and hazed with static, but she was sure she'd understood the substance of the message. The sense of unease which had begun to oppress her intensified as she considered the implications.

'I think so,' Horst replied, looking equally troubled. They seemed to have arrived somewhere close to where the shaft they were looking for was located, or, Keira corrected herself, at least they were somewhere aboard the same derelict hull. Starships were big, even when they weren't fused together to form a spacegoing leviathan like the *Misericord*. Once again they seemed to be walking on walls, avoiding deep wells of blackness where old corridors plunged into lightless depths, and their progress had become slow as they clambered around them. 'And I'm not sure I like the implications.'

'Me neither,' Drake put in. 'If those wyrds weren't passengers, who the hell were they? Raymer seems convinced they weren't crew.'

'Well, he ought to know,' Keira said, without much confidence. In her experience, local law enforcers weren't exactly quick to spot signs of heresy, even when they should have been blindingly obvious. 'Could they have come aboard with the thralls?'

'I doubt it,' Drake said. 'They were dressed like Secundans from one of the minor houses. If they tried to blend in with the serfs, they'd have stood out like an ecclesiarch in a bordello.' He glanced at Jenie, belatedly realising that the simile was probably rather tactless given their guide's profession, but the girl didn't seem to have noticed. She was sticking close to Vex, apparently paying more attention to the dataslate in his hand than to their immediate surroundings.

'Jenie.' Keira raised her voice a little to attract the harlot's attention, and listened to the echoes it raised with detached interest. After a moment the girl's head turned. 'Do you ever get stowaways on a vessel like this?'

'Stowaways?' Jenie stared at her in blank incomprehension. 'How could they possibly get aboard?'

'I was hoping you could tell me,' Keira said, with a faint shrug.

Jenie shook her head emphatically. 'They just couldn't. They'd be discovered as soon as the shuttles were unloaded.'

Keira nodded, recalling the bustle which had surrounded the *Righteous Indignation* when it arrived aboard. No one could possibly have slipped away unobserved through that maelstrom of activity. 'You're right,' she said. 'Stupid question.'

'There's no such thing as a stupid question,' Jenie said. 'If you don't know something, how else are you going to find out?'

Keira nodded. She should despise the young harlot, she knew, but in spite of the fact that the girl was a professional sinner, she couldn't help finding her likeable. After all, she'd been born into a rigidly enforced caste system, which had compelled her to hawk her body to the passengers; it wasn't as though she'd ever had much of a choice. 'Good point,' she said.

'Watch your step,' Vex cautioned, from somewhere up ahead. He was poised on the lip of another of the shafts spaced along the canted corridor, where cross passageways had once intersected it. 'We need to climb down here.'

'Oh good,' Drake said, with heavy sarcasm. 'That looks easy.' He aimed his lasgun down the pit, the bright beam of his luminator playing across the walls. Two sides of it were smooth metal, studded at intervals with rivets and cross bracing, while the side which had once been the floor was surfaced with metal mesh. The fourth side had the remains of luminators attached to it, long since burned out, and connected by some heavy-duty cable. 'Do you think that'll hold?'

'It should do,' Vex said, reaching across the void to grab it, taking a cautious step onto the lintel as he did so, and tugging experimentally on the hanging wires. They held his weight, even when he swung out and prepared to scramble down.

'Next time, wait until we've rigged a safety line before you try something like that,' Horst said, failing to mask an undercurrent of anger in his voice.

'The risk was negligible,' Vex assured him, his voice as even as ever. 'The breaking strain of electrical conduit of this diameter would be in the order of several tonnes, and the supporting brackets are clearly capable of bearing a good deal of weight.'

'If you say so,' Horst said, sounding dubious. 'Do we follow this all the way to the bottom?'

'I hope not,' Vex said. 'There's a side passage about twenty metres down, which seems to offer a more reasonable route. If we attempt to descend directly, we might well grow tired enough to fall, which, from this height, would be inconvenient to say the least.'

'Which is?' Keira asked, more from idle curiosity than anything else. Being native to Ambulon she had no fear of heights, and she didn't feel the faintest flicker of apprehension at the prospect of the vertiginous descent. You wouldn't be any deader if you fell a thousand metres than if you only fell ten.

'Approximately three hundred and fifty metres,' Vex said, as if that was no more than stepping off the kerb beside a carriageway, and began to scramble down the wire.

'You next,' Horst said to Jenie, and the girl shook her head, backing away from the dizzying shaft.

'No,' she said, licking her lips nervously. 'No, I can't.'

'Fine.' Horst nodded to Drake. 'Danuld.'

'Here goes nothing,' Drake said, slinging his lasgun with the barrel pointed down, to light his progress. He inched his way out onto the lintel, and grabbed the cable, with a reassuring smile at Jenie. 'See? Nothing to it.' He began to work his way down with every appearance of confidence, until only the bobbing halo of his luminator was visible above the lip of the pit.

'I just can't. Sorry.' Jenie backed away another step. 'We'll all be killed.'

'Well, it's your choice,' Horst said. 'I'm sure you can find your way back.' He turned towards the shaft.

'You can't just leave me here!' Jenie protested, her voice cracking a little. She looked from Horst to Keira and back again, as if hoping to find some indication that he was bluffing.

'Yes we can,' Horst said. 'You're here as a guide. If you won't guide us, we've no further use for you.'

'Then swive you,' Jenie snarled, making a convulsive grab for the cable. She clutched at it with the jerky movements of someone fighting their own body, and began to let herself down hand over hand, her eyes tightly closed. 'Oh Throne on Earth, swive the lot of you...'

Keira followed, finding the descent easy enough, particularly once Drake gained the cross-corridor they were aiming for and the light cast by his luminator steadied again. She tried to keep a hand free in case Jenie slipped, even though there was little chance of being able to grab her if the worst happened, but in the event she never had to try.

'Keep going,' Drake called encouragingly. 'You're almost there.'

'Swive off,' Jenie answered, her breath coming in ragged gasps. She let go of the cable with one hand and reached out desperately. 'Don't just stand there, grab me for Throne's sake!'

'It's all right, I've got you.' Drake anchored himself with a firm grasp on a convenient stanchion, and reached out towards her. After a moment of flailing, he took hold of her wrist. 'All you've got to do is let go and jump.'

'Let go? Are you insane?' Jenie shouted.

'It's either that, or stay there for the rest of your life,' Keira pointed out. 'Which, considering you're blocking me from getting any further, is liable to be short.'

'All right!' Jenie let go of the cable, pushing off awkwardly, and shrieking as she began to fall; but Drake had a firm hold on her wrist, and hauled her into the sanctuary of the cross-corridor with a single convulsive movement. 'Oh, thank the Throne! Thank you!' She clung to him, trembling, which Drake didn't seem to object to at all. 'I thought I was going to die!'

'Everyone does eventually,' Keira pointed out, somersaulting neatly through the opening to land beside them. Drake began to detach the girl, to Keira's unspoken relief; the sight of them reminded her of the brief, impromptu embrace she'd shared with Horst after he'd hauled her to safety when the bridge collapsed, and the memory disturbed her in ways she didn't feel comfortable with. 'What was all that about anyway?'

'I don't like heights, all right?' Jenie snapped, then recovered her composure as best she could. 'Never have done.'

'Then it was very brave of you to make the descent anyway,' Horst said, joining them at last.

Unable to meet his eye, for reasons she couldn't quite articulate, Keira went to join Vex.

'Will we have to do that again?' she asked.

'Not for a while,' the tech-priest said, consulting the screen of his data-slate. He indicated a point on the display. 'We're here.' His finger moved. 'And we need to be here.'

'Looks right to me,' Jenie agreed, joining them, and glancing at it in a cursory fashion. The ordeal in the shaft seemed to have boosted her confidence, Keira thought, which was probably all to the good. She began to lead the way into the darkness. 'Are you coming, or what?'

Scintil VIII Void Station, Scintilla System
247.993.M41

THE LOWER ARM was never particularly quiet, but there were rhythms to the pattern of any human activity, and the Ordo Xenos team had timed their incursion to take full advantage of one of the periodic lulls. The corridors were emptier than usual, and many of the businesses closed, which made the network of outer pickets around Voyle's warehouse easier to spot; which, in turn, made them all the easier to neutralise. Out of the corner of his eye, Quillem saw a flicker of movement down one of the side passages, heard a faint sigh and the slither of a falling body, and a moment later Rufio trotted up to join him, the habitual easygoing grin on his face.

'Another one down,' he said cheerfully, his blond ponytail brushing against his back as he tilted his head a little to talk to the taller man. Rufio was a feral worlder, who'd grown up hunting creatures more dangerous than he was amid vegetation scarcely less lethal, and relished the chance to use his stalking skills whatever the environment. Quillem had worked with him a few times, but never warmed to the man; he'd killed in the service of his patron too, of course, but purely because it was necessary, or in self-defence. Rufio enjoyed that sort of thing too much for his liking: not because he was a sadist, or even particularly callous, but simply because he was good at what he did, and took a craftsman's pride in doing it well. 'He had this on him.'

Quillem took the short-range comm-bead from the assassin's outstretched hand, and nodded in approval. 'I take it he never got the chance to use it?'

'Course not,' Rufio said, with complete confidence. 'I got him with a janus thorn.' He slipped the thin spike of wood, harvested from one of the most toxic trees of his home world, into a protective sheath, his dexterity unhampered by the thick leather gloves he wore. 'He was dead as soon as it broke the skin.'

'Good,' Quillem said. 'Then they still don't know we're coming.' He pulled a data-slate from his jacket pocket, and glanced at it, noting the positions of the sentries they'd already taken out, and adding Rufio's latest victim to the tally. With a sense of relief, but little surprise, he realised that they'd all been stationed precisely where they'd been predicted to be: one of the many advantages of having a Deathwatch kill team attached to Inquisitor Grynner's entourage was the matchless tactical expertise the veteran Astartes were able to bring to this kind of enterprise. No doubt they'd have preferred to take a more direct hand in the affair, but for the moment the inquisitor preferred a more subtle approach, which meant that Quillem and his companions had been given the job.

All five of them were dressed the same, in dark jackets and trousers, conventional enough in style to escape all but the most casual notice, while still being cut generously enough to conceal the weapons and other essential equipment they carried. Even so, they each managed to imbue the nondescript clothing with some trace of their own personality.

Rufio, for instance, had his jacket unfastened, revealing a singlet of the same charcoal-grey, along with a necklace of teeth from some predator he'd faced and bested as part of a tribal rite on whichever backwater planet he'd come from. Malven, by contrast, kept his jacket firmly closed, partly to conceal his array of augmetics from casual passers-by, but mainly, Quillem suspected, because he simply didn't feel comfortable in anything other than the vestments of a tech-priest. The white robe of his calling would have attracted too much attention on a covert operation like this, though, so, despite his manifest reluctance, the mechwright had agreed to don something less noticeable.

Carys, the only woman in the group, simply fitted the clothes as though they'd been tailored for her, a happy knack she seemed to have whatever she wore. A striking redhead in her middle thirties, Carys was a thief, and quite an exceptional one; a talent she'd been happy to turn to the services of the Inquisition after her arrest, particularly once the alternatives had been pointed out to her. If anything was hidden in Voyle's premises, Quillem was certain she'd be able to find it.

The fifth member of their party was the most enigmatic, and the one who, though he did his best to conceal it, Quillem felt the least comfortable around. Arken was a cadaverous young man, with a nervous manner and a faint, rasping voice, which grated on the interrogator's nerves. He seemed to be huddled inside his cocoon of garments, which hung loosely on his spare frame, as though the ambient temperature was colder than he liked, although Quillem knew that the winds he felt were those of the immaterium rather than the void station's recirculators. Arken was a sanctioned psyker, sensitive enough to feel the presence of any more blasphemous artefacts like the wraithbone which had slipped through their fingers in the Halo Stars; if Voyle was indeed working for the Faxlignae, and had somehow managed to obtain more of the stuff, they'd know almost as soon as they arrived on the premises.

'Was that the last of them?' Carys asked, and Quillem nodded.

'All the ones we were told to look out for,' he agreed. 'But keep your eyes open. There may be others.' He doubted it, having worked with the Deathwatch team often enough to have complete faith in their expertise, but you never knew. Heretics didn't play by the rules, and they weren't predictable. Besides, there was always the human factor to consider; sooner or later someone would stumble across the bodies of the sentries they'd taken out, and the Franchise would be roused. He took a final look at the plan on the screen of the slate, checking the gap in the cordon around their objective which Rufio had so carefully opened up, and stowed the small device in an inside pocket, where it bumped against his bolt pistol in its shoulder rig.

'I can't feel any unusual disturbances,' Arken said, and Quillem nodded again.

'Then let's go and do some disturbing ourselves,' he suggested, setting off down a passageway leading in the direction of their objective.

The *Misericord*, the Warp, Date and Time Meaningless

'BETTER LET ME take point,' Drake said, catching up with Jenie. 'I've been trained for this.'

'Be my guest,' she said, dropping a pace or two behind him with evident relief. 'I'm beginning to think I'm in way over my head.'

'You get used to it,' Drake told her, sweeping the beam of his luminator along the passageway ahead of them. It

had evidently been used for access originally, rather than
the main corridors they'd been following up until now; it
was wider than it was high, forcing him to crouch a little,
although the girl beside him was still able to walk more or
less upright without banging her head on the ceiling.

'Do you really do this sort of thing all the time?' Jenie
asked, sounding sceptical, and Drake nodded.

'Pretty much,' he agreed. Now he came to think of it, an
awful lot seemed to have happened since that fateful day
in the forests of Sepheris Secundus.

'I don't know how you stand it,' Jenie said.

'Neither do I,' Drake said, only half-joking. At least
there weren't any shafts along here to negotiate; he'd had
more than enough of swinging around and over chasms,
where one misstep would mean falling to a very messy
death. He kept the beam of his luminator moving, covering every wall, the ceiling, and the floor, and his finger
on the trigger of the lasgun. Something about one of the
shadows up ahead didn't seem right, and he held up a
hand to forestall the others.

'What is it?' Horst asked quietly.

Drake edged forwards, trying to bring the shadow into
focus. 'There's a grille in the floor,' he said. He deflected
the beam upwards, to illuminate another, identical, rectangle of mesh in the ceiling. 'And another above it.'

'Part of the ventilation system,' Vex said. 'Don't forget,
they'd have been in the walls originally.'

'I know that,' Drake said. He'd already stepped over
several similar ones. 'But this one's been moved.' It
wasn't quite flush with the floor, which was why it had
cast the shadow that had seemed subtly wrong to him.

'Receivers scavenging?' Keira suggested, and Jenie
shook her head.

'They'd have taken the grille, if they'd been able to
remove it,' she pointed out.

'It doesn't look as though it's been booby trapped,' Drake
said, edging closer. There were no telltale twists of wire,

which might lead to an improvised detonator, but he drew his Guard-issue combat knife and probed it carefully in any case. The grille moved slightly as he prodded it. 'Something's under there, too bulky to let it drop back into place.'

'A Receiver's stash?' Keira suggested.

'Could be,' Drake agreed. 'Looks like a bundle of rags, wrapped around something.' He coughed, as the repellent stench of decay caught the back of his throat. 'Whatever it is, it smells pretty rank.'

'Better check it anyway,' Horst said, moving up to join him. 'If it's any of our stuff, we'll know we're on the right track.'

'Right.' Drake squatted on one side of the grille, while Horst took the other. To his surprise it felt lighter than he'd expected, unwieldy rather than heavy, and they lifted it easily between them. 'Holy Throne!'

'What is it?' Keira asked, stepping forwards, her hand dropping to the hilt of her sword.

'One of the missing Riggers, I think,' Horst said, flinching from the stench, which had intensified more than Drake would have believed possible now that the grating had been removed. 'But it's hard to be sure.' A metal duct, about two-thirds of a metre wide and deep, ran beneath the floor, intended to circulate fresh air, as Vex had deduced. Now it was choked with the ragged remains of a human cadaver, which looked as though it had simply been stuffed there.

'That looks like their livery,' Jenie said, edging closer, then recoiling as she caught a clear sight of the corpse for the first time. 'Emperor on Earth!' She turned aside, and was noisily sick.

'What did that to him, do you suppose?' Keira asked, curiously. Swathes of muscle tissue had been flensed from the corpse, revealing glimpses of the bone beneath. 'Looks like a blade of some kind, but pretty crude.'

Vex nodded. 'A knife would be my guess, too, but a very primitive one.' He leaned closer, examining the body with every sign of interest. 'And there are quite clearly teeth marks on parts of the exposed bone.' He pointed. 'Particularly around there, where the flesh has been torn rather than cut.'

His scalp prickling, Drake swept the luminator beam up and down the corridor, but there was no sign of movement.

'Plague zombies, do you suppose?' Keira asked, and Vex shook his head.

'The ones we dealt with on Scintilla wouldn't have used knives,' he said. 'But some victims do retain a vestige of intellect. I'd be more inclined to suspect mutants, though.' He turned to Jenie, who was just straightening up after a further bout of dry heaving. 'Have you ever heard rumours about things like that infesting the out-hulls?'

'I've no idea what you're talking about,' she said, her face grey in the light of the luminators. 'And I don't want to either. Let's just get the warp out of here before whatever ate the poor bastard comes back.'

'That does seem quite likely,' Vex agreed. 'Given the way the corpse was concealed, and the remains of its clothing were wrapped around it, I'd imagine who or whatever is responsible intends returning for further meals.'

'Anything that tries snacking off us is in for a big surprise,' Keira said, with easy confidence, and Drake nodded his agreement.

'Damn right,' he agreed, checking that the power pack of his lasgun was fully charged. Nevertheless, as they set out again, despite a complete absence of both sound and movement, he couldn't quite shake the uneasy feeling that they were being watched.

NINE

**The *Ursus Innare*, Scintilla System
247.993.M41**

ELYRA FELT THE *Ursus Innare* make the transition back to the material universe like the sudden cessation of a nagging migraine. Even mundanes, she knew, could sometimes feel the pressure of unreality scrabbling against the void shields during warp travel, but for psykers the experience was unrelenting, and deeply unpleasant.

'What happened?' Kyrlock asked, looking faintly puzzled in the perpetual half-light, and she smiled as reassuringly as she could. She wasn't sure how the psychically deaf perceived the shift between the realms of Chaos and the Emperor, but some of them had spoken of a momentary sense of disorientation at such times, and Kyrlock had clearly found his first experience of warp travel disturbing.

'Isn't it obvious?' Trosk cut in before she could speak, his voice taking on a tinge of derision. 'We've arrived.' Since the fight with the bandits he'd been tacitly challenging her authority at every opportunity, although so far he'd stopped short of outright rebellion. That could be a problem; she needed him and his friends if she was going to follow the trail any further once they got to Scintilla. At least Zusen still seemed to trust her, though, and Ven was too far out of it most of the time to really count as either an obstacle or a potential ally.

'Good,' Kyrlock said, refusing to let the juve's tone get under his skin, although it probably galled him to let it go. He'd made his point after the fight, and didn't seem to feel the need to return to the topic, to Elyra's relief. He had a volatile temper, she knew, but fortunately he seemed able to keep it under control in the interest of the mission. Though she'd hardly known the man when they set out on this assignment together, she'd come to trust him, and his judgement. 'The sooner we're off this barge the better.'

'How soon's that likely to be?' Zusen asked, looking up from her ration pack. The franchisers had made another delivery of food a while back, although how long ago that had been Elyra wasn't too sure; mired in this unremitting twilight it was all too easy to lose track of the time even without the peculiar tricks the warp played on the mind. If the gangers had noticed the absence of a handful of their passengers they'd made no mention of the fact, presumably expecting a certain amount of attrition before the freighter reached its destination. The other refugees certainly had, though, eyeing Kyrlock and herself with a wary mixture of gratitude and fear as they took their turns to collect their food, and giving the other members of their party as wide a berth as possible.

'A few more days,' Elyra told her. 'We'll have left the warp on the fringes of the system, so we'll be coasting in towards Scintilla for a while yet.'

'Except we're not going to Scintilla,' Trosk said. 'Maybe you and the cattle are, but we're getting off at the void station.'

'Since when?' Elyra asked, and Trosk smirked.

'Since we started out on this trip,' he said.

Zusen nodded. 'It's true,' she confirmed, 'they told us back on Sepheris Secundus. We're being taken off in a shuttle.'

'And you've only just thought to mention this?' Kyrlock put in, sounding more resigned than irritated.

Trosk shrugged. 'You never asked,' he pointed out reasonably, turning to Elyra. 'And you've made it pretty clear from the moment we met that you've got your own plans once we hit Scintilla. Why would you care where we go?'

'Because I promised to get you there in one piece,' Elyra said. 'When I've done that, and talked to your babysitters, I might stick around; or I might go bounty hunting with Vos after all.' She shrugged. 'Depends on what they're offering.'

'But you must come with us,' Zusen said earnestly. 'The Sanctuary can help you too, I know they can.'

'Sanctuary?' Kyrlock asked, with a clear lack of interest in whatever the answer might be. 'Is that some religious thing?'

'It's the people helping us,' Zusen said. 'The Sanctuary of the Blessed. They find people with special talents, and protect them from persecution.'

'What's in it for them?' Elyra asked, still playing her role to the hilt, and allowing no hint of the quickening of interest she felt to rise to the surface of her face.

'Nothing,' Trosk said, with a hint of impatience. 'They're psykers too, looking after their own. Isn't that enough?'

'In the galaxy you live in, maybe,' Kyrlock said, stepping in instinctively to draw the juvies's attention back to himself before they realised how much they were giving away. 'But over here in the real one, nobody takes that kind of risk without expecting some serious payback. Usually with interest.'

'Well, that's where you're wrong!' Zusen said vehemently, with enough emphasis to tell Elyra that she must have entertained doubts about this herself, and was desperate to suppress them. 'All they've asked is that we use our gifts to help people, and save more psykers from the Black Ships if we get the chance.'

'Lovely.' Elyra shrugged. 'Well, I'll talk to them. But if I don't like what I hear, I'm gone.'

'Can't say fairer than that,' Trosk agreed, with elaborate uninterest.

The *Misericord*, the Warp, Date and Time Meaningless

'THAT'S ODD,' VEX said, looking at his data-slate in some perplexity. 'This bulkhead should be sealed.'

'Well, it's not,' Keira said, unnecessarily, while Drake flashed his luminator along the length of the corridor beyond the open door. Nothing moved in the darkness except a startled rat, which squeaked and fled the moment the light speared it. Drake's finger twitched on the trigger, but he overrode the impulse to fire, Keira noted with approval. Letting panic dictate your actions was a sure way to get killed.

'Do we need to go that way?' Horst asked, and the techpriest shook his head.

'No. That leads to the impact site.' A faint look of puzzlement crossed his face for a moment. 'The hull can't have been breached after all, or we'd feel the air moving towards the leak.'

'Maybe the Riggers patched it before ending up in the larder,' Keira said impatiently. 'But that's not really important, is it?'

'It's not immediately relevant to the mission, no,' Vex agreed. 'But it is anomalous. Perhaps we should investigate.'

'And perhaps we should keep our minds on what we're doing down here in the first place,' Horst said. 'Recovering the manuscript.'

'Works for me,' Drake said, sweeping the luminator around the chamber they'd just arrived in. There were several potential exits ranged around the walls, all of them choked with shadows. He turned to Jenie. 'Where's the bottom of that shaft from here?'

The girl looked around, with a hint of uncertainty. 'Hang on a minute,' she said, 'I just need to get my bearings.'

'I believe this way would be the optimum route,' Vex said, pointing to a narrow conduit, and Jenie nodded.

'Me too,' she agreed.

'Well then, let's get to it,' Horst said.

'I'd better go first this time,' Keira offered. 'I'm more used to moving around in tight spaces.' Horst nodded his agreement, and she clambered up to the service duct Vex and the harlot had indicated. It was cramped, as she'd expected, but there was still room to move freely, and she wriggled inside without difficulty, flashing the beam of her luminator ahead of her.

The duct was dusty, but clear of obstructions, and she moved forwards at a rapid crawl; a moment later the clangour of metal against metal informed her that Drake was behind her, and finding his lasgun a little difficult to handle in the confined space. Ignoring the distraction, she kept moving, her eyes fixed on a metal grille in the distance; it reminded her of the one they'd found the corpse behind, and she tried to ignore the mental image of a similar blockage abruptly appearing in front of her.

'I think this is it,' she said, her voice echoing around her, and pressing her face to the grille. The space beyond was vast, she could tell that at once from the quality of the silence, like the nave of a cathedral, and she struck at the rusting metal with a force which could shatter bone. It popped out abruptly, and fell away; a moment later a carillon of overlapping echoes confirmed her first impression of the size of the chamber.

'Looks like it,' Drake agreed, doing his best to peer past her rump, and she leaned outwards, shining her luminator down towards the floor. 'How big's the drop?'

'Just a couple of metres,' Keira said, diving head first through the gap, and twisting in mid-air to land softly on the soles of her feet, bending her knees as she landed to absorb the impact and deaden the noise. She raised her luminator to the duct, picking out Drake's shock of blond hair and pale face in the gloom.

'Mind where you're pointing that,' he protested, squinting, and began to wriggle out of the hole like a tube worm in search of food. He descended reasonably quickly, and hurried to join her, the lasgun back in his hands with an evident sense of relief. 'See anything?'

'We're definitely in the right place,' Keira said, picking out the mangled remains of a handcart in the beam of her luminator. A tangle of metal beyond it had probably once been the bridge; she directed the light upwards, finding a rectangular hole in the high ceiling which looked about the same dimensions as the shaft she remembered so well.

'It looks like another hold,' Horst agreed, joining them, and adding his light to theirs. Doorways could be seen halfway up the walls, where other corridors had presumably once joined the vast room. 'Like the lake chamber, but unflooded.'

'I suggest we split up and search the area,' Vex said, standing aside to make room for Jenie as she scrambled awkwardly down from the open grille.

Drake snorted with derision. 'Why not? It worked so well the last time.'

'The circumstances are entirely dissimilar,' Vex said. 'Unlike the Gallery of Sin, there are clear lines of sight, and no crowd to get lost in.'

'And no rogue psykers trying to part your hair with a fireball,' Drake added.

'Spread out,' Horst instructed, stepping in to curtail the discussion before it became acrimonious. 'Make sure you can see whoever's on either side of you at all times. And keep your weapons handy; you might not run into any rogue psykers, but someone dismembered the poor bastard we found back there.'

'Or something,' Keira added, the image of the daemon Adrin's coven had inadvertently raised suddenly appearing in her mind.

'You're looking for a box, right?' Jenie asked, and Keira nodded. 'Like you told Verren?'

'That's right,' the young assassin confirmed. 'But if you find anything else that looks interesting, sing out anyway. It might help to point us in the right direction.'

'All right.' Jenie still looked out of her depth, but rallied fast. 'And there was a reward, you said?'

'You'll be well paid for helping us, I can assure you,' Horst said.

'After what I've been through, I'd better be,' Jenie replied tartly, and wandered over to take her place in the line, between Keira and Drake.

Combing their way across the chamber was a slow and frustrating task. An awful lot of detritus had accumulated at the bottom of the shaft over the centuries, and the Angelae had to pick their way through and around it, constantly alert for treacherous footing and jagged edges.

'I've found something!' Jenie called, holding up the battered remains of a valise Keira recognised as having once contained most of Horst's clothing, including a few items they'd recovered from Cuddy's stall.

'Well done,' she called encouragingly. 'It shows we're on the right track.'

'It shows we're out of our rutting minds,' Drake grumbled. 'We'll never find it among all this cack.'

'Trust the Emperor, and He will guide your steps,' Keira quoted, refusing to be disheartened.

The Guardsman shrugged. 'Well, He might try guiding them a bit quicker, that's all I'm saying.'

Keira felt her hand flexing over her sword at the casual blasphemy, before pragmatism overrode the instinctive reaction. Drake was as pious as the next man, she knew, and not everyone was as pure in outlook as the Redemptionists. These days she wasn't even sure if she was, uncomfortably aware of how many little compromises she'd had to make to get the job done. Then all her doubts were swept away, as the beam of her luminator picked out the unmistakable outline of the cogitator case they were looking for; if that wasn't a clear sign of the Emperor's favour, she didn't know what was.

'I've got it!' she yelled, keeping the precious box pinned in the circle of light, irrationally afraid that if she moved the luminator away from it the case would disappear.

'Well spotted,' Horst said, hurrying as best he could through the hindering debris to join her, and Keira felt strangely cheered by the compliment. 'Is it intact?'

'Of course not,' Keira said. 'But I'm not poking about in what's left of it until Hybris has taken a look. You know how many wards and hexes he's put in the thing.'

'A wise precaution,' Vex said, stooping to examine the case. 'Although I'm afraid none of the mechanisms remain functional.' He lifted a corner of the box carefully, and a cascade of small cogwheels and broken glass rattled against the floor. 'It also appears that the machine-spirit has departed to the eternal files.' He made the sign of the cogwheel, and muttered a brief benediction in binary.

'What about the manuscript?' Horst asked, and the tech-priest lifted the lid, peering inside with an expression of hopeful expectation, which vanished as suddenly as a slamming door.

'It's gone,' he said flatly.

Scintil VIII Void Station, Scintilla System
247.993.M41

THE LOCATOR THE Deathwatch Techmarine had given Quillem guided them to a small, unregarded access hatch in a rusting metal wall between an apothecary's stall and a vendor of bushmeat, both shuttered for the slack period. Taking advantage of the cover the two ramshackle structures provided, Malven extended a mechadendrite from beneath his swaddling jacket and probed the latch, muttering a brief incantation in binary as he did so. As always, the twittering chant set Quillem's teeth on edge, but it was over mercifully quickly, and seemed to have done the trick; a moment later the slab of metal swung outwards, squealing a little on hinges unoiled for decades.

'Ladies first.' Carys stuck out a hand to check his movement, then grinned, eager as always to see what someone was taking such pains to keep her away from. 'Don't want to set off any alarms now, do we?'

'No, we don't,' Quillem agreed, stepping aside to let her go first. This was what he'd brought her along for, after all. The service conduit ought to be clear of any unpleasant surprises, but if it wasn't, she'd be the one most likely to spot them. Carys scooted inside, then the interrogator ducked his head and followed her.

The narrow duct was even more cramped and claustrophobic than he'd imagined, and he felt a sudden flare of panic, which he fought down after a moment. The others were looking to him for leadership, and he couldn't show any sign of weakness in front of them. The passage was tight and airless, his shoulders brushing the walls on either side, and he couldn't straighten up either, forced into a low crouch by the closeness of the ceiling. Conscious that the others would be hard on his heels, he shuffled awkwardly along, until he collided with something warm and yielding.

'Oi! You might at least buy me dinner first,' Carys said, clearly amused at his clumsiness. Shuffling and slithering sounds behind him told Quillem that the rest of the team was following, and a moment later a resonant boom of metal against metal confirmed that Malven had closed the hatch. Somehow that seemed to intensify the darkness, and the air grew thicker, permeated with the choking odours of dust, rust and rodent droppings.

'Hang on a minute,' Carys said, scrabbling for something in her jacket judging by the sound, and a moment later Quillem found himself squinting as she kindled a small luminator. It wasn't all that bright, but in contrast to the pitch darkness surrounding them it seemed more than adequate, and after a moment his eyes adjusted enough to take advantage of the glow it cast.

Now he could see his surroundings, the conduit turned out to be every bit as unpleasant as his imagination had pictured it, patches of damp raising blisters of rust on floor, walls and ceiling, which broke off whenever anyone brushed against them; shattered, they sublimed into tiny flakes of brown dust, which scratched at his eyes and left his mouth coated with the bitter taste of old, dried blood. In places the traces of moisture were more pronounced, and Quillem's knees and elbows were soon coated with thick ochre slime, where small puddles had coagulated into an offensive porridge of corrosion, mould and faeces.

'That's better,' Carys said, attaching the tiny light to an elasticated headband, which left her hands free, and setting off at a rapid crawl, apparently undeterred by the filth littering the floor.

'I liked it better when we were navigating by smell,' Rufio said, from somewhere behind Quillem. 'It's like a hrud's nest in here.'

'Well, if you see one, feel free to poke it with your stick,' Quillem said, trying to sound relaxed, and sticking as close to the thief as he could. Rufio was perfectly trustworthy, of course, or Inquisitor Grynner would never have recruited him, but he always felt more comfortable where he could see the man.

'Shamefully neglected,' Malven said from the rear of the column. 'These power relays haven't been sanctified in a generation.'

'You mean those box things?' Rufio asked, ducking past something the size and shape of a rust-shrouded rucksack. His attention called to the periodic protrusions in the walls as something other than just an irritating obstacle, Quillem examined the next one as he passed it: an anonymous metal chest, to which a few flakes of paint still clung, connected to its fellows by a cable as thick as his forearm.

'I do,' Malven confirmed, as incapable as most of his brethren of recognising when his leg was being pulled. 'This must be part of the energy distribution grid for the old docking bays.'

'So don't mess about with anything,' Quillem added, unnecessarily, trying to keep as far from the cables as he could. If anything went wrong down here, they'd be lucky if the inquisitor even found their ashes.

'Bit of quiet back there, if you think you could manage it,' Carys said, a hint of irritation entering her voice. 'Sound carries a long way in these ducts, and I'd rather not let the heretics know we're coming.' She waited a moment, apparently anticipating some kind of argument, then resumed her progress, muttering under her breath. 'Mum was right. Never work with amateurs…'

After that they moved on in relative silence for a while, punctuated only by their ragged breathing, and the scraping of cloth against metal. Just as Quillem was beginning to wonder if they'd ever reach their objective, Carys turned, holding up a hand.

'Wait,' she whispered, so quietly Quillem barely heard her; he glanced back, and relayed the message, just in time to prevent Rufio from colliding with him. Judging by the short burst of murmured profanity which followed a moment later, the assassin hadn't been quite so quick to inform Arken of the unexpected stop.

'What is it?' Quillem breathed, moving a little closer, and trying to peer over the woman's shoulder.

'Motion sensor. Set into the ceiling, where you'd be most likely to miss it crawling along like this.' She glanced up, the luminator attached to her headband illuminating a crudely welded metal box about the size of a data-slate.

'Unsanctified work,' the tech-priest said, a faint edge of distaste forcing itself into his voice, despite his best efforts to filter his utterances of emotional content. 'Put together by some heretical dabbler.'

'I don't care who built it; what does it do?' Quillem asked.

'It senses motion,' Carys told him, accurately but unhelpfully. 'In this case ours. Don't worry, I know how to deal with it.'

'That would be a matter for a properly sanctified acolyte of the Omnissiah,' Malven objected.

'Except you can't get to it,' Carys pointed out in a whisper.

'If it's unhallowed, I don't see that it matters who deactivates it,' Quillem said.

'Its sanctity isn't the issue,' Malven said. 'The correct incantations...' He broke off as Carys extracted a small aerosol from her jacket, and sprayed the box, paying particular attention to a tiny aperture in the underside. A moment later, choking fumes began to fill the narrow tunnel. The tech-priest suppressed a surprisingly delicate cough. 'But I suppose that might work too.'

'What in the Emperor's name is that stuff?' Quillem asked, his eyes streaming.

Carys shrugged, and returned the spray to her pocket. 'Molecular acid. Dissolves pretty much anything. Don't get it mixed up with your breath freshener.'

'And don't get dripped on,' Quillem counselled, as they resumed their progress past the slowly melting booby trap.

'At least we know they've definitely got something to hide now,' Carys said, sounding positively cheerful at the prospect. 'No point putting alarms down a hole like this otherwise…' She broke off, the light she carried picking out a ladder ahead of them in the darkness. 'I think this is it.' Before Quillem could stop her she'd swarmed up it, vanishing into the shadows above them.

Quillem followed, relieved to be able to stand at last, and found himself climbing a narrow shaft a little more than twice his own height. At the top of the ladder was a corridor large enough to stand upright in, and he stretched his back gratefully, glancing round at their surroundings while he waited for the rest of the team to join them.

'Look at this,' Carys whispered, the light from her luminator flickering around the passageway. At first Quillem wasn't sure what she meant, seeing little apart from the greater headroom that was any different from the conduit they'd crawled along so laboriously, then it suddenly hit him. The floor was almost clear of detritus, the coating of filth hard-packed by the passage of innumerable feet.

'Rufio.' Quillem gestured to the assassin as he stepped from the ladder. 'Scout down that way, see where it goes.' He had no need to explain any further; the feral worlder's tracking skills would already have told him everything he'd just deduced with a single glance. Rufio nodded, and loped off into the darkness, his jungle-honed senses evidently not needing anything so crude as a luminator to assist them.

Arken clambered up the ladder a moment later, glancing around with an air of distraction, which Quillem found vaguely disquieting, as he first set foot in the corridor.

'Are you all right?' he asked the psyker in an undertone. So far as he knew Arken didn't suffer from claustrophobia, but it was surprising what hidden weaknesses would sometimes emerge under stress.

'I'm not sure,' Arken replied. 'I'm sensing some kind of residue here. It's… disturbing.'

'What sort of residue?' Quillem asked, fighting the urge to draw his bolt pistol. If the seer was uncomfortable, that meant there was probably warpcraft going on somewhere in the vicinity, or there had been recently enough for the fabric of reality to still be feeling the bruises. 'Something xenos?'

Arken shook his head. 'Human, I think. Elation and madness and hatred, all tainted with the stench of the warp.' He looked directly at Quillem. 'Something very bad was here, not too long ago. Hellishly powerful in the aggregate, but fragmented, divided.' He shrugged. 'Sorry, that's probably not making a whole lot of sense.'

'We'll find out what it is before we leave,' Quillem assured him, with more confidence than he felt.

Arken shrugged again. 'I'm not sure I want to,' he admitted.

Before Quillem could reply, the tech-priest joined them, glancing around the corridor with his habitual neutral expression. 'Are we orientated?' he enquired dryly.

'We are,' Carys assured him, leading the way along the passage, in the opposite direction to the one taken by Rufio a few moments before. 'Just a few score metres down here.'

Her voice had dropped to a barely audible murmur, and Quillem had to strain his ears to make out the words, but he wasn't about to chide her for that; they were almost on top of their objective now, and caution was paramount. 'Spread out,' he instructed the others, almost as quietly. 'Let Carys go first.'

The call was a good one; almost as soon as he'd finished speaking, the woman held up a hand, motioning her companions to stay back. Once again she plied her bottle of acid, grimacing as the fumes tainted the air around her, then gestured the rest of the party forwards.

'Another alarm?' Quillem asked, when he got close enough to speak to her in an undertone.

Carys shook her head. 'Booby trap this time. Directional mines in the walls. Anyone they don't know who gets this close, they want dead.'

'Life's full of little disappointments,' Quillem told her, and the thief suppressed a chuckle.

'Isn't it just?' she said, her attention on the floor. 'Thought so. Look.'

Quillem followed the beam of her luminator. A few metres further on, the trampled floor gave way to the familiar scattering of loose-packed detritus they'd struggled through in the conduit. He nodded.

'We've arrived,' he said quietly.

'And not before time,' Carys agreed. She began to examine the walls on either side of the corridor, looking at them so closely Quillem began to wonder if she was about to get a smear of rust on her nose, to supplement her natural freckling. 'Oh, this is class work. Very nice. You'd never realise it was there if you didn't know where to look.' She shrugged. 'Of course the footprints kind of give it away, but you can't have everything.'

Stooping to join her, Quillem was just able to discern a faint line in the patina of rust coating the walls. 'Hidden panel, do you think?' he asked.

'Does the Emperor sit on the Throne?' Carys asked rhetorically. She gestured to Malven. 'Can you do anything with this? Preferably quietly?'

'To the Omnissiah, all things are possible,' the techpriest said, moving up to join them; as he began to probe the slab of metal delicately with his mechadendrites, Quillem and Carys stepped back a pace to give him room to work. 'Most elegant. Unsanctified, of course, but well crafted nevertheless.'

'Which means?' Carys asked, with a hint of impatience.

Malven turned his head to answer, although his metallic tentacles continued to work on the concealed panel as if under their own volition. 'The locking mechanism is tied to a genecode scanner. Only six people are authorised to trip it. If anyone else makes the attempt, the alarm will be raised.'

'Can you do anything about it?' Quillem asked, and Carys shook her head.

'Nothing subtle. Sorry. Genecoders are a bitch to get past, unless you've got a sample from an authorised user. We'll just have to blow the hatch, and go in shooting.' She shrugged. 'Never a Deathwatch team around when you need one.'

Quillem raised a hand to the comm-bead in his ear, then let it fall. The Astartes squad were on standby, he knew, but there was no way he could call them in for backup. He pictured the sable-armoured giants double-timing it through the startled crowds in the thoroughfares of the lower arm, and shook his head. The news of their presence would be all over the station in moments, the system in days, and any hope of keeping the operation secret would be gone. The heretics they were hunting would go to ground, the Faxlignae would slip through their fingers, and the mysterious agenda their prey was pursuing might well come to fruition before they could pick up the trail again.

'We'll just have to do the best we can without them,' he said, beginning to reach for his bolt pistol.

'Or we could trust our intellect,' Malven added dryly. A moment later the panel moved, with a barely perceptible click, and a faint current of cleaner air began to waft past their faces.

'What did you do?' Quillem asked, trying not to smile at Carys's expression of astonishment.

'Interfaced directly with the control circuitry,' Malven said, withdrawing his mechadendrites. 'I simply added my own genetic code to the file of authorised users.'

'Smart,' Carys admitted, with a nod of the head. 'If you ever feel like a change of career, I know a couple of vaults I could introduce you to.'

'The Adeptus Mechanicus provides for all of my physical requirements,' Malven replied evenly, 'which would render thievery a singularly pointless endeavour.'

Not for the first time, Quillem found himself wondering if the tech-priest was entirely devoid of a sense of humour, or possessed a dry and ready wit which few gave him credit for. There was no time to think about that now, though, as the unmistakable sound of footsteps could be heard hurrying along the tunnel behind them. Drawing his bolt pistol, he turned, then relaxed: it was Rufio, as he'd already surmised, but right now would be a bad time to take anything for granted.

'Only me.' The assassin grinned at him, as if amused at the idea that Quillem would actually be able to harm him if he ever really wanted to, then tilted his head back down the tunnel. 'The travelled area peters out about half a kilometre that way. I couldn't get right to the end, because there was another of those box things Carys took out, but it looks as though there's an exit of some kind about where the footprints end.'

Quillem nodded, recalling the plans he'd studied on the screen of his data-slate. As he'd expected, that would put the other end of the clandestine corridor they'd infiltrated somewhere among the docking bays, but precisely where would have to be determined at a later date. Right now they had more pressing concerns to worry about.

'Good work,' he told Rufio, then nodded at Malven. 'Whenever you're ready.'

The bolt pistol was a comforting weight in his hand, and he flicked the safety off, glancing at the others as he did so. Arken said nothing, but followed his lead, drawing the laspistol he normally favoured, his face set. Rufio smiled, disdaining anything so crude as a firearm, but tapped the blowpipe tucked into his belt with a fingertip, reassuring himself that he knew precisely where it was, and could ready it for use in an instant. Carys, too, preferred to leave her hands free, but opened her jacket, revealing a holstered autopistol among the tools of her trade arrayed around her belt.

'Now would seem an appropriate moment,' the tech-priest said, and opened the panel.

The *Misericord*, the Warp, Date and Time Meaningless

'GONE?' HORST ECHOED, unwilling to believe it. After travelling so far, and overcoming so many obstacles, he refused to believe that they could be cheated of their goal so close to its completion. 'Gone where?'

'I lack sufficient information to offer an opinion,' Vex said, sounding as disgruntled about the fact as a tech-priest would ever admit to feeling.

'Could it have been scattered by the impact?' Drake asked, and Vex shook his head.

'No. The case retained sufficient structural integrity to have contained the papers. The only plausible inference is that someone removed them after it fell.'

'Verren,' Keira said, and Horst nodded, reluctantly coming to the same conclusion. 'We should have asked him a few more questions while we had the chance.'

'Well, it's too late for that now,' Horst said, wishing he'd been a little less precipitate in ordering her to tidy up that particular loose end.

'It can't have been him,' Jenie offered, a little hesitantly, and Horst turned to look at her, trying to conceal his eagerness for her answer.

'Why not?' he asked, and Jenie shrugged.

'He's a sot, but he isn't stupid. He knows who you are, and that you're after that box. If he'd found it first, he would have tried to sell you whatever was inside.'

'That makes sense,' Drake agreed.

'Which raises the obvious question of who took it, and where they are now,' Vex concluded.

'Another Receiver, probably,' Jenie said, and shrugged. 'The only trouble with that is finding out which one. There are hundreds, looking for salvage all over the ship.'

'Which means there aren't that many working this particular section of the outhulls,' Horst said. 'We'll contact the guild officially when we get back, and find out who's been down here since the ship left Sepheris Secundus.'

'Should narrow it down,' Keira agreed. 'What's our fastest way back?'

'The way we came, I suppose,' Jenie said, with a side-long glance at Vex, who was consulting his data-slate.

After a moment, the tech-priest nodded. 'Technically, that's true, although if we make a small diversion to take advantage of the open passageway we passed, we can avoid having to climb the cable in the shaft we descended.'

'That gets my vote,' Drake declared, and Keira nodded her agreement.

'Mine too,' she said, with an amused glance at Jenie.

'Then that's the way we'll go,' Horst declared, noticing the expression of relief on the face of their guide. He might have made some kind of remark about it, but before he could say anything a metallic clatter echoed through the gloom.

'We've got company,' Keira said, swinging her lumina-tor in the direction of the sound, and Drake followed suit. Shadows were moving among the debris, roughly human-sized, but scurrying like rodents, avoiding the light. 'At least a dozen.'

Horst drew his bolt pistol, and peered through the gloom, trying to get a good look at one of the creatures.

'More over there,' Drake called, sweeping his own light to a different section of the hold, in response to a fresh outburst of scuffling.

This time he caught one of the skulkers in the open, and Horst stared at it in revulsion. It was vaguely human in size and shape, but its jaw was overlarge, and studded with sharp, pointed teeth. Its fingers ended in long, curved talons, but it carried a club fashioned from a length of pipe, to which vicious, rusting spikes had been fixed. It quailed back from the light, shrieking, and Drake shot it, taking it cleanly through the head.

Instantly, more of the abominations appeared, swarming all over the still-spasming corpse, slashing and tearing at it with their own fangs and claws in an insensate feeding frenzy. None were exactly alike, Horst noted, some sporting fur or scales, but all shared their unfortunate fellow's resemblance to humanity.

'Mutants,' Keira said, revulsion curdling her voice, and began to draw her sword. Horst forestalled her.

'Pull back,' he ordered, 'and find some cover. If they swarm us, we'll never be able to hold off that many.'

'Speak for yourself,' Keira said, but she replaced the blade in its sheath, and readied her crossbow instead.

'Works for me,' Drake agreed, and turned to Jenie. 'Which way?'

'I don't know!' The girl's voice was shrill with panic, and she glanced around frantically, like a small animal with its leg in a trap. 'I've really no idea!'

'Well you'd better get one fast,' Keira said, planting a crossbow bolt neatly in the eye of a mutant a little bolder than the rest, which had begun to lope towards them, 'unless you're planning to end up as indigestion.' Her victim pitched backwards, becoming a meal for its fellows as rapidly as the first had done.

Horst took out a couple more from the main group with his bolt pistol, noting with rising apprehension that fewer of the bestial abhumans stopped to feast on the corpses of the fallen, and that they seemed to be losing their fear of the light. It was only a matter of time before the whole pack descended, and they could never hope to fight them all, out in the open like this. He rounded on the terrified joygirl. 'Keira's right,' he said. 'You're supposed to be a guide, so guide us. We need to go somewhere defensible.'

'I really don't know!' Jenie was almost hysterical by now. 'I'm sorry, I lied, all right? I've never been deeper than the Fringes in my life!'

'Rutting great,' Drake said, laying down a burst of suppressive fire, which forced a handful of mutants to duck back behind a pile of scrap. 'Should have known better than to trust a whore in the first place.'

'We'll discuss this later,' Horst said, hoping they'd get the chance to. He turned to Vex, who had abandoned the data-slate for his autopistol. 'Hybris? Any recommendations?'

'None for the present,' the tech-priest said, sending a couple of heavy-calibre slugs after Drake's las-bolts. They ricocheted, whining off into the dark, and eliciting a howl of inhuman agony from behind a pile of detritus. 'The original doorways are some twenty metres above our heads, which rather precludes their use as a refuge, and the mutants appear to be using all the service ducts which give access directly to this level.'

'In other words, we're swiven,' Drake said, firing again.

'It would certainly appear so,' Vex agreed.

'This way!' an unfamiliar voice yelled, and something shattered on the metal floor, spreading a pool of flame. The mutants howled, drawing back from it, and two more of the makeshift incendiary devices followed, filling the cavernous space with flickering orange light. Horst turned in the direction they'd come from, to see a rope descending from one of the open doorways high above their heads. 'It's your only chance!'

It was hard to argue with that assessment, and he gestured towards it. 'Keira, you go first.' She glanced at him curiously, probably wondering if the unresolved issues between them were clouding his judgement, and he explained hastily. 'We don't know who's up there, and I know I can count on you to make sure they play nice.'

'They will,' she assured him, and swarmed upwards with a rapidity and grace which no one else he'd ever met could have matched. As she disappeared, the mutants howled again, in rage and disappointment, and a few of them began to edge around the puddles of burning liquid, beginning to lose their fear of the flames.

'Hybris,' Horst said, discouraging them with a couple of well-placed pistol bolts. The explosive tips turned chunks of the scrap they were hiding behind into shards of shrapnel, which bit deep into abhuman flesh, and he was rewarded with more shrieks and howls. 'You're next.' The tech-priest's autopistol was adding the least to their firepower, and keeping him safe was their only chance of finding their way back to the *Beyonder's Hostelry*.

'Your turn,' Drake said, discouraging another rush with a burst of automatic fire as Vex began to climb the rope. 'I can keep them suppressed a lot better with this than you can with a pistol.'

'True,' Horst said, 'but I'm in command. I go last.'

'I'm not arguing,' Drake said, failing to conceal his relief. 'I'll set up again as soon as I get to the top, and cover you as best I can from there.'

'Then you'd better not hang about,' Horst said. The Guardsman sprinted for the rope, slinging his lasgun as he did so, and began to swarm his way up, adrenaline more than compensating for his lack of technique.

'What about me?' Jenie asked anxiously, as a trio of mutants charged forwards, drool spraying from their distended jaws, flourishing makeshift weapons as they came. Horst felled them with a blizzard of pistol bolts, the misshapen bodies bursting apart in a shower of blood and viscera. The weapon's clip was almost empty by now, and he knew with a stone-cold certainty that he'd never be able to reload it before the next charge brought him down. 'For Throne's sake, you can't just leave me to them!'

'I can,' Horst said, 'but I'm not going to. We still have things to discuss.' He smiled, without humour. 'I can always throw you back if I don't like your answers.'

'Grab hold!' Drake called, from the doorway above their heads. 'We'll pull you up!' He opened fire with the lasgun again, single shots this time, picking off the boldest of the mutants.

'You heard him,' Horst said, emptying the rest of the clip as the main body of the pack began to surge forward, the prospect of losing the last of their prey apparently overcoming their fear of the Angelae's weapons. Holstering the gun, he leapt for the rope, and began climbing.

With a yelp of fear, Jenie grabbed the line beneath him, and Horst felt it sag a little as it took her weight; then they were both rising, hauled upwards by whoever had lowered it in the first place. It had been some time since Horst had had to make a climb like this, but he kicked off instinctively, using his legs to accelerate his progress, all but running up the wall.

Seeing their prey eluding them, the whole pack ran forwards, screaming and howling like the damned, but it wasn't that which sent a shudder of pure horror down Horst's spine; interspersed with the bestial ululation, he could clearly discern phrases in some form of debased but recognisable Gothic. 'Meat run, kill it quick!'

'Get them off me!' Jenie screamed, and he glanced down to see one of the largest of the mutants leap high enough to grab hold of her leg. For a moment, it seemed, its weight would be enough to break her grip, and send the girl crashing to a hideous death, but she'd taken the precaution of wrapping a loop of rope around her upper arm. It constricted, making her scream again, and she kicked out frantically with her other foot, catching the debased creature in the muzzle. It howled with rage and pain, but didn't let go, and, to his horror, Horst felt the rope slipping backwards under the added weight of the furious creature.

Then he felt rather than heard a faint hiss of displaced air passing close to his face, and the mutant abruptly fell backwards, a crossbow bolt embedded in its throat. The rope began to rise again, and Horst glanced upwards to see Keira's grinning face looking down at him.

A moment later she reached out a hand, which he took gratefully, and helped him up to the metal floor of the passageway.

'Thanks,' Horst said, suddenly wanting to say a great deal more, but realising this was hardly the time or the place to say it.

'You're welcome,' Keira said, maintaining the pressure for another fraction of a second, before turning to drag Jenie over the edge of the drop.

Horst looked around, taking in the half-dozen people on the other end of the rope. They were a strange group, dressed, for the most part, in the patched and faded remnants of guild liveries, no two alike. Two were women and four were men, although whether that fact was significant, he had no idea, and all were carrying bundles or bags.

The man at the front of the group stepped forwards, clearly the leader, judging by his air of calm authority. His hair was grey, but he carried himself with the ease of a man much younger than his apparent age, and unlike his male companions, his beard was neatly trimmed. He smiled at Horst. 'I thought we'd lost you there for a moment,' he said, his voice the one which had shouted the warning.

'I thought you had too,' Horst said. He glanced again at the motley group behind the man. 'I take it you're the Malcontents?'

'Some of them,' the man said. 'My name's Simeon, formerly of the Suturer's Parliament, so, as you can imagine, I see most of the rest from time to time.'

'You're really Malcontents?' Jenie was staring at them in something like awe. 'Emperor be praised, I came down here to find you.'

'And the rest of you?' Simeon asked, taking in the weapons the Angelae carried in a single pointed glance.

'Something else entirely,' Horst said, with a glare at the joygirl. 'But this is hardly the time to discuss it.'

'Of course not,' Simeon agreed, relaxing a little, and Horst moved away to join Drake, who was sweeping the floor of the upended hold below with the luminator attached to his lasgun. The mutants were still congregated beneath them, glaring up with angry eyes, and Horst wasn't quite able to suppress a reflexive shudder as he looked down at the seething mass of malformed flesh.

'There's something else down there,' Drake said, swinging the beam in a methodical search pattern. 'Hanging back from the pack.'

'Are you sure?' Horst asked. That didn't make much sense that he could see, but by now he trusted Drake's instincts almost as much as he did Keira's or his own. 'It could just have been a rat or something moving around.'

'Don't think so,' Drake said. 'It was too large for that.' Then he tensed, as a human figure, in the garishly patterned clothing Horst had grown so used to seeing on Sepheris Secundus, walked calmly into the circle of light, and bowed mockingly. The Guardsman pulled the trigger, but the las-bolt hit a stanchion millimetres from the fop's head as he turned, almost imperceptibly, and the following two rounds missed by an equally improbable margin as the man moved again. 'Holy Throne, it's him!'

'The psyker who escaped in the Gallery?' Horst asked, and Drake nodded.

'I'd recognise the warp-touched bastard anywhere.'

'It's unquestionably him,' Vex confirmed. As he joined Horst and Drake at the mouth of the tunnel, the distant figure waved to the tech-priest as though to an old friend.

'I'm glad you've still got it with you!' he called. 'My pets won't have so far to come to collect it!' Then he turned away, apparently oblivious to the las-bolts striking sparks all around him.

As the man disappeared, the mutants at the foot of the wall fell silent, and began to drift away after him. A moment or two later the hold was as quiet as it had been when the Angelae first arrived.

'Well,' Keira said, folding her crossbow and replacing it on her thigh, 'at least we know what happened to the manuscript. The wyrd must have found it.'

'Which would explain how he knew the artefact was on board,' Vex agreed. His voice grew speculative. 'Perhaps he can tell us what it is, and where it came from, when the interrogators at the Tricorn put him to the question.'

'We'll have to catch him first,' Drake said. He looked from one of his colleagues to the other. 'Any ideas about that?'

TEN

The *Misericord*, the Warp, Date and Time Meaningless

'IT'S NOT MUCH,' Simeon said, as he conducted the Angelae into another echoing chamber roughly the size of the one they'd just left, 'but it's home.' He shrugged, and smiled ruefully. 'At least for now.'

'You move around a lot, then?' Drake asked, taking in the temporary nature of the outlaws' camp. Sheets of fabric had been erected to create small areas of privacy, and a small stove, burning the same volatile liquid which the Malcontents used in their incendiary bombs, had been set up between them to provide warmth, light and heat. A pan was bubbling away on it, and he regarded it suspiciously, wondering whether the mutants were the only ones down here who'd reverted to cannibalism.

'All the groups do,' one of the women said, glancing up from the pot, after stirring it with a spoon which looked as if it had been crudely fashioned from something else. 'Resources are limited down here. Stay too long in one place and they run out.'

'That's true,' Simeon said. He indicated their surroundings with an expansive gesture. 'This is better than most; there's water and algae here, and the rats are abundant.'

'I'm happy for you,' Drake said, even more determined not to try the stew. 'Shame about the neighbours, though.'

Simeon nodded. 'They just appeared out of nowhere, a short while ago. Now they're spreading. Time we pulled back to a higher level.'

'How's that possible?' Keira asked. 'We're aboard a starship. No one can just appear on it.'

'There was an impact a while back,' Simeon said. 'Near one of the sealed levels, left over from a debris strike about a century ago. Some of the old welds broke, and a couple of hatchways sprung.' He indicated one of the other men. 'Jared was going to take a look after the Riggers had finished patching the new damage, but then the muties started showing up, so he lost the taste for exploration.'

'Damn right,' Jared said. 'The smell was bad enough down there, never mind the creatures.'

'Smell?' Horst asked, and Jared nodded.

'It stank. Hardly surprising, as the whole deck had been sealed off for over a hundred years, but I wasn't keen to go down there, let me tell you. Probably just as well as it turned out. I wouldn't want to run into a whole tribe of those things.'

'Could you show me?' Vex asked, and produced his data-slate. Jared nodded, and went into a huddle with the tech-priest, poring over the map together in muttered undertones.

'What about the wyrd?' Keira asked, her hand falling to the hilt of her sword, as it always did at the thought of an enemy of the Imperium to be purged.

Simeon shrugged. 'Never seen him before.' He looked troubled. 'But if he really can control those things, you're going to find it hard to get to him.' There hadn't been much point in hiding the fact that they were Inquisition agents, as Jenie was bound to blurt it out sooner or later, so Horst had explained who they were on the short walk back to the Malcontents' camp.

'We'll find a way,' Horst said. He glanced up, surprised, as a drop of water fell on his face. 'When you said there was water down here, I didn't think you meant that it rains.'

'You'd be surprised,' Simeon said. 'There are spaces in the outhulls so high that water condenses near the ceiling, and falls back to the floor. But that's just a leak from up there.' He pointed above his head, and Drake raised the luminator.

As he'd expected, there was another open portal in the ceiling, where a pressure door had once sealed a corridor, and the beam hazed away into what seemed like infinity. Just before it petered out, though, he thought he could discern the shape of a heavy bulkhead door, like many others they'd passed, sealing the end of the shaft. As he peered upwards, trying to resolve more detail, another drop of water fell, landing on his cheek, and he flinched.

Gradually a nascent suspicion began to grow in the back of his mind, and he called across to Vex. 'Hybris. Is that the lake we crossed up there, or have I got turned around again?'

'No, you're quite correct,' the tech-priest assured him, after a cursory glance at the data-slate display, and resumed his conversation with Jared.

'Lovely,' Drake said, trying not to picture the thick slab of metal giving way under the pressure of the tonnes of water above it.

'They said I can stay,' Jenie said, settling beside him with a metal bowl of whatever the cooking pot had contained. She blew on it, and began eating, with the curious expression of someone determined to like it whatever the taste.

'Well, I guess that's what you want,' Drake said, trying not to sound surly, and Keira drifted over to join them. 'You certainly went to enough trouble to get here.'

'Would you mind explaining why?' Keira added, sounding genuinely curious. 'There aren't many people who'd risk lying to Inquisition acolytes to get what they wanted.'

'There aren't many people as desperate as I was,' Jenie said. 'I was a Gatherer of Diversity. Believe me, you've no idea what that's like.'

'No, I haven't,' Keira agreed evenly.

Drake snorted. 'I might have known even the joygirls had a fancy name on this jinx barge. Everyone else seems to.'

'Is that all you think I am?' Jenie asked, then shrugged. 'Of course, that's what beyonders are supposed to believe, so I suppose that makes me good at my job.' She chewed moodily for a moment. 'The ship's an enclosed community. We know all too well what a stagnant gene pool leads to. Which is why we have the Gatherers.'

'You mean you're supposed to...' Drake broke off, incredulous.

'Let the beyonders treat you like a piece of meat, get pregnant, and refresh the gene pool,' Jenie confirmed bitterly. 'And as soon as you've given birth, do the same thing again. Boys get adopted by the other castes, and the girls are condemned to be Gatherers in turn.' She rubbed her stomach absently. 'Well, not my daughter. She's going to have some choice about her life.'

'I see.' Running around in the dark eating rat stew didn't seem like much of a choice to Drake, but he could see why Jenie might think so. To his astonishment, Keira was gazing at the girl with something like respect.

'The Emperor truly walks with you,' Keira said. 'To risk so much to cleanse your soul...' Then she stood abruptly, and was gone.

'What did she mean by that?' Drake asked, and Horst shrugged, having listened to the end of the conversation.

'Some kind of Redemptionist thing,' he said. 'They're very big on turning your back on sin, whatever the cost. And she'd think Jenie here was sin on legs.'

'There's only one sinner I'm interested in,' Drake said. 'And he's out there laughing at us. How do we bring down a wyrd we can't shoot?'

'I've been thinking about that,' Horst said. 'And I think there just might be a way.'

Scintil VIII Void Station, Scintilla System
247.993.M41

LIGHT FLOODED THE hidden passageway, bright as the luminators normally found throughout the station, and Quillem blinked his eyes clear of the sudden glare. No alarms blared, and no one shouted; after a moment he emerged cautiously into the warehouse.

His first reaction was one of surprise. The luminators in the ceiling blazed down on an area roughly the size of a scrumball pitch, but instead of the stacked crates full of merchandise or contraband he'd been expecting, the vast space was all but empty. A few shipping containers stood off to one side, next to a staircase leading up to an office area overlooking the main floor of the warehouse from a mezzanine gallery, but apart from that there was no sign at all that cargo ever came through here.

'Someone's been living here,' Rufio said, stating the obvious.

Quillem nodded. 'Rather a lot of someones,' he agreed. The floor was covered in bedrolls, arranged in neat rows, although their rumpled appearance indicated that they'd been abandoned in haste, and that their occupants hadn't expected to return. He glanced around warily, aware that the lack of cover in the cavernous space was leaving them dangerously exposed. 'We need to know who, and we need to know why.'

'No personal effects,' Carys reported, rifling through a few of the nearest bedrolls with the speed of a lifetime's practice.

'One hundred and forty-seven,' Malven suddenly remarked at Quillem's elbow, and the interrogator turned to look at him.

'One hundred and forty-seven what?' he asked. Arken was the only member of the team not to have emerged from the hidden panel yet, and he glanced back at the rectangle of darkness with renewed unease.

'Individuals quartered here,' the tech-priest elucidated. 'That's only the most likely number, of course; there are always variables, but there are a hundred and fifty bedrolls, of which three appear to be undisturbed, which leads me to conclude…'

'I see, thank you.' Quillem cut him off, and took a step towards the concealed entrance. It would have been all but invisible from this side too, he thought, which meant that Voyle and his friends had probably been exploiting the breach in the station's security for a very long time. Certainly the precautions they'd observed on their way in spoke of meticulous planning, and a sophistication far beyond most Shadow Franchise operations, which were generally aimed at making as much money as possible before the authorities noticed and moved in to close them down.

Before he could reach the rectangle of darkness, though, Arken appeared, stepping into the echoing chamber as though being forced to wade through a cesspool. He looked around, his face paler than ever. 'Madness and death,' he mumbled, gripping Quillem's arm so tightly that the interrogator wasn't surprised to find a bruise there the next time he removed his shirt.

'Arken.' Quillem spoke clearly and calmly. 'I need you to focus. Can you feel anything like the wraithbone?'

'No.' The psyker regained a measure of composure, with an effort Quillem could see etched on his face. 'Too much residue. Like in the tunnel.'

'You mean all these people were psykers?' Carys's voice was incredulous. 'How's that possible?'

'I don't know.' Arken shook his head. 'But that's how it feels.'

Quillem felt a momentary flare of primordial terror, then reason reasserted itself. Even if that many wyrds had somehow been able to congregate here, they were long gone. The priority now was to find out where, and there was an obvious place to start looking. 'Carys, with me,' he said. 'Let's check out the office.'

'I'll take a look at the cargo containers,' Rufio said, beginning to move away.

Malven took out a data-slate. 'I'll try communing with the genecode reader,' he said. 'With the right incantations, it might divulge the identities of the people it's set to recognise.'

'Sounds good,' Quillem agreed, with another glance at Arken. 'Will you be all right?'

'Of course,' the seer said, although Quillem was far from convinced of that. Since there was nothing he could do about it anyway, he turned, and began to follow Carys up the echoing metal stairs towards the office.

'It's locked,' she informed him cheerfully as he joined her outside the door. She took a couple of picks from a pouch on her belt, and began to work on the mechanism with every sign of enjoyment. Leaving her to it, Quillem leaned on the railing, looking down at the floor of the warehouse below.

Rufio glanced up from the nearest cargo container, and waved. 'Empty,' he said, using his comm-bead rather than raising his voice. 'But it used to hold food.' He moved on to the next, then recoiled hastily. 'The other end of the process. Portable sanitary units. Definitely not empty.'

'Almost there,' Carys murmured at his elbow, then straightened up with a satisfied smile. 'Done.' She pulled the door open, but stayed outside, examining the frame carefully. 'Ooh, thought so. Haven't seen one of those in a while.' She extracted a small pair of pliers from her tool-belt, and began to work on something Quillem couldn't see. 'Your Mister Voyle has a nasty mind.'

'What is it?' Quillem asked.

'Microwire, stretched across the door. So thin you can hardly see it. But if you walk straight in, it'll cut you in half.' She closed the jaws of the pliers carefully, and something parted with a barely audible twang. An expression of consternation crossed her face. 'Sorry, boss. That was dumb.'

'What was?' Quillem asked, feeling his stomach knot. She only ever called him that when something was badly wrong.

'We should just have ducked under; I felt a mild shock when I cut it.'

No need to ask what that meant: if the wire had been carrying a current, it was a trap within a trap, and in disposing of the obvious threat, Carys had just tripped an alarm. Quillem tapped his comm-bead. 'Everyone up here now!' No one argued, knowing him well enough to recognise the urgency in his voice, and he hurried to the railing of the balcony to see what was going on.

Within seconds, it seemed, the main door of the warehouse was cranking open, a slab of metal about three metres high and four wide, and he cracked off a couple of bolts at the widening gap, hoping to dissuade whoever was coming to investigate long enough to allow the others to reach safety. The only real refuge would be the office, he thought, trying not to wonder if there were any other booby traps up here they didn't have time to locate. Arken and Malven began to run, while Rufio settled himself behind the cargo containers, and drew his blowpipe.

To Quillem's surprise, instead of quailing behind the door as he'd expected, the guards began to return fire with expert precision, and he was forced to duck back behind the railing of the mezzanine, grateful for the metal mesh between the upright bars. A las-bolt scorched the air, close enough for him to smell the ozone, and something clattered against the protective palisade like a handful of coins falling on a resonant surface, accompanied by a sinister hissing sound.

Recognising it, Quillem's blood turned cold. 'They've got…' he started to vox, but before he could complete the warning, Arken suddenly jerked, as though he'd run into a wall, and then fell sideways, his torso reduced to a rain of shredded meat fragments.

'An eldar weapon,' Malven confirmed, sounding more intrigued than frightened. A faint nimbus of blue lightning started to play around him, as his augmetic enhancements switched to battle mode; in a moment, Quillem knew, he'd unleash an energy bolt of devastating power at their attackers. 'Fortunately, I can repel the discs with an internal magnetic…'

Before he could finish the sentence a pair of plasma bolts struck him almost simultaneously, the energy discharge fusing every augmetic component in his body, while reducing the flesh parts to charred and smoking ruin. He was dead before he hit the decking, where his mechadendrites clattered like so much scrap, barely audible over the echoes of the gunfire.

'Hound one to kennel,' Quillem said, tapping his comm-bead again, and trying to come to terms with the barely conceivable. 'We're under attack with xenos weaponry.' Armoured figures were fanning out across the floor of the warehouse now, eight, ten, a dozen, laying down covering fire as they advanced with the precision of Imperial Guardsmen. None were armoured or equipped precisely the same, but they all moved with professional skill. As well as the eldar and tau weapons which had felled his companions, Quillem noted, the majority were equipped with Imperial-pattern lasguns, and one seemed to be carrying a kroot rifle, its long barrel surmounted by the blade of a primitive polearm unmistakable among the rest. 'Extraction paramount, repeat, paramount.' Nothing else he could do now except wait for rescue, and hope they could survive long enough for it to arrive.

'Emperor's Justice responding,' the resonant voice of Ullen, the Deathwatch Techmarine, replied a moment later, and Quillem risked popping up to crack off a few more bolts at the advancing mercenaries. He hit one, the man's flak armour no protection against the explosive projectiles, and watched him fall with grim satisfaction. It wouldn't bring Arken or Malven back, but the act of vengeance made him feel better anyway.

'Rufio's still down there!' Carys shouted, grabbing him by the shoulder as he ducked back, just ahead of a blizzard of return fire. 'We've got to help him!'

'Don't even think about it,' the assassin advised. Glancing down, Quillem saw him fitting a janus thorn into the end of his blowpipe. 'I'm going to take out their leader. That might knock them back a bit.'

'Good luck,' Quillem said. 'The Emperor protects.'

'He'll have to,' Rufio said, sounding as amused as he always did. 'You think it's the one in the funny hat?' One of the mercenaries was wearing an eldar helmet and torso armour, although he was clearly human, moving without a trace of the lithe grace of the xenos breed.

'That'd be my guess,' Quillem said, unable to imagine how a human had been able to get hold of such things in the first place, let alone turn them to his purposes. He turned to Carys. 'Cover him. Give him the best chance we can.'

'Right.' The woman nodded grimly, drawing her autopistol, and sending a blizzard of unaimed fire down into the floor of the warehouse. She didn't manage to hit anything, so far as Quillem could tell, but the bullets whined and ricocheted from the metal floor with a satisfying amount of noise, which distracted the mercenaries nicely, especially after a couple of his pistol bolts detonated as well.

Rufio's aim was as true as it always was; Quillem saw the deadly splinter flick through the air, striking the eldar-costumed leader precisely at the vulnerable point where helmet and torso armour met, slipping easily through the minuscule gap. Then, to his astonishment, the dart stopped moving, hanging in the air for a second before withdrawing, turning and retracing its path as quickly as it had come.

'Psyker!' Carys gasped, but the warning came too late: even before she'd finished speaking, the janus thorn had returned precisely to its point of origin, speeding back down the blowpipe still held between Rufio's lips. Despite the astonished assassin's phenomenal reflexes, he had no time to react; he toppled backwards, dead before he hit the metal floor.

Quillem felt a spasm of dread as the helmeted figure turned to look up at him, its posture one of disdainful amusement. The blizzard of incoming fire intensified, and Quillem crawled into the relative safety of the office, nudging Carys ahead of him. Las and plasma bolts scorched and dented the metal walls, shattering the observation windows, showering them with shards of glass which lodged painfully in hair and skin.

'I'm sorry,' Carys said, as the firestorm abated, and running feet began to clatter against the metal stairs. 'This is all my fault.'

'No,' Quillem said, taking aim at the door, 'it's theirs. And they're going to pay. The inquisitor will see to that, even if we don't.'

A shadow moved in the frame of the doorway, and his finger tightened on the trigger; but before he could pull it, the air thickened around him. The familiar wrenching sensation of a teleport field swept across his senses, as reality blurred and twisted around them, and the enemy disappeared in a welcome haze of nausea.

The *Misericord*, the Warp, Date and Time Meaningless

JARED HADN'T BEEN exaggerating about the smell, Keira thought. She'd found her way into the sealed section with little difficulty, following the directions the tech-priest and the Malcontent had given her, moving with all the stealth her training had made her capable of. She'd only encountered a couple of the mutants so far, dispatching them swiftly and silently, and she was confident that her intrusion into their territory remained undetected. She tapped the comm-bead in her ear.

'The passageway's clear,' she voxed, keeping her voice as low as she could. That was something of an exaggeration; whatever catastrophe had led to this part of the ship being cut off for so long had more than left its mark, but at least up and down here corresponded to the direction of gravity again. She ducked under a fallen ceiling beam, which loomed up out of the gloom surrounding her as a patch of greater darkness, and straightened, listening for any telltale signs of movement. 'Which way now?'

'Straight on for about ten metres,' Vex said, his voice attenuated slightly by the intervening kilotonnes of metal. 'You should come to a crossway, leading straight into the heart of the section.'

'And the muties' camp, probably,' Horst added. 'There's a large open space up ahead, probably a cargo hold or a hangar bay.' He hesitated a moment. 'So be careful.'

'Count on it,' Keira assured him, pleasantly surprised by his concern. She turned her head a little, almost relishing the darkness enshrouding her. She'd enhanced her natural night vision with eyedrops from her Assassinorum operative's kit, which had dilated her pupils completely, and was able to pick out her route well enough to move with complete assurance, despite the lack of any source of light beyond the occasional splash of phosphorescent mould or the status displays of long-forgotten devices, which continued to signal wanly for the attention of crewmen long since crumbled into dust. The luminators her companions had relied on during their descent seemed crude by comparison, and would simply have betrayed her presence to her quarry in any case.

A few more cautious steps took her to the passageway, and she paused, feeling a faint current of air on her face. The stench intensified, carried on the breeze, and she suppressed the gag reflex without conscious thought. There were sounds too, the curious admixture of guttural speech and more bestial noises she'd heard picking her way past mutant camps on her scouting expeditions into the Shatters beneath the Gorgonid mine on Sepheris Secundus. She was on the right track.

The corridor here was broader and wider than the one she'd just left, and she was able to pick up her pace a little. She dropped her hand to the hilt of her sword, making sure it was loose in the scabbard, and that her throwing knives were ready for use. The sounds were getting louder, and she was beginning to see her surroundings a little more clearly, a diffuse glow up ahead growing steadily brighter with every step.

'I'm getting close,' she reported, instinctively moving towards the nearest wall, where the shadows were thickest.

'Acknowledged,' Horst said, sounding more tense than she was, and she melted into the patch of darkness around the jamb of an open doorway at the end of the corridor, her cameleoline bodyglove making her all but invisible as she scouted the space beyond.

She'd expected to find herself at floor level, but this entrance opened directly onto a mezzanine gallery, floored with metal mesh, running the full width of the hold. A staircase descended just beyond the doorway, matched by another at the far end, and the wide platform of a cargo lift was visible halfway between them; it had obviously not moved in decades, and by now had rusted immovably into place, transmuting itself into a balcony which projected out over the huge space beyond.

Keira ventured cautiously onto the metal walkway, placing her feet carefully to minimise the noise. She need hardly have bothered, though, the racket of the mutants below more than sufficient to drown out any sounds she might make. There were far more of them than the group which had attacked the Angelae; by her initial reckoning there must have been at least three score of the abhuman monstrosities shuffling around the vast space, tending to the flickering fires which fitfully lit it, hammering at pieces of metal to form crude tools or weapons, or rutting bestially wherever they happened to be. Horst's guess that this was the site of their camp was clearly accurate, as a few sheets of fabric had been draped over makeshift supports to form tents, although, since the debased creatures clearly had no idea of decorum or privacy, she couldn't see why any of them had bothered.

There was no sign of her quarry, though, and she moved further along the gallery, trying for a better vantage point. As she did so, a pattern came into view on one of the crude tents, which had evidently once been a banner of some kind. She activated her vox.

'The DeVayne Incorporation's symbol is a hand, isn't it?' she asked.

'It is,' Vex confirmed. 'Why do you ask?'

'Because it's in the hold here.' Now she knew what to look for, she quickly made out the same logo in several other places around the cavernous space, stencilled onto cargo containers long ago broken into and stripped of whatever they'd held.

'Interesting,' Vex replied, his voice thoughtful. 'Their ancestors must have been thralls in transit, cut off by the earlier impact, and forgotten about when the section was sealed. After several generations exposed to the warp...'

Before he could elaborate further, Keira caught sight of her quarry at last, walking away from one of the ramshackle pavilions.

'Target in sight,' she said crisply.

That could be a problem. If the wyrd was living down there, it would be almost impossible for her to reach the tent to search for the precious manuscript without being spotted by the creatures surrounding it.

Keira held her position, and observed the man analytically, as she'd been trained to do. He was walking purposefully, towards the stairs at the far end of the gallery, but she was confident that her cameleoline bodyglove and the shadows enfolding her would be enough to evade detection, and remained perfectly still. The human eye registered movement above all else, and, as she knew from experience, it was possible to escape notice even in the open if you simply remained immobile.

After a moment or two of watching her quarry, she was able to discount the possibility of the manuscript being anywhere in the camp with a fair degree of certainty. The man moved easily among the mutants, but his body language was redolent of disdain and contempt; clearly he was willing to use them, but despised them as much as any other pureblooded human would. Keira smiled coldly, relishing the irony of one kind of abomination looking down on another. That being so, he was highly unlikely to be sleeping among them, and she doubted that he'd leave anything as precious as the manuscript where it could be casually despoiled by bestial hands while his back was turned.

Which made the whole thing very simple. Follow him back to his own lair, find where the document was hidden, and take it. Preferably killing him in the process. She had no doubt that she could eliminate him easily, despite his apparent ability to predict attacks, but if she couldn't, there was always Mordechai's plan to fall back on.

The psyker began to climb the stairs at the far end of the gallery, and Keira waited until he'd reached the top and disappeared through the open doorway at the far end before making her move. As the darkness swallowed him, the glow of a luminator flickered into life, and she breathed a silent prayer of thanks to the Emperor; he could hardly have made it easier for her if he'd tried.

ELEVEN

The *Misericord*, the Warp, Date and Time Meaningless

'ARE YOU SURE you can do it?' Horst asked, and Vex nodded, trying not to seem irked at the interruption. He'd had a great deal of practice in dealing with unmodified humans in the years since he'd left the ordered existence of the Mechanicus shrine, for what he'd intended to be no more than a brief sabbatical, so he was able to reply without a trace of irritation inflecting his voice.

'I believe so,' he said, wondering why Horst seemed to think the answer might have changed at all in the five minutes and twenty-seven seconds since the last time he'd asked the same question. 'It should be a simple matter to determine the correct codes.' He had absolutely no doubt of his ability to do so; the only problematic variables lay in the physical condition of the ship itself, which he was unable to predict with any degree of certainty, and whether Keira would be able to carry out her part of the plan. On balance, he was inclined to be optimistic about that, as the young assassin was commendably efficient, and seemed able to survive most things the galaxy threw at her. Given the data to hand, he would assess her chances of escaping death on this occasion at around sixty-seven per cent, and sustaining serious injury at no more than forty.

Perhaps it would be tactful to keep these particular musings to himself for the time being, however. Horst seemed particularly concerned about the young assassin of late, for reasons he couldn't quite fathom, and verbalising them would probably distract the team leader unnecessarily.

'We're going to be making rather a mess of your camping ground, I'm afraid,' Horst said, turning to Simeon, and the Malcontent shrugged.

'We'll manage,' he said. The small group of nomads were packed up and ready to leave, which Vex could hardly fault them for under the circumstances, carrying their possessions on their backs, or slung on poles which two of the men carried between them. Jenie seemed as laden as the others, though considerably more awkward under her burden, and Vex found himself wondering if she was finding her new life quite as congenial as she'd imagined. 'Everything changes eventually, except for the Emperor.'

'Right,' Jared agreed. He glanced around the echoing chamber, as if fixing the image of it in his mind for the last time. 'By the time we come back, you might even have improved it.'

'There'll definitely be fewer mutants down here to worry about,' Drake promised him, cradling his lasgun, and Vex nodded his agreement.

'None at all, if everything goes as well as we hope,' he said.

KEIRA FOLLOWED THE glow of the luminator through the warren of passageways, keeping well back from her quarry; the light he carried was visible for quite a distance, reflecting eerily from the grime-encrusted metal walls, so she tried to stay at least two turns behind him. Nevertheless, on a couple of occasions, when the corridors down which he walked were particularly long, she caught a fleeting glimpse of the man, striding out confidently ahead of her. His arrogance, no doubt born of the conviction that he was beyond the reach of the Emperor's vengeance, infuriated her; it was an affront to everything she believed in as a Redemptionist, and she silently promised the Golden Throne that she'd deliver his soul to judgement before the hour was out.

So thinking, she began to turn another corner, then froze: the reflection of the luminator was steady, which meant that her target had stopped moving. Fearing that he had somehow become aware of her presence, she began to draw the sword at her belt, and peered cautiously round the angle of the walls.

Her quarry had stopped at the end of the corridor, where a heavy bulkhead had once sealed the passageway off from whatever lay beyond. Now, however, the thick metal had been bent, the door sprung from its guide channels, creating a narrow gap. As Keira watched, the man wriggled through it, the corridor descending at once into almost impenetrable darkness, apart from the thin crack of light where he'd disappeared. After a moment, this too began to grow dim as he moved away.

Keira waited for her eyes to adjust again, and padded forwards, reaching the buckled door. The gap was easily enough to pass through, and she stepped across the threshold, noting with some relief that the air was fresher on the other side; struck by a sudden thought, she turned and looked at the jamb. It had indeed been welded shut, a long time ago, the seam split by whatever had caused the door and the wall surrounding it to buckle.

'Mordechai,' she whispered, activating her comm-bead, 'I've passed right through the old sealed section. By the look of things, I'm approaching the new impact site.'

'Acknowledged,' Horst said. 'We're almost set here.' He didn't repeat the words of caution he'd spoken before, but Keira hadn't really expected him to, and told herself she wasn't disappointed.

'Can you estimate how severe the impact was?' Vex asked.

'Very,' Keira told him. 'The bulkhead door's been sprung from its runners, just like Jared said, and the walls are severely buckled.' She took a few paces forward, compensating for the sudden unevenness of the deck plates without conscious thought. 'The floor too.'

'Interesting,' the tech-priest said thoughtfully. 'Given the nature of the material, for deformation of that magnitude to have occurred, the impacting object must have been of considerable mass.'

'I'll let you know,' Keira said. The damage was getting noticeably more pronounced as she advanced down the corridor. 'What's down here?'

'A thermal vent, leading to the heat exchangers,' Vex said. 'It should appear to you as an open shaft, about five metres across. I'd advise caution before attempting to access it, as the hull plating above is particularly thin, to enable the fusion core of one of the tertiary powerplants to be vented that way in the event of a plasma breach; an impact as severe as the one you indicate might well have ruptured it.'

'Well, I'm not breathing vacuum, so I guess it's all right,' Keira said, picking her pace up. Light was visible through the access hatch ahead, a steady gleam this time instead of the randomly fluctuating hand luminator, and she trotted forwards to gain a better view. 'Sinning hell!'

The exclamation of astonishment escaped her unbidden, as she stared into the shaft, hardly able to believe the evidence of her own eyes. It had indeed been breached, only to be plugged again as neatly as a cork in a bottle by the vast bulk of an ore shuttle, like the ones she'd seen arriving and departing from the Gorgonid on

Sepheris Secundus. If this was what had collided with the *Misericord* just before her entry into the warp, no wonder the crew had simply decided to seal the section, and deal with the problem once they reached Scintilla; sorting this mess out would be a massive undertaking.

'Say again,' Horst replied, an edge of anxiety entering his voice.

Recovering her composure, Keira drew her sword, certain that she'd found the heretic's lair. 'Sorry,' she said. 'Bad vox discipline.' She took another look at the huge cargo lifter apparently suspended just above her head. 'But this is incredible. There's an ore shuttle jammed in here. It must be how the heretics got aboard.'

'That's right, it is.' The voice spoke right behind her, and Keira spun, aiming a strike at where she knew the man's heart must be, but the sword met only empty air. She turned again, finding the garishly dressed fellow from the mutants' camp in front of her, and advanced, unleashing a flurry of blade strokes, but somehow none of them managed to connect. The man laughed, an ugly sound, in which the taint of madness scratched like a broken nail. 'Unfortunately our pilot expired on the way in, so our landing was rather harder than we'd expected. But we survived.'

'For a short while,' Keira said, advancing onto the narrow catwalk which spanned the shaft. It didn't occur to her to glance down, and see how deep it was; all that mattered was the smug popinjay in front of her, and the urgent desire to spill his blood.

'Vogen and Drusus got careless,' the man said. 'Over-confident in their gifts. Your friends, Drake and Vex is it? They were good. A credit to the Inquisition.'

Incredibly, the fellow was still managing to evade every strike she made, and every time he did so, her anger grew. She fanned it, honed it, the way the Collegium had taught her, refining it into a weapon as sharp as the blade she wielded. Behind it all, her rational mind wondered how he'd known her colleagues' names, and the man smiled patronisingly.

'I can see them in your mind, you half-witted trollop. Along with your precious faith, with all those cracks in it you try to pretend aren't there, and those guilty little dreams about Mordechai you wake from sweating, and the document you came here to steal, and everything else there is to know about you.'

'If you think you know me,' Keira said, shaping the anger, feeling it become a pure weapon of the Emperor's wrath, 'then you know I'm going to kill you.' She let the white heat of it flow like molten gold across the surface of her mind, and saw the psyker flinch, burned by it in a foretaste of his eternal damnation. For the first time he began to look uncertain, and started to back away in earnest. 'My name is Keira Sythree, and I am death, and the hand of the Emperor Himself. You are nothing, and you are dust, and you are *dead!*'

She struck on the final word, hard and true, and the psyker yelped in pain and surprise as her blade spiked flesh. Only his arcane ability saved him from a mortal wound, but his confidence was gone now, and he leapt back, through the access hatch on the other side of the narrow bridge. Snarling, Keira tensed her muscles to follow, but before she could make the jump a trio of abhuman monstrosities crowded past the terrified heretic, charging onto the narrow catwalk towards her, brandishing the crude weapons they favoured.

Keira barely checked her pace, dispatching all three in a flurry of blade strokes, which sent them plummeting into the depths below in a rain of bloody chunks, but the brief delay had been all the respite the wyrd had needed. By the time she'd run forwards across the blood-slick floorplates he'd vanished into the darkened labyrinth beyond, only the overlapping echoes of his footsteps giving her a clue as to his whereabouts.

'He's running,' she reported briefly. 'But he can't hide
forever.' He'd had the sense not to kindle his luminator
this time, but a graduate of the Collegium Assassinorum
didn't need anything so crude as sight to track her prey.
She turned her head, listening to the diminishing scurry
of his flight, trying to pinpoint the direction it was coming from.

'Break off,' Horst replied. 'Search the shuttle. If you
recover the manuscript, he'll come to us.'

'Acknowledged,' Keira said, letting the righteous fury
which had sustained her drain away, and turned back to
the heretic's vessel. Horst was right, of course, safeguard-
ing the document was their primary goal, although it
rankled to let a target escape his just retribution. No, not
escape, she reminded herself, merely postpone it. She
hesitated. 'About the things he said…'

'He was trying to distract you,' Horst said, 'that's all.
Don't give them another thought.'

'Already forgotten,' Keira lied, and began to make her
way back to the crippled cargo lifter. However much she
might wish to deny it, the dreams the psyker had taunted
her with were real enough, and she couldn't help wondering how much else he might have seen in her that was
true.

The *Ursus Innare*, Scintilla System
248.993.M41

THE ATMOSPHERE IN the cargo hold was different now, the
transition to real space marking the end of the voyage in
all but name, and their fellow passengers seemed as
relieved as Elyra felt to be out of the warp. Intellectually,
she supposed, everyone still realised that they were going
to remain cooped up in here for several more days, but
the nagging sensation of wrongness that had pervaded
the very fabric of the vessel during its passage through
the anteroom of hell was blessedly absent, and spirits

among the scattered huddles of refugees were definitely beginning to rise. Voices had returned to conversational levels, instead of being hushed and muted, and she'd even heard laughter a couple of times, although Emperor knew there was little enough to laugh about down here.

'Vos,' she said, casually picking up her pack, and reaching inside it for the laspistol. 'Something's moving behind that pile of rocks.' The skittering of the rodents had intensified, several of them moving to avoid something which hadn't come into view yet, and she trusted nothing here that she couldn't see. Come to that, she trusted precious little aboard the *Ursus Innare* that she could.

'I hear them,' Kyrlock said, equally casually, and picked up the shotgun. He glanced at Zusen, feigning uninterest. 'Getting anything?'

'Not really, sorry.' The girl looked pleased and surprised to be addressed directly, though probably not as surprised as Elyra was to overhear the remark. Kyrlock had been uncomfortable around the young wyrds ever since they'd first encountered them in the mine shaft the Shadow Franchise had been using to hide the people they were smuggling off-world, Zusen in particular as she tended to stay close to him as much as she could, and his apparent willingness to trust in their abilities was a startling new development. Then again, he was a pragmatist above all else; the young wyrd had been able to guide his aim in the dark during the skirmish with the bandits, and whatever he might feel about her and her friends, he would be happy to make use of whatever advantages they could give him if whoever was approaching meant trouble. 'Whoever it is out there isn't feeling any strong emotions.'

'Well, that's something,' Kyrlock said, smiling at the girl in a slightly less forced manner than usual. 'When people want to kill you, they're usually keyed up about it.' He kept his weapon ready for use in any case, Elyra noted approvingly: in her experience, killers didn't always feel strongly about their victims. Keira, for instance, would snuff out a life without a second thought if it seemed expedient, and she'd met plenty of certified psychopaths in her time who didn't seem capable of any kind of emotion at all. Zusen returned the smile, a trifle uncertainly, her thin face taking on a brief moment of animation before returning to its usual, slightly haunted expression.

'It's Greel,' Elyra said, catching sight of a flicker of movement at the bottom of the nearest ore heap. She let go of the butt of the handgun, but left the pack slung across her shoulder, where she could draw the weapon quickly at the first sign of treachery.

Kyrlock nodded and followed suit, lowering the barrel of the shotgun, but keeping his hand on the butt rather than slinging it. The franchiseman was accompanied by two thugs, both carrying shotguns themselves, although by this stage of the voyage they couldn't have been expecting any real trouble. Elyra smiled to herself. The weapons were symbolic as much as anything, intended as a visible sign that the bearers were in charge down here rather than for actual use, but they could still make a mess if things turned ugly.

'Looks like our ride's here,' Trosk said, turning to pick up his pack, and nudge Ven to his feet. The young seer looked mildly confused, but there was nothing unusual about that, and after a moment he started to collect his meagre belongings together. Trosk turned to Elyra and grinned, in a manner she found faintly irritating; it was as though he didn't feel the need to even pretend to defer to her any longer. 'Better make up your mind whether you're coming with us or not.'

'Of course she is,' Zusen said, then glanced at Elyra herself. 'Aren't you?'

'Let's just see what the man wants before we start planning the rest of our lives, shall we?' Elyra suggested. Greel and his minders were picking their way across the rubble with a distinct lack of urgency, so far as she could tell.

'That's far enough,' Kyrlock said in a conversational tone, as soon as the franchisemen had approached close enough to hear him. The three men stopped moving, the two with guns looking distinctly unhappy, but refraining from bringing them up; that meant they'd been told to remain on their best behaviour, Elyra thought, which was probably a good sign.

Greel closed the distance another pace or two before halting his advance, separating himself from the minders and any implicit threat they carried, subtly underlining who was in charge here. He spread his hands, to show he was unarmed. 'No need for that,' he said. 'I'm just here to talk.'

'What about?' Elyra asked.

Greel shrugged. 'Oh, several things. A business arrangement you might be interested in, for one.' He glanced pointedly at the three wyrds. 'When you've a few moments to yourself, of course.'

'You'll have plenty of time to chat once we're on the shuttle,' Trosk said, and Greel looked at him as though one of the rocks had just had the temerity to speak.

'Yes, well, that's the other reason I'm here,' he said. Trosk looked expectant. 'There's been a change of plan.'

'There can't be!' Trosk looked outraged. 'It was all arranged before we left Sepheris Secundus!' He looked narrowly at Greel. 'If you're planning to renege on our agreement, I'd advise you to think again. The people we're with...'

'Are a very long way from here,' Greel reminded him, apparently unmoved by the implicit threat. 'And I know a great deal more about them than you do, boy.'

Elyra had assumed as much already, but mentally noted the fact for future use. Chances were that Greel had only the sketchiest idea of who he was actually dealing with, but it wouldn't be the first time that the minions of

organised crime had allowed the wealth of a Chaos cult
to blind them to the true nature of their business part-
ners, and aware of the truth or not, he'd still be able to
name his contacts with the Sanctuary. On the other
hand, maybe he did know precisely who and what they
were, and simply didn't care so long as the arrangement
remained profitable. Either way, the interrogators of the
Tricorn would be able to extract any useful information
he had without too much difficulty if Carolus decided to
have him brought in, she was sure.

'What kind of a change?' she asked, contriving to
sound barely interested in the answer. Greel glanced at
her with an expression of mild curiosity, and she
shrugged. 'I promised your friend with the expensive hair
oil I'd look after them until they got where they were
going,' she explained casually. There was no guarantee
that Greel had actually met the man who'd escorted
Zusen, Trosk and Ven to the cavern, but she was pretty
certain that he'd know who she meant; he'd set up the
deal to carry them personally, cutting the expeditor who
normally handled the people wanting clandestine passage off-world out of the loop entirely.

'I see.' Greel nodded, as though something trivial suddenly made sense. 'I wondered why you were letting the
juves hang around with you.' He clearly assumed the
arrangement had been purely financial. 'Lucky for them
you were here to hire. They'd have been eaten alive otherwise.' Reminded of the juvies' existence again, he
turned back to them. 'There's been a complication on the
void station. Our usual transfer arrangements for passengers like you have been compromised, so you'll have to
stay with the others until we reach Scintilla.'

'Compromised how?' Trosk asked.

'That's all I was told.' Greel shrugged, philosophically.
'Got caught evading import duties, probably. That's the
trouble with smugglers, sooner or later they get too
greedy and attract attention. But it was a good

arrangement while it lasted.' He turned back to Elyra. 'So it looks as though you'll be babysitting for a while longer.'

'No problem,' Kyrlock said, trying to match Elyra's unconcerned exterior. 'We thought that was what we'd signed up for anyway. No one mentioned a shuttle trip to us.'

'Which rather raises the question of what you're going to do once we make orbit,' Greel said, beginning to walk slowly away from the camp. Taking the hint, Elyra and Kyrlock fell into step with him, moving out of earshot of the trio of wyrds. Only Trosk seemed to be taking the news of the change of plan particularly badly, kicking moodily at a lump of rock; Ven was staring into space as usual, adrift in his expanded consciousness, and Zusen looked pleased, if anything, probably because it gave her a little more time with Kyrlock.

'Find a good fence,' Elyra said, with a meaningful glance at her pack. Most of the jewellery she'd supposedly absconded with was still there, as Greel well knew. 'Any recommendations?'

'If you're serious, I can think of a couple of names,' Greel said. 'I could introduce you, for a modest commission.'

'Three per cent's pretty modest,' Elyra said. To her surprise, Greel laughed, with every sign of genuine good humour.

'Three per cent's not modest, it's pathologically shy,' he said. 'Try ten.'

'On top of the fence's cut?' Elyra shook her head. 'Five, take it or leave it.'

'Seven,' Greel said, apparently enjoying himself; it was probably a long time since he'd brokered a personal deal, Elyra thought, franchisemen of his status usually living off the tithes paid to their superiors by the lowly gangers further down the food chain, and he was relishing the chance to relive a bit of his youth.

After a show of consideration, Elyra nodded. It wasn't that bad a deal, when you came down to it, and if she was really who she was pretending to be she'd want to convert the loot in her pack to cash as quickly as possible. Besides, Greel would be a useful contact for someone like her, and it would be out of character not to try to cultivate him. 'All right, seven,' she said, injecting just the right amount of sullen acquiescence into her voice.

'Good decision,' Greel said cheerfully. He glanced round. 'All right, you've got a buyer for your shinies. What's the next thing?'

'Whatever comes along,' Kyrlock said. He glanced at Elyra, as though wondering if he ought to speak. 'We talked about chasing some bounty warrants.'

'Money to be made there,' Greel conceded. 'But it's chancy.' He looked from one to the other appraisingly. 'You'd probably make out all right, though. I've been hearing quite a bit about you two lately.'

'Thought you might,' Elyra agreed, as though she'd been expecting something of the sort. Greel would be well aware of their abilities, and the reputation they'd earned among their fellow passengers. 'There isn't that much to talk about down here.'

'Don't sell yourselves short,' Greel said. 'I saw what you did to Kantris back in the Gorgonid, and I gather you've made a few fresh enemies on the trip as well.'

'We haven't got any enemies aboard that I'm aware of,' Elyra said, and Greel laughed again.

'My point exactly. I know talent when I see it, and I can always find an opening in the Franchise for someone with the right abilities.'

For a moment Elyra felt a thrill of apprehension, wondering if the franchiseman was hinting that he knew that she was a psyker; but he'd shifted his gaze to Kyrlock before he finished the sentence, making it clear that he was including them both in the offer.

'It's tempting,' Kyrlock said, as if any other answer was possible. He looked at Elyra. 'Working for the Franchise means money, contacts…'

'And lawdogs on your arse every hour of the day,' Elyra finished. She allowed herself to look as though she was considering the offer anyway. Greel wouldn't know she'd already been offered refuge by the Sanctuary, and the woman she was pretending to be would at least be tempted by the proposal. 'I've done all right so far by keeping a low profile.'

'Unless you count sleeping with your employer's husband and stealing her jewellery,' Greel said, with a trace of amusement.

Elyra inclined her head a little, acknowledging the justice of the remark. 'Well, yes, apart from that,' she conceded.

Greel laughed again, his good humour apparently unfeigned, although Elyra was well aware that to have achieved the eminence he apparently had within the Franchise he would have raised deceit to the level of an art form.

'Think about it anyway,' he suggested. 'And don't worry too much about the dogs. I never do.'

He probably didn't, Elyra thought. Criminals tended to deal with what was in front of them, forgetting that actions had consequences until they turned round and bit. Something Greel would probably be reminded of quite forcibly once she'd found a way to report to the Tricorn.

'We will,' she said, and shrugged. 'I don't suppose we'll be getting a better offer before we dock, anyway.'

The *Misericord*, the Warp, Date and Time Meaningless

'HIS NAME'S TANCRED,' Keira said. 'I found his personal data-slate aboard the shuttle. Along with this.' She held out the precious manuscript, and Horst took it, covertly assessing her demeanour as he did so. It appeared as businesslike as ever. Despite the concerns he'd tried so hard to suppress, it seemed she hadn't been unduly affected by her encounter with the rogue psyker after all.

'Hybris.' He glanced over to where the tech-priest was communing with his own data-slate. As Vex glanced up, he held out the document. 'Your area of expertise, I think.'

'Thank you,' Vex said, taking it, and riffling through the pages before stowing it somewhere inside his robe. 'It appears to be intact.' A tinge of regret flickered in his voice. 'This hardly seems the time or the place to peruse it, however.'

'You got that right,' Keira agreed. 'When Tancred discovers it's missing, he'll be right behind me.' She glanced at Horst with a flicker of amusement. 'I made sure I left enough of a trail for him and his animals to follow.'

'Good,' Horst said. 'We're all set here.' He glanced across at Vex. 'Aren't we?'

'We are,' the tech-priest confirmed. 'All the relevant systems are interfaced, and awaiting activation.'

'Good.' Keira produced a gold-plated data-slate from a pouch on her belt. 'Then you can take a look at this while we're waiting.' An expression of distaste flickered across her face. 'Most of the files appear to be nothing more than pornography, but there are a few encrypted ones, which might contain something we can use.'

'I'll see what I can extract,' Vex said, activating the slate. 'It's unlikely that any of the ciphers are particularly sophisticated.' He busied himself with the arcane rituals of his calling, leaving Horst and Keira alone.

'Are you all right?' Horst asked, feeling a little awkward at asking so bluntly.

'Fine, thank you,' Keira replied, apparently just as uneasy as he was.

'Good.' Horst nodded briskly. 'We'll all need to stay focused if this is going to work.'

'Taking on an army of mutants without backup, you mean?' Drake asked sarcastically, approaching from the tunnel entrance Keira had returned by at a rapid trot, his lasgun already in his hands. 'What could possibly go wrong?'

'Nothing,' Keira said firmly, apparently heartened by the Guardsman's display of confident cynicism. 'We're doing the Emperor's work, so He stands beside us.'

'I'd rather have Him standing in front of me,' Drake said, happily oblivious to the way Keira's jaw knotted at the impious jest.

'Did you get everything rigged?' Horst asked, and Drake nodded. 'Good. Then you'd better take up your position.' Which would get him out of the way before he distracted Keira any more than he had done already with his misplaced sense of humour. Horst knew it was a common enough way of coping with stress, particularly among soldiers preparing for combat, but if it began to undermine the cohesiveness of the team, he was going to have to intervene. Far better to keep them separated as best he could.

'On my way,' Drake assured him, and began to scale one of the rope ladders the Malcontents had left hanging from the two cross corridors which pierced the walls about halfway up, in the same manner as the upended hold where the Angelae had first encountered Tancred and his mutants. In a moment he'd gained the mouth of the passageway, and gone prone, training his lasgun on the mouth of the tunnel.

'Hybris, you too,' Horst said. Now Keira had recovered the manuscript, it was even more important to keep the tech-priest safe.

'Very well,' Vex said, looking up from the screen of Tancred's data-slate. 'Are you coming too?'

'No.' Horst shook his head. 'A trap's not a trap if it hasn't any bait in it.'

'Then I'm staying down here too,' Keira said, as if she expected him to argue. 'There's no point in making it obvious, either.'

'No, there isn't,' Horst agreed. 'And there's no one I'd rather have with me.' Though he spoke purely for form's sake, it belatedly occurred to him that it was no more than the literal truth.

The *Emperor's Justice*, Scintilla System
248.993.M41

'A RATHER UNFORTUNATE outcome,' Inquisitor Grynner said, glancing up from the data-slate containing the interrogator's report. Not trusting himself to speak, Quillem merely nodded. He still felt nauseous from the after-effects of the teleporter, and a sick, dull headache hammered at his temples. Krypen, the Death-watch Apothecary, had given him something to ease the discomfort of being abruptly folded through the fringes of the warp, but it didn't seem to have helped a great deal.

'Most unfortunate,' Grynner repeated. 'I trust you're recovering, Pieter?'

'As well as can be expected,' Quillem replied, wondering if this was how a heretic felt when the inquisitor began an interview with them. Then he dismissed the thought; most heretics were fooled by the pose of vagueness Inquisitor Grynner so successfully cultivated, at least until they'd let something incriminating slip. He was under no illusions about the formidable intellect facing him across the polished wooden desk.

Grynner nodded, as though that was precisely the answer he'd been anticipating: most likely it was. Quillem had been working with him long enough for the older man to be able to predict his responses with a fair degree of accuracy. 'I'm pleased to hear it,' he said. 'And Carys?'

'Not too good,' Quillem admitted, after a momentary hesitation he was certain his patron had registered. 'Apart from the effects of the teleport, she's still blaming herself for the operation going klybo.'

'Perhaps with good reason,' Grynner said, glancing at the data-slate on which Quillem could see his own report reproduced in glowing, upside-down letters. Composing it through the haze of nausea and disassociation which continued to dog him after the teleport had been difficult, but he'd persevered, knowing the inquisitor would want all the pertinent details to hand as quickly as possible. 'She was the one who tripped the alarm, was she not?'

'It wasn't her fault,' Quillem said, sensing the trap a lesser man might have fallen into, and evading it without thought or hesitation. 'She was following my orders, and had every right to expect that I knew what I was doing. They all did.' Arken, Malven and Rufio had paid dearly for that assumption, and he wasn't going to leave Carys to carry the burden of it on his behalf. 'I should have kept them safe.'

'A noble sentiment,' Grynner said dryly, 'but a singularly unrealistic one given our calling and responsibilities.' Suddenly, the blue eyes behind the unnecessary spectacles were hard, and focused, and Quillem felt as though he was staring down the barrel of a plasma gun. 'I do hope you're not going to let this little setback compromise your efficiency, Pieter. You've shown a fair amount of promise so far. It would be rather inconvenient if I felt I couldn't rely on you to the same extent in the future.'

'I won't let you down, inquisitor,' Quillem said, hoping he didn't sound too disconcerted by the implied threat. Once lost, Grynner's confidence could only be regained by long and hazardous service, a route he'd already taken once to rise to his present position, and was by no means keen to repeat. If he even survived the experience.

'I'm pleased to hear it.' With the abruptness of a card sharp making the Abbess disappear, the mask of pedantic prissiness was back. Grynner picked up another of the data-slates arranged neatly on his desk, activated it, and handed it to Quillem. 'Anything here strike you as familiar?'

Suppressing the pounding in his temples as best he could, Quillem squinted at the display screen, and read a paragraph or two. Then he nodded, regretting the abrupt gesture instantly. 'It's one of the reports your friend's agent filed from Sepheris Secundus,' he said, as soon as the flashes of light stopped dancing across his retina. 'The follow-up statements from the two Guardsmen he had seconded to his team.'

'Quite,' Grynner said. 'Specifically, their description of the heretic forces which attacked the Black Ship holding pen.'

Quillem returned his attention to the screen, concentrating with rather more effort than he would normally have required on the shuddering letters. After a moment he nodded again, a little more cautiously this time. 'It sounds like the same group of mercenaries that attacked us,' he said. 'The same mixture of Imperial and xenos equipment, and the same psyker in eldar armour.'

'Which means we now have all the confirmation we needed that the Faxlignae are behind this affair,' Inquisitor Grynner said. 'No other renegade group has access to so many xenos artefacts, or would risk using them so openly, if they could make them work at all.'

'It also seems to confirm their connection to the psyker underground,' Quillem said, to show that he was paying attention. 'A wyrd with eldar wargear; that's a combination you don't see every day.'

'For which we should all thank the Emperor,' Grynner concluded dryly. He sat back in his seat, and steepled his fingers. 'Unfortunately we seem to have lost our most promising lead. Before pulling out, the mercenaries did a very thorough job of destroying the datafiles in the office you found.'

'There must be secondary records,' Quillem suggested. 'Traffic control, berthing fees, stuff like that. If we can get the name of a ship, that might get us somewhere.'

'Possibly.' Grynner looked thoughtful. 'But it's just as likely that they left their carrier vessel in the outer system; the chances are it never docked at Scintil VIII at all.'

'I'll try running it down anyway,' Quillem said. 'You never know, we might find something.' He was beginning to feel more like his old self again, the nagging sense of guilt at the deaths of so many of his team receding under the comforting dictates of duty; at least for now.

The inquisitor nodded. 'I'd also suggest,' he said, in a tone which made it clear that he fully expected the suggestion to be followed, 'that you find out what Carolus's people are up to. They should be arriving in-system about now, and it seems quite clear that we're following different strands of the same conspiracy.'

'Consider it done,' Quillem assured him. 'Do you want me to make direct contact with them?'

'Not for the time being,' Grynner said, after a momentary reflective pause. 'We still don't know why Carolus decided to invoke Special Circumstances, and until we do it might not be wise to advertise our own interest in the affair. Discretion, I think, would be the best way to proceed.'

'Discreetly it is, then,' Quillem agreed.

The *Misericord*, the Warp, Date and Time Meaningless

THE WAITING WAS the worst part for Drake. Once combat was joined, he could let instinct take over, the immediate-action drills he'd practised in the Guard and the Royal Scourges taking the place of introspection, but until that happened his imagination kept supplying worst-case scenarios, each one more disturbing than the last. If Kyrlock had been with him it wouldn't have felt so bad; they'd have taken refuge in the profanity and banter which had sustained them on the battlefield, but his friend was Emperor knew where. Not for the first time, Drake wondered how he was faring, and hoped that he was all right.

'Getting anywhere with the data-slate?' he asked, reflecting wryly that he must be getting desperate for distraction to attempt small talk with Vex.

'I believe I've succeeded in decrypting the files,' the tech-priest replied, 'but their contents still require detailed perusal and analysis. Most appear to be concerned with unremarkable business dealings, and similar personal contacts.'

'Anything relating to Adrin or Tonis?' Horst asked; he'd kept the comm-bead network open, so the whole team could respond instantly as soon as the attack came.

'No mention of Tonis, although Adrin appears several times in the business files. He seems to have been facilitating the purchase of some merchandise from Scintilla on Tancred's behalf. The sort of pointless expenditure the Secundan nobility habitually indulge in, so I see nothing particularly suspicious in that.'

'Everything's suspicious where heretics are concerned,' Keira reminded him sharply. Drake turned his head a little, trying to spot her, but she'd chosen her ambush point well, and remained invisible from his position. Horst was stationed towards the middle of the space below, taking cover behind a tangle of fallen metalwork, where he would have a good field of fire as the mutants advanced, and a clear line of retreat to the rope ladder.

'I stand corrected,' Vex replied dryly. 'Nonetheless, the importation of wines, rugs and decorative automata seem less probable avenues of heretical endeavour than the meetings of Adrin's coven of wyrds. Most of the cargoes were routed through the same shipping agent, a man named Voyle, so that connection might be worth following up when we get to Scintilla, however.'

'Is there anything about the coven itself?' Drake asked, and the tech-priest nodded.

'Several references to a group Tancred refers to as the Sanctuary of the Blessed. There are few details, but Adrin is clearly connected to it, and the final dated entry on the data-slate is a summons to a meeting of the Sanctuary at his mansion on the evening we raided the premises.'

'That seems pretty definite–' Horst began, only to be interrupted by an explosion in the depths of the tunnel, where Drake had rigged a couple of frag grenades attached to tripwires. The booby trap was crude enough, but he hadn't expected the muties to be overly bright, and it seemed he hadn't underestimated them.

'Incoming,' Drake warned, catching the first sight of movement from his elevated perspective, and began shooting at the first group of mutants to make it as far as the hole in the wall. Smoke and dust from the explosion billowed out behind them as the misshapen parodies of humanity lurched forwards, and for a moment he found himself hoping that Tancred had been caught by the blast. In that he was disappointed, however; a moment or two later he caught sight of the Secundan fop emerging from the hole behind the first wave, evading every las-bolt the Guardsman sent in his direction with the same infuriating ease.

'I see them,' Horst said, his voice calm, and began firing too, each bolt from his pistol claiming a mutant life in a spray of blood and viscera.

'Holy Throne,' Drake said. 'He's sent the whole rutting tribe this time!' He continued to shoot until his power-pack ran dry, then ejected it and snapped in a replacement; as he did so the shambling horde below took advantage of the brief lull to surge forwards like a tidal wave.

'Looks like it,' Keira agreed, ghosting into visibility at last, to dispatch a small group of mutants, which had just run past the shadows concealing her in their eagerness to get to Horst, in a single flurry of blade strokes. Ignoring the expiring abhumans littering the ground at her feet, she charged forwards, carving her way through the next wave as though they were no more substantial than smoke. 'He must really want that book.'

'How's it coming?' Drake asked, glancing briefly at Vex before sighting his recharged weapon on the largest group of mutants he could find. Every time he squeezed the trigger another one fell, but it was like trying to punch holes in water; the gap would fill instantly, and there still seemed no end to the horde pouring into the upended hold. 'We can't hold them off for ever.' He switched his aim, taking out a group a little more tactically minded than the rest, which had bypassed Horst in an attempt to cut him and Keira off from the ladder.

'You won't have to,' Vex assured him, his own data-slate back in his hand. A green 'ready' icon pulsed reassuringly on the screen. 'I can activate any time you're ready.'

'Just a couple more minutes,' Horst said. 'We need to make sure Tancred's taken the bait.'

'He's moving,' Drake reported, switching his attention back to the wyrd puppet master. Tancred was trotting towards Horst, behind a bodyguard of heavily muscled mutants, although what help he thought brute strength would be against an explosive-tipped pistol bolt was beyond Drake. He was running awkwardly, his left arm hunched in close to his body, and the Guardsman was heartened to see a smear of blood on his sleeve where Keira had pinked him at their last encounter. 'Heading for Mordechai.'

'Hoping I'm carrying the document,' Horst said dryly. 'Makes sense; heretics aren't very big on delegation. Too much trust involved.'

'Pull back,' Drake urged. 'While I can still cover you.'

'On my way.' Horst turned and sprinted for the ladder. 'Keira, pull out.'

'I can still get to him!' Keira snarled. She was slashing her way relentlessly towards the wyrd, heedless of the number of brutes surrounding her. If she wasn't careful, she was going to be cut off and pulled down by the sheer weight of numbers.

'Stick to the plan!' Horst said, picking a couple of attackers off her back with well-placed pistol shots, and she nodded, a trifle reluctantly, before turning away from her target to begin hacking her way towards the ladder. They reached the hanging avenue of escape almost simultaneously, and Horst waved her up. 'Go! I'll be right behind you!'

'You'd better be.' Sheathing the sword, she began swarming upwards, while Horst defended the foot of the ladder for a few vital seconds, his bolt pistol barking death at the onrushing horde.

'She's here!' Drake yelled, switching to full auto, and hosing down the first wave as they closed on Horst's position. There was no point in picking targets now, the whole floor just seemed to be a seething mass of frenzied, misshapen flesh, intent on killing them all. 'For Throne's sake move!'

'Hybris, do it!' Horst instructed, and started to climb, the bestial pack hard on his heels. The first few mutants to arrive started scrambling up after him, and Drake seethed with frustration at his inability to pick them off.

'I can't get a clear shot around Mordechai!' he snarled, emptying the powerpack in the general direction of Tancred instead, who seemed as unconcerned as ever by the blizzard of las-bolts, even as his bodyguard was cut down around him.

'I can,' Keira said, hanging upside down over the lip of the passageway by her knees, her back to the wall and her crossbow in her hand. She took the shot, then flipped herself upright again, to land on her feet in the corridor.

'Thanks,' Horst said, as the leading mutant fell, screaming, into the mass of his fellows below, Keira's bolt
embedded in his neck. Then the arbitrator's head and
shoulders appeared over the rim of the drop, and Drake
leaned down to take his arm, hauling him to safety with
as much strength as he could muster.

'System activated,' Vex said, glancing upwards with an
air which, in anyone but a tech-priest, would have
looked to Drake suspiciously like anxious anticipation. A
loud metallic booming noise echoed though the chamber, and the mutants hesitated, milling uncertainly for a
moment before renewing their attack.

'Sin off,' Keira said, striking down with her sword at the
first mutant to appear at top of the ladder. Blood foun-
tained as she sheared through both his arms, and he
toppled backwards, an expression of dull-witted astonishment on his face. The ropes parted too, and the ladder
followed, taking its cargo of abhumans with it.

'It appears to be working,' Vex said. 'The door mechanism is functioning as I expected.'

No sooner had he spoken than the water arrived, bursting like a bomb on the floor below, scattering mutants
and detritus alike. The noise was worse than Drake had
expected, the thunderous roar drowning out all other
sounds, battering him with an almost physical force; if it
hadn't been for the comm-beads in their ears, conversation of any kind would have been impossible.

Incredibly, the torrent just seemed to increase in power
as the hold began to fill, surging up the sides of the
chamber; within seconds the Angelae were drenched
with spray and the backwash surging around their feet.

'I would recommend expeditious withdrawal,' Vex said.
'This is becoming rather too reminiscent of the Fathomsound.'

Drake nodded. 'What he said,' he agreed, looking in
awestruck horror at the boiling, foam-flecked cauldron
which filled the space below. A few of the hardier

mutants were still struggling to remain above the surface, but most of the bodies he could see were motionless, floating among the other flotsam.

'Wait,' Horst instructed. 'I want to make sure of the wyrd.'

Drake nodded, scanning the surface of the water around the roaring column which still rose in the centre of the chamber; flecks of debris and mutilated corpses appeared and disappeared around it, churned to the surface and sucked back down again by the relentless waterfall in a matter of seconds.

'There!' Keira pointed to a feebly kicking figure, its garish Secundan clothing unmistakable, as it surfaced, and began to sink again.

'Something's wrong,' Drake said, a nameless foreboding descending on him. The way the wyrd was moving didn't seem right, somehow.

Even before he'd finished speaking, Tancred spasmed, then seemed to tear open, as something huge and formless began to force its way out from inside him. Tentacles thrashing, flickering in and out of corporeal existence, and battered by the boiling waters, it struggled to find a purchase in the material world.

'Throne on Earth, it's another daemon!' Keira yelled, taking up a guard stance with her sword.

Drake fumbled a fresh powerpack into his lasgun, mouthing the litany against the warpspawned he'd memorised from the *Infantryman's Uplifting Primer*, and hoped that the blessing Vex had performed on the weapon was still holding. He'd taken down another of these monstrosities with it, he reminded himself, which must surely have endowed it with some enduring virtue.

He pulled the trigger, praying to the Emperor to keep his aim true, the stream of las-bolts raising clouds of steam as they sliced through the sleeting spray. Where they struck home, they gouged ichorous craters in the abnatural flesh, but the majority of the shots passed straight through the entity; tormented by the roiling waters, it seemed to be having trouble taking form, and the more it solidified, the more it seemed to be finding itself at the mercy of the currents in the maelstrom. A moment later, still pursued by Drake's dogged marksmanship, it was dragged under the column of water pouring from the lake chamber above.

Pounded by tonnes of plummeting liquid, the terrifying apparition emitted a high-pitched keening which somehow managed to cut through the rumble of the waterfall, and vanished, sucked back into the warp at last.

'Can we go now?' Drake asked. 'He looks pretty dead to me.'

Horst nodded, and they began the long trek back to the *Beyonder's Hostelry*.

'Was that the same one?' Drake wondered aloud, as the boom of the falling water diminished behind them. 'Or the third of those things we've encountered?'

Horst shrugged. 'Offhand,' he said, 'I don't know which of those possibilities worries me more.'

TWELVE

The *Misericord*, Scintilla System
249.993.M41

'WE'RE LIFTING,' BARDA informed them from the cockpit, and Horst felt a gentle pressure against his spine as the *Righteous Indignation* began to rise. The vista of the hangar bay dropped away as the young pilot fed power to the engines, and began nudging them towards the vast brass hatch set into the ceiling of the cavernous chamber. The noise outside would have been appalling, reinforced by the echoes rolling back from all sides, and Horst found himself suppressing a grin as he caught sight of Tweendecker covering her ears, her robes flapping as they were caught in the backwash from the shuttle's engines. Her face was still invisible behind her mask, but Horst hadn't needed to see it to know she was heartily glad to see the back of them. He still wasn't entirely sure if the small honour guard which had assembled to see them off was a mark of respect, or just to reassure the ship's company that the Inquisitorial party had unquestionably left.

A moment later the shuttle had risen too high to see anything other than the throat of the boarding shaft, the gate in the hangar ceiling swinging ponderously closed beneath them; Barda began to tilt the little craft back as it rose, shifting the point of balance towards the main engines, and Horst swallowed, feeling the first faint twinges of the void sickness which usually afflicted him when travelling in space. The shuttle had its own gravity generator, so he remained comfortably settled in his seat, but the shifting perspectives outside were playing havoc with his inner ear regardless. Light began to enter the shaft as another huge door began cranking open ahead, pure sunlight edged with the knife-sharp shadows only visible in vacuum, and Horst found himself squinting in the sudden brightness.

'Emperor be praised!' Drake said, with every sign of sincerity, as the shuttle passed through the portal, and gained the freedom of open space at last. He looked back at the misshapen lump of the *Misericord* with visible distaste, then glanced across the narrow aisle at Horst. 'Still think her reputation's just gossip?'

'She was bad luck enough for us,' Horst agreed. 'But we're out of there now.' He stood, cautiously, waiting for his inner ear to stop spinning, and took a step towards the flight deck.

'Is something wrong?' Keira asked, and he shook his head, trying to ignore the inevitable twinge of nausea which followed.

'No. But if Barda's going to set us down at the Tricorn, he's going to need the proper clearances. I can arrange that better from the cockpit.'

'That would be the most efficient course of action,' Vex agreed. 'Their resources will be invaluable in furthering our investigation, and we should avail ourselves of them at the earliest opportunity.'

If anything, the view through the armourcrys shielding the pilot's station was even more vertigo-inducing than travelling in the cabin had been, but Horst fought off the queasiness which afflicted him, and settled into the co-pilot's seat next to Barda. Most of the controls facing him were completely unfamiliar, but he recognised the vox-unit he needed, and began to enter the necessary codes.

'Do you want to head for the orbital docks?' Barda asked, pulsing the manoeuvring jets to slip around the steady stream of heavy cargo shuttles already beginning to pillage the vast holds of the *Misericord*. The immense structure was visible ahead of them, a miniature galaxy of lights leaking from uncountable viewports and airlocks, tied together by a city-sized conglomeration of metal and other materials, hanging in the sky between the shuttle and the planet below. Several small asteroids, long since pillaged of any extractable minerals, were embedded somewhere among the accumulated flotsam, along with a couple of early void stations; rumour had it that even a few starships which had docked there had failed to break away again, becoming slowly digested as the stellar reef system had grown inexorably around them.

'No,' Horst said, beginning to transmit a coded vox pulse which identified the tiny shuttle as an Inquisition vessel. 'Hive Sibellus. We're heading straight for the Tricorn.' A luxury they wouldn't have had, if they'd left Barda and the shuttle on Sepheris Secundus; instead they would have had to transfer to the dock, find passage to the surface and make their way to the headquarters of the Calixian Conclave from the nearest star port. Even if everything had gone according to plan, it would have taken the best part of a day before they could report to Inquisitor Finurbi, and in Horst's experience, things seldom worked out as easily as that. Even with the advantage the shuttle gave them, he'd taken the precaution of sending a vox digest of the events aboard the *Misericord* to their patron's office as soon as the Chartist vessel had emerged from the warp; time was of the essence, and the inquisitor needed all the information they could provide if he was to decide on their next course of action.

'Northern continent. Right.' Barda looked across at Horst, a faint trace of amusement on his face, and the arbitrator realised that the surprise he felt must have been visible. 'I read up on Scintilla on the voyage here.' The young pilot glanced through the viewport, a faint trace of wonder on his face. 'The picts don't do it justice, though; all that water.' The grey-green mass of the polluted oceans was visible through the banding of cloud, the darker mottling of the continents standing out clearly by contrast, and Horst remembered that Barda's home world, the only one he'd ever seen from space before, was perpetually shrouded in cloud.

'Very commendable,' Horst said. 'Unfortunately, the rest of us didn't have time to relax with a slate...'

Hive Sibellus, Scintilla
249.993.M41

ALTHOUGH BARDA WAS fascinated by Horst's account of events aboard the *Misericord*, he was too good a pilot to allow himself to become distracted by it; as he listened, the bulk of his attention remained on the instrumentation arrayed in front of him, and the panorama of the hive city towards which they were descending. His reading aboard the shuttle during the long voyage here had prepared him to some extent for the wonders unfolding below, the details gradually becoming visible as they descended through the main mass of cloud blanketing the ground, but the actuality of it was more than he'd been able to imagine. Hive Sibellus was vast, dominating the continent on which it stood, eight thousand kilometres at its widest point, and its central spire rose almost to the stratosphere. That led to some interesting wind patterns; not to mention the thermal currents rising from the manufactoria of the middle hive, and, for all Barda knew, the sheer conglomerate body heat of its billions of inhabitants.

'So what are you going to do with this bone thing?' he asked, once Horst had finished speaking.

The team leader seemed more comfortable now they were back inside the atmosphere, and he turned his head slightly, apparently looking for some landmark he recognised, as he replied.

'Turn it over to the inquisitor, of course. There are facilities in the Tricorn for storing that kind of thing.'

'I suppose there would be,' Barda agreed, never having had any occasion to think about matters like that before. It seemed reasonable to him, though; no doubt acolytes like Horst and the others would come across unhallowed artefacts all the time in the course of their duties, and they could hardly leave them lying around in the bottom of a drawer somewhere. He made a minute adjustment to the shuttle's trim, bringing the nose up a barely perceptible amount, and relaxed a little, sensing that the airflow around the fuselage was optimised again in a fashion he couldn't have managed to put into words even if it had occurred to him to try.

'There's the Lucid Palace,' Horst said, as Barda banked the shuttle in a wide, slow turn over the artificial landscape below. By this point they'd descended so low that the sprawl of the hive filled the horizon, although according to his altimeter they were still closer to the vacuum of space than to whatever passed for ground level here.

Barda turned his head in the indicated direction, and, after a moment, was able to make out the city-sized citadel in the froth-churned ocean which marked the residence of the Sector Governor. Reluctant to fly directly over the central spire of the hive, he widened the turn a little, drifting towards the towering artificial cliffs, where the fringes of Sibellus tumbled like setting lava flow into the sea which bordered it. 'Impressive,' he said, as the minute course adjustment brought the palace more clearly into view. Though dwarfed by the main mass of the hive itself, it passed beneath them like an artificial mountain, surrounded entirely by turbulent water. Its surface, fashioned in the likeness of the petals of a vast flower, the original of which was long extinct anywhere on Scintilla, was festooned with gaudy banners, uncountable thousands of them, which made the whole structure appear to ripple as the winds roared around it.

By now their steady descent was bringing them into the upper levels of the air traffic over the main mass of the hive, uncountable thousands of shuttles, aircars and heavy cargo dirigibles swarming over and around the towers like flies attracted to a choice piece of carrion. Out of long habit, honed on the approaches to Icenholm, which were frequently choked with heavy cargo lifters shuttling between the Gorgonid and the ore barges in orbit, he kept part of his attention on the auspex, and an ear alert for the collision alarm. To his vague surprise, though, none of the dense traffic came close enough to trigger it, moving aside instead to make way for the shuttle, which remained surrounded by a small bubble of unimpeded air; after a moment's thought, he realised that the Inquisition ID Horst was broadcasting was probably the reason for that.

Horst nodded, when he asked about it. 'Yes,' he said. 'Everyone in Hive Sibellus knows the Inquisition has its headquarters here, so they tend to keep out of our way if they can.' He smiled ironically. 'One of the main advantages of working for them. There are others, but precious few; apart from the satisfaction of knowing you're doing the Emperor's work, of course.'

'Isn't that enough for anyone?' Barda asked, and Horst's smile grew a little less strained.

'I thought so when I was your age,' he said. 'Now...' His voice trailed away, and a pensive expression drifted across his face. 'These days, things seem a lot less clear-cut than they used to.'

Barda didn't really understand what he meant by that, but there was no time to ask, and he wasn't sure Horst would elaborate even if he did. 'I'm taking us over the eastern fabrication zone,' he said instead. 'There may be a little turbulence from the thermals above the manufactoria, but it'll shave a few minutes off our arrival time.'

'Then do it,' Horst agreed, and Barda turned the shuttle's nose towards the thick plume of smoke drifting across the artificial foothills of the hive slope like a low-lying thundercloud. Navigating was becoming a little trickier now, as their steady descent had brought them closer to some of the lesser spires which surrounded the main one, dwarfed by it like weeds round a tree, although they still rose a kilometre or two from the fissures and canyons of the main upper hive, and the air currents were getting a little choppy. Though modest in comparison to the towering gnomon which turned the entire megalopolis into a continent-spanning sundial, they still seemed to compete with one another to outdo their neighbours in garish ornamentation; as Barda piloted the shuttle over two of them, linked by a vertiginous bridge, he noticed that their outer surfaces were encrusted with mosaics and statuary.

'They like their decoration here,' he remarked, and Horst nodded.

'It's a status thing. All the really wealthy and powerful families have estates on the main spire, of course, but the parvenus and the merchant classes make do with these, and they want everyone to think they've got just as much good taste as the upper levels.' He smiled sardonically. 'It's probably true, too. Sibellans like to flaunt it if they've got it, and flaunt it even more if they haven't.' His knuckles whitened briefly on the armrest of his seat as the shuttle abruptly dropped a couple of hundred metres, before Barda levelled off again with casual ease. 'What was that?'

'Just a bit of clear-air turbulence,' Barda assured him. 'Although I wouldn't call this air exactly clear.' The armour-crys was becoming spotted with motes of ash as they descended through the pall of smoke, and he concentrated on the controls, feeling the faint shuddering in the fuselage his years of experience had led him to expect. The thermals he'd anticipated came roaring up from the forges and workshops below, and he balanced on them instinctively, varying the power to the engines and the repulsor fields without conscious thought, keeping their forward progress almost as smooth as if they were still coasting through the vacuum of space. Horst watched him narrowly, but Barda barely noticed, completely engrossed in the intricate dance of mingling forces.

'Nicely done,' Horst said, as the industrial zone slipped behind them at last, and the shuttle's flight became smoother again without the need for constant vigilance.

'It's not that hard,' Barda said, acknowledging the compliment. To him, that was no more than the literal truth, although he supposed his skill must seem arcane to a man unfamiliar with the rituals of spaceflight. 'You just have to listen to what the bird's telling you.'

'Which bird would that be?' Horst asked, an expression Barda couldn't easily interpret flickering across his face.

'The one you're sitting in, of course,' Barda explained, bemused, then suddenly understood. 'I meant the shuttle. It's Cloudwalker slang. Means having a feel for how the ship's responding.' He smiled, amused by the misunderstanding. 'I haven't started hearing the void voices, if that's what you're worried about.' Like most shuttle pilots he'd spent quite a lot of time around starship crews, and had heard plenty of tales about the insidious whispering in the mind people sometimes claimed to have been plagued by while transiting the warp, although the only voices he'd heard on the voyage here apart from his own and the Angelae had been the ones on the vox-channels he'd been monitoring.

'I'm glad to hear it,' Horst said, sounding as though he meant it.

The main spire was looming up ahead of them now, dominating the skyline, and Barda adjusted their course a little to bring them around the artificial mountain in a tightening curve. As they rounded it, close enough to make out individual people bustling about their business on innumerable terraces and balconies, Barda could see that it was, if anything, even more encrusted with ornamentation than the subsidiary spires had been. Gardens had been planted on several of the terraces, which had been glassed in to preserve the foliage from the cold prevailing at these altitudes. It was the first vegetation he'd seen on Scintilla, and he wondered briefly how the builders had managed to get the necessary soil to where it was needed; by air, presumably.

'They must like their plants very much,' he remarked, and Horst shrugged.

'Maybe some of them do,' he said. 'But they like impressing the neighbours more.' He indicated the nearest construction site, one of many clinging to the outer surface, where spirejacks in breather masks toiled despite the thin atmosphere, apparently heedless of the abyss beneath their feet. 'Everyone's trying to have the biggest and the best estate on their level, just so the rest of the spirers can pretend they don't care.'

'I don't see the point,' Barda admitted, and Horst shrugged.

'Neither do I. But then we're not rich and bored.' His posture straightened subtly. 'Over there. See it?'

'Yes.' Three linked towers had come into view round the curve of the central spire, shrunk to the scale of a child's building blocks by distance, but still unmistakable, standing out clearly from the northern boundary of the sprawling hive. Barda felt his heartbeat speed up. This was it, the fortress from which the will of the Emperor was enforced throughout the sector. The Tricorn. 'Do I need to contact traffic control?'

Horst shook his head. 'They know who we are,' he said, with a quick glance at the vox-unit, still sending the ID code he'd entered. 'If they didn't, they'd have shot us down by now.'

'Really?' Barda wasn't sure if the senior acolyte was joking or not. The ruthlessness of the Inquisition was legendary, of course, and very little he'd seen of the Angelae and Inquisitor Finurbi had contradicted that impression, but a shuttle crashing into the sprawling hive below would claim countless innocent lives along with the crew it contained.

Horst nodded, apparently able to appreciate his doubts. 'Really. The security of the entire sector rests on the Tricorn. No amount of collateral damage can outweigh the need to protect it.'

'Of course not,' Barda agreed. It was a larger-scale version of the same choice he'd made back on Sepheris Secundus, when he'd used the white-hot flare of the shuttle's engines to breach the walls of the heretic's mansion, knowing that the man's misguided household retainers would be immolated along with the stonework. It had been regrettable, but necessary. If he hadn't acted as he did, Horst and the others wouldn't have been in time to kill the daemon the cultists had been raising, and the damage to his home world would have been incalculable. 'You told me when I signed up for this that there'd be hard choices along the way; I just hope the Emperor guides my hand again when the time comes.'

'He always does,' Horst said, in the tone of a man who was trying to convince himself as much as his listener.

The triune towers had drifted closer while they spoke, dominating everything in the northern sprawl now that the central spire was behind them, and Barda was able to make out a little more detail. Unlike the other edifices he'd seen, they were relatively devoid of ornamentation, only the Imperial aquila and the stylised letter I giving any clue as to who the grim fortress belonged to. A high curtain wall, in the same black stone, connected the three towers, and a scattering of smaller buildings lay between them.

Right in the centre of the complex was a landing field, and it was only as he caught sight of the shuttles and drop-ships parked there that Barda finally grasped the cyclopean scale of the Inquisitorial citadel. With the sight of something familiar to cue his sense of proportion, the realisation dawned that the Tricorn was at least three times the size he'd first estimated.

'Impressive, isn't it?' Horst said, with a hint of amusement, as Barda began their final descent.

'Very,' the pilot agreed, as they passed over the curtain wall. 'Which pad should I use?'

Vehicles of some kind were patrolling it, the smooth upper surface as broad as a highway, and the small red dots crewing them glanced up as they slid smoothly overhead. Turreted lascannons emplaced at regular intervals rotated slowly, bracketing the shuttle, alert for any sign of treachery, their barrels depressing as the small craft continued to descend. This close to the edge of the hive a little of the landscape beyond could be seen, and Barda caught a brief glimpse of a desolate wilderness, choked with the detritus of the manufactoria, through which a river of vivid chemical waste wound its way towards the distant ocean. Then the walls rose around them, cutting off the sight of everything beyond, and the universe outside the Inquisition redoubt effectively ceased to exist.

'Any of the empty ones,' Horst said. 'The cogitators will log us in from the ident beacon.' He pointed. 'Somewhere towards that edge of the field would be best.'

'No problem.' Barda selected an empty berth, between a sleek Aquila in crimson and grey livery, and a battered-looking utility transport no one would normally look at twice, which he suspected was the whole point. Powering down the main thrusters, he vectored the manoeuvring jets just enough to nudge them into position, and settled the shuttle gently into its nest. 'Any particular reason?'

'The west tower's the one we want,' Horst told him. 'No need to walk any further than we need to.'

'I see,' Barda said, trying not to look too hard at the neighbouring Aquila, the kind of vessel he'd flown until the terrifying night it had been shot down by heretics attempting to kill Inquisitor Finurbi and his team of Angelae. The memories the sight of the elegant vessel brought back weren't pleasant. To escape them he took refuge in the familiar routine of powering down the ship, listening to the whine of the engines as their note deepened to an idling murmur.

'There are three different ordos of the Inquisition,' Horst told him. 'Inquisitor Finurbi is of the Ordo Hereticus, which works out of the west tower.' He paused, as if waiting for Barda to ask what the other ones were, and when the young pilot didn't speak, he carried on anyway. 'The Ordo Xenos has the east tower, and the Ordo Malleus the south one.'

'I see,' Barda said, although the names added nothing useful to his knowledge of the organisation he now served. He already knew Horst and the others hunted heretics, which was what he'd always thought the Inquisition was for in any case, so the designation of that particular section hardly came as a surprise. The Ordo Xenos sounded equally self-explanatory – he assumed they must deal with the alien threats which continually beleaguered humanity – but he couldn't for the life of him imagine what the Ordo Malleus did. He had a vague idea from the fragments of High Gothic his childhood tutors had tried to instil in him that their name referred to a tool of some kind, although he'd long since forgotten everything about the ancient language beyond the few phrases necessary to converse with the tech-priests who maintained the guild's aerospace fleet, and the rote-learned catechisms required to propitiate the machine-spirits of his onboard instrumentation.

'The Malleus are daemon-hunters,' Keira said, leaning in through the narrow doorway to the passenger compartment, almost as if she could read his thoughts, 'and probably best avoided. They're not exactly safe to be around.'

Barda tried to imagine the kind of men and women who would seek out the worst horrors of the warp by choice, and decided to follow Keira's advice. 'Do you want me to leave the engines running?' he asked.

'Not this time,' Horst said, stretching as he stood. 'I think it would be better if you came in with us.'

'It's not as if anyone's going to steal it while we're gone,' Keira added, as Barda began to take the engines off-line.

DRAKE HADN'T BEEN sure what he expected the Tricorn to be like, but if he'd thought about it at all, he would probably have pictured something along the lines of the citadel he and Kyrlock had been sent to defend in the wilds of Sepheris Secundus. The reality was overwhelmingly different, though, the isolated outpost he'd seen in the Forest of Sorrows seeming little more than a fortified camp in comparison to the mighty fortress they were walking through now. The Tricorn was the size of a small town; larger, if anything, than some he'd seen on his native world.

At least he wasn't gawping at everything like Barda was, he told himself, as the Angelae passed through the cordon of storm troopers who'd surrounded their shuttle as soon as it grounded; the soldiers had kept their weapons trained on the newcomers while they disembarked, standing down only after the sergeant in charge had examined Horst's rosette minutely, both by eye and with the aid of a small slate-like device which downloaded a stream of genetic and biometric data to confirm the identity of its holder.

Still possessed of a soldier's instincts, he found a detached part of his mind assessing everything he

passed for a potential weakness in the fortifications surrounding them, and he wasn't sure whether he felt
relieved or not that so far he'd failed to find any. No
doubt the garrison at the Citadel of the Forsaken had
felt completely secure too, until the night the band of
mercenaries had descended from the skies in their blasphemous alien spacecraft and all but levelled it to the
ground, freeing hundreds of malignant witches in the
process.

Red and grey uniformed storm troopers were everywhere, mounting guard at strategic locations, or
double-timing from place to place with an air of grim
purpose, and for a fleeting moment he wondered how
the few survivors of his old regiment were faring; they'd
all been inducted into the Inquisition's private army,
having seen too much of the unhallowed to be allowed
to return to the Imperial Guard, and, had it not been for
Inquisitor Finurbi's snap decision to make use of their
local knowledge, both he and Kyrlock would have gone
with them.

Come to that, they still might; the inquisitor had made
it very clear that the chance to become permanent members of the Angelae would depend on their performance,
and if he wasn't satisfied with his new recruits' conduct
since being seconded to the team, Drake might find himself returning to the ranks before the day was over.

'Picturing yourself in uniform?' Keira asked brightly,
and he realised he'd been staring at a storm trooper
detachment in the distance. Something of his nervous-
ness must have shown on his face, despite his best efforts
to hide it, because she smiled encouragingly at him. 'I'm
sure you'd look very dashing.' Then she shrugged, and
added, 'I don't think you're going to get the chance to
find out, though.'

'Neither do I,' Horst assured him. 'In my opinion, you
and Vos have proven to be exemplary field agents, and I
intend commending you both to Inquisitor Finurbi.'

Drake felt the smile broaden. He'd be willing to serve in the ranks again, if that was what the Emperor willed, but he'd come to like the other Angelae a great deal, and the prospect of becoming a permanent member of the team was considerably more appealing.

'I hope we can justify your confidence,' he said, wondering briefly how his friend was faring. Speculation would be fruitless, however, so he appealed mentally to the Emperor to guard Vos and Elyra, wherever they were, and returned his attention to the matter at hand.

They were approaching the entrance to the west tower now, a forbidding portal more than three times the height of a man, and wide enough to have driven a couple of Chimeras through in line abreast without slowing down. All the traffic entering or leaving the gateway was on foot, though, and now his attention was no longer on the relatively small proportion of the citadel's population obviously bearing arms, Drake was surprised to note that most of the people bustling about them wouldn't have excited much notice in the streets beyond the walls. The vast majority were robed in the day-to-day vestments of the various adepta, only the sigil of the Inquisition displayed discreetly on some item of jewellery distinguishing them from their colleagues engaged in more prosaic lines of endeavour; scribes of the Administratum for the most part, although there were several tech-priests among them, and more members of the Ecclesiarchy than he'd expected to see. The rest were dressed in the garb of ordinary citizens, as nondescript as that worn by the Angelae.

'Who are these people?' Barda asked, to Drake's unspoken relief, as he was damned if he was going to look impressed by any of this.

'People like us,' Horst told him. 'Acolytes working for one of the inquisitors based here, coming in to report to them.'

'Actually,' Vex said, 'that would be only a small proportion of the total. The Tricorn employs over eight thousand ancillary staff, who work here full-time, in the archives or some other support capacity.' He permitted himself to infuse a trace of eagerness into his tone. 'And speaking of the archives, I'm confident that, with enough time, I should find the information we need here.'

'Good,' Horst said.

By this time the group had all but reached the huge portal, which seemed to Drake to be rather more impressive than defensible. On closer examination, however, he was able to pick out the narrow firing slits in the thick walls, carefully concealed among the bas-relief carvings of the Inquisitorial seal which formed a sombre decorative frieze above the lintel, and the murder holes over the gateway, through which lethal surprises could be dropped on anyone foolhardy enough to assault the tower itself. Which would, he reminded himself, already have required an attacking force to have carried the formidable walls, in the face of whatever active defences the outer perimeter was able to bring to bear. More guards were visible here too, accompanied by tech-priests, who swept the passing crowds with portable auspexes, and a few quiet men and women with haunted eyes; momentarily meeting the gaze of one, Drake shivered, feeling the sanctionite peering deep into his soul for any sign of taint.

As they stepped inside the structure itself he almost stumbled, and Keira reached out, as quickly and surely as a striking serpent, to take his arm. 'Watch your step,' she said, a spark of mischief in her voice. 'That gets pretty much everyone on their first visit.'

A shallow channel, no more than a couple of centimetres deep and just over a metre wide, ran across the floor from one wall to the other. It had no purpose that Drake could determine, but on both sides it terminated in a niche running from floor to ceiling, in which an identical pair of life-sized statues of power-armoured warriors appeared to have been installed.

Then the coin dropped. The niches were nothing of the kind, they were the recesses into which massive blast doors had been retracted. Which either meant that someone had been unforgivably cavalier about the possibility that the last-ditch defences would ever be needed, or what he'd taken for statues were...

'Emperor on Earth!' he said, forgetting all about his resolution to appear unimpressed by anything he saw here. 'Are those really Astartes?'

'Adepta Sororitas,' Vex said, apparently taking the startled exclamation as a genuine request for information. 'Each of the towers has a permanent honour guard from the chamber militant of the ordo it houses. The Sororitas guards the Ordo Hereticus, the Deathwatch the Ordo Xenos, and the Grey Knights ward the Ordo Malleus. In more ways than one, if the rumours are to be believed.'

Drake didn't ask what the rumours were: he was quite sure he didn't want to know.

Despite himself he turned his head for a better look at the legendary warriors, taking in every detail of their burnished, midnight-black ceramite, inlaid with gold devotional icons, and the richly worked fabric of their surcoats. The crisp white cloth was embroidered with a black goblet, containing a vivid yellow flame, an image echoed on the shoulder guards of the Battle Sisters' power armour. Their guns appeared huge, but the Sororitas held them as easily as Drake carried his lasgun; after a moment he identified them as heavy-calibre bolters, like the ones he'd seen mounted on Imperial Guard Chimeras, although none of those had been decorated with images of the Emperor wrought in precious metals.

A second channel in the floor marked the inner limit of the gatehouse, flanked as before by a second pair of impassive, immobile figures, their blank-visaged helmets decorated with the same fleur de lys as those of their sisters. Beyond the silent warrior women, the fortress opened up into a massive antechamber, through which the bustling crowd of acolytes flowed with ceaseless motion. The floor here was tiled, in an intricate abstract pattern, which both drew and repelled the eye.

'Best not to look too closely at the mosaics,' Keira advised. 'They incorporate wards against warpcraft. You don't want to meet the inquisitor with a nosebleed, do you?'

'Don't the sanctioned psykers find that a bit inconvenient?' Drake asked, and the young assassin shrugged.

'Elyra's never complained.'

'It's my understanding,' Vex said, 'that the patterns are supposed to dampen the kind of raw warp energy drawn on by wyrds. Sanctionites are blessed by the Emperor, so find the effects a great deal less unpleasant than a witch would.'

'Where to now?' Barda asked, looking around with manifest amazement at the dozens of doorways through which people were hurrying, with all the random energy of a turbulent pool.

'Over here,' Horst replied, leading the way to a polished wooden counter at one end of the room, behind which a handful of the Administratum scribes Drake had noticed before were seated on high stools, paging through documents or the displays of data lecterns set into the woodwork. The nearest looked up as the Angelae approached, her expression one of polite uninterest.

'Can I help you?' she asked, evidently unconcerned as to what the answer might be.

'We need to see Inquisitor Finurbi, at his earliest convenience,' Horst said, slotting his rosette into a recess in front of the scribe's lectern. The lectern hummed for a moment, then disgorged a slip of paper, which smudged the tips of the scribe's purple-stained fingers with an additional layer of ink. Drake tilted his head, reading the elegant, and slightly smeared, cursive script.

PETITIONER IDENTIFIED: MORDECHAI HORST.
PATRON INQUISITOR: CAROLUS FINURBI.
HOLD FOR SPECIAL INSTRUCTIONS.

This was evidently an unexpected development, Drake thought; Horst's momentary frown made that perfectly obvious.

'Something wrong?' he asked, as Horst retrieved his rosette, and the scribe rolled the slip of paper into a cylinder, which she stuffed into a metal tube, and hung from a cable above her head. She pulled a lever set into the wall, and the metal capsule disappeared into the distance with a faint whirring sound.

Horst shook his head. 'I don't think so. Usually the inquisitor just clears us for access to his chambers, but I suppose he wants to meet us somewhere else this time.'

'Maybe he isn't in the Tricorn at all,' Keira suggested. 'You know what he's like when he's got a lead he can follow up.'

'Could he have gone to meet Vos and Elyra?' Drake asked, and Horst frowned.

'It's possible, I suppose. That ore barge they were on should have got here ahead of us, but you can never really be sure of anything where warp travel's concerned.'

'Right.' Barda nodded. 'I heard about this voider once, his ship arrived back in-system about thirty years before it left, and what with one thing and another he ended up becoming his own father.' He caught sight of Keira's expression, which could have frozen helium at thirty paces, and trailed off lamely. 'Just stories, of course. I never met anyone who actually... um...'

'Isn't that servitor coming to meet us?' Drake asked, mainly to throw the poor lad a lifeline, but the flesh and metal construct continued to plod towards the little group of Angelae with all the fixity of purpose of its kind, and after a moment he realised that he was right. Its metal components were brightly burnished, its flesh ones ruddy with what, in a living creature, he would have considered good health, and its body was draped in a crimson tabard worked with the sigil of the Inquisition in gold thread.

'It is,' Horst said, sounding surprised.

'It's holding something,' Barda said, seizing on the change of subject with grateful alacrity. A moment later the construct had reached the counter, its head turning slightly as the imagifers set into its skull scanned all their faces in turn.

'Biometric parameters matched to template,' it announced at last, in the flat tones of a vox-coder unit. 'You are Mordechai Horst, please confirm.'

'I am,' Horst said, as calmly as if he held conversations with constructs like this every day.

'Voiceprint confirmation accepted,' the servitor droned, and held out a small, polished wooden box. 'Designated recipient identified within acceptable margins of error. Please take the specified item.'

Wordlessly, Horst took the proffered casket, and the construct turned and walked away, its function discharged. The box was small enough for him to hold in one hand, its surface inlaid with the Inquisitorial sigil, the stylised letter I comprising it chased in some glowing azure mineral unknown on Sepheris Secundus. Horst and Keira stared at it, and even Vex seemed disconcerted, although Drake was at a loss to understand why.

'What is it?' Barda asked after a moment, ingenuous as ever.

'Trouble,' Horst said shortly, slipping the casket into his jacket pocket.

'How can you tell?' Drake asked, no longer caring about seeming blasé. He'd realised that much already, without needing to be told, and been a soldier long enough to know that the more information you had when trouble came calling, the better equipped you were to deal with it.

'The sigil's blue,' Keira said, as if that explained everything.

'Which means what, exactly?' Drake asked.

'It means we don't even think about opening it until we're back aboard the shuttle,' Horst said, looking around as though expecting to find an enemy lurking here, in the heart of the Inquisition headquarters. Meeting his gaze as she glanced up from an intense discussion with the next scribe in line, a red-headed woman smiled a brief greeting, before resuming her argument.

Well, if Horst was worried, so was Drake; the Guardsman checked the impulse to reach for his Scalptaker. Probably not the wisest place in the sector to start waving firearms around, he thought wryly.

'Blue means Special Circumstances,' Keira explained, glancing around with the same hunted expression Horst had just acquired, and beginning to follow the team leader back towards the gatehouse. 'The inquisitor doesn't trust the ordo any more, and that means neither do we.'

'I see,' Drake said, although that was something of an overstatement, falling in at her shoulder as he spoke. 'So what do we do now?'

'We complete our mission, of course,' Keira said, as though that was both simple and obvious.

'Oh, right,' Drake said, hoping her evident confidence wouldn't turn out to be misplaced.

No ONE SAID anything else until they were back aboard the shuttle, with the hatches sealed. Barda disappeared into the flight deck as soon as the atmosphere seals had hissed into place, and began reciting the catechism of engine activation, his voice echoing faintly from the cabin speakers. The whine of the engines grew louder, and, after a moment or two, the vessel lifted from the ground; as it did so, Drake saw his colleagues relax perceptibly.

'Right. Let's see what we've got.' Almost as soon as they passed over the outer wall, Horst opened the box, and the rest of the Angelae crowded round to see whatever it contained. Drake had expected some further elaborate security precaution, a genecode scanner built into the locking mechanism at the very least, but there had been nothing like that: simply a metal catch, worn shiny with generations of thumb pressure, which clicked as Horst released it.

'What's in there?' Keira asked, leaning forwards to get a look inside.

'Just this.' Horst withdrew a slip of paper, seeming faintly surprised to find nothing else. He scanned it briefly, then passed it to Keira, who handed it to Drake. Out of courtesy, the Guardsman angled it so that Vex could read the note too.

It was short, to the point, and written in a clear and confident hand.

The conspiracy reaches further and wider than I could possibly have imagined. Trust no one in the Calixis Conclave: even there, treachery may lurk. I will contact you at the earliest opportunity.

Until then, may the Emperor walk with all my Angelae.

Carolus Finurbi.

THIRTEEN

THE FIRST INDICATION that the *Ursus Innare* had finally made it to its destination was a series of reverberating booms, like the tolling of a great bell far off in the bowels of the ship, which echoed through the hold like distant thunder. Kyrlock glanced up from his position by the firepit, reaching instinctively for the shaft of his chainaxe, and looked over to Elyra, who hadn't moved a muscle. As the sound died away, the murmur of distant voices could be heard echoing round the mineral heaps, as the alarmed passengers began arguing among themselves about what was going on.

'What was that?' Trosk asked, his habitual pose of uninterest undermined a little by the higher than usual register of his voice.

'A step on the road,' Ven told him, unhelpfully, while Elyra rose slowly to her feet, her expression of unconcern a great deal more convincing than the young psyker's. Heartened by this, Kyrlock followed her lead, and stowed the chainaxe in its sling across his shoulders, hoping that his companions would assume that was why he'd picked it up in the first place. Trosk and Ven hadn't noticed anything out of the ordinary in his demeanour, he was sure, although Zusen smiled shyly at him as he glanced in her direction, probably having sensed his momentary flare of alarm.

'It's just the docking clamps,' Elyra said, beginning to gather her belongings, and after a moment Kyrlock followed suit, picking up the pack he'd been using as a pillow. 'They must have brought us in to Tarsus High for unloading.'

'That's the orbital docks, right?' Kyrlock asked, and Elyra nodded.

'In geostationary orbit over Hive Tarsus, which makes it the most important economic hub in the system. Hardly a thing moves on or off the planet without coming through here.'

'Which means it's being watched all the time for people like us,' Trosk said. He glanced at Elyra, as if wondering how much he should take her into his confidence. 'That's why we were supposed to go through the void station.'

'Well, we're here now,' Elyra said. 'Better just hope your friends in the Sanctuary have a back-up plan.'

'Of course they do,' Zusen said, beginning to sound more like the self-confident young woman they'd first met in the depths of the Gorgonid, now the long, arduous trip appeared to be over. She turned to Elyra. 'I told you, they can keep us safe for ever. You too, if you'll trust them.'

'I don't trust anyone,' Elyra said, then glanced at Kyrlock. 'No offence, Vos.'

'None taken,' Kyrlock assured her. According to their cover story, their alliance was one of expediency rather than friendship, and that was the best way to keep playing it. Elyra would go with the Sanctuary when the time came, of that there was no possible doubt, and if they refused to accept Kyrlock too, there couldn't be any suspicion of Elyra's apparent willingness to part from him.

'Were you given any contact details for a situation like this?' Elyra asked, addressing the question to Zusen, presumably because she knew Trosk wouldn't give her a straight answer anyway.

The young empath shook her head. 'No. We were just told we were being taken off by shuttle in the outer system.'

'By someone from the void station, presumably,' Elyra said.

Trosk shot her a sharp look, then nodded slowly. 'Presumably,' he agreed.

'They weren't very specific,' Zusen said, a trifle apologetically.

'Which was very sensible of them,' Kyrlock said, 'but rut all use to us now. What do we do, just sit around and wait for a vox call?'

'No,' Elyra said, 'we wait for Greel to get one.' She smiled at the young wyrds, without a trace of humour. 'If he's making as much money as I think he is from letting your babysitters use his network, he'll have been trying to arrange an alternative rendezvous with them ever since things went paps up on the void station.'

She might have said more, but attempting to speak suddenly became pointless. With a grating sound, punctuated by squeals like the shrieks of the damned, the main cargo hatch began to crank open. The clear yellow light of powerful luminators began to seep in through the widening gap, and Kyrlock found himself squinting, unused to normal levels of illumination after spending so long confined in the semi-darkness of the mineral hold.

'Up and out, come on, let's go.' A trio of franchisemen appeared, chivvying the rest of the apprehensive passengers in front of them, clearly in no mood to delay.

Despite the shotguns they carried, they hesitated when they came to Elyra's group, and she smiled in a manner calculated to leave them thinking they were wise to do so.

'Where to, exactly?' she asked.

'The docking arm,' one of the franchisemen explained, glancing warily at her pack, which she'd left hanging from her shoulder where she could draw the laspistol inside it in a heartbeat. Word of her emasculation of Kantris had no doubt got around fast, and no one was keen to provoke her. 'We can get you aboard the harbour through one of the utility shafts. But we have to be quick, before they open the discharge hatches.'

'Works for me,' Elyra said, turning away even as she spoke. She began to follow the rest of the nervously milling refugees without so much as a backwards glance.

Trusting her judgement, Kyrlock fell in beside her. 'Will the juves follow?' he asked quietly.

'They will if they don't want to make a return trip to Sepheris Secundus,' Elyra said, remaining in character despite the minimal risk of being overheard. She shrugged, indicating the megatonnes of fractured stone surrounding them. 'Besides, they're about to unload this lot the same way they got it in here. It'll all fall through a hatch in the floor, and it'll be damned uncomfortable for anyone left behind.'

That was something of an understatement, Kyrlock thought, picturing the sudden torrent of displaced rubble. It would make the rockslide Trosk had started look like a scuffed pebble. Anyone still left in the hold would be crushed to death almost instantly.

As that alarming thought struck him, he glanced round involuntarily for Zusen, and was relieved to find the young wyrd picking her way cautiously over the stones in their wake, the other two following a few paces behind. Noticing the movement of his head, she smiled wanly at him for a moment, then returned her attention to the

tricky matter of not stumbling on the treacherous surface.

Having spent a large proportion of his life among the
spoil heaps of the Tumble, Kyrlock had no such concerns, his stride almost as sure-footed as if he was on
solid ground. Sure for the moment that the trio of psykers were out of earshot, he returned his attention to Elyra.
'If you've anything to say, better make it fast,' he said.
'They'll be able to hear us again in a minute.'

'Right,' Elyra said. 'First thing: this information has to
get back to the Tricorn. If we get separated, that'll be up
to you.'

'Got it.' Kyrlock nodded once. 'How do I do that? I
don't think you can just walk up to the door and ask to
see an inquisitor.'

'You'd be surprised.' Elyra smiled at some private joke.
'But there's a vox-code Carolus gave us for emergencies.
You can use that if you don't want to break cover.' She
reeled it off, not quite managing to hide her astonishment when he repeated it back verbatim on the first try.
'It connects to a safe house in Sibellus middle hive, and
the warden there can pass on the message.' She looked
thoughtful for a moment. 'You might not need to use it,
though. I'm sure Mordechai's reports got here long
before we did, so chances are you'll be contacted by
another Angelae cell before long. Or maybe Mordechai
himself, if they were able to follow us.'

Kyrlock didn't bother to ask how she expected their
colleagues to know which ship they were on; she evidently did, and she knew them better than him, so that
was enough.

They were approaching the main door of the hold now,
and he was able to catch a glimpse of the interior of the
starship itself for the first time. The franchisemen they'd
spoken to before remained behind, completing a sweep
of the cargo space for any stragglers, but another armed
man was waiting by the hatch, and directed them down

the corridor outside with a wave of his shotgun. It seemed vaguely disappointing, just a grimy, nondescript passageway; if he hadn't known they were aboard a vessel capable of transiting the warp, Kyrlock might have taken it for part of a barrack block or a manufactorium.

Another equally bored guard directed them though a narrow gap where a panel had been removed from the wall, and down a cramped, winding staircase, which Kyrlock assumed was normally the domain of the vessel's engineers, judging by the number of exposed conduits and yellowing prayer scrolls they passed; the other passengers were bunching up a little in the confined space, and the two Angelae hung back slightly, although the babble of voices rising up the stairwell meant that the risk of being overheard was minimal. After descending about a hundred metres, the staircase abruptly terminated in another corridor; as they ducked through the open inspection hatch to reach it they brushed past a rack of hostile environment suits, their enclosed helmets and life support packs shelved neatly nearby. Kyrlock eyed them apprehensively.

'We're not going to need those, are we?' he asked. Jumping from Icenholm with the glidewings had been bad enough; the thought of crossing the outer hull, where a single misstep could send him spinning off into open space, was a thousand times worse.

Elyra shook her head. 'No, they're all still in place.' Kyrlock exhaled noisily with relief as she continued, glancing around as though this was an environment she was perfectly comfortable in. 'We must be in one of the dorsal utility locks. They'll have made a hard seal with one of the external hatches on the station.'

She was right: beyond the airlock chamber, both doors of which had been propped open to let the passengers disembark as quickly as possible, a flexible tunnel connected the vessel to an almost identical portal a few metres away.

As they stepped up onto the lip of the hatch, and he was able to see the interior of the ore chute beyond for the first time, Kyrlock felt a momentary twinge of vertigo. The far wall of the chute was at least five hundred metres distant, and the metal catwalk they found themselves on swayed alarmingly as it took their weight, suspended by chains over a drop of at least thirty metres.

'You said the first thing,' Kyrlock reminded her, as their bootsoles rang on the metal mesh. Despite himself, he was unable to resist the impulse to glance up, and see a little of the starship which had brought them here. It didn't look like much, a blank metal ceiling, dull and corroded, the outline of the discharge hatch etched clearly into the pitted surface, and with a thrill of horror he realised that the docking port was normally open to the vacuum of space, only the fabric of the ship itself sealing in the air they needed to breathe. The fear of it drifting away, leaving them to suffocate, was completely irrational, he knew, but nonetheless real for all that, and he quickened his pace involuntarily. 'What was the second?'

They were halfway along the catwalk by now, and he was able to see that it terminated in another doorway, identical to the one they'd just entered the station by. The notion of solid decking under his feet again was an almost irresistible lure, but he checked the impulse to break into a run. There was no telling what lay beyond, and he had no intention of finding out the hard way if it was dangerous.

'The void station,' Elyra said, planting her feet with a faintly exaggerated care which told Kyrlock she was as uncomfortable on the swaying bridge as he was. The chains seemed to be attached to a boom, tens of metres above their heads, and after a moment he realised that it could be swung out of the way of the cargoes being dumped down the chute. 'Most of the freight handled there is trans-shipped for forwarding to other systems.

Maybe our psykers weren't heading for Scintilla after all.'

'Which means you could be on your way to Emperor knows where before too much longer,' Kyrlock said.

'Exactly.' Elyra nodded soberly. 'If I'm right, I'll try to get a message to Carolus as soon as I know our final destination, but there are no guarantees.' Without a word being said, somehow, it seemed, they both accepted that this was going to be the parting of the ways.

Kyrlock made a last attempt to puncture the mood. 'If the Sanctuary take us as a team,' he said, 'I'll be there to watch your back. If not, I'll follow the Franchise connection. Maybe Greel knows where everyone's going.'

'I doubt it,' Elyra said. 'The Sanctuary might have been using the Franchise smuggling operation to get its own people off Sepheris Secundus, and possibly other worlds in the sector, but if they trust them with the next stage of the pipeline, my mother's a virgin.'

'We won't let you down,' Kyrlock said, vaguely surprised to discover that he meant it. He wasn't used to the idea of duty, or responsibility, or even loyalty to anyone other than Danuld, but he liked Elyra, and the idea of her being cut adrift without any backup was disturbing.

There was no more time for discussion, however, as by now they'd reached the end of the catwalk. Kyrlock stepped through the metal doorway facing them, to find another identical portal a couple of metres beyond it, also open.

'Coming?' Elyra asked, turning to check on the progress of the three wyrds, underscoring the fact that they were now too close for the Inquisition agents to discuss their business openly.

'Right behind you,' Trosk said, shepherding Ven as usual. The young seer seemed to be in one of his more lucid phases at the moment, much to Kyrlock's relief, walking along the narrow catwalk in a reasonably straight line, and with his eyes focused on his surroundings. Zusen was a pace or two ahead of them, and took his arm as she caught up. She was clearly sensing his unease, as she smiled at him reassuringly.

'You can't have spent much time in Icenholm,' she said.

'No.' Kyrlock shook his head. None of the wyrds had said much about their backgrounds, but the lack of facial tattoos, marking them out as the vassals of one or other of the barons, had been enough to tell him that none were of peasant stock. It was hardly surprising if Zusen had grown up in the suspended city, as indifferent to the void beneath her feet as Drake would have been. For a moment he wondered if she was of noble blood, or merely the offspring of servants, but he didn't particularly care; there were far more pressing matters to concern himself with at the moment. 'I was a forester before Elyra fell on me. Most of the time, anyway.'

He stepped through the doorway on the far side of the airlock, trying to hide his relief at finally being on a solid deck. Elyra was already in the room beyond, and was talking to a man he didn't recognise; they both looked up as he entered the chamber with Zusen, which, judging by the piping and conduit running through it, was some sort of utility space. 'Here they are,' she said. 'As promised.'

'We were told three,' the man said. He was short, but muscular, and carried himself like a man used to trouble. He seemed to have found some recently, too, if Kyrlock was any judge, the mottling on one side of his face looking suspiciously like the residue left by the fragments from a nearby detonation. He was wearing a loose jacket and trousers in hive-pattern camo, though he clearly didn't feel comfortable in them.

'The others are right behind us,' Zusen said, breaking away from Kyrlock, and staring at the newcomer with an expression of delighted surprise. A moment later Trosk and Ven appeared, stopping short as soon as they entered the chamber.

'He's one of us,' Ven said, confirming Kyrlock's suspicion. Psykers seemed able to recognise one another, and he couldn't imagine any other reason why Zusen would suddenly lose interest in clinging to him.

'Mister Voyle here claims to be a representative of the Sanctuary,' Elyra said.

'So,' Trosk said. 'Are you coming with us, or not?'

'That's what we've been discussing,' Elyra said. She turned to Kyrlock. 'The one we met in the Gorgonid was right. They were surprised to see me, but grateful to us for looking after the juves.'

'Grateful enough to offer us a job, like he said?' Kyrlock asked, trying to sound indifferent. It was hardly likely that the man in the mine had been able to send an astropathic message about their encounter, or would even want to, so implying that he'd been included in whatever arrangement Voyle thought they'd made wasn't much of a risk.

Elyra shrugged. 'Sort of,' she said. 'He thinks they can use me, at any rate.'

'But not me.' Kyrlock nodded his understanding, having expected as much from the outset.

'Do you have a problem with that?' Voyle asked, addressing him directly.

Kyrlock shook his head. 'I preferred Greel's offer anyway,' he said. He glanced at Elyra. 'It's a good deal,' he reminded her, as if hoping to persuade her to reconsider.

'So's not having to look over my shoulder for the Inquisition every hour of the day,' Elyra replied.

'Well, I can't argue with that,' Kyrlock said. A sudden loud clanking sound from beyond the doorway drew everyone's attention, and the catwalk beyond began to swing towards the wall of the ore chute. He started to take a step towards the hatchway, intending to close it before the discharge hatches opened, but before he could complete the motion the door swung closed of its own accord, thudding firmly into place. He turned towards

Trosk, thinking the young wyrd must have been responsible, but the shaven-headed youth was staring at Voyle
with undisguised envy.

'If you hurry, you can catch up with the others before
the shuttle leaves,' Voyle said, gesturing towards the only
other door to the chamber.

'Sounds like a plan,' Kyrlock agreed. He nodded to
Elyra. 'You ever get tired of babysitting, get in touch.'

'Take care of yourself, Vos,' she said, her tone perfunctory.

'Yeah, you too.' No point in delaying any further: it
would only make Voyle suspicious, so he turned away,
walking towards the exit.

'Goodbye, Vos,' Zusen said, and he turned back, trying
to hide his surprise. The girl was looking at him with a
peculiar expression on her face. 'And thank you for pretending to like me.'

'I do like you,' Kyrlock protested automatically, completely taken aback, and a faint, sad smile ghosted across
the girl's face.

'I know exactly what people are feeling, remember?
Every time I got close to you, it made your skin crawl. But
you tried to hide it, and that was kind.' The smile flickered, like a wind-blown candle flame. 'So, thank you.'

'You're welcome,' Kyrlock said, and, moved by an
impulse he couldn't explain, raised his hand in farewell.
'Look after yourself, kid. 'Cause I guarantee you, no one
else will.' The same advice his brother had given him,
when they parted for the last time.

'I'm not a kid,' she said, the smile spreading, and her
voice devoid of petulance despite the words.

Kyrlock shook his head. 'No, I don't think you are any
more,' he said. Then he turned and walked through the
hatchway Voyle had indicated, fighting the impulse to
turn and check on Elyra for one final time. She was an
experienced Inquisition agent, he knew; he'd just have to
hope that would turn out to be enough.

Even so, as he hurried down the narrow passageway towards a swelling babble of voices, he wasn't quite able to shake the dreadful certainty that he'd never set eyes on her again.

The *Emperor's Justice*, Scintilla System
255.993.M41

'PIETER, COME IN.' Inquisitor Grynner glanced up from his desk, noting the data-slate in his apprentice's hand with a faint nod of his head. 'You have some additional information?'

Quillem nodded, and held out the reports he'd just finished collating. 'The *Ursus Innare* docked at Tarsus High less than an hour ago. Some of our assets are keeping an eye on it, but the only people who've disembarked so far are members of the crew.'

'I hardly think they're likely to usher a herd of illegal passengers through the main concourse,' Grynner said, a tone of mild reproof creeping into his voice as he paged rapidly down the screen.

'Quite so,' Quillem said. 'So I've been going over the schematics of the docking bays. You'll notice there's a potential route directly from the freighter's hold to the service passages, which could be used to move a large group of people relatively quickly.'

'Well done, Pieter,' Grynner said, selecting the indicated file, and skimming the contents. 'It would require careful timing, but I'm sure that's how they get their people aboard.'

'There's more,' Quillem said, trying not to look too pleased with himself, and certain that the inquisitor wouldn't be fooled for a moment by his pose of dispassion. 'The ship reported a minor systems failure, which delayed the discharge of her cargo for nearly seven minutes. And according to the port logs, which Mal... I mean Ullen, obtained access to, the same thing has happened on two out of her last three visits.' He was certain that the Deathwatch Techmarine had found the request to tap into the port's datacore a distasteful one, a misuse of his abilities, but with Malven dead, there hadn't been anyone else on the inquisitor's staff able to do the job. Not quickly and cleanly enough, anyway.

'From which we can infer that she's been smuggling people on a regular basis,' Grynner said.

'Quite.' Quillem nodded his agreement. 'There are only a few likely exits from the service tunnels, and I've asked Ullen to monitor the systems for any signs of unauthorised access.'

'Then all we can do is await developments,' Grynner said, placing the data-slate carefully on the surface of his desk. He steepled his fingers, and looked thoughtfully at his apprentice. 'And speaking of which, how are Carolus's people getting on?'

'They've gone to ground, as you anticipated,' Quillem reported. 'Carys tagged them at the Tricorn without any trouble, but they seem to have brought their own shuttle and pilot with them from Sepheris Secundus, so she wasn't able to follow them when they left. Something of an unexpected development, needless to say. Nevertheless, we do have a lead to their whereabouts.'

'The shuttle, presumably,' the inquisitor remarked.

'Exactly,' Quillem confirmed. 'She got word back to the *Justice* fast enough for us to be able to track it with our auspex suite when they took off again; they landed at a small commercial pad in the middle hive, close to the western industrial zone.'

'That hardly narrows it down much,' Grynner said. 'There are about seven million inhabitants of that district.'

'But their pilot appears to be very conscientious,' Quillem told him. 'He's either living aboard the vessel, or visiting it to run systems checks every few hours. Either way, he can lead us to the others.'

'No doubt.' Grynner looked up at his pupil, his expression grave. 'But be discreet, Pieter. We're dealing with experienced and resourceful acolytes, and we don't want to alarm them unduly. The consequences of that could be unfortunate, to say the least.'

'Of course, inquisitor,' Quillem assured him. 'Discreetly it is.' He handed Grynner a second data-slate. 'We've also intercepted the vox report Horst made to the Tricorn after the *Misericord* emerged from the warp. They seem to have had an eventful trip.' He waited for the inquisitor to skim through the file.

'Eventful indeed,' Grynner said, setting the slate down at last, in an uncharacteristically abstracted manner. 'This fresh encounter with a daemon is extremely disturbing, Pieter. It pains me to admit it, but we're out of our depth. We need advice from the Ordo Malleus.'

'Something of a problem when the information we're dealing with is subject to a Special Circumstances edict,' Quillem reminded him. 'We still don't know if we can trust anyone in the Calixian Conclave with it.'

'Karnaki's discreet enough,' Grynner said thoughtfully after a while. 'And he has little enough to do with his colleagues in any case. I'd already considered consulting him, but now, I think, we have no choice.'

'Then I'll make the arrangements,' Quillem said. He smiled, wryly, anticipating his patron's next remark. 'Discreetly, of course.'

Hive Sibellus, Scintilla
255.993.M41

'EVERYTHING QUIET OUTSIDE?' Horst asked, as Drake entered the living room of the apartment.

'As the grave,' Drake replied, inaccurately. This close to one of the industrial zones which generated the wealth and power for which Hive Sibellus was famous throughout the sector, silence was a luxury denied the labourers

who toiled around the clock in its furnaces and manufactoria. Day and night had little meaning to any of the
locals, as sunlight never penetrated this deep into the
middle hive: the street outside had once been open to
the sky, but millennia of subsequent construction had
buried it beneath almost a kilometre of masonry. Now
luminator poles burned unceasingly, and ducted fans in
the ragged ceiling did their best to suck the promethium
fumes farted by the lorries which rumbled along the carriageway every few minutes, laden with raw materials for
the manufactoria, away to the outside air: or, more likely,
Horst thought, to some other part of the hive, where it
would simply inconvenience someone else. 'Preferably
not mine.'

'Can't blame a girl for being careful,' Keira said, lowering the pistol crossbow she'd been aiming at the door
ever since she'd heard the first faint scuff of Drake's key
in the latchplate.

'Or a man,' Drake agreed, shrugging off the shapeless,
dull green hooded coat he'd bought from a local street
trader to help him blend in more easily with the local
population. As he discarded it, he revealed the Scalptaker
in its shoulder rig, angled for a fast draw. He and Keira
both glanced in Horst's direction as he spoke.

Nodding an acknowledgement, Horst let his hand fall
away from the butt of his bolt pistol. Keira's weapon
would have been far more discreet if Drake had turned
out to be an enemy after all, but around here, he suspected, no one would have heard the bolter being fired
over the general background noise in any case.

The strange thing was, no one else seemed particularly
bothered by it. Keira and Drake both slept soundly
enough, and Vex seemed able to ignore the noise completely, tapping away on the keyboard of the cogitator in
the corner of the room with unbroken concentration. Or
perhaps he actually enjoyed it, discerning some hymn to
the Machine-God in the never-ending racket. Only Horst

found the constant thrumming in the background, the periodic growling of the trucks, and the sporadic thuds and crashes from the manufactoria a perpetual irritation.

Perhaps he should just give up trying to ignore it, he thought, and take to sleeping in the shuttle, like Barda did. Despite the fatigue which had afflicted him ever since their arrival here, he smiled at the absurdity of the idea; that would be an abrogation of his duty to the Angelae, and to the Inquisition itself. Inquisitor Finurbi would expect to find them here, of that he was certain, and when their patron required their help, he was determined to be ready.

The apartment was one of several nondescript properties the Angelae network maintained in Hive Sibellus, but he'd chosen to take refuge in this one for several reasons. The fact that it was in the most densely populated of the districts in which Inquisitor Finurbi maintained a safe house was a major one, of course. Here, the Angelae could come and go completely unremarked; even Vex's distinctive robe was only one among the thousands worn by the small army of tech-adepts who laboured ceaselessly to keep the fabrication units turning out their quota of whatever it was they made.

The fact that many of the smaller, more valuable products left by air, and some of the essential equipment the Mechanicus acolytes required came in the same way, was also an advantage; the shuttle his team had arrived aboard would excite little comment, and they'd been able to rent a berth at a minor, and apparently struggling, commercial pad at a slightly less extortionate rate than he'd anticipated. They'd paid for a month up front, access to the inquisitor's coffers apparently still being available to those of his acolytes who required it despite his disappearance; mindful of the need for secrecy, he'd had Vex reroute the funds several times before claiming the money. He wasn't naïve enough to believe that a sufficiently determined researcher couldn't follow the trail back to them eventually, but he was sure they'd have moved on long before anyone managed to complete so complex a task.

His eyes moved momentarily to the firmly closed door at the far end of the room, where the main reason he'd chosen to go to ground in this particular bolthole was currently doing whatever it was he did all day. Marrak Vorn was the oldest surviving member of the Angelae Carolus, and one of the inquisitor's closest associates; only Elyra, who had undoubtedly shared his bed at one time, had an equal claim to their patron's confidence.

Vorn was one of the inquisitor's most crucial assets. He collated the reports of all the active cells, whether delivered in person, or by astropath to the Tricorn, and condensed them into digests suitable for retransmission to wherever Finurbi happened to be. If anyone knew the whereabouts of their missing patron, it would be Vorn.

Unfortunately, he'd turned out to have no more idea about that than Horst did, but had agreed with his assessment that when the inquisitor did break cover, this would be the first contact he made.

'So you might as well stay here for a while,' he'd said, shrugging, before returning to the array of vox receivers and data looms cluttering the back room, and at which Vex had stared with undisguised envy on their arrival.

'Speaking of being careful,' Horst said, 'I take it you made sure you weren't being followed?'

'I took all the usual precautions,' Drake assured him. Although the streetcraft required to spot and evade a hidden watcher had been strange to him at first, radically different from the battlefield skills he'd been trained in as a soldier, he'd been a willing pupil, and learned fast.

'How's Barda?' Keira asked, and Drake shrugged, dropping onto a sofa barely any cleaner than the one in their old suite in the *Beyonder's Hostelry*. Checking in on the young pilot was a regular and necessary chore, as Horst didn't trust the vox not to be monitored by whichever shadowy enemies had forced their employer underground, and had been the main reason he'd gone out that day.

'Fine, so far as I can tell.' It had been a risk leaving the Cloudwalker alone with the shuttle, but bringing him here with them would have been equally problematic; on balance, Horst felt, if they needed the little spacecraft they were likely to need it in a hurry, and the time saved by having Barda already aboard, ready to power up the engines before their arrival at the pad, might be crucial. 'But if you ask me, that boy needs to get out more.'

'Maybe he does,' Horst agreed. Barda's competence as a pilot was beyond question, but in most other respects he was dangerously naïve about life in the wider galaxy. He glanced at Drake. 'Do you think you can do something about that?'

'Not a problem,' Drake said, a peculiar mixture of eagerness and reluctance entering his voice. No doubt he'd relish the chance to get out of the claustrophobic apartment again, but Barda was hardly the companion he would have chosen for an evening's entertainment. 'I'll take him for a drink or something. Try and ease him gently into real life.'

'Somewhere quiet,' Horst counselled, and Drake nodded judiciously.

'Good idea. I'll leave the brawling and the joygirls for next time.' He smiled, clearly joking, and Horst felt a flare of irritation, which he quickly suppressed. This was no time for levity.

'Maybe I ought to make a recon sweep,' Keira said. 'Just to check that the street's clear.' She glanced at Drake, and brushed her purple fringe back out of her eyes. 'Danuld's getting good at spotting possible tails, but you never know.'

'Good idea,' Horst said. He doubted that anyone would have been able to find them as quickly as this, only two days having passed since they received Inquisitor

Finurbi's disquieting message at the Tricorn, but sending her out to make sure couldn't hurt, and would prevent her from becoming too restive. She was wearing a loose blouse and knee-length skirt, in muted shades of brown and grey, typical of the attire worn by the women of this quarter, so she should blend almost invisibly into the crowds in the street outside. 'Take care.'

'Always,' she replied, folding the crossbow with a neat economy of motion.

'Getting anywhere?' Drake asked, wandering past Vex to reach the small kitchen area, which an open counter separated from the rest of the room. Traces of an intricate mosaic were still visible on the wall there, between the larger patches of crumbling plaster and exposed brick where seeping damp from the levels above had broken most of the design away over the centuries, and Horst tried again to work out what it had once depicted. Rural scenes of some sort, he thought, of a kind which had ceased to exist on Scintilla millennia ago, if they ever had at all. Between the deserts and the jungles, and the sprawling hives, most of the planet was far too barren to even consider growing crops. All the food here, with the possible exception of the vermin hunted in the under-hives, had to be imported from nearby agri-worlds, thousands of shiploads a day arriving at the orbital docks for trans-shipment to the surface. If a warp storm ever hit the sector, Scintilla would die a protracted, agonising death, along with the billions of souls which thronged its hives.

'Not so far,' Vex said, his voice abstracted, continuing to work the keypad in front of him. 'I've been attempting to find some reference to archeotech finds matching the artefact we recovered from the Fathomsound, but there are no records in any of the archives I've been able to obtain access to.'

'We need more recaf,' Drake said, setting a pot on the stove.

'We need more of everything,' Horst replied. Vorn appeared to have frugal tastes, and hadn't been expecting so many visitors; after two days here, the meagre supplies they'd found in the kitchen were all but gone.

'I'll pick something up while I'm out,' Keira said, looking up from checking that the fall of her skirt didn't reveal the outline of the throwing knife strapped to her left thigh. She'd have another up each sleeve, Horst knew, the loose-fitting blouse concealing the scabbards on her forearms, and would probably be regretting that the local costume didn't offer her anywhere to hide her sword. She hitched up her skirt to clip the crossbow to the quiver full of quarrels already in place on her right thigh, any lingering Redemptionist scruples about modesty swept away by the dispassionate precision of the professional assassin. Horst averted his eyes politely nonetheless; as he did so, she glanced in his direction, with an expression which in anyone else he would have taken for flirtatious. 'Seen anything you'd like? In the market, I mean.'

'Just use your own judgement,' Horst said, then fearing he was sounding too priggish, he added 'but don't forget the recaf. If we run out of that, Danuld might decide to move in with Barda instead.'

'Damn right,' Drake said, infusing the last scrapings of gritty brown powder from the bottom of the can with the water he'd just boiled. Horst suspected that a fair amount of rust had gone into the beverage too, but if Drake could live with that, he certainly could. 'I'd move in with Horus himself if he could guarantee me a mug in the morning.'

Keira's jaw tightened, clearly unhappy with the casual mention of the arch-heretic who'd struck down the Emperor, but controlled the impulse to chide Drake for his irreverence with an effort only Horst, with an arbitrator's affinity for the subtle cues of body language, had been able to spot.

'Then I'd better do my best to find some,' she said. 'Even Horus wouldn't deserve Danuld as a house guest.' Apparently satisfied that her weapons were invisible, she waved a farewell, and left the flat.

THE STREET OUTSIDE was bustling, as always, and Keira took a moment to orientate herself, standing in the narrow entranceway to the apartment building. Out of habit she scanned the crowds passing by in both directions, the two flows of humanity interpenetrating with an ease only hivers could match, having grown up dodging their way through uncounted numbers of their fellow citizens. No one seemed to be loitering, observing the doorway, or keeping a covert eye on the building from further down the street. The sidewalk on the far side of the traffic-choked carriageway was harder to check, being obscured every few seconds by thundering lorries or an omnibus packed with manufactoria hands shuttling between hearth and shift, but her training and experience enabled her to discount the possibility of hidden watchers behind the cover they afforded rapidly enough.

It took a while longer to calm her own mind, however. Danuld hadn't meant anything by his tasteless little joke, she knew, but it rankled nonetheless; then a sudden doubt assailed her. Instead of reacting with righteous anger, as she certainly would have done until recently, she'd let the matter go; she had even responded with an impious witticism of her own.

She was changing, she could feel it, and a sudden, unfamiliar sensation uncomfortably like panic suffused her, rooting her feet to the pavement. All the comforting certainties she lived by were shifting; although that had been happening to some extent ever since Inquisitor Finurbi had taken her away from the crusade in Ambulon, and set her feet on a different path. Bringing the unrighteous to the Emperor's judgement had always been relatively uncomplicated in the past, though, the holy work enough in itself to justify the moral compromises she'd been forced to make to carry His retribution to those who deserved it, but now the words of the psyker she'd confronted aboard the *Misericord* rushed back to haunt her: was her faith really flawed, and if it was, were her barely acknowledged feelings for Mordechai to blame?

Taking refuge in the demands of duty, even one as mundane as replacing the dwindling supply of recaf, she slipped easily into the turbulent throng of humanity. Sure-footed as only a graduate of the Collegium Assassinorum could be, she passed through the dance of intersecting bodies as though they were no more substantial than mist; only one passer-by, a local habwife whose red hair stood out in stark contrast to her drab surroundings, actually touched her, brushing past with a reflexive and insincere apology, which she couldn't be bothered to acknowledge.

There was a small cluster of market stalls in a square a few hundred metres from here, she recalled, in what had apparently once been the ballroom of the palace of some aristocratic family when this district had been at the crest of a spire, towering over the bulk of the main hive. The porticoes surrounding her were encrusted with coats of arms, identifying the long-forgotten owners of mansions long since built above and forgotten, into which the middle-hive workers had seeped as insidiously as the water which now saturated every vertical surface, trickling down to erode the faces of the statues, and shroud everything in a clinging miasma of damp. Now the magnificent rooms were split into smaller apartments, like the one Vorn occupied, or their walls crudely broken through to make way for new thoroughfares.

Halfway to her destination, Keira hesitated. A heavy handcart was rolling along the pavement, a tottering pile of furniture balanced precariously on top, and a family orbiting around it, bickering among themselves in shrill voices while they attempted to keep the load from falling into the gutter by hopeful random shoves at anything which seemed particularly loose. It was a common enough sight in the mid-levels; lodgings were often lost due to structural failure, increases in rent, or the appearance of the owner or their agents in some previously overlooked corner of their holdings with visible weapons and scant sympathy for squatters. A bow wave of displaced pedestrians were moving ahead of the miniature juggernaut, and Keira stepped aside reflexively, unwilling to be caught in the crush or forced into the carriageway.

A pair of double doors stood open to her left, and she took another step inside the building, away from the commotion. It occurred to her that she'd never noticed this particular entrance before, taking it for the front of another apartment house on the few occasions she'd passed it, but the reality of its interior was very different.

Warm candle flames lit the space beyond the narrow hallway she found herself in, casting yellow light across a cloth-shrouded altar, and an icon of Him on Earth mounted above its centre. Keira felt the breath catch in her throat, and made the sign of the aquila as she continued walking into the modest little chapel with no more volition than thistledown on the wind.

'Can I help you, young lady?' The speaker seemed hardly any older than she was, but she let that pass, and nodded anyway. He could only have been in his twenties, straight out of the seminary probably, and his robes seemed as new to the priesthood as their owner; despite his youth his hair was already beginning to thin, and a wispy blond fringe hung over his forehead like a theatre curtain waiting to descend. He was trying to grow a beard, probably in an attempt to give himself an air of gravitas, but it hadn't taken very well, and clung to his face in patches, like the fragments of mosaic in Vorn's kitchen.

'I think so, yes,' Keira said, looking back at the icon of the Emperor again, so lost in the wonder of the moment that she barely noticed the crash of falling furniture and the raised voices in the street outside. He had guided her here, she was suddenly certain of it. 'I've been having doubts. About the right thing to do.'

'Perhaps you should simply trust the Emperor to guide you,' the priest said. 'He cares for us all, as a father does for his children.'

'That means he punishes us when we do the wrong thing, though, doesn't it?' Keira said.

The priest looked troubled for a moment. 'I prefer to think he gives us the choice, trusting us to do the right thing, and lets us take the consequences if we don't,' he said carefully, after pausing just long enough to formulate a sufficiently simple answer to a complex theological question. 'If your intentions are pure, He gives you His blessing.'

'That's just it,' Keira said, feeling a tremendous surge of relief, as she was finally able to put her doubts into words. 'I'm not really sure if my intentions are pure any more.'

'I see,' the priest said, glancing towards a curtained-off recess in the corner. 'If you'd feel more comfortable in the confessional, we could always...'

'Here's perfectly fine,' Keira said, reluctant to leave the benevolent gaze of the man above the altar.

'Good.' A faint air of relief washed over the priest. 'Then what seems to be the problem?'

'I work with someone,' Keira said, allowing her clothing to lie for her, and let the priest think she was one of the local labourers. 'And, recently, I've started to have these feelings about him. Ones I think might be wrong.'

'I see.' The young man looked at her, with what he probably hoped was a grave and understanding expression, but which merely made him look well-meaning and a little simple-minded. Under the circumstances, Keira was happy to settle for that. 'Is he married?'

'Throne on Earth, no!' Keira said, so outraged that she forgot for a moment where she was, and who she was speaking to. 'What do you take me for?' Her left hand was already dropping to receive the knife up her sleeve, and she checked the motion just in time; killing a priest, particularly on holy ground, would have damned her for eternity without a doubt.

'Nothing at all,' the priest said hastily, then realising how that must have sounded, he shook his head. 'I mean, not blameworthy in any way. You're clearly unmarried yourself.' Round here, it seemed, if you were married, you advertised the fact with a nose stud, although whether that was true of the whole hive, or just this particular district, Keira had no idea. 'So if he's free too, I must confess I don't really see what the problem is.'

'The problem is, I used to be sure of what the Emperor wanted of me,' Keira said. 'Now I've started to doubt my own judgement. People rely on me to do the right thing, and I'm not sure I know what that is any more.'

'I see.' The priest clearly didn't, but wanted to help, which was something at least. 'Have you prayed for guidance?'

'All the time,' Keira said.

'Then Him on Earth will undoubtedly show you the right way to proceed,' the priest replied, manifestly happy to pass the problem on to a far higher, and unassailable, moral authority. He must have sensed Keira's disappointment, because he added, 'After all, He brought you here.'

'Yes,' Keira agreed. 'I really think He did.'

'So listen to what He tells you,' the priest advised. Then he smiled, a little wistfully. 'But it's my opinion that love is His gift to us all, if we're willing to receive it. Or have the courage to take it when it's offered.'

Keira considered this. If courage was the absence of fear, then she'd proven her possession of it countless times in her short and violent life. But the hesitancy she felt now was completely different from the way she'd felt before going into combat against the Emperor's enemies. Well, perhaps this was a battle too, against some aspect of herself. The only question was, what kind of a test was she being faced with? The courage to act on the feelings she'd started to experience, or the courage to turn her back on them forever, dedicating herself entirely to the path of destruction?

FOURTEEN

Hive Tarsus, Scintilla
256.993.M41

'IT'S ALL RIGHT, I know him. Let him in.' Greel looked up from behind a plain wooden desk, which had probably been chosen to fit the image he liked to project of a moderately prosperous businessman, with an air of polite curiosity. The only thing spoiling the impression was the hand he kept hidden behind an open drawer, undoubtedly containing a gun. It seemed there were plenty of men like the one he pretended to be in Hive Tarsus, the economic, and, thanks to the presence of the Cathedral of Illumination, spiritual centre of the Scintilla System. On his way here, Kyrlock had passed innumerable offices just like this, every one dealing with the storage, forwarding, or dissemination of the trade goods which flowed through the mercantile hive like blood through a beating heart. Where better for an agent of the Shadow Franchise to base himself, he thought, where his clandestine business would be hidden among uncountable legitimate movements of goods and people?

The thugs who'd been attempting to bar his way fell back at once, except for the groaning one he stepped over as he crossed the threshold, and Kyrlock smiled as he nodded a greeting. 'I've come about that job you offered me,' he said.

'I assumed as much.' Although it was the first time Kyrlock had been able to see him clearly, in the daylight flooding through the heavily tinted windows, Greel seemed just as much a creature of the shadows as he always had. His hair was indeed grey, although his face was darker than the Secundan had expected, browned by the sun which managed to penetrate even this deeply into the middle hive, and his eyes were a startling blue, like distant lightning. His clothes were blue as well, a pale, pastel shade, which would be better at reflecting the light and heat, cut loosely to facilitate the flow of air around his limbs.

Kyrlock had already known a little about the conditions here before he arrived, as Elyra had spent a fair amount of time on Scintilla in the past, and had taken care to fill him in as best she could on the most important aspects of all the main hives: at least the ones she'd had occasion to visit. Fortunately, one of them had been Tarsus, so he'd landed with some idea of what to expect.

Perhaps because of this, despite the brightness of the sky, which had struck him at once as being so different from the perpetual cloud cover of his home world, and the suffocating heat which had enveloped him the moment he'd set foot on the baking surface of the shuttle pad, Kyrlock felt quite at home here already. He'd discarded the heavy furs he'd been wearing throughout the journey at once, leaving them in the hostel he'd found lodgings at shortly after disembarking, secure in the knowledge that no one here was likely to steal them. What had happened to his fellow passengers, he had no idea, and cared even less; he'd spent a few moments conversing with one of the franchisemen he recognised as having accompanied Greel on his visit to the hold, getting directions to his office, and by the time he'd left the cargo pad where the shuttle had grounded, they'd all disappeared.

Despite its size, and the very different temperature, Hive Tarsus reminded him quite strongly of Icenholm. He hadn't spent long in the suspended city, but he'd been there long enough for the similarities to be obvious as soon as he'd begun to orientate himself.

Tarsus was a huge tangle of buildings, streets and infrastructure, slung between vertical support columns so vast that, on most worlds, they would have been considered hive spires in their own right. Set in the middle of a baking, inhospitable desert, the further down and deeper inside the complex web of interwoven structures a location was, the more comfortable it felt; so, in contrast to most such communities, the rich and powerful reserved the lowest levels for themselves. Here, in the middle hive, conditions were tolerable enough; but out towards the skin, Kyrlock knew, they grew hellish.

'Here on your own?' Greel asked, his eyes staying on the doorway as his unexpected guest advanced into the room. A faint air of disappointment seemed to hang about him for a moment, as his battered minion finally staggered to his feet and pulled the door closed, with a last, venomous look at the former Guardsman.

'For the moment.' Kyrlock sat in the visitor's chair in front of the desk without waiting to be invited. He knew Greel's type well, the Tumble back home was full of them, although none were quite so successful as the franchiseman appeared to be. The key to dealing with them was not to seem too deferential; any sign of weakness would be pounced on like a tree weasel scenting blood. 'Elyra decided to carry on babysitting for a while.'

'I see.' Greel nodded, and poured himself a glass of water from a decanter on his desk. He didn't offer Kyrlock one, but then the Guardsman hadn't expected him to. He'd taken the initiative, and now Greel was subtly underlining who was really in charge around here. 'And you didn't.'

'I didn't get the chance,' Kyrlock said. 'Voyle only wanted Elyra.' He wasn't sure whether the man across the desk knew that he'd been smuggling wyrds, but suspected not; if he was wrong, Greel would probably be able to deduce the reason for the Sanctuary's interest in his travelling companion. Either way, it wouldn't make a lot of difference to his story. He shrugged. 'The juves have got used to her, I guess.'

'I suppose so,' Greel said, his obvious indifference adding weight to Kyrlock's assumption that he really had no idea who or what he'd been dealing with.

Having given the franchiseman enough time to get used to the idea that he wasn't going to get a percentage of the jewellery Elyra was carrying after all, Kyrlock carefully baited his hook. 'She did say to let you know she's still interested in that bit of business you discussed, though,' he said, as if he'd only just recalled the message. With a bit of luck, motivated by greed, Greel would contact the Sanctuary to arrange a meeting with her. That would allow him to keep track of Elyra after all, despite their enforced separation.

'Very sensible of her,' Greel said. 'Voyle's contacts are mostly on the void station, and you need planetside pull to shift what she's carrying.' He shrugged, a wintry smile elbowing its way onto his face. 'I hope she's getting paid in advance for whatever she's doing. I'm afraid our friend's operation took a bit of a dent last week, so he might not have the cash reserves he's used to.'

'Did you find out what happened yet?' Kyrlock asked, trying not to sound too interested. This might be information Horst, or even the inquisitor himself, could use.

'Someone hit his warehouse on Scintil VIII,' Greel said, sipping at his drink. 'There are all kinds of rumours flying around, but it sounds like the Arbites to me. They cleaned the place out, and left a lot of damage; I don't know of anyone else who could have brought that amount of firepower to the party.'

'Then it sounds like she'll be needing that job sooner than she thought,' Kyrlock said. He paused for a moment. 'Come to that, I want to know where I stand. If you've got some work for me like you said on the ship, I want it. If not, sorry about your people. I don't think I broke them much.'

'Not as much as I will, if they don't start doing the job I pay them for,' Greel said, smiling faintly. 'But getting past them was a pretty impressive audition. Without weapons, too.'

'Chainaxes tend to get noticed in the street,' Kyrlock said. 'Shotguns too.' There were people walking around out there with visible weapons, but they were a small minority, and most of them had stared at him in implicit challenge as he'd passed. Franchise operatives, probably, posted to keep the regular gangers from getting in the way of the serious business of making money. A couple had even accosted him, but Greel's name had been enough of a passport to avoid any more serious confrontations.

Not that he'd have been particularly concerned if it hadn't been; he was certain he could take care of himself if he needed to. Even so, he preferred to avoid conflict if he could: Elyra was relying on him to contact the other Angelae, and he couldn't risk getting hurt in a pointless brawl before doing that. The shotgun was still with him, in case things got ugly, comfortably cocooned in the grox-hide holdall he'd purchased from a street vendor outside his lodgings, and which he carried casually in one hand; he hadn't had to draw it to get past Greel's watchdogs, but it had made a handy club.

'Sometimes that's useful,' Greel said. 'But not today.' He leaned back in his chair, his hand moving away from the drawer at last, and looked at Kyrlock appraisingly. 'All right, you want to work. Fine by me. I've got a little job needs doing, and judging by the noise I heard a few minutes ago, the man I had in mind for it needs to see a medicae now.'

'Big fellow with an ear missing?' Kyrlock asked, and Greel nodded.

'That's the one. Pyle. You'll like him when you get to know him, everyone does. Great sense of humour. Doesn't bear grudges either, you'll be glad to hear.'

Kyrlock nodded too. 'I think I broke his arm. Hit it with a shock maul.'

Greel's eyes narrowed a little. 'You're not carrying a shock maul.'

'No.' Kyrlock shook his head. 'He was. I sort of borrowed it.'

'I see.' Greel chuckled quietly to himself, although his eyes never left Kyrlock's face. 'What did you do with it afterwards?' His eyes flickered towards the holdall, although Kyrlock was sure he'd correctly divined its contents the moment he'd arrived.

'I gave it back,' Kyrlock said. 'I'd finished with it.' Pyle hadn't been in any condition to use the weapon, and he'd no further use for it himself; he preferred the greater reach the chainaxe gave him when it came to close combat. Besides, it had intimidated the hell out of the franchisemen still standing in Greel's outer office, which had been the whole idea; no one discarded a functional weapon in the middle of a brawl unless they had something better to hand, or were supremely self-confident. After that, no one had been keen to tackle him, and find out the hard way what he had in reserve.

'Then you're either a suicidal idiot, or precisely the man I've been looking for,' Greel said. 'No doubt time will tell which it is.' He reached inside the drawer again, and produced a thin sheaf of papers, to which a pict had been clipped. It showed a faintly worried-looking young man with dark hair and earnest brown eyes, which reminded Kyrlock incongruously of a hound hoping for a titbit. He was wearing a padded jacket, which meant he was from a long way further down the hive; either minor nobility, or a high-ranking servant in somebody's household.

'Who's that?' he asked, feeling he ought to show a little interest.

'Marven Dylar. He owes me some money, which he's been rather slow to repay.' Greel shrugged. 'True, I've been off-world for a while, but he knows where my office is.'

'Do you want me to kill him?' Kyrlock asked, trying to sound casual about it. He'd taken lives before, in self-defence, or in the heat of combat, but he was by no means certain that he could commit cold-blooded murder. To his well-concealed relief, Greel was shaking his head.

'Of course not. I want my money back. Or what he originally offered in exchange, which would be preferable.' The franchiseman shrugged. 'If you can't manage to extract either, then by all means, make an example of him if you like.' Another thought seemed to strike him. 'You can read, I take it.'

'Well enough,' Kyrlock said, taking the sheaf of papers, and stuffing them into the bag next to the shotgun. 'Do you want me to get in touch when it's done?'

'If you see the need,' Greel said. 'Otherwise, just come back here. You shouldn't have any more trouble getting in.'

Hive Sibellus, Scintilla
256.993.M41

As an initiate of the Cult Mechanicus, Vex was supposed to be above such petty human frailties as frustration, but right now that was pretty much what he was beginning to feel. Not that he would ever have admitted it in such plain and simple language. The manuscript, which they'd gone through so much to recover, had nothing to say about the origins of the bone fragment, and little about its arcane properties that they hadn't already deduced for themselves. That had left him with no other option than to go looking for clues elsewhere, and the search had not been going well.

'The data I need is proving particularly elusive,' he said, keeping his voice uninflected with rather more effort than usual. He was certain that the archives of the Tricorn would have the answers he sought, but Inquisitor Finurbi's message had effectively curtailed that avenue of investigation, and he'd already wrung dry the few other repositories of information on archeotech available to him.

'Is there anywhere else you could try?' Horst asked, with the air of a man knowing the question is both foolish and futile, but determined to ask anyway in case he turns out to be wrong.

'Not from here,' Vex said, turning away from the cogitator keyboard for the first time in days. Communing with the data-net had been stimulating at first, but by now he was beginning to feel fatigued, too many of his superfluous fleshly components demanding rest and nutrition. Drake was making recaf in the kitchen unit, and his mouth suddenly flooded with saliva as he caught the scent of it.

'Where then?' Keira asked, placing a steaming mug and a plate full of sandwiches on top of the main data loom, and Vex had to force himself not to snatch at them straight away. Ingesting nutrient was a distasteful necessity, the pangs of hunger and thirst a lingering human weakness, and it would be unseemly for a member of his order to give in to their dictates without interposing a little reason to master them first. Nevertheless, he appreciated the gesture, even overlooking the egregious disrespect towards so fine an example of the Omnissiah's bounty that using it as a table implied.

'The Temple of the Omnissiah in the upper hive has an extensive archive,' he said, trying to ignore the excessive sensory input being provided by the nourishment. 'Not all of it accessible remotely by technotheological means. Some of the older records only exist in hard copy, and there are rumoured to be artefacts there of great antiquity.' Feeling that he'd demonstrated the superiority of reason for long enough, he took one of the sandwiches and bit into it. If his companions were amused at how quickly the food disappeared, they concealed it well; Vex simply felt quietly pleased with himself for dealing with the matter as expeditiously as possible. 'It may be that one of those will be sufficiently similar to the one we recovered to enable us to deduce its origin and purpose,' he concluded, a trifle indistinctly.

'Can you get in there without any risk?' Horst asked.

For a moment Vex wondered what he meant; shrines to the Machine-God were havens of order and efficiency in a complex and muddled galaxy, and although they contained their fair share of perils for the unwary, one of the Omnissiah's anointed would have little to fear from random electrical discharges or the like. Then he realised what the team leader was driving at.

'The risk of being observed is acceptably low,' he said, reflexively trying to calculate the odds of an unseen watcher identifying him as he entered the shrine. 'Hundreds of members of my order enter and leave the premises every day, and I would simply blend into the aggregate.'

'It's who you might meet inside that worries me,' Drake said, looking up from preparing more sandwiches. 'We know at least one senior tech-priest's involved in the conspiracy.'

'Magos Avia,' Vex confirmed. 'I hadn't forgotten.' Nor was he likely to. Corruption among the Adeptus Mechanicus was almost unthinkable, the very notion an affront to all the principles he'd espoused on first donning the white robe of his calling. Nevertheless, Technomancer Tonis had built the mysterious psychic amplifier on Sepheris Secundus, apparently with the connivance of the mentor who'd brought him into the order in the first place.

'What have you been able to find out about him?' Horst asked, accepting a plate of food and a steaming mug from Keira with a nod of acknowledgement. Keira smiled back, rather more than the simple exchange would seem to warrant so far as Vex could see, and settled on the dusty sofa.

'Very little,' Vex said. 'He has visited Scintilla in the past, but not for at least eighty years, and has spent the vast majority of the last two centuries on the Lathe Worlds. No doubt the records there would be considerably more helpful, but unfortunately they're unavailable to us without a voyage of significant duration.'

'I'll ask Vorn to contact any Angelae there,' Horst said. 'They might be able to dig something up.'

Vex rather doubted that, but nodded anyway. 'There may be some traces of his last visit in the physical archives of the shrine,' he said. 'Nothing so dramatic as the ones he left in the Fathomsound, of course, but if he was researching the artefact at the time, I should be able to follow the trail he left. Even if he wasn't, we should gain a clue as to his wider agenda.'

'Tonis was a psyker before he joined the Mechanicus,' Drake said, emerging from the kitchen with a pair of plates and a couple of mugs wobbling precariously as he tried to balance them in his overfull hands. He handed one of each to Keira without mishap, and sat, beginning to tackle his own food with evident relish. 'Could Avia have been one as well?'

'Highly unlikely,' Vex said, trying not to show how uncomfortable he felt at the notion. The idea that even one of his brethren had been tainted by the warp was bad enough, let alone that he hadn't been the first.

'Maybe he's possessed by a daemon,' Keira said, a trifle indistinctly. 'Tonis was, so maybe his mentor is too.'

'Tonis's case was completely unprecedented,' Vex said, keeping his voice level with an effort, despite the manifest absurdity of such an idea. 'It's inconceivable that Avia could be equally afflicted.'

'Unless the bone thing had something to do with it,' Drake put in morbidly, staring at the pocket in Vex's robe where the mysterious artefact currently resided. 'We still don't know what it is, or where it came from. Maybe it does attract daemons.' He looked around as he spoke, apparently unhappy with the disquieting thought which had just struck him.

'When I find the appropriate records, perhaps I'll be able to answer that question,' Vex said, a trifle more sharply than he'd intended. As so often, the conversation was getting bogged down in pointless speculation and ludicrous flights of fancy.

'Maybe they're not the records we should be looking at,' Keira said, with a thoughtful expression. 'Perhaps we should be trying to find out more about the daemon.' She looked directly at Horst. 'If Hybris is right, then this is the first time ever a tech-priest has been possessed. If we find out how and why, maybe we can start to see what's going on here.'

'Good point,' Horst said. 'The only problem is, we don't know anything about daemons, or where to go to find out.'

'Don't be so dense, Mordechai.' Keira shook her head, looking faintly amused. 'We know exactly where to go. The south tower.'

'Let me get this straight,' Drake said. 'You want us to break into the Tricorn, sneak past hundreds of acolytes, dozens of inquisitors and an honour guard of Space Marines, then raid the archives of the Ordo Malleus?'

'Don't be silly, Danuld.' Keira glanced up at him, smiling in the way she always did when someone told her that what she wanted to do was impossible; and, to her credit, they hadn't been right all that often. 'You'd be killed before you took a dozen paces.'

'Quite,' Horst agreed, nodding quietly. 'It would be suicide to try.'

'Exactly,' Keira said soberly. 'Which is why I'll be going in alone.'

QUILLEM WAS GETTING bored, and didn't mind admitting it; but he'd been an acolyte for long enough to know that the periods of tedium on an investigation tended to outweigh the running and shooting by a considerable margin. Just as well, too, he thought sourly: after the fiasco aboard the void station, a bit of tedium was positively welcome.

He was loitering as close as he dared to the Angelae's safe house, on the corner of the street, where he could remain half-concealed if any of the missing inquisitor's agents happened to emerge. A mass-transit station stood close at hand, and he blended easily into the inchoate mass of passengers waiting to board; if any of the passersby streaming past had noticed that the service he wanted never seemed to come, they kept the thought to themselves.

The noise and the stench surrounding him had long since faded into the background of his consciousness; he'd grown up somewhere not dissimilar to this, although, unlike most of his friends, he hadn't been content to remain there, trudging to the manufactoria every day until he died. Instead, he'd volunteered for the hivesteading programme, lured by the prospect of carving out a new life for himself in some newly reclaimed tranche of the underhive, only to find that it hadn't been reclaimed nearly as much as the authorities in the far-distant spire seemed to think; mutant raids were still frequent, and justice turned out to be the personal property of anyone with enough gelt to hire a bounty hunter.

Much to his surprise, Quillem had thrived in this unpromising environment, swiftly acquiring both a gun and a reputation for being able and willing to use it; talking his way into a job as a caravan guard had been easy, and after a year or two he'd started collecting bounties as a sideline. It hadn't been a bad life, all told, and he'd probably still have been enjoying it if Inquisitor Grynner hadn't turned up one day looking for a guide into the lower deeps. The young Quillem had acquitted himself well against the genestealer cult which turned out to be lurking down there, and when the inquisitor moved on, he'd taken a new protégé with him, eager to learn all he could from his new mentor.

Well, he'd certainly done that, Quillem thought wryly. Grynner had shown him how to use his intellect as well as his weapons, eventually placing him on the path to inquisitorial status himself, although he was well aware that many interrogators never proved themselves worthy to take that final step. Even so, he'd come a long way from a place like this; all in all, he had a lot to be thankful for.

A flurry of movement near the house he was watching caught his eye, a mere eddy current in the endless stream of pedestrians, but it was enough: someone had left the building, moving with evident purpose. He allowed himself to drift with the flow of bodies surrounding him, angling towards the street corner, where he'd be able to see more clearly, but without creating any answering ripples in the crowd which an astute observer would be able to notice in turn.

'Holy blood!' The exclamation slipped unbidden from his lips. Instead of a single subject to keep under observation, there were three of them, all leaving at the same time. He began to regret ordering Carys to take some rest, although Throne alone knew, she could clearly do with it. Then the habit of dispassionate analysis his mentor had taken such pains to inculcate in him began to take over.

Sythree was wearing a jacket and skirt indistinguishable from those of the other women in the crowd, although her purple hair and Redemptionist bandana were still visible from this distance. If she hadn't changed her clothes, she was probably still carrying the tracer Carys had planted on her when they'd brushed past one another in the street outside the temple; good enough, he'd just have to vox the *Emperor's Justice* and ask them to monitor the signal. Drake was with her, moving towards the funicular leading to the upper levels; that meant he was probably on his way back to the shuttle, to check in with their pilot again. Plenty of time for Carys to pick him up en route, if she hadn't turned her comm-bead off, but he doubted that; she prided herself on her professionalism at all times, and would have left it activated while she slept. In fact, she'd probably kept it in her ear, for just such a contingency.

That left the tech-priest, who had parted from the others, and begun to walk up the street towards him. Fine, he had his target.

'Hound one to kennel.' He spoke quietly, a hand raised to conceal the fact that he seemed to be talking to himself, and feigned interest in a display of hand tools in the grimy shop window in front of him. 'Three hares started, repeat three. Active trace on one, hounds tracking both the others. Acknowledge.'

'Acknowledged, hound one. Trace confirmed.' To his surprise, the unmistakable voice of Ullen the Techmarine responded. Malven was proving difficult to replace, none of the other tech-priests aboard the *Emperor's Justice* having his specialised skills, which meant the Deathwatch Techmarine was still having to fill in for the fallen acolyte at moments like this. Quillem hoped he wasn't finding the distraction from his regular duties too onerous.

'Hound two. I heard that.' Carys cut in almost at once, confirming his assessment of her readiness. 'Who and where?'

'Drake, the funicular. Sythree's with him, but disregard if they split up; the *Justice* is tracking her.' His target, the tech-priest Vex, was getting closer now, but he just had time for one more transmission before closing the link. 'Smart move with the tracer, Carys.'

'Thanks.' The thief cut her connection, apparently cheered by his encouragement. Good, he needed her sharp.

Quillem turned away from the hardware store, and glanced at his chronograph, as if wondering how long his connection would be. He'd timed the motion exactly, keeping his face averted from Vex without appearing to deliberately avoid him, but he needn't have bothered with subtlety; the tech-priest's attention was entirely on the timetable attached to the pole supporting the illuminated sign which marked the embarkation point for services to the adjacent sector.

The interrogator smiled, and joined the queue, waiting until a couple of smelters, an overseer and a habwife had taken their places behind Vex before moving into position. It seemed this was going to be easier than he thought.

Tarsus High Orbital Docks, Scintilla System 256.993.M41

'ENJOYING THE VIEW?' Voyle asked.

Elyra nodded. 'Impressive,' she said. Mindful of her assumed persona, she inflected it to sound as though she was anything but impressed, but in truth she had been. After Kyrlock had parted from the little group of psykers she'd wondered what sort of hellish bolt hole they'd be conducted to next, picturing something akin to the hold aboard the *Ursus Innare*, but their eventual destination, after an indeterminate time spent scuttling through the warren of service tunnels which riddled the vast structure, had been completely different.

It was the smell she'd noticed first, a damp, heavy odour like wet loam after rain, seeping round the seals of a heavy door like dozens of others they'd passed; she'd expected to move on, but Voyle had paused, gazing intently at the locking plate. A moment later the hatch had swung open, and their guide vanished into the space beyond.

Elyra followed, with a glance back at the trio of juvies; Zusen was hard on her heels, while Trosk was shepherding Ven in the right direction, his attention mostly taken up with the mumbling seer. Thanks to the momentary distraction, she'd already taken a couple of steps after Voyle before her surroundings truly registered.

'This is amazing!' Zusen had said at her elbow, her voice tinged with awe.

Elyra had nodded. 'Beats the last place they stuck us,' she agreed, choosing her words carefully. She and Kyrlock had made their own contact with the Franchise smuggling ring, rather than relying on the Sanctuary as intermediaries, but the phrase made her sound a part of the group herself, rather than a chance-met stranger; and, if challenged about it, as she half-expected Trosk to do, she could plausibly claim to have meant Greel and his Franchise operatives.

'Needs must,' Voyle said, glancing back at his quartet of charges with a faint air of amusement, which led Elyra to suspect that he'd anticipated an awed reaction. 'We needed the ore scow to get you off-planet, but there's no reason you can't be a bit more comfortable now you've arrived.'

Comfortable was hardly the word Elyra would have used, but it was certainly an improvement on the hold of the *Ursus Innare*. They were walking on grass, which yielded beneath her feet in the fashion which, being void-born, she always found faintly peculiar. The floor was covered in a thick layer of soil, which had leaked from corroding knee-high containers arrayed in what

had once been a neat grid, but which was now looking
distinctly irregular. The grass was everywhere, underfoot,
and choking the raised beds, in which a variety of weeds
and straggling vegetable crops competed for space.

'I never get tired of looking at it,' Voyle said, bringing
her back to the present.

Elyra could certainly see why. The derelict agrideck
he'd conducted them to was on the outer skin of the
orbital dock, protected from the void by a geodesic dome
of metre-thick armourcrys. The disc of Scintilla was visible above them, cloud wreathing its pastel face, through
which patches of the surface could be glimpsed, like the
visage of a dowager behind a veil of lace.

Familiar with the world they were orbiting, Elyra was
able to make out the brighter smudges of the three continents, and the pale, sickly oceans surrounding them,
whose grey and polluted waters blended into the lowering clouds, imparting a pearl-like sheen to the whole
globe. The sere equatorial continent was right below, and
she tried to make out the position of Hive Tarsus, but
there was no real clue; the sun was almost exactly behind
the docks, which meant it would be close to noon on the
surface below. If she was going to spot the megalopolis
with the naked eye, she'd have to wait until the sun was
rising or setting down there, casting a shadow tens of
kilometres long.

'I take it you spend a lot of time here, then,' Elyra said.

'You're fishing,' Voyle replied, with a trace of amusement.

'Sorry,' Elyra said, making sure the apology sounded
insincere. 'Old habits. I'm not used to trusting people.'

'Then I hope we can convince you to, given time,' Voyle
said.

'Maybe you can,' Elyra said, her eyes still on the disc of
the planet. The northern continent was comparatively
free of cloud, and she tried to pick out the location of
Hive Sibellus, wondering if Carolus was down there,

marshalling his forces from his chambers in the Tricorn, or had already begun to move against the network she'd infiltrated. The more information she could pass on to him when she finally found a way to get in touch the better: they'd hunted heretics together long enough to know just how true the old adage that knowledge is power really was. 'So what exactly is this place?'

'An old agridome,' Voyle said, producing a lho-stick from an engraved silver case which had floated out of his pocket, and was now hovering in mid-air in front of him. 'Got hit by the blight a few years ago, and we pulled a few strings to make sure no one ever got round to rescinding the quarantine order.' The silver case rotated towards Elyra, and she shook her head.

'No thanks, I don't.' Voyle's casual use of his powers for something so trivial shocked her profoundly, but it seemed to be part of the ethos of the Sanctuary that the psykers affiliated to it should simply take them for granted, rather than regarding them as a curse, or at the very least a potential danger. Concealing her own unease, Elyra focused her will on the end of the thin tube, and kindled it, while Voyle was still reaching for his lighter.

'Thank you.' He smiled, and inhaled the smoke. 'Feels good, doesn't it? Being able to be who you really are, without some vacwitted prole screaming "Witch!"'

'Is that why you joined the Sanctuary?' Elyra asked. 'To be yourself?'

'Something like that,' Voyle said, inhaling more of the fragrant smoke. 'I'd spent most of my life hiding what I could do, and when they found me, the relief... Well, I don't have to explain that to you. They offered me refuge, in the Sanctuary itself, but I thought I could do more good here.' He shrugged. 'On Scintil VIII, I mean.'

'Do more good how?' Elyra asked.

'Helping the rescued.' He glanced at Elyra, a trifle embarrassed. 'That's what we call you, the people we

save. I had a small cargo brokerage on Scintil VIII, and
like most businessmen there, I was evading the odd tariff
and paying protection money to the Shadow Franchise. It
didn't take much to convince them that I wanted to
diversify into smuggling, and they agreed to bankroll me.
Which meant they could move their merchandise on and
off the station more easily, and we could shift some of
the rescued through their network.' He smiled. 'Oddly
enough, we both ended up making money out of it,
which was a bit of a bonus. Although I suppose that's all
at an end now. They'll be looking for a new partner on
the void station.'

'What happened, exactly?' Elyra asked, seeing a flicker
of hesitation in the man's eyes before he answered. 'If
we're supposed to start trusting each other, we could start
with that.'

'We got hit,' Voyle said. 'We'd just moved a lot of people on to the Sanctuary, more than we'd ever tried
rescuing before. Luckily they'd gone by then, but their
escort was still around, and they decided to make a fight
of it. Things got messy.'

'Well, at least you finally made it to the sanctuary yourself,' Elyra said. To her surprise, Voyle laughed.

'This isn't Sanctuary,' he said. 'Nowhere in the
Imperium is safe for our kind. This is just another waysta-
tion, like the hole in the Gorgonid where you met the
others.'

'So where is it?' Elyra asked, and Voyle shrugged.

'I've no idea. Out there, somewhere.' He gestured
vaguely in the direction of the stars above their heads.
'The Inquisition have ways of getting information out of
you. Better not to know in the first place.'

'Better for everyone else,' Elyra said. 'Not so good for
you if you get picked up.'

'Yes,' Voyle said, his good mood of a few moments
before thoroughly deflated. He ground out the stub of

his lho-stick on the corroded edge of a weed-choked vegetable bed, leaving a faint grey mark. 'We'd better make sure that doesn't happen then, hadn't we?'

FIFTEEN

Hive Sibellus, Scintilla
257.993.M41

'SHE SHOULD BE getting close by now,' Barda said, replacing his tankard on the table between them, and pitching his voice low enough not to be overheard by anyone else in the bar.

Drake nodded. They'd returned to their usual berth after flying Keira to a shuttle pad on the northern fringes of the hive, generally used for short suborbital hops to Tarsus or the docking ports above it, where she'd be close enough to the Tricorn to make her way to her final destination without difficulty. It was heavily used, particularly by passenger vessels, and Barda had hoped they'd avoid attracting any undue attention by blending in among the constant stream of arrivals and departures.

Keira had disappeared into the mass of passengers thronging the terminal like a raindrop into the sea as soon as they'd landed, and Drake tried not to wonder if he'd ever see her again. He would have preferred to remain where they were, in case she needed backup, but the risk of detection would have been too great, so they'd returned to the mid-hive almost as soon as she'd left the boarding ramp.

Grounded, with nothing to do except wait for further orders, the shuttle had begun to feel claustrophobic, and it hadn't taken long for Drake to start chafing under the enforced inactivity. Mindful of his promise to Horst to begin introducing Barda to the world beyond his cockpit, and quietly desperate for some displacement activity, he'd suggested finding a tavern somewhere in which to kill a little time.

Much to his surprise, the young pilot had agreed, and now sat opposite him in a quiet booth towards the rear of an establishment Drake's greater experience of such things had led him to consider a suitable one for his first attempt to acclimatise his charge to the ways of the galaxy. The furniture was solid, iron-grey plastek worn smooth by generations of buttocks, with few signs of damage, and the carpet on the floor still clung grimly to the majority of its nap. Somewhere for the clerks and overseers to stop for a bit of light refreshment, and maybe a plateful of food that actually tasted more or less like it was supposed to, on their way to and from their shifts. The bars frequented by the factory hands would be a great deal livelier, and a great deal more to his own taste, but they'd be a minefield for someone as socially inept as Barda, and a shuttle pilot wouldn't normally set foot in a place like that anyway.

'How's the ale?' Drake asked, trying to deflect the conversation onto a safer, more neutral topic. He was as certain as he could be that they weren't being overheard, but the more experienced Angelae had made it abundantly clear that the Special Circumstances under which they were now operating meant that very little could be taken for granted. Better safe than sorry was a maxim he'd learned the truth of very quickly in his first firefight, and he'd been applying the lesson religiously ever since.

'Pretty good,' Barda said, taking another swallow from his mug. 'But I'd better not have too much. If we need to fly again today…'

'You'll need a clear head,' Drake agreed, hoping the call to pick Keira up would come soon, and drained his own tankard. It wasn't that strong, compared to the stuff he'd been used to drinking in the Imperial Guard, but it had a pleasant, light flavour, with a lingering hint of caba nuts.

'Can I get you another?' A woman was hovering beside the booth, a couple of empty tankards in her hand, and she reached down to add Drake's to her collection.

'Yes, thanks,' Drake said. He glanced across at Barda. 'You too?'

'Why not?' The young pilot swallowed a couple of times, and handed his own mug to the barmaid. 'Just the one.'

'I'll be right back.' The woman smiled, and departed towards the bar, the angle of the booth taking her out of sight in a moment. Her hair was red, unlike most of the people Drake had seen here, and for a moment he felt a formless flash of *deja vu*; then he shrugged and dismissed it, trying instead to find some safely neutral topic to discuss.

THERE WERE MORE ways into the Tricorn than most people realised, but Keira had dismissed all the obvious ones before she started. Simply landing the shuttle there, as they had when they first arrived, would have been easiest, but the risks were too great; if the shadowy enemies Inquisitor Finurbi had gone blue to evade really had infiltrated the Calixis Conclave, they would undoubtedly have identified the sturdy little craft on its previous visit, and be on the alert for its return. Besides, that would have left Danuld and Barda dangerously exposed while they waited for her, and if it all went klybo, as she was only too well aware that it might, they'd be caught in the crossfire. No point in them getting killed as well.

The main gate was a little more plausible, but she wasn't keen on that idea either. Though hundreds of people passed through it every day, they were scanned, checked, monitored and observed by dozens of Inquisitorial functionaries, any one of whom could be a dupe of the conspirators their patron was hunting, or an active member of the cabal in their own right.

That left the postern gates, through which inquisitors and their acolytes arrived and departed on clandestine errands of their own, and which were monitored, if anything, even more closely than the main one. Clearly none of those would do either. Not normally, at any rate; but if she was bold, and the Emperor was with her, there just might be a way.

Keira shrank into the shadows cast by the setting sun, which was glowing a rich, blood-red, like the coals of a furnace, and smiled, still enough of a Redemptionist to take the sight as a good omen. Above her, the triune towers loomed, thrown into stark silhouette by the crimson orb.

Working quickly, she shed the skirt and blouse which had allowed her to blend in with the mid-hive drones, fading even more into the background as the cameleoline synsuit she'd worn beneath them began to imitate her immediate environment. From habit, she checked the feel and fit of her weapons, although she was so precisely attuned to them that she would have known at once if anything was amiss: knives strapped to each forearm, her left thigh, and in the small of her back, the pistol crossbow and its clip of quarrels at the top of her right leg. She'd carried her sword bundled up in a carryall, which she abandoned too, slipping the scabbard into its accustomed place with a sense of rightness, the subtle weight, missed for so long, making her feel properly balanced again.

This was going to work, she could sense it, as surely as if the Emperor Himself was standing at her shoulder.

Smiling at the thought, she held herself still, waiting for the right moment to strike, like the predator she was.

Hive Tarsus, Scintilla
257.993.M41

KYRLOCK HAD WAITED until nightfall before setting out on the commission Greel had given him. The air was cooler after dark, more bearable for a man who'd spent most of his life either trudging through snow or watching more of it fall. The delay had given him time to catch up on a little sleep, grab some food, and become better orientated in the strange latticework hive he supposed he'd better start to call home.

At night, the vast construction took on a strange and majestic beauty, the complex warp and woof of the interwoven streets and thoroughfares lit from all directions, so that it felt almost as if he was walking though a multifaceted jewel of incredible proportions. Looking up, he could see the complex tangle above him glowing with diffused light, layer upon layer of it, open and airy, but dense enough to block out any hint of the darkling desert beyond. Shortly after dawn, the light of the sun would begin to seep through again, bringing its suffocating heat with it, but for now Kyrlock breathed the cool air gratefully.

Greel's dossier on his target had been thorough, though mercifully brief; although he'd been telling the truth when he told the franchiseman he could read, Kyrlock had neglected to add that it was a skill his life as a Secundan peasant had left him with little time or inclination to hone. Being able to make out the warning signs around the Gorgonid, and the occasional baronial proclamation, had been enough intellectual exercise for him up until now, and the effort of scanning the sheets of paper, with their minuscule print, had left him with a faint headache, which the fresh night air was beginning to dissipate at last.

Well, cool air, at any rate: he didn't suppose it would taste particularly fresh anywhere in a hive city like this one.

According to the information he'd been at such pains to decipher, Dylar lived in a far more affluent district, almost a kilometre downhive from where he was standing. There were transport networks he could have used, looking rather like the cable cars which had linked the various levels of Icenholm back on Sepheris Secundus, though on a much bigger scale, but Kyrlock decided not to avail himself of them; not while he was descending, at any rate. He'd spent long enough cooped up on the ore scow getting here, and relished the chance to stretch his legs properly again. Besides, he'd lived in the wilderness long enough to know that you could only really get the flavour of a place by feeling it beneath your feet. This environment might be new and strange, but he was sure he'd be able to master it before too much longer; after all, his life might depend on it.

A short distance ahead of him a huge staircase fell away to one side of the road like a petrified waterfall, soaring across a vertiginous gap to a street about twenty metres away and twice that below; dozens of people were ascending and descending it, and a couple of bushmeat stalls were doing reasonable business on the wide landing about halfway down.

Well, down was the way he wanted to go; calm and unhurried, he started to descend.

Hive Sibellus, Scintilla
257.993.M41

THE SHRINE OF the Omnissiah had been everything Vex could have hoped for: a haven of logic and order, in sharp and welcome contrast to the swirling maelstrom of disorganised humanity in the hive outside. He'd entered the precinct unchallenged, the white robe of his calling mingling with the others moving around the premises with evident purpose, and he'd had to exert a modicum of reason to remain focused on the purpose of his visit instead of becoming distracted by the dazzling examples of the Omnissiah's bounty displayed about the imposing entrance hall.

Gaining access to the archives had been a mere formality; after a quick exchange in binary, the callow technographer manning the altar of information had directed him to the appropriate vaults, and left him to his own devices. That had been a welcome surprise: Vex had expected to repeat the ritual of identification he'd had to undergo on his previous visit, some years before, but the Machine-God had smiled on him, and the security protocols still recognised his biometric parameters.

His researches into the provenance of the peculiar artefact had been fruitless so far, although he had to confess to enjoying them; he'd examined a good deal of arcane lore, and even been permitted to handle a few so-far unclassified fragments of revenant technology, which the custodian of the vaults had assured him almost certainly pre-dated the Heresy, if not the Imperium itself.

He'd had a little more luck in his secondary goal of trying to find traces of Tonis's mentor, the mysterious Magos Avia. The magos had indeed been following a line of research which tended to suggest that the artefact had been in his possession during the occasion of his previous visit, and that he'd been as much in the dark about its origin and properties as Vex currently was; even more so, in fact, since the Angelae already knew that it could affect psykers in some fashion, a fact Avia had evidently discovered somewhere else in the decades between consulting the records here and forging an alliance with his ill-fated protégé.

There seemed little point in lingering, but Vex remained anyway, reluctant to depart; the old hunger to discover one more fact, to make one more connection, was on him, and he continued to work at the data lectern he'd found, sifting through the mountain of information one dust mote at a time.

KEIRA WASN'T SURE how long she'd been waiting, but the passage of time didn't matter in any case. Nothing did, beyond the calming mental discipline of watching, immobile, from her vantage point in the shadows. For the first time in days she felt truly at peace, the storm of confusion which had ruffled her composure for so long replaced by the reassuring certainties of instinct and action; even the reflection that her life was on the line, with death a more probable outcome than survival, carried with it the comfort of the familiar.

She heard the approaching vehicle long before she saw it, the growling of an engine approaching along a road most of the locals shunned; though broad, and well paved, it led to the postern gate in the wall of the Tricorn through which those suspected of heresy, or the assistance of its perpetrators, were taken to be interviewed. A few of them even returned the same way, their innocence established to the satisfaction of the interrogator assigned to their case, although all would be profoundly affected by the experience. Most, however, remained inside the bastion for the rest of their lives, which, on the whole, tended to be short.

As the transport came into view, Keira could feel the Emperor smiling on her again, His approval of her plan more than evident. Why else would He have arranged things so that the snatch squad approaching were driving a modified civilian vehicle, like several she'd ridden in herself on the occasions she'd been operating out of the Tricorn?

Externally, it looked like nothing more than a battered utility van, indistinguishable from thousands of others in this sector alone, with twin rear doors giving access to an enclosed cargo compartment. The right front grimeguard was painted in ochre primer, the rest in grubby white, and the logo of the florist's shop to which it ostensibly belonged was beginning to flake away.

Internally, Keira knew, it would be very different. Tech-priest acolytes would keep the mechanical systems at the peak of efficiency, and thick armour plate would protect both the crew compartment and the box in the back where the suspects rode, chained to steel mesh benches, and surrounded by wards designed to dissipate any warp-spawned powers they might possess. Fortunately, she didn't need to get through the armour plate to get the result she wanted.

The tiny crossbow was already in her hand, the string drawn back and locked. Normally she wouldn't have considered wasting a quarrel on so solid a target, but she wasn't out to destroy it; just inconvenience the crew a little. If she missed her mark, they'd never even know she'd been there.

But she wasn't going to miss, she knew that, just as surely as she knew that faith in the Emperor was the path to redemption. The shot felt right, and she took it, her finger tightening on the trigger before her conscious mind had even registered the fact. The thin dart struck the metal mesh covering the air intake, and penetrated, lodging itself deep in the guts of the engine.

As the van got nearer, the steady growl deepened in pitch, and it began to lose speed, moving forwards in a series of increasingly violent jerks. If she correctly remembered what Vex had once told her, the quarrel would have jammed the fan keeping the engine cool, and once it stopped, the mechanism would rapidly overheat.

Time for the next part of her plan. Moving rapidly, as the crippled van was almost abreast of her hiding place by now, she pulled up the sleeve of her synsuit, and drew her sword. A single stroke was all it took to open up a shallow gash in her forearm, which wouldn't affect her fighting ability if she turned out to need it, but provided enough blood to smear the bright metal in a convincing enough manner. She added a few patches to her face and bodyglove too, then ran out into the road.

She'd timed it perfectly, which she took as further proof of divine approval, arriving in the driver's field of view just as the abused engine finally coughed and died.

'Inside! Quickly!' Keira shouted, brandishing her bloodstained sword in one hand, and her rosette in the other; reassured that the apparition facing him was another Inquisition operative, the driver bailed out of his cab, a heavy-calibre autopistol held ready for use. He kept her covered in any case, Keira noted approvingly, while a second acolyte, a vulpine-faced woman with hard eyes, remained behind the armoured door, her lascarbine seeking a target in the shadows beyond. 'They're right behind me!'

'Who are?' the man demanded, making sure he got a good look at her rosette. Forged ones weren't exactly common, but had been known, although the difference would be immediately obvious to anyone familiar with the genuine article.

'You think I stopped to ask their names?' Keira asked, with waspish incredulity. 'Heretics, four or five of them, all armed. They had a wyrd with them too. He must have jinxed your truck before I cut him down.'

'It did just stop for no reason,' the woman agreed. She was wearing a comm-bead, and tapped it. 'This is Sharyn. Contact with solo acolyte, possible heretic band pursuing. Vehicle disabled. Requesting backup.' She listened for a couple of seconds, then nodded curtly. 'They're on their way,' she said, glancing at her partner.

'Good.' He nodded too, his eyes on Keira. 'So who the hell are you?'

'Vanda Shawn,' Keira said, reverting to an alias she'd used once on Quaddis, and which she was sure no one here would have heard of. 'I was just on my way in to report, and ran across the pack laying in wait for you. Who's in the back worth rescuing?'

'Throne knows.' Sharyn scanned the shadows uneasily. 'Just the usual scofflaws so far as I could see.'

'We can sort that out later,' her partner said. The postern was opening even as he spoke, and a squad of storm troopers boiled out of it in skirmish formation, fanning out to secure a perimeter around the stalled truck, their hellguns at the ready. 'Let's get the meat in for processing before their friends take another crack at us.'

'Not much chance of that now,' Sharyn said, apparently a lot happier behind a screen of Inquisitorial troops than exposed in the middle of the street. A second squad had followed the first, breaking down into individual fireteams, to advance up the alleyway Keira had appeared from in short bursts of alternating movement, while their comrades kept them covered. 'Not if Vanda got the wyrd. They'll have been counting on him to give them an edge.'

'So you say,' the man said, apparently unconvinced. He unlocked the rear doors of the van, and threw them open. 'Heretics are insane by definition. I wouldn't put it past them to have a go anyway.' A blast of foetid air, redolent of fear, sweat and worse swept over them. Evidently several of the prisoners had been unable to control their bladders, and at least one had soiled him or herself in their terror. 'Everybody out. One wrong move and I'll shoot the lot of you.'

'What's up, Kal?' A pair of guards armed with shotguns and shock mauls were seated reasonably comfortably on the ends of the benches closest to the doors, training their weapons on the widening gap. They both relaxed when they recognised the driver, although Keira was pleased to note that they kept a wary eye on her. Both were wearing carapace body armour and storm trooper-pattern helmets with integral respirators, although whether that was for additional security in case of an attempted breakout using chemical weapons or simply due to the stench she couldn't have said.

'Ambush, apparently.' Kal gestured impatiently towards the open gate. 'If you want to debate it, let's do it inside.'

'Sounds good to me.' The guard who'd spoken before unlocked the chain securing the prisoners' shackles to the bench on his side of the van, and after a moment's hesitation his colleague followed suit on hers. He man-handled the first prisoner to his feet. 'Out.' The man took a hesitant step, hindered by his leg irons, and, like all the others, unable to see through the thick grox-hide hood covering his head. 'Faster than that.' The guard shoved him hard in the small of the back, and he fell out of the van, landing with an audible smack on the rockcrete roadway, unable to break his fall with his hands mana-cled behind him. Although most of the others merely stumbled as they disembarked, several of them fell too; one of them, a young woman in a satin gown, the qual-ity of which marked her out as a member of the aristocracy, cracked her head against the kerbstone as she went down, and lay inert for a moment, evidently stunned, until the female guard goaded her into motion again with the shock maul.

'Come on, up, you dozy bitch.' Seizing the opportu-nity, Keira grabbed the dazed debutante, yanking her roughly to her feet, heedless of the hysterical sobbing behind the muffling hood. 'Get moving.'

The stratagem was working, just as she'd hoped; the confused mass of prisoners was being driven towards the open gate like grox to the slaughter pen, and she was right in the middle of the group. The encircling storm troopers were pulling in to form an escort around the inchoate mass, their attention still focused outwards in anticipation of an attack, and the effort of herding the blind, shuffling captives was keeping the guards from the van too busy to bother her with any further questions. Kal even glanced in her direction with a brief nod of thanks before moving in to separate a couple of prisoners who'd collided, threatening to bring the whole sorry cavalcade to a halt.

Their storm trooper escort hurried them through the outer door in a matter of moments, then redeployed to cover the return of the scout detail. Keira glanced around. She knew the layout of this entrance well, having delivered her share of recidivists to the oubliette on previous tours of duty at the Tricorn, and abandoned her whimpering charge in the middle of the floor without a second thought. The guards were still distracted by the business of counting heads and preparing their prisoners for processing, while the storm troopers' attention was directed outside, and the gatekeepers were too busy booking in the new arrivals to take any notice of one of the escorting acolytes.

Perfect. A handful of strides took her to a small side door leading directly to the interrogation suites, generally only used when time was of the essence in an investigation, and a suspect needed to be put to the question immediately. The soundproof door thudded closed behind her, cutting off the echoing babble of the gatehouse, and she padded down the connecting corridor, sheathing her sword as she went. From here on, she simply had to look as if she belonged, which wasn't difficult; this was a part of the Tricorn she knew well.

The Emperor continued to smile on her; only a couple of the suites were in use, judging by the volume of screaming, and she passed through the rest of Information Retrieval without meeting anyone she knew. A well-remembered door led to the main courtyard, and a few moments later she was comfortably lost in the throng of other acolytes going about their business.

Dusk was falling in earnest by this time, and Keira picked up her pace a little, hurrying towards the looming bulk of the south tower. She'd been lucky so far; now things were about to become really difficult.

* * *

PERHAPS THIS HADN'T been such a good idea, Drake thought, leading the young pilot's stumbling steps up the boarding ramp of the grounded shuttle. The ale hadn't been that strong, he was certain, and the Cloudwalker had definitely been watching his intake: nevertheless, Barda was legless. He must have less of a head for alcohol than Drake had realised.

'Are you going to be all right?' he asked, steering Barda towards his bedroll, and the pilot nodded, grinning broadly.

'Never better. Need the head, though.'

'Well you can sort that out for yourself,' Drake told him, and sat in a nearby seat while his young charge disappeared into the small washroom at the rear of the passenger compartment. Come to that, he was feeling a little light-headed himself, which seemed strange; he definitely knew he'd only had a couple. Well, three. The one he'd bought at the bar, and the two extra rounds the barmaid had brought over to their booth.

Barda was still busy, and, judging by the sounds emanating from the tiny chamber, was liable to remain so for some time. Drake settled back in his seat with a contented sigh, and thought about the barmaid. A bit old, maybe, thirty standard at least, but a nice figure nevertheless. If he hadn't been babysitting, he might have tried his luck there. That smile when she turned away the last time, that had been the next best thing to an engraved invitation. Almost like a piece of home, too; redheads were quite common on Sepheris Secundus, but he'd hardly seen any since he'd arrived on Scintilla. Not since…

'Oh, nads,' he said, suddenly feeling very sober indeed. A pin-sharp fragment of memory was floating on the surface of his mind: the hall in the Tricorn where Horst had received the box from Inquisitor Finurbi. The team leader had glanced up from the counter, and for a fraction of a second had made accidental eye contact with a woman a few paces away. A redhead.

He reached for the comm-bead in his ear. 'Mordechai,' he began without preamble, 'I think we have a problem.'

SIXTEEN

Hive Sibellus, Scintilla
257.993.M41

THE MAIN HALL of the Ordo Malleus tower was the same size and shape as the one Keira was familiar with in the redoubt of the Ordo Hereticus, but the crowd of bustling acolytes she'd expected to find there was largely absent. She'd tensed inwardly as she passed the outer guards, feeling the sanctioned psykers scratching at the surface of her mind, but the blocking techniques she'd been taught at the Collegium had repelled them as she'd hoped; all they'd been able to pick up was a litany of devotion to the Emperor, hardly the thing a heretic would have had at the forefront of their thoughts.

The towering figures of the Grey Knight Astartes flanking the main entrance were another matter, and she observed them covertly as she passed, alert for the faintest flicker of movement which might betray their intention to attack. They were more colourfully armoured than she'd expected, holy images and bright crimson purity seals encrusting the smooth ceramite, and their Chapter badge, a book pierced by a dagger, was bordered in red on gilded shoulder guards. The bolters they carried were twin-barrelled, even bigger and more intimidating than the ones she'd seen in the hands of the Sororitas, and she felt a warm stirring of righteousness as she pictured the havoc they were capable of wreaking on the Emperor's enemies. Despite her apprehension, none of the towering warriors moved a millimetre, but as she passed them she could feel their scrutiny, and a faint chill seemed to follow her into the depths of the citadel they guarded.

Despite herself, Keira shivered. The cavernous antechamber was dimly lit, votive icons and warding sigils everywhere she looked, and the mosaic in the floor seemed to writhe like smoke, its details obscured by the enshrouding darkness. Probably just as well too, she thought. The few Ordo Malleus operatives in sight moved quietly about their business, in ones and twos, occasionally conversing in hushed tones, like pilgrims in a cathedral.

The young assassin had never thought of herself as particularly imaginative, but a faint miasma seemed to cloy the air in here, as though something unwholesome was pushing against the fabric of reality, and the echo of its presence was somehow able to seep through into the material world.

'Can I be of assistance?' a reassuringly supercilious voice asked, and she looked up to find an Administratum clerk of indeterminate age and gender peering at her over a counter like the one in the Hereticus tower where Mordechai had been told to wait for the servitor.

'I need information,' Keira said, having discovered a long time ago that the best way to get what she wanted was to act as though she was perfectly entitled to it. 'About cases of possession involving members of the Adeptus Mechanicus.'

'The library is on level seven, section three,' the scribe said, apparently taking it for granted that her mere presence was all the authorisation she needed. Not for the first time, the young assassin blessed the lack of imagination which the Administratum seemed to consider a prerequisite for advancement among its ranks. 'The staff there should be able to direct you to the material you require.'

'Thank you,' Keira said, hoping she sounded sufficiently bored. 'And section three would be...'

'The second doorway to the left,' the scribe said, indicating one of the shadowy portals allowing access to the depths of the tower.

Keira nodded, and set off in the indicated direction, fighting the impulse to look back and see if the scribe was tripping an alarm. There was no point in fretting about all the things that could go wrong. If she was discovered, she'd just have to bluff or fight her way out as best she could.

Luckily the internal layout of the tower was very similar to the one she was already familiar with, and she was able to orientate herself reasonably quickly. The corridors were as shadowy as the main concourse had been, and the few people she passed engrossed in their own affairs; it was all uncannily reminiscent of the early stages of the Angelae's descent into the bowels of the *Misericord*, and she shivered in spite of herself, hoping that wouldn't prove to be an omen.

Level seven was at the bottom of a wide flight of stairs, and as she descended, Keira was heartened to see that the low levels of illumination she was growing used to were beginning to rise, which meant she must be getting near her destination. You needed light in order to read, after all. A few more minutes were sufficient to confirm that her guess was right, and that the library was just ahead.

She pushed her way through a pair of wooden doors, carved with a snarling visage which made her palms sweat to look upon, to find herself in front of a small desk. Instead of another Administratum scribe, as she'd expected, a woman in a green robe looked up at her, and Keira found her breath knotting for a moment. Only one of the woman's arms was there, the entire right side of her body contorted and diminished, like the wax dropped by a melting candle. The human side of the bisected face, in which a single blue eye was visible, looked at her appraisingly.

'Yes?' the crippled acolyte asked, her voice rasping a little as it forced its way past the ruin of her throat.

'I'd like to see anything you've got about possessed tech-priests,' Keira said, in the same matter-of-fact tone she'd employed with the scribe in the entrance hall.

To her surprise, the recognisable part of the woman's mouth twisted in a parody of a smile. 'I get it,' she rasped. 'You've just started working for the ordo, right?'

'It's my first time down here,' Keira admitted, and the librarian nodded.

'Thought so. Some of the senior acolytes think it's funny to send a rookie on a pointless errand. When you get back upstairs, tell them to come and see me. I take a very dim view of people treating my archives as a joke, and they really don't want me to come looking for them.'

'Nevertheless,' Keira said, trying not to wonder what the woman thought she could do if sufficiently provoked, and suddenly sure she didn't want to find out, 'I'd be grateful if you could check. Just so I can say I've been thorough.'

'If you insist on wasting your time,' the woman said, moving her sole remaining shoulder in what might have been a shrug, 'you can use that data lectern over there. Just enter "tech-priest", "possession", and hit the cross-reference icon. I'll say the incantations for you from here, as they're a bit technical. But I guarantee you won't find anything.'

'I wouldn't be too sure about that,' a new voice said, and Keira turned, to find a man standing behind her. He appeared to be in late middle age, although his hair was still dark, and his narrow face had an air of brooding intensity about it. He wore the robes of an inquisitor, the sigil of his calling hanging on a gold chain around his neck, and his eyes, as black as his hair and vestments, seemed to look through her, to some distant realm.

The librarian inclined her head in a gesture of respect. 'Inquisitor Karnaki,' she said. 'How can we be of service?'

'I think you could start by granting this young lady her request,' the inquisitor said, 'as we appear to be engaged on the same line of research.' He looked at Keira narrowly. 'Then perhaps we can discuss the matter of daemons, Miss Sythree.'

Hive Tarsus, Scintilla
257.993.M41

THE CHILL IN the air grew ever more marked the deeper Kyrlock descended, until, by the time he found himself approaching his destination, his breath was becoming visible, faint puffs of vapour appearing with every exhalation. After a lifetime spent in the frozen forests of Sepheris Secundus, this was nothing new, but it was only when he observed the phenomenon that it struck him how used he'd become to not seeing every breath he took; and how much his life had changed in so short a time for that to be so.

The streets here were wider and quieter, and the passers-by dressed in thicker fabrics than the ones he'd seen uphive, flaunting the wealth and social status which allowed them to live in the chillier regions. Elyra had told him that the real aristocracy were supposed to dwell in palaces carved from solid ice, deep in the hive roots, although, knowing a little more than she did about sub-zero temperatures, Kyrlock doubted that. He'd taken the precaution of bringing his furs with him, jammed into the holdall along with his shotgun, and decided to don them as soon as he'd first noticed the vapour condensing in front of his face. A lifetime of experience had left him all too aware of how easily the growing chill could sap his strength by almost imperceptible degrees, and he felt ever more grateful for his foresight as the temperature continued to fall.

That his clothing marked him out as an off-worlder didn't bother him in the slightest; his red hair did that already, as did his facial tattoos, neither of which he'd seen anyone else sporting since his arrival. If anything, the furs worked to his advantage, most of the people he passed apparently assuming they meant that he was from the really cold regions still far below, and stepping out of his way with respectfully averted eyes. The irony of that, highborn locals deferring to a Secundan peasant, amused him greatly, but he wouldn't allow himself to enjoy it too much. He was here to do a job, and doing it well would consolidate Greel's confidence in him, helping to further his mission for the Angelae. On the other hand, some things were just a gift from the Emperor...

'You there!' he called, gesturing in a peremptory manner to a couple of men loitering at the corner of the street, who had clearly been taking a covert interest in his approach. They were dressed alike, in dark tunics of a deep burgundy hue, with gold piping on the sleeves, and a similar streak of shiny decoration down the seams of their trouser legs. Local watchmen, employed by the neighbourhood households to keep the riff-raff from encroaching on the precincts of their betters. Both carried lascarbines, slung from their shoulders in a casual manner which would have earned them a flogging from Sergeant Claren, Kyrlock's late and unlamented superior in the Imperial Guard, although he doubted that either would be able to hit the broad side of a starship from inside the hold if they actually had to use them.

Reassured that the man approaching was really entitled to be there, because no one who wasn't would have accosted them, the two watchmen pulled themselves into a semblance of attention. The older one appeared to be in charge, and bowed, with an overelaborate flourish. 'Delegated to meet your acquiescence, your worship,' he said. 'How may we be of assurance?'

For a moment Kyrlock wondered if he'd be better off just shooting the pair of them, then shrugged. 'I want directions,' he said. 'To Lower Chrysoprase. Fifty-third level, south terrace.'

'Ah,' the senior watchman said. 'That's alimentary from here. Deduct your steps to the temple yard, and you'll see Chrysoprase from the South Present. Across the causistry to your left, and you'll arraign at the fifty-second littorel, one down from your destitution.'

'Thank you,' Kyrlock said, wondering if this was some patois peculiar to the portion of the hive he now found himself in, or if the man was just simple-minded. The latter, he suspected, as the younger of the two watchmen spoke up for the first time.

'You won't find many of the scholastical gentlemen there at this time of night, though,' he said.

'Not a problem,' Kyrlock assured him, barely managing to suppress a grin. 'I'm not after many of the scholastical gentlemen. Just the one.'

'Would that be one particulate indivisible, sir,' the senior one asked, 'or by way of a germane inquiry?'

'One in particular,' Kyrlock said, turning to follow the road towards the visible outline of a temple, some hundred metres or so in the direction they'd indicated. 'One very much in particular.'

Hive Sibellus, Scintilla
257.993.M41

DESPITE HIS SLOW progress, Vex was feeling quite satisfied with his work so far. He'd managed to eliminate a considerable number of dead ends, and, although he hadn't managed to discover anything new about the mysterious fragment of ivory, the data he had collated was quite fascinating in its implications. It seemed several attempts had been made in the last few millennia to control psychic phenomena through technotheological means, and, although the details remained elusive, all had apparently ended in failure. Some of the new information might help him to make more sense of Tonis's manuscript, however, and uncovering the principles behind the operation of his infernal machine might enable him to deduce more about the properties of the artefact.

'Hybris.' Horst's voice was in his comm-bead, and, judging by the edge of asperity in it, the team leader had been attempting to attract his attention for some time. 'For Throne's sake, respond!'

'I'm here,' Vex said, tearing himself away from the dizzying dance of fact and conjecture with the greatest reluctance. 'I'm afraid I've only been able to make the most cursory–'

'We've been compromised,' Horst said, cutting him off before he could complete the sentence. 'Get back here. We're pulling out as soon as we hear from Keira.'

'Acknowledged,' Vex said, abandoning the lectern, and erasing all the files he'd been perusing. It wouldn't take long for a sufficiently skilled datasmith to reconstruct them, but if their shadowy enemies were able to trace him here, at least the delay might buy the Angelae a little more time to identify them and prepare a response. 'I'm returning at once.' With a last, regretful glance at the workstation he'd been using, he turned away; whatever he'd learned so far would just have to be enough.

QUILLEM'S VIGIL OUTSIDE the shrine of the Machine-God had been as tedious as he'd expected. For some hours he'd drifted around the plaza fronting the temple of the Omnissiah, concealed among the perpetual crowds who congregated here bearing cherished or malfunctioning devices to be blessed by the tech-priests, fortifying himself as best he could with barely identifiable viands and bitter recaf dregs purchased from the swarm of street traders inevitably drawn to any large gathering of people.

'Carys.' He leaned casually against a girder supporting an overhead walkway, wondering if he dared drink any more of the contents of the paper cup in his hand, and pretending to do so to conceal his use of the comm-bead from anyone who happened to glance in his direction. This was a good vantage point, one he'd used several times in the hours since he'd arrived here and seen Vex disappear through the gaping bronze doors embossed with the cogwheel symbol of the Adeptus Mechanicus. 'Anything happening your end?'

'Nope. Drake and the flyboy are staying put aboard the shuttle.' She sounded as bored as he felt. 'I spiked their drinks in the tavern they went to, and stuck a microvox under the table, hoping they'd let something slip, but they're too good to start talking shop in the open, even with a bit of help. Sorry about that.'

'Well, it was worth a try,' Quillem said, trying not to feel uneasy about the risk she'd run. Carys clearly felt she had something to prove since the fiasco aboard the void station, and it was making her reckless. 'But we need to keep a low profile, remember.'

'Don't worry,' Carys assured him. 'I'll be careful.'

'Good,' Quillem said, hoping she would, and cut the link, letting his cup of bitter sludge fall unheeded to the age-worn cobbles of the square, where the contents splashed his boots. Vex was leaving the shrine, with an air of evident purpose, and Quillem began to follow, making full use of the crowd to keep himself concealed. Either the tech-priest had got what he'd come here for, or something urgent had redirected his attention; and whichever it was, Quillem intended to find out.

* * *

Hive Tarsus, Scintilla
257.993.M41

THE WATCHMEN'S DIRECTIONS turned out to be surprisingly accurate, once Kyrlock had mentally translated the gibberish, and he crossed the causeway into the Chrysoprase district at the same unhurried pace he'd maintained since starting out on his errand some hours before. Unusually, the roadway here was unlined by shops or houses, soaring over a vertiginous drop, and he had to fight the temptation to linger and admire the view, reminded of the vast pit of the Gorgonid back home on Sepheris Secundus. Traffic was relatively light at this hour, mostly limousines or transcabs, and he was the only pedestrian crossing the vast span; feeling exposed, he maintained a careful watch for any observers, but noticed none. On reaching the far side he found himself in a prosperous-seeming district, where mansions surrounded by high walls sat back from the roadway, and the shops sold things nobody he'd ever met before needed, at prices none of them could possibly afford.

If Tarsus was a tangle of intersecting angles, like a vast ball of twine, Chrysoprase was a particularly obdurate knot. Streets, buildings and alleyways clumped together, folded in and around one another, although from the cyclopean bridge he'd crossed to get here it had been possible to discern the semblance of a pattern. Like the district of Icenholm where the Angelae had made their headquarters, multiple terraces piled atop one another, although on a much bigger scale than they had in the Secundan city, to create the impression of a gradual slope when seen from a distance. Up close, however, the illusion of a regular ziggurat was shattered, in a frozen explosion of stairways, balconies and spiralling roads.

Kyrlock found a street sign, where a broad boulevard met a quiet residential sideroad, and, to his relief, recognised the name. He was close to his destination, and pressed on, looking for more of the landmarks helpfully detailed in the sheaf of papers Greel had given him.

A small formal garden was right where it was supposed to be, and he cut across it, making for a narrow stairway rising between two buildings. One was an anonymous-looking apartment block, apparently home to some of the students from the university for which Elyra had told him the Chrysoprase quarter was famed, and even at this time of night sounds of revelry could be heard emanating from several of the windows. The other had a stout wooden door, next to which a discreet brass plate had been fixed; Kyrlock knew what it was supposed to say, but glanced at it as he passed to make sure nevertheless.

The Conclave of the Enlightened, he read, in an elaborate cursive script. There was nothing else, not even the name of the lodge, but that was hardly necessary; anyone who needed to know it already would. That included Kyrlock, although he had no doubt that if any of the members ever realised the fact, they'd be quietly appalled.

The Conclave liked to think of itself as a gathering of the sector's intellectual elite, although according to Horst's briefing on the subject back in Icenholm, it was more of a social club for wealthy and aristocratic dilettantes who liked to dabble in esoterica. The ill-fated Technomancer Tonis had been a member of the lodge in the Secundan capital, which had first brought the organisation to the attention of the Angelae; for a moment Kyrlock found himself wondering how his colleagues were faring, and if they'd discovered anything useful there. Then he dismissed the thought as fruitless, and returned his mind to business.

Already aware that the Conclave had apparently played some part in the conspiracy Inquisitor Finurbi had left them to investigate, Kyrlock had been surprised to find it mentioned in Greel's dossier too; it seemed that Dylar was a member, and he had wondered for a moment if that meant he was a heretic as well. But that hardly seemed likely; every major hive or significant city in the sector seemed to support a lodge of the Conclave, at least if there were enough rich idiots in the vicinity who fancied themselves philosophers, so on balance it was probably no more than a coincidence.

Dylar lived close to the top of the stairway, in a modest town house set back a little from the street behind a wrought-iron fence over which some neglected climbing plants straggled, and a narrow strip of garden which seemed to consist mainly of raked gravel and weeds. Kyrlock, who saw no point in subtlety given the nature of his errand, marched up the tiled path and pounded on the door with his fist.

At first, nothing happened, and he had to repeat the operation a couple of times before a light went on, somewhere in the depths of the house. He was just raising his hand to knock again, when he heard the rattle of a bolt being drawn back, and stilled the motion.

'Yes?' The servant who opened the door had evidently been roused from a deep sleep, and resented the fact. He was short and florid, and glared at Kyrlock over the crumpled ruin of a hastily knotted cravat; his cerulean tailcoat was creased, and his trousers sagged over a pair of battered bedroom slippers. If he was taken aback by the outlandish appearance of the unexpected visitor, he gave no sign of it.

'I'm here to see Dylar,' Kyrlock said, raising a hand to push past him. To his surprise the servant refused to yield, merely bracing himself against the pressure. Reluctant to injure the fellow for merely doing his job, Kyrlock simply stared at him in the intimidating manner which had worked so well when he'd had occasion to face down gangers in the Tumble.

'The master is abed. I suggest you return in the morning.' The servant obviously didn't know a dangerous man when he saw one, or was too well paid to care.

Kyrlock smiled, without warmth. 'He'll see me. Or Mr Greel will be very upset.'

'Your employer's disposition is no concern of mine.' The servant made to close the door in his face, and Kyrlock's fist bunched: it seemed he'd have to do this the hard way after all. Fortunately, before he could draw his hand back to strike, a new voice cut across the entrance hall.

'It's all right, Brabinger, let him in. I've been expecting him.' Dylar was descending a wide, curving staircase, still knotting the cord of a silk dressing gown. He was a little taller than Kyrlock had expected from the pict, although the faint air of unworldliness it had captured still hung about him. He reached the bottom of the stairs, and looked appraisingly at the former Guardsman. 'Someone like him, anyway.'

'Very good, sir.' Brabinger stood aside to admit Kyrlock, with ill grace, then slammed the door with unnecessary emphasis. 'Will that be all?'

'I believe so. You may return to bed.' Dylar glanced at Kyrlock, with the kind of faint curiosity he might have exhibited towards something unexpected on a microscope slide. 'We'll talk in my study.'

'If it makes you more comfortable,' Kyrlock said, recognising his type at once. Born and raised on a feudal world, he was intimately familiar with the innate arrogance of the aristocracy towards anyone of inferior rank, although it was only since joining the Angelae that he'd discovered it was possible to resent it, and even pay them back in their own coin on occasion.

'This way,' Dylar said, leading the way towards a door on one side of the marble-floored entrance hall. It had a touch plate set into the wall next to it, and as his fingertips brushed against the smooth metal surface, a lock clicked.

The study was larger than Kyrlock had expected; clearly his unwilling host spent a great deal of time in here.

Bookshelves lined the walls, their contents spilling over onto every available surface, and clumping up into forlorn little dunes in quiet corners of the carpet. A compact cogitator stood on a glossy wooden desk, its brass cogs still, and its pict screen dark, while a litter of papers and a couple of data-slates hid most of the rest of the rich, brown surface.

Without waiting for an invitation, Kyrlock dropped into the chair behind the desk. 'Mr Greel was expecting to have heard from you by now,' he said.

'You must understand that these things take time,' Dylar replied, in a studiedly reasonable tone, as though he expected immediate agreement and an apology for the franchiseman's impatience. If he resented the implicit usurpation of his personal domain, he was too sensible to let it show, or challenge the insult; the first impression most people formed when they met Kyrlock was that he was trouble just waiting for someone to happen to, and the self-styled scholar had clearly come to the conclusion that it would be better to be nobody in that regard. Instead, he just cleared a pile of books from another chair, and sat down himself.

'All I have to understand is that you owe Mr Greel something he wants, and I've been sent to collect it,' Kyrlock said, letting the statement hang significantly in the air between them.

'I see.' Behind the pose of aristocratic detachment, it was plain that the man was very nervous. With good reason, too: the Shadow Franchise was not an organisation it was wise to cross. He gestured towards the desk. 'The black data-slate.'

'What about it?' Kyrlock asked, picking the thing up. It looked and felt like every other slate he'd ever handled.

Dylar licked his lips nervously. 'It's all on there. Everything I've managed to uncover so far, anyway. I was hoping to cross-reference the information with a couple of other sources, but most of the useful texts are on the proscribed list, so of course I haven't been able to gain access to them.'

'Have you tried?' Kyrlock asked, masking his surprise with a show of belligerence. It sounded as though Dylar was all but confessing to heresy, and, new as he might be to the ranks of the Inquisition, he could hardly ignore something like that.

'Of course not!' the aristocrat blurted, looking both shocked and terrified. 'If anyone ever found out, I'd be hauled off to the Tricorn! Everything on there's from legitimate sources, I swear!'

'They'd better be,' Kyrlock said. 'Mr Greel wouldn't like the Inquisition sniffing around.' Though he spoke primarily for effect, he found himself considering his own advice. If the franchiseman ever discovered his new recruit was an agent of the Throne, he'd be dead in a heartbeat.

'We're all square, now, then?' Dylar asked hopefully, as Kyrlock stood, and pocketed the data-slate.

Kyrlock shrugged. 'You'd have to ask Mr Greel,' he said, watching something deflate inside the man across the desk. If he'd really believed providing the Franchise with what they wanted would get them off his back, he was too naïve to be let out in the street without a nursemaid. 'No doubt he'll be in touch.'

'No doubt.' Dylar rallied with an effort, and stood to usher him out, as though he'd simply been playing host to a business discussion. 'Would you like me to get Brabinger to call you a transcab?'

'No thank you,' Kyrlock said. Typically, the aristocrat seemed to have forgotten that he'd sent his servant back to bed; no doubt if roused again he'd do what was asked of him without complaint, but Kyrlock had spent too long being treated like that by people like Dylar to be comfortable with the idea. 'It's a pleasant night for a walk.'

More to the point, he'd pass plenty of public vox terminals on the long climb back to the upper hive, and now he had something to justify using the code Elyra had given him. The weight of the data-slate seemed suddenly heavy in his pocket, and he found himself wondering what secrets it concealed.

I

SEVENTEEN

Hive Sibellus, Scintilla
257.993.M41

THOUGH HE'D DEDICATED his life to the notion that pure reason was the only sure basis on which to proceed, Vex was forced to conclude that he was feeling perturbed. If the Angelae's enemies really had become aware of their location, they could be anywhere, even merging into the crowds thronging the streets of the middle hive through which he walked. In fact it was perfectly possible that they were watching him now...

Irritated by the inescapable inference, he had to exert all his reserves of dispassionate analysis to prevent himself from turning his head in what was bound to be a fruitless search for unseen observers dogging his footsteps. If anything, such a reaction would be counterproductive, achieving nothing beyond warning anyone trailing him that he was aware of their surveillance.

Not for the first time, he wished he'd asked Horst for more details about the security breach. If he'd known why the team leader was so concerned, he would have been able to analyse the situation effectively, instead of sending his thoughts skittering down one blind alley after another. As with so many things, it all came down to a lack of information.

The transit terminal he'd used to get to the shrine was still some distance away, and he turned down a side street, intending to take the most direct route he could to the transport hub. It was a high-ceilinged thoroughfare, lined with manufactoria and warehousing units, and he should have been safe from attack there; lorries were entering and leaving in a steady stream, and by his initial estimate there must have been at least three score workers in sight along its length, dotted sporadically about the narrow pavement. Far too many potential witnesses to be casually disregarded.

Which made the attempt on his life all the more disturbing when it came. It was skilfully executed, and carefully planned, although the real shock was the identity of the perpetrators.

His enemies struck without warning as he passed a small, narrow door, set into a much larger one intended to provide vehicular access to one of the warehouses. The big cargo door was closed, rolled down to the ground, but the personnel one had been propped open with a makeshift doorstop which looked as though it had once been a paint tin, any indication of its contents long since obliterated by a rash of rust. Vex had just moved level with it when a nimbus of electrical discharge enveloped him.

Surprised, he tried to react, but the unexpected overload was wreaking havoc on his augmetic enhancements. His meat muscles went into spasm, inducing considerable discomfort, and most of his implants shut down, autonomic failsafes protecting them from the sudden power surge. Instinctively, he tried to channel the worst of it into his capacitors, but there was far too much excess energy to bleed off that way, and he collapsed on the pavement, twitching feebly.

'Get him inside,' a voice said, with the level inflection of a vox-coder. Hands grabbed him, and he was obscurely reassured to realise that they were augmetic rather than flesh and blood. His vision was still blurred, but as he was half-helped, half-carried into the dim, echoing warehouse, he was able to make out the swirl of white robes like his own.

He attempted to greet the strange tech-priests, but the appropriate implanted systems were still shut down, leaving him unable to communicate in binary with his peers. That was galling; he was used to being able to exchange information almost instantaneously with others of his calling, instead of having to rely on the slow and clumsy channel of conversation in Gothic which he was forced to use with his fellow Angelae. Fighting down a surge of embarrassment, he tried to speak, but it seemed his biological systems were still grievously impaired as well; all that emerged from his mouth was a strangulated gurgle.

'He's still functional,' the tech-priest who'd spoken before said, and as Vex's vision began to clear, he could see that he was holding a vox-unit in his hand. Mechadendrites were waving in the air above the man's shoulders, and one of them suddenly snaked out to start rummaging through the pockets of Vex's robe.

'Then deactivate him as soon as you've secured the wraithbone,' whoever was on the other end of the vox-link directed, and Vex began to feel seriously alarmed.

'If he's actually got it,' another voice said; it spoke in the carefully modulated fashion that Vex himself cultivated, and which was common among acolytes of the Omnissiah who had been unable as yet to replace their original larynxes with augmetic ones. The higher register suggested to him that its owner was female, and, as she let him fall to the floor and took a step backwards, he was able to confirm that impression.

'You said that was the most logical inference,' the voice on the vox said, in tones which implied very strongly that it didn't want to hear any suggestions to the contrary at this stage.

'Roughly ninety-seven per cent,' the male tech-priest assured his superior. 'In the absence of Inquisitor Finurbi they had no one at the Tricorn to give it to, and a member of the Adeptus Mechanicus would be less likely to find handling the substance disturbing than any of his colleagues. It's possible, but unlikely, that he would have left it wherever his team has found refuge–' He broke off suddenly, then withdrew his mechanical tentacle, the sliver of ivory grasped in the handling filaments at its tip. 'We have obtained it.'

'Then deactivate him and return at once,' the voice directed, before cutting the link from the other end.

'I comply,' the female said, miniature lightning arcs beginning to crackle between her fingers.

Vex tried to move, reach for his autopistol, but his meat muscles were still knotting, refusing to obey. A detached part of his mind began to calculate the voltage the woman was able to generate; she'd managed to disable him at a distance of at least three metres, possibly more. If she touched him directly, she'd burn out every augmetic component he had, and that would be the end of him; he'd been upgraded so much since joining the Adeptus Mechanicus that he seriously doubted his remaining flesh could continue to function without them. Even if he could survive the trauma, he wouldn't want to, cut off from the perfection of the Machine, to be imprisoned in a mere bag of meat again.

Trying not to flinch as his murderer bent smoothly towards him, her hand outstretched, he prepared himself for transfer to the eternal files.

'Desist in the name of the Emperor!' someone shouted, and the female straightened abruptly, stretching out her hand towards the doorway; but before she could discharge the lightning sparking around her fingers, the unmistakable *hissss crack* of a miniature bolter echoed through the cavernous space, and her torso erupted in a crater of viscera and shredded augmetics. The energies she'd been hoarding earthed themselves suddenly, arcing through her remaining metal implants, and she toppled to the rough rockcrete floor in an unpleasant miasma of scorched insulation and charred meat.

'Mordechai?' Vex asked, managing to regain a measure of control over his body at last, and rolling to a semi-recumbent position. No one else he knew carried a bolt pistol, but he couldn't imagine how Horst had even known he was in trouble, let alone managed to get here so quickly.

Then he caught sight of the man who'd saved his life. He was a complete stranger, but the crimson sigil of an Inquisition rosette gleamed in his raised left hand.

Vex reached for his autopistol, unsure who he intended using it on. The stranger might indeed be an ally, but Inquisitor Finurbi's note had been quite unequivocal: no one in the Calixis Conclave could be trusted.

Abruptly, the decision was taken out of his hands. The male tech-priest was already running, making for the back of the warehouse, the artefact still gripped in his mechadendrite. No doubt there was another entrance there, leading Omnissiah knew where in the labyrinth of the middle hive. If he got away now, they'd never recover the sliver of ivory, or be able to determine its purpose. He squeezed the trigger.

Normally, Vex took a quiet pride in his standard of proficiency with firearms, which, although nowhere near as high as a professional gunfighter like Horst or Drake, was sufficient for him to be reasonably confident of hitting the mark with a single aimed shot. This was no time to indulge in self-aggrandisement, though; his enfeebled state was bound to degrade the accuracy of his shooting, so he flicked the seldom-used selector to the burst setting.

It proved to be a wise precaution. The hail of bullets cut the air around his erstwhile assailant, but only two struck their mark. The renegade tech-priest staggered, then rallied, feeding power to his legs.

'Halt or die!' the stranger shouted, and when the fugitive made no response except to take another couple of steps, fired the bolt pistol again. The explosive projectile detonated between the tech-priest's shoulder blades, pitching him forwards, and detaching the mechadendrite holding the artefact. The metal tentacle clattered to the floor.

In severe discomfort, Vex dragged himself to his feet, and staggered towards the gleaming sliver of ivory. He was going to have to carry out a considerable number of repairs before his systems were able to operate at anything like an acceptable standard of efficiency again.

Noticing the movement, the stranger walked forwards too, an unmistakable expression of stunned surprise appearing on his face as he registered the presence of the artefact. Tucking his rosette away inside his jacket, he bent down and picked it up carefully.

'I'll take that,' Vex said, bringing up his gun.

The stranger shook his head. 'I don't think so. We've been looking for it for a very long time.' He brought his own weapon round to cover Vex. 'I'm sure you're well aware that if you shoot me, my finger will tighten on the trigger purely by reflex. At this range, we'll both be dead before I hit the floor.'

'I could say the same,' Vex replied, unable to find fault with the logic of the man's position.

'Precisely.' The stranger nodded. 'So rather than make saving your life a pointless waste of effort, I suggest we talk.' He smiled, in a manner Vex felt far from reassured by. 'My name's Pieter Quillem, and I work for a friend of your employer. With a bit of luck and common sense, I think we can help one another.'

Tarsus High Orbital Docks, Scintilla System
258.993.M41

ALTHOUGH TARSUS HIGH kept the same time as the hive below, in order to facilitate the never-ending flow of commerce, the concept of day and night had no more relevance aboard the orbital than it did on any of the starships constantly arriving and departing from it. That made it hard for Elyra to reliably estimate the number of other psykers sharing their refuge, as they tended to sleep and eat whenever they felt like it. There weren't that many, she was sure; apart from Zusen, Trosk, Ven and Voyle, she'd only met a handful, most of whose names she didn't know, although she suspected there were an additional few who preferred to remain completely concealed among the sprawling vegetation. All the ones she had come into contact with were wary, radiating the same aura of general distrust that Trosk did, and were reluctant to engage in conversation with anyone.

Though she might have found this frustrating, given her determination to gather as much information as she could, in some ways it came as a relief. The less contact she had with the wyrds, the less chance there was of letting something slip which might unmask her as an Inquisition agent. The real fear she had was that one of the rescued might turn out to be a sufficiently powerful telepath to break through the carefully constructed barriers in her mind, and lift the truth of her mission directly from her thoughts, but fortunately the only 'paths she'd encountered here so far were epsilon-grade at best: a pale young woman with dark hair, who seemed to spend most of her time talking to the plants, and a man of about her own age, whose main topic of conversation was how frustrating he found it being surrounded by people who knew of his gift, and were accordingly reluctant to play cards with him for money.

Her cover story, too, didn't exactly lend itself to worming information out of her fellow refugees: having gone to some lengths to establish a reputation for being a paranoid sociopath, she could hardly start trying to be everybody's new best friend. To her barely concealed relief, Trosk seemed as keen to stay out of her way as she was to avoid him, spending most of his time with Ven, while Zusen, though as friendly as ever, knew no more about the setup here than she did, and seemed content to leave things that way.

All of which left Voyle as the only possible source of the information she wanted, and Elyra determined to cultivate him, without appearing too obvious about it. It helped that he was evidently attracted to her, though understandably wary, given what he thought he knew of her nature, so she played on that as subtly as she could, managing to give the impression that his interest might possibly be reciprocated without ever actually saying so.

Accordingly, when he clambered out of his bedroll while she was preparing a makeshift stew from vegetables scavenged from the surrounding beds, over a fire she'd kindled from the surfeit of dried-out twigs littering the floor, she waved him over to join her.

'Eaten yet?' she asked.

'No, I haven't.' Voyle ambled over, apparently agreeably surprised by the invitation, and warmed his hands at the flickering flames. 'You're not getting tired of the view, then.' He reached out and plucked a stunted ploin from a nearby espalier, which he bit into, and grimaced.

'Not yet.' Elyra glanced up at the disc of Scintilla, where the terminator line had just reached the position of Hive Tarsus, bisecting the planet neatly between day and night. The night side was speckled with the lights of minor settlements, and she was able to pick out the greater glow cast by the furnaces of Gunmetal City without difficulty. Part of the larger moon was just visible behind the nightside limb, a ghostly fingernail paring of reflected sunlight, its craters thrown into stark relief by the harsh illumination. 'I'm not sure I ever will.'

'Better enjoy it while you can, then,' Voyle said, abandoning the unripe fruit in favour of the steaming bowlful of vegetable mush Elyra ladled out for him with visible relief. 'We'll be moving on soon.'

'How soon?' Elyra asked, and Voyle shrugged. 'As soon as they can arrange a ship for us. No more than a day or two, I hope.'

'Well, that's good.' Elyra ate a spoonful of her own stew, trying to mask her shock. She'd expected a little longer than that to try and find a way of contacting the Tricorn. When she spoke again, she made sure to inject the right amount of scepticism into her voice. 'Assuming your patron can just whistle one up whenever he feels like it, of course.'

'He should be able to.' Voyle smiled, apparently amused at having predicted her reaction so accurately. 'He owns one of the biggest merchant fleets in the sector.'

'Really?' Elyra chewed a piece of tuber, and smiled with just enough warmth to encourage him. If true, this was vital intelligence for Carolus. It made sense, she supposed: the owner of a shipping line would be in the perfect position to organise a sector-wide network like the one the Sanctuary apparently maintained. The Shadow Franchise were probably unaware that they were being manipulated, used as a smokescreen by a wider conspiracy, although if they were making enough money out of the arrangement she didn't think they'd object too much even if they did discover the truth. 'I guess you must trust me a little to share something like that.'

'A little,' Voyle agreed, smiling.

'But not enough to tell me his name.'

'Alaric Diurnus.' Voyle smiled again. 'All you had to do was ask.'

'Diurnus,' Elyra repeated, nodding thoughtfully. 'I suppose if anyone could set up an operation like this, it would be him. But what's the catch?'

'The catch?' Voyle laughed, in an open, friendly manner, which under other circumstances she would have found engaging. 'Why would there be a catch?'

'Because Diurnus is a Rogue Trader,' Elyra said, 'and they're not exactly known for their altruism.' She felt safe enough revealing this degree of knowledge about the man, as his activities were widely known throughout the sector. On some worlds, particularly ones where Diurnus Lines held a virtual monopoly on shipping, he was even something of a folk hero, a popular subject for pict dramas and story texts.

'He expects a little something back from us,' Voyle admitted. 'Psykers are obviously useful to him, and the Adeptus Terra keep their sanctionites on a tight leash. Sponsoring the Sanctuary gives him a useful pool of talents like ours, without any bureaucratic restrictions on their activities.'

'I see,' Elyra said, trying not to let the concern she felt at the prospect of a cadre of wyrds in the personal service of a ruthless and powerful man like Diurnus enter her voice. 'Seems like a fair trade to me.' Contacting Carolus and telling him what she'd learned was now more urgent than ever. But, as she smiled and ate stew, she couldn't imagine how she was going to manage that.

Hive Sibellus, Scintilla System
258.993.M41

HORST WAS FEELING angry, worried and confused, and trying to keep all three emotions from his voice. He wasn't sure how well he was succeeding, but the man who called himself Pieter Quillem seemed relaxed enough; if he was picking up on the undercurrent of tension in the room, he was too good an operative to show it.

'So it was one of your people Danuld spotted,' he said, and Quillem nodded, in a matter-of-fact fashion.

'Carys isn't usually inclined to take unnecessary risks, but she isn't quite herself at the moment. I'm sorry if she alarmed you.'

'Alarmed isn't quite the word,' Horst said, still trying to take the measure of the man Vex had so unexpectedly returned with. 'How long have you been keeping us under surveillance?'

'Since you arrived in-system,' Quillem admitted, as though that was a perfectly reasonable thing to have done. 'Inquisitor Grynner was understandably concerned about his friend's disappearance, and wanted us in a position to respond quickly if he needed help.' It sounded plausible enough to Horst, as it would to anyone familiar with the shadowy world inhabited by acolytes of the Inquisition, where even allies were seldom to be completely trusted, but that didn't necessarily make it true. 'And we do seem to be involved in the same investigation, exactly as Inquisitor Grynner surmised.'

Horst nodded. Inquisitor Finurbi had returned to Scintilla in response to a message from his old friend, requesting assistance, and it did indeed appear as though the two groups had been following separate threads of the same tapestry of heresy. None of which did anything to dispel the real source of his unease. 'Which doesn't change the fact that we were specifically warned not to trust any other members of the Calixis Conclave,' he said.

'That shouldn't be a problem,' Quillem replied, a hint of amusement appearing on his face. 'Inquisitor Grynner isn't one. He's a free agent. The Faxlignae don't confine their activities to a single sector, and neither do we.'

'The who?' Horst asked. The name didn't mean anything to him.

'The Faxlignae,' Quillem repeated. 'An extremely perni-cious and well-resourced network of heretics, who scavenge any xenos artefacts they can. We still don't know what their primary agenda is, but recently they seem to have started collecting psykers too, which is why Inquisitor Grynner felt we could do with the assistance of a witch hunter.'

'The mercenaries who attacked the Black Ships holding pen on Sepheris Secundus were equipped with xenos weaponry,' Vex said, glancing up from the cogitator he'd begun working at the moment they'd arrived back at Vorn's apartment. Horst noted the spark of interest in Quillem's eyes, and inwardly cursed the tech-priest's lack of discretion.

'Then it seems an exchange of information would be to everyone's benefit,' the interrogator said. 'We'd be partic-ularly interested to hear where you recovered the wraithbone from.'

'The what?' Horst asked, wrong-footed for a moment.

'The artefact,' Vex supplied helpfully. 'He knows what it is.'

'Really?' This time Horst didn't bother to disguise his scepticism. 'Despite the fact that you've been getting nowhere running it down?'

'It appears that I've been consulting the wrong archives,' Vex admitted, his habitually level tones not quite managing to conceal his chagrin at having made so elementary a mistake. 'I've been labouring under the mis-apprehension that the artefact was a piece of archeotech, whereas in fact it's of xenos origin.'

'Eldar, to be precise,' Quillem said. 'We were tracking this fragment when it went missing from the freighter transporting it. Stolen, so far as we could tell, by power-ful psykers.'

The implication was obvious, Horst thought. Tonis's group had snatched it, to use in their infernal psychic booster. Which raised the question of how they'd known it was aboard the vessel in the first place.

Before he could consider the question further, to his astonishment, the door leading to Vorn's room opened, and the elderly acolyte hobbled out, carrying a portable vox receiver. He glanced curiously at Quillem, then turned to Horst.

'Message for you,' he said, proffering the device.

'Who from?' Horst asked, glancing at Quillem as he spoke. He'd immediately assumed that it would be some sort of communiqué from Inquisitor Grynner, but the man from the Ordo Xenos seemed as surprised as he was by the interruption. Drake or Keira would have contacted him directly using their comm-beads, and he couldn't imagine who else knew they were there.

'Says his name's Kyrlock. Wanted the inquisitor, but says you'll do.' Vorn shrugged, his greying hair tumbling around his shoulders, and Horst found himself thinking that the old man wasn't nearly as frail as he liked people to think.

'Vos?' Heedless of Quillem's presence, Horst took the communicator at once. 'Where are you? Is Elyra there?'

'Hive Tarsus. We got separated, but I hope I can get a message to her. She's with a heretic group calling themselves the Sanctuary of the Blessed. Mean anything to you?'

'No.' Horst glanced at Quillem, who shrugged; clearly he'd never heard of them either. 'Do you want picking up?'

'Not yet. I'm supposed to be working for a Franchise fixer named Greel, who has some dealings with the heretics; if I stay put, I might be able to find out where Elyra's gone.'

'Good,' Horst said, pleased to find Inquisitor Finurbi's instincts had been right about Kyrlock as well as Drake. A lesser man would have been tempted to accept the offer of relative safety, but the former Guardsman hadn't even hesitated before answering. 'We'll wait for your call.'

'There's something else,' Kyrlock said. 'Greel sent me to collect a data-slate from a scholar in the local lodge of the Conclave of the Enlightened. I don't know what's on it, but it could be important.'

'Just a moment,' Vex interrupted, looking up from the cogitator in the corner. 'I'm setting up a direct data-link. Can you activate it?'

'I think so,' Kyrlock said. 'It's just a standard slate.' After a short pause he spoke again. 'How's that?'

'Puzzling,' Vex said. 'The data's coming through, but I'm not sure what it means. This will take some consideration.'

'Just so long as we've got it,' Horst said. He glanced at Quillem. 'We'll think about your offer.'

'I hope so,' Quillem said, too practised, or too confident, to press the matter. He stood. 'We've both got a lot to gain from cooperation. I'm sure you'll see sense.'

For a moment Horst considered trying to prevent him from leaving, but there seemed little point: Inquisitor Grynner's people obviously knew where they were anyway. 'We'll think about it,' he repeated instead.

KEIRA'S CONVERSATION WITH the black-garbed inquisitor had been a series of surprises, the first of which had been an invitation to discuss matters in his private quarters, rather than the interrogation suite she'd expected. They were as Spartan as she'd inferred from his demeanour, although the living room had included a fire in an age-blackened hearth, and a scattering of worn armchairs, one of which she'd selected after being prompted with an airily waved hand and a perfunctory 'Sit, sit. You're making the place look untidy.'

Her choice had been prompted by two factors; it faced the door by which they'd entered, and its padding made it seem natural for her to remove her sword from her belt, resting its scabbard between her knees, where she could draw the blade instantly if she felt the need.

'As you've probably realised by now,' the man said, dropping into a chair facing her, and steepling his fingers, 'you've piqued my curiosity. What exactly were you hoping to achieve by breaking in here?'

'I can't discuss it,' Keira said. 'If you know who I am, you know we're operating under Special Circumstances.'

'Then let me speculate,' Karnaki said. 'You were hoping to find some clue as to the nature of the warp entities you encountered on Sepheris Secundus and aboard the *Misericord*. Which I suspect very strongly weren't actually daemons at all, by the way, but you could certainly be forgiven for thinking so. It's probably also occurred to you that the case of Tonis's apparent possession was extremely unusual, and that any other instances of tech-priests so afflicted might provide you with a fresh lead.'

'I can't discuss it,' Keira repeated, masking her shock and surprise as best she could. If this man knew as much as he appeared to about their business, the only explanation that she could see was that he was one of the shadowy enemies Inquisitor Finurbi had cut himself off from the Conclave to evade. She steeled herself for the ordeal she was certain was coming, knowing all too well that once the interrogators started, no one could hold out indefinitely; but she'd been trained to resist, and was determined not to break until the others would have had enough time to reach safety. If necessary, there were ways to end her own life no one could prevent, although she'd be loath to use them; the longer she could hold out against the torturers, the more time she could buy for the other Angelae.

'Of course not,' Karnaki said, nodding. 'But there'll be no need for that kind of unpleasantness. If necessary, I can simply take what I need directly from your mind.'

'Then why don't you?' Keira asked, gripping the hilt of her sword. She could reach him easily from here, and she clearly had no choice now other than to kill him. But however hard she tried, she couldn't complete the motion; her body refused to obey her will, simply sitting passively in the overstuffed chair. It seemed Karnaki was a formidably strong psyker, perhaps even as strong as her own patron.

'Because at the moment I don't see the need,' Karnaki explained calmly. 'You would find the experience extremely uncomfortable, perhaps even more so than the physical methods of coercion you were picturing so vividly a moment ago. And so deep a probe against so disciplined a mind would leave you severely damaged.' The matter-of-fact tone in which he spoke sent shivers down her spine, in spite of the calming litanies she began to subvocalise, in an attempt to keep him from reading any more of her thoughts.

'What do you want, then?' Keira asked.

'For the moment, merely to assure you that you and your colleagues have nothing to fear from me,' Karnaki said. 'You'll recall that Inquisitor Finurbi left Sepheris Secundus to consult with a trusted colleague, Inquisitor Grynner. Not surprisingly, Grynner was perturbed by his friend's disappearance, and consulted me about the apparent daemonic aspects of the case.'

'I've heard of Grynner,' Keira conceded. There was no point in attempting to conceal that. 'But the boss never mentioned you.'

'Probably because we've never met,' Karnaki said. 'The connection is merely through a mutual friend.' He looked at her appraisingly. 'Tell me about the warp entities you saw.'

'I can't discuss...' Keira began, but she couldn't prevent the flood of memories his words released from surging to the surface of her mind, and after a moment Karnaki leaned back in his chair with an unmistakable air of satisfaction.

'Thank you. That's all I needed to know,' he said, and Keira found that she was able to move once more, as easily as if the paralysis which had afflicted her had never been. She was on her feet instantly, the sword hissing from its scabbard; then suddenly her muscles locked again, and she froze into immobility, the keen edge millimetres from Karnaki's throat. 'Please don't do that, it's unconscionably rude.'

Keira tried to fight his will, battering it down as she had done the rogue psyker aboard the *Misericord*, but the effort was futile; the inquisitor's mind was honed, sanctified by the Emperor, and infinitely more powerful. She found herself moving with no more volition than a clockwork toy, an impotent and furious passenger in her own body, sheathing the sword and turning towards the door.

'I'll be in touch,' Karnaki said, 'once I've been able to confirm the conclusions I've come to. Now out you go.'

And, seething inwardly, unable to do anything else, Keira went.

EIGHTEEN

Hive Sibellus, Scintilla
258.993.M41

'WHICHEVER WAY YOU look at it, things have gone klybo,' Keira said, in her usual forthright fashion. She'd arrived back at the safe house to find a lively debate already in progress about Quillem's offer of an exchange of information, and her account of her interview with Karnaki had simply made matters worse.

Horst nodded. 'The question is, what are we going to do about it? Inquisitor Finurbi's instructions were perfectly clear. We were to avoid all contact with the Calixian ordos, and now we have two of their inquisitors breathing down our necks. I think we should cut and run, while we've still got a chance.'

'I don't reckon that'll work,' Drake said. 'This Inquisitor Grynner's people are good. I don't give much for our chances of evading their surveillance now they know where to find us.'

'We're pretty good ourselves,' Horst reminded him. 'And we've still got the shuttle.'

'Which they can track from orbit the second we lift,' Drake replied gloomily. 'They know where it's berthed, and they've got a starship. Not what I'd call an even match.'

'The proposed alliance would offer us a number of advantages,' Vex put in. 'It's clear that they possess a great deal of information which we don't, and would be grateful for our assistance.'

'Two words,' Drake said. 'Special Circumstances. The inquisitor said not to trust anybody.'

'Well, we know he trusted Grynner,' Keira said. 'Sharing information with him was the main reason he was coming here. Karnaki's the one who worries me.'

'Then perhaps we can play one off against the other,' Horst said, the germ of an idea beginning to take shape in his mind. 'If we can't get out from under Grynner's surveillance anyway, we might as well play along with his people for as long as it suits us. If nothing else, whatever information they're sitting on might give us another lead to Elyra. Vos is working on it from his end, but if he can't make the connection after all, she's going to be left flapping in the breeze.'

'Good point,' Keira agreed, nodding. 'But what about Karnaki?'

'If he's working with Grynner anyway, we'll be able to keep an eye on him at the same time,' Horst said. 'And perhaps we can exploit any tensions there might be between them.'

'I'm still not happy about any of this,' Drake said doggedly. 'It all seems very convenient this Quillem guy just happening to be there when Hybris was attacked. How do we know he didn't set the whole thing up himself to gain our confidence?'

'It's possible, of course,' Vex said. 'But the balance of probabilities is against that. It's far more likely that the tech-priests who assaulted me were working for Magos Avia. They were clearly intending to abscond with the artefact, whereas Quillem was extremely surprised to find it in my possession.'

'Then how did they know where to find you?' Keira asked.

'Deductive reasoning, of course,' Vex said, evidently happy to be back on the firmer ground of pure intellect. 'That street was the most logical route for me to take back to the transport hub. Once they knew I'd entered the shrine, they merely had to wait for me to leave again, and walk past the point they'd chosen for their ambush.'

'All right,' Drake said, 'I'll buy that. But how did they know you were visiting the shrine in the first place?'

'My biometric data was already on file there,' Vex said. 'Anyone with access to the system would know I'd entered the building to consult the records.'

'Fair enough,' Horst said. He sighed. 'Are we agreed, then? Accept Quillem's offer, and watch our backs carefully?'

'That's the most rational course of action,' Vex said, nodding faintly.

'I suppose so,' Drake conceded, with visible reluctance. 'But I don't like it. It feels like we're being manipulated.'

'Of course we are,' Keira said. 'But if it makes you feel any better, we're using them at least as much as they're using us.'

'Oh good,' Drake said, with heavy sarcasm. 'That makes it all right, then.'

'Keira?' Horst asked. Technically, he didn't have to ask her opinion; as team leader, the decision would be his alone to make. Nevertheless, he found himself wanting to know how she felt, more than any of the others.

'Make the call,' she said, shrugging. 'If they are part of the conspiracy, at least we can watch them while they're watching us.'

'Pretty much what I was thinking,' Horst agreed, and went to find Vorn.

* * *

Hive Tarsus, Scintilla
258.993.M41

GREEL'S OFFICE WAS exactly as Kyrlock remembered it, although this time no one made the mistake of attempting to bar his way, simply glancing at him as he passed through the outer layers of security with wary respect. It seemed that either word of his last visit had got around, or Greel had made it clear that he was to be left alone the next time he appeared on the premises. Nevertheless, if there was going to be trouble, he was sure he'd be ready for it; after calling the vox code Elyra had given him, he'd returned to his room at the hostel and slept for a few hours, wanting to be sharp when he next spoke to the franchiseman.

The discovery that the other Angelae were also on Scintilla had been a welcome one; used to fending for himself, he'd been surprised to find how much the idea that he had backup again if he needed it had improved his outlook.

'You took your time,' Greel said, glancing up from a data-slate as Kyrlock entered his office.

Kyrlock shrugged. 'You didn't say it was urgent,' he pointed out reasonably, dropping into a nearby chair without waiting to be invited.

'No, I suppose I didn't.' Greel set the slate aside, and looked at him appraisingly. 'Did he pay up, or did you have to hurt him?'

'Neither.' Kyrlock pulled the data-slate Dylar had given him out of his pocket, and leaned forwards to place it on the desk. 'He said you were waiting for this. If he was lying, I can always go back and smack him about a bit.'

'I don't think that'll be necessary,' Greel said, picking the slate up, and paging through it avidly. 'Not this time, anyway. I know someone who'll pay real money for this.'

'Good,' Kyrlock said. 'And speaking of money…'

'Of course.' Greel smiled, and threw a heavy purse at him.

Kyrlock caught it easily, one-handed, an instant before it would have hit him in the face, and smiled back. 'Thanks.' He'd been expecting something like that, another test, or a reminder not to get too cocky with the boss. Hive or Tumble, it seemed, the rules were the same wherever you went. The two men shared a glance of mutual understanding.

'Any more little errands you'd like me to run, before I go and squander this on ale and whores?' Kyrlock asked, tucking the purse inside his shirt without bothering to count the contents. The first payment would be generous, he knew, calculated to reinforce his loyalty, and hint at bigger things to come. Subsequent ones would be far more dependent on results.

'I'll let you know,' Greel said, effectively dismissing him, and Kyrlock stood, taking the hint. On the way out, he paused in the door, as if struck by an afterthought.

'If you're seeing Elyra soon,' he said, 'remind her she owes me ten credits.' Then he stepped outside, without waiting to see if the franchiseman had risen to his carefully baited hook. Mentioning the woman's name in connection with a trivial amount of money might just be enough to remind Greel of the considerably greater sum he stood to gain from contacting her.

Emperor willing, of course. As he regained the stifling street, and narrowed his eyes against the glare filtering through the outermost kilometres of the hive, Kyrlock found himself fervently praying that He would be.

The *Emperor's Justice*, Scintilla System
258.993.M41

'DO YOU THINK they'll cooperate?' Inquisitor Grynner asked, and Quillem nodded, prepared for the obvious question.

'I don't think we've left them any choice,' he said. 'They might opt to go underground again, but they must know if they try we'll pick up their trail without too much trouble. And the tech-priest will certainly argue for allying with us, if only to find out more about the wraithbone.'

'Which is where, at the moment?' the inquisitor asked dryly. 'I presume you didn't allow them to keep it?'

'Throne on Earth no,' Quillem said, unable to completely suppress a smile at the absurdity of the idea. 'I gave it to Brother Paulus as soon as I docked.' The Deathwatch Librarian was a powerful psyker, even more so than most Astartes of his calling, and was the most fitting custodian of such a tainted artefact. 'He's attempting to determine whether it's the same one that went missing from the *Eddia Stabilis*.'

'That would seem to be the most likely hypothesis,' Grynner agreed. 'Which, unfortunately, raises a number of new questions, of course.'

'Like how it got to Sepheris Secundus,' Quillem said.

'Quite.' The inquisitor's head inclined in a vestigial nod. 'We've been extremely remiss, Pieter. We had copies of their reports to young Carolus. We should have realised that this artefact they kept referring to was the wraithbone.'

'We had no real reason to make the connection,' Quillem pointed out. 'The *Eddia Stabilis* was attacked in the Halo Stars, not the Calixis Sector. The psykers who took it must have had an exceptionally fast ship to get it to Sepheris Secundus so quickly.'

'Indeed.' Grynner nodded thoughtfully again. 'The timing is quite anomalous, Pieter. Even if the warp currents were particularly favourable, they couldn't have made the journey much faster than we did, yet this wretched man Tonis clearly had his hands on the wraithbone for some considerable time.'

'Perhaps we can learn more when we debrief the techpriest properly,' Quillem said. 'He's been studying the manuscript they recovered from the heretics quite intensively, so he may be able to shed a little more light on the matter.'

'Perhaps,' Grynner replied. 'I must confess I'm agreeably surprised that he relinquished the wraithbone quite so readily.'

'It was a matter of logic,' Quillem said. 'We're Ordo Xenos, and it's a xenos artefact. Therefore, it's our responsibility.' He smiled faintly. 'And, I imagine, he was getting rather tired of people attempting to kill him to obtain it.'

'Yes, I imagine so too,' Grynner said.

Tarsus High Orbital Docks, Scintilla System
258.993.M41

THE NOVELTY OF a garden on an orbital habitat, even one as derelict and overgrown as this one, still astonished Elyra. After the privations they'd endured aboard the *Ursus Innare*, she found herself enjoying the simple pleasures of grass underfoot and the warmth of the sun on her neck, despite the sense of urgency and imminent danger she was never quite able to shake.

'I brought you a hat,' Zusen said, breaking into her reverie. 'You're starting to burn.' The young empath scratched absently at a phantom itch on the back of her own neck, just where Elyra was beginning to feel the first faint tingle of overexposure to the sun. The older woman's albinoid skin, common to the void-born, succumbed easily to the ultraviolet, and she took care to remain covered up in the open on most worlds, but it was hard to remember to take the same precautions aboard an orbital.

'Thank you,' she said reflexively, remembering to inflect it with a tone of indifference at the last minute.

'You're welcome.' Zusen grinned, her mood light, probably for the first time in her life. 'Do you think Sanctuary will be anything like this?'

'I haven't a clue,' Elyra said truthfully, her taciturn response evidently precisely what the teenager was expecting. 'But I doubt it.' In her experience, psykers falling into the hands of heretic groups were unlikely to be left alone to enjoy the scenery. Zusen's sense of contentment wasn't going to be punctured that easily, though.

'Oh well.' She shrugged. 'This'll be a nice memory to take with us when we go.'

'There is that,' Elyra agreed. No point in spoiling the girl's happiness; whatever happened, it was going to be fleeting enough. If she managed to get through to Carolus, Zusen would be on a Black Ship to Terra before the month was out, along with the rest of the wyrds hiding here, and if she couldn't, the reality of the so-called sanctuary the girl hoped to find would almost certainly turn out to be equally unpleasant. Of course in that event Elyra would probably be dead by then, or, knowing what she did of heretic cults, devoutly wishing that she was...

'I don't know why you're so worried all the time,' Zusen said. Like most of the wyrds taking refuge here, she seemed to be using her powers more and more casually, heedless of the potential danger to her soul, and had clearly picked up on the anxiety Elyra was trying so hard to suppress.

Elyra shrugged. 'Just waiting for the boom,' she said.

'What boom?' Zusen asked, a faint frown of puzzlement appearing on her face.

'There's always a boom,' Elyra said. 'Sooner or later. Everything seems to be going well, then... Boom. Better not to forget it. Then at least it won't take you by surprise.'

'You can't really believe that,' Zusen said. A faintly pitying expression crossed her sharp features as she thought about the feelings she was picking up from the older woman. 'Holy Throne, you probably do. What a sad, bleak life you must lead.'

'Works for me,' Elyra said. 'You try looking over your shoulder for the next few decades, then come and tell me about the simple joys of existence.' Despite herself, a thread of amusement at the idea of being told how to live her life by a girl a third of her own age began to filter through her pessimistic musings. 'Till then, when I want the opinions of a cocky adolescent, I'll tell you what they are, all right?'

'All right.' Detecting the lightening of her mood, Zusen refused to take offence, and trotted away, traces of the poised and confident woman she'd one day become beginning to manifest in her posture, and Elyra sighed. One way or another, that destiny was going to be brutally snatched away from her, and there was nothing she could do about it.

'There you are.' Voyle was walking towards her, and she adopted a neutral expression as she turned in his direction. He seemed to be hurrying, and as the obvious explanation occurred to her, she fought down a sudden stab of panic. 'I've been looking for you.'

'Have they found us a ship already?' she asked, managing to mask her fear of the answer behind the tone of scepticism she'd been cultivating since they met. To her well-concealed relief, he shook his head.

'Not yet,' he said. 'But maybe tomorrow.'

'What do you want then?' she asked.

Voyle looked a little puzzled. 'It seems our friend Greel wants to talk to you. Any idea why?'

'The jewellery I stole,' she said, jumping to the obvious conclusion. 'Before I decided to go with you, he offered to fence it for me. I guess he still wants to deal.' She shrugged, slipping easily into the assumed persona of self-obsessed thief. 'Maybe I should think about it; I might need the money later.'

Voyle laughed. 'I doubt that. The Sanctuary takes care of its own. But the Franchise are useful, and it wouldn't hurt to throw Greel a bone if you feel like it.'

'Fine,' Elyra said. 'Then I'll set up a trade with him.' This could be the chance she'd been praying for to contact Carolus, and she intended to seize it. But she'd have to play things very carefully. 'On one condition.'

Voyle looked at her curiously. 'What's that?'

'Vos makes the contact. I know him, and I don't trust Greel.'

Voyle laughed. 'You don't trust anyone, do you?'

'Maybe you, a little,' Elyra said, looking at him appraisingly. As she'd expected, Voyle looked both pleased, and somewhat taken aback.

'Then let me take the package for you,' he suggested. 'I've got some business with Greel myself before we leave.'

Elyra shook her head. 'I said a little. Not that much. The shinies stay with me until I see the cash. And Vos.'

Voyle smiled, and sighed tolerantly. 'I can't do that. If Diurnus ever found out I let you leave here, he'd have my head.'

'Then don't tell him,' Elyra said reasonably. 'I wasn't planning to; he might want a cut.'

'By all the powers, you're a piece of work,' Voyle said, seeming genuinely amused.

Elyra echoed the smile. 'It shouldn't take long. Maybe when we get back here we can celebrate.' It was far from the first time she'd used the prospect of sex to get what she wanted since becoming an agent of the Throne; a lot of men, and a surprising number of women, had short-circuited their brains and their sense of self-preservation over the years at the idea of joining her in bed. Generally, to their disappointment, the promised tryst had either failed to materialise, or turned out to involve rather more people with guns and brusquely asked questions than they'd anticipated. On a few occasions, however, she had made good on the promise, either to maintain a cover story, or, if she was honest with herself, simply because she found her target pleasant enough company and thought she might as well take advantage of the situation. She wasn't sure if Voyle would fall into the latter category or not, but in any event, the hint seemed to be having the desired effect.

'Well, I won't tell him if you won't,' Voyle said. He glanced at the dome overhead, through which most of the planet was now revealed, only a faint sliver of darkness arcing across the easternmost limb of the world. 'I'll go and get the shuttle sorted out.'

NINETEEN

Hive Sibellus, Scintilla
259.993.M41

'YOU MIGHT WANT to take a look at this' Quillem said, taking a data-slate from his pocket, and trying to read the expressions on the faces of the Angelae surrounding him. Openly suspicious, for the most part, which hardly came as a surprise, only the tech-priest seeming indifferent to his presence. 'It's a fairly comprehensive summary of our investigation so far.'

'Thank you.' Horst took it, a trifle stiffly, and handed the device to Vex, who tore himself away from communing with the cogitator, and began to scan the files it contained with evident interest. 'Hybris can cross-check it for anything which might relate to what we've discovered.' He picked up an almost identical slate from a nearby table, and handed it to Quillem. 'You might find something useful here, too. Copies of all the reports I've compiled for Inquisitor Finurbi, brought up to date this morning.'

'Much appreciated,' Quillem said, deciding that it wouldn't be tactful to mention that he'd already read

most of the material it contained. Context was everything, as Inquisitor Grynner was fond of pointing out,
and it wouldn't hurt to begin again from first principles
in any case. They'd already missed the reference to the
wraithbone, and there was no telling what else might fall
into place from a careful rereading in light of the latest
information.

'You're welcome,' Horst said, a trifle grudgingly, but
clearly determined to make the effort. 'I got Hybris to
add a copy of the data we got from Vos as well. Perhaps your people can make more sense of it than we
could.'

'Dylar appears to have been collating rumours and
reports of eldar sightings in and around the sector,' Vex
said, glancing up from the data-slate Horst had handed
to him. 'Paying particular attention to the oldest and
most exaggerated. Which would certainly fall under the
remit of the Ordo Xenos.'

'We'll take a look at that too,' Quillem said, his interest
piqued. 'Maybe there's a clue there to the origin of the
wraithbone fragment.'

'Recaf?' Drake asked, emerging from the kitchen section with several steaming mugs. To Quillem's vague
surprise the former Guardsman offered him one, along
with his colleagues, and he took it, even though he didn't
really want the drink. It was the gesture which was
important, consolidating the fragile alliance with a token
acceptance of him as a part of their group.

'Thank you,' he said, sipping the bitter beverage. There
was little else to say or do here, and he'd depart as soon
as he'd finished it. Inquisitor Grynner would be eager to
begin analysing the fresh intelligence the Angelae had
brought to the fledgling partnership, and he didn't want
to keep his patron waiting.

'That's interesting,' Vex said, glancing up from the data-
slate Quillem had brought. 'The freighter you boarded,
the *Eddia Stabilis*, was owned by Diurnus Lines.'

Quillem shrugged. 'So are half the merchantmen in the sector,' he pointed out.

The tech-priest shook his head. 'The actual number would be more in the region of thirteen per cent,' he corrected pedantically, evidently as incapable as most of his brethren of recognising exaggeration for effect. 'So it could simply be a coincidence. Nevertheless, it might be significant that Diurnus also owns the *Ursus Innare*.'

'Which brought your friends to Scintilla,' Quillem said. He took another swallow of the recaf, which seemed suddenly more palatable. 'Possibly a coincidence, as you say. But one which might well be worth looking into.'

Hive Tarsus, Scintilla
259.993.M41

THE MEETING GREEL had arranged with his buyer took place in the most Emperor-forsaken part of the hive Kyrlock could imagine, close to the outer skin. At first, as they'd descended, he'd felt relieved, anticipating some respite from the suffocating heat; but the franchiseman had led him away from the cool of the shadowed interior towards the scorching wilderness of the desert itself. Now the interlacing infrastructure was porous enough for him to see the sere kilometres of windblown sand surrounding the single island of humanity, their altitude still great enough to discern the curve of the horizon in the distance.

'Stay out of the sunlight,' Greel advised, ducking to avoid a dazzling beam. 'This close to the shell, it'll cook you to the bone.' That was probably an exaggeration, Kyrlock thought, but not much of one; Elyra had told him that only a few minutes' direct exposure could be lethal. She'd apparently been here before, with the other Angelae, but had glossed over the details.

'I thought it was supposed to get cooler further down,' Kyrlock grumbled, deciding it would be best to feign ignorance of everything he'd been told aboard the ore barge. If Elyra had decided to pretend this was her first visit, he didn't want anyone wondering how he knew so much about the place.

'That's in the centre,' Greel said, with a trace of amusement at his apparent naïveté. 'The outer skin goes all the way down to the ground.'

'Yeah,' Kyrlock said. 'I suppose it must. Lucky us.'

'It is if we don't want anyone noticing our business,' Greel said.

Kyrlock shrugged. 'That makes an awful lot of nobodies around,' he pointed out. To his surprise, even this hellish layer of the hive seemed to be home to an awful lot of people, wrapped, for the most part, in loose, hooded robes, apparently designed to protect them as much as possible from the lethal rays of the sun.

'That's why I chose this place,' Greel said, with surprising good humour. But then he thought he was going to make two big scores today, so Kyrlock supposed he was entitled to be cheerful. 'No one will recognise us in these.' He held up a pair of the enveloping garments, plucked from a nearby street stall, and threw one to Kyrlock.

'I suppose not,' Kyrlock said, struggling into it, while the franchiseman haggled with the stallholder, eventually parting with a handful of small change.

There was no doubt about it, the loose fabric made him feel noticeably cooler, and he pulled the hood over his head gratefully. Greel followed suit, becoming almost indistinguishable from anyone else in the crowd thronging the souk, and Kyrlock resolved to watch him carefully; a moment's inattention, and he could lose both his guide, and his only chance of contacting Elyra.

His stratagem, it seemed, had worked: piquing Greel's cupidity had prompted him to set up a meeting with her, in the hope of obtaining the jewellery she was carrying. Better still, the people she was with were apparently the ones interested in buying the data-slate he'd collected from Dylar, which meant that he'd done the right thing in passing a copy of its contents on to Horst.

'Where to now?' he asked.

'Just a few levels down,' Greel assured him, shaking the fine layer of gritty sand, which seemed to get everywhere here, from the folds of his voluminous garment. The two men began to move off together, weaving their way through the milling crowds, and Kyrlock began to feel a tingle of unease.

'We're being followed,' he said a few minutes later, sure that at least two of the cowled, anonymous figures surrounding them were sticking too close for coincidence.

'I hope so,' Greel said, amusement colouring his voice. 'You didn't think I'd come down here without some backup, did you?'

'I hadn't thought about it,' Kyrlock said, shrugging, although it was far from true. 'Planning's your department.' He'd been hoping for a more visible show of force, though. When he spoke to Elyra, he wanted to be sure that no one could overhear them.

Greel laughed. 'I like your attitude,' he said. 'You don't give a rut about anything much, do you?'

Kyrlock shrugged, a little awkwardly under the enveloping robe. 'Not so long as I get paid,' he said.

The brief exchange had taken them down two flights of steps, and across a small square of roughcast hovels, their bleached and sand-scoured surfaces indicating that they were exposed to the full fury of the sun for at least a few hours a day. They all looked pretty much alike to Kyrlock, so he was taken aback when Greel suddenly stopped in front of one, outside which a faded awning flapped in the breeze in a desultory manner.

'In here.' The franchiseman vanished abruptly, ducking to pass through a narrow doorway, over which a blanket had been nailed to pass muster as a curtain.

Kyrlock followed, trying to ignore the memories of his brother's drinkhole in the Tumble, which had boasted a similar arrangement. It seemed his earlier impression had been correct: wherever you went in the galaxy, things were a lot more alike than you might think. As he let the curtain fall behind him, he caught sight of the figures he'd seen before taking up positions where they could easily cover the door.

'You're still here, then,' he said, nodding to Elyra and Voyle, who were seated at a roughly carved wooden table in the middle of the room. There was no sign of whoever normally lived here, if anyone actually did; perhaps the Franchise just kept it for clandestine meetings like this one.

'Not for long,' Elyra said, and Voyle shot her a warning glance. 'So let's make this quick.' She took a small cloth bag from the recesses of her robe, and spilled the contents onto the table. Flickering lamplight flashed from the facets of gemstones, and gleamed dully from their settings of precious metal. She smiled sardonically at Greel, who stared at the small heap of jewellery as if hypnotised. 'I haven't got time for you to fence them and pass back a percentage. You buy, and sell them for whatever you can get. Do we have a deal?'

'Depends on the price,' Greel said, tearing his eyes away from the glittering hoard, not quite able to conceal his avarice. 'I could front you maybe ten, possibly twelve thousand. That should give me a reasonable return on my investment.'

'Add a nought to that, and maybe we'll talk,' Elyra said, starting to scoop the jewellery back into the bag.

Greel shook his head. 'I know this hive. I could get fifty for a stash like that, and not a throne more. Twenty-five.'

'You could get twice that without breaking sweat,' Elyra said, and scowled. 'Which would be a neat trick in itself in a hellhole like this. Do you think I just fell off the tree?'

'I think you just arrived from off-world,' Greel said, try-ing to sound reasonable. 'I don't know what contacts you had on Sepheris Secundus, or wherever you were before then, but this is my turf, and I know what's possible. One wrong move trying to shift merchandise like this, and I'll have the lawdogs down on me like fleas on a dreg. I can't get more than fifty, and I'm not sticking my neck out for anything less than twenty off the top.'

'I'm sure you can live with ten,' Elyra riposted.

Greel hesitated, his indecision almost succeeding in looking genuine, then nodded. 'All right, forty K it is.'

'Has a nice ring to it,' Elyra agreed. 'You've brought cash?'

'Not that much,' Greel said.

'That needn't be a problem,' Voyle interjected, having watched the negotiations with undisguised amusement. 'We still have to reach an arrangement about the mer-chandise you're selling. If you deduct your forty thousand from the price we agree, I'll give Elyra the cash myself, on your behalf.' He glanced at Elyra, apparently sharing some private joke. 'I presume you trust me that much, at least.'

'I guess so,' she said, shrugging. 'It's not like I don't know where to find you.'

'Where is that?' Kyrlock asked, and Voyle and Elyra both stared at him, her feigned suspicion no less con-vincing than his genuine one. Kyrlock spread his hands. 'All right, stupid question. Forget I asked.' He smiled at Elyra. 'So, now you're rich, any chance of that demiscore you still owe me?'

'Reckon so,' she conceded, playing along effortlessly, and rising to join him. Greel immediately slipped onto the stool she'd vacated, and began negotiating with Voyle about the data-slate in hushed and urgent tones. 'I've probably got a few thrones on me somewhere.'

She pulled out a purse, and extracted a handful of coins with an easygoing smile. As she pressed them into his hand, she palmed a small piece of paper from somewhere up her sleeve, and added it to the money.

'Thanks,' Kyrlock said, tucking the cash away without looking at it.

'You're welcome,' Elyra said. She might have been about to say more, but never got the chance; Voyle and Greel were rising from the table, their own deal evidently concluded to their mutual satisfaction.

Greel glanced at Kyrlock. 'Come on, we're leaving.'

'If you say so,' Kyrlock agreed, with a last look back at Elyra. As the curtain fell across the narrow doorway, and the glare and noise of the hiveskin souk burst around him again, she was already turning back to Voyle.

'Stupid bitch,' Greel said, with some amusement. 'I can get a hundred and fifty for this stuff easy.' Then he glanced at Kyrlock, an incipient challenge. 'Oh, I was forgetting, she's a friend of yours. You have a problem with that?'

'Why would I?' Kyrlock asked. 'You're the one paying me, not her.' Then he shrugged, his fingers closing around the little stash of coins in his pocket, and the tightly folded note. 'Besides, I got what I came for.'

The *Emperor's Justice*, Scintilla System
259.993.M41

'THEY'VE ENCOUNTERED KARNAKI?' Jorge Grynner raised an eyebrow. 'A most intriguing development. I never expected them to attempt to obtain access to the archives of the Ordo Malleus.'

'But a logical one,' Quillem pointed out, 'given the number of times they've encountered daemons in the course of their investigation.' Catching his patron's eye, he corrected himself hastily. 'Or what they believed to be daemons at the time. Karnaki seems less than convinced about that.'

'Well, the warp and its denizens are his area of expertise,' Grynner said, musingly. 'I'll be interested to hear what else he thinks they might have been.'

'No doubt he'll let us know as soon as he's sure,' Quillem said. 'I could contact him, and ask for an interim assessment, if you like.'

'Let's give him a little longer to complete his researches. He's somewhat reclusive, and tends to resent what he sees as unnecessary interference.' Grynner picked up the data-slate Horst had given the interrogator. 'This information Kyrlock intercepted, regarding the eldar, is quite remarkable. Considering its compiler didn't have access to most of the sources we do, it's surprisingly comprehensive.'

'I'll have it cross-referenced against the standard texts,' Quillem said. 'Is there anything in particular the analysts should be looking for?'

'There are a disproportionate number of references to the legend of the *Voidwraith*,' Grynner said. 'He appears to be attempting to deduce its location.'

'But the *Voidwraith's* just a myth,' Quillem objected. 'A dead craftworld, abandoned by the eldar, drifting through space for aeons... The whole idea's patently absurd.'

'On the face of it,' Grynner agreed. 'Nevertheless, if you wouldn't mind asking Castafiore to drop in for a word, I'd like to hear his opinion.'

'Of course,' Quillem said, trying to mask his reluctance, and knowing full well that it would be a wasted effort: Inquisitor Grynner was well aware of how little he'd relish speaking to the ship's Navigator. Like every other member of the Navis Nobilite, Jaquamo Castafiore was arrogant, opinionated and treated everyone outside his precious guild as little better than orks with pretensions to culture. Quillem could already picture his reaction to being consulted about a children's story, and braced himself for the coming storm. 'I'll see that he's informed.'

'Thank you,' Grynner said, his attention already absorbed by the words on the slate's tiny screen.

Hive Sibellus, Scintilla
259.993.M41

As KEIRA ENTERED Vorn's apartment, laden with supplies from the market, she was immediately struck by how quiet it seemed. Instincts honed on the belly of Ambulon, and refined by the Collegium Assassinorum, kicked in, and she lowered her burden silently to the floorboards. The street clothes she wore effectively concealed her knives, and she drew two, feeling instantly more comfortable with the weight of their hilts against her palms.

There was no one in sight. Vex's cogitator was dark and deactivated, and the only trace of Drake's presence was the scattering of empty recaf mugs which generally marked where he had been. She had joked once that she was able to track his movements by them, but it might actually be possible, by using the residual heat of the dregs to assess how long each one had been there.

She began to move warily into the main living area, as stealthily as if she was stalking a target.

'What kept you?' Horst asked, emerging from the kitchen area, and she relaxed at once, slipping the blades back into their scabbards.

'You weren't getting worried, were you?' she asked, beginning to wonder if the others had gone out to search for her.

Horst shook his head. 'After your little escapade in the Tricorn, I'd expect you to come back unscathed from the Eye of Terror. With Abaddon's head in a bag.'

Keira grinned, acknowledging the compliment. 'I stopped off at the chapel down the street,' she said. 'I must have lost track of the time.'

A faint expression of puzzlement crossed Horst's face. 'I didn't think Redemptionists went in for chapel,' he said.

'They don't. More the blood, fire and damnation stuff,' Keira said, vaguely surprised to hear her own flippant tone about matters she used to take so seriously. But something had changed in her, and she hurried on, reluctant to analyse them too much. 'But I've been in there several times. It feels… I don't know. Welcoming.'

'I suppose it should do,' Horst said. 'It's the house of the Emperor, after all.'

For the first time, it occurred to Keira that she knew very little about the tenets of his faith; the Ecclesiarchy was home to a bewildering variety of practices and beliefs, many of which agreed on little or nothing beyond the divinity of Him on Earth. She nodded. 'It's a side of Him I never knew before. It's making me question a lot of things I always just took for granted.'

Horst nodded. 'I can see that it would,' he said cautiously.

Emboldened, Keira hurried on. 'I've been praying for guidance about some things that have been troubling me lately.'

'Oh.' Horst nodded again. 'Perhaps I should drop in there too.' He looked at her, as if wondering what to say next. 'I've been confused about a few things myself recently.'

'Perhaps they're the same things,' Keira said, keeping her voice neutral, although her heartbeat was suddenly loud in her ears.

'Perhaps they are,' Horst said. He took a hesitant step towards her, but before he could say anything more, Vex appeared from the doorway leading to Vorn's inner sanctum. His robe was off, revealing the patchwork of metallic implants the fall of the cloth generally concealed, and a few cables trailed from plugs inserted into diagnostic sockets. It seemed he'd finally found the time to finish restoring the damage he'd sustained in the attack by Avia's renegade tech-priests.

'A message from Vos,' he reported, an edge of excitement he couldn't quite suppress nudging its way into the carefully modulated tones he habitually employed. 'He's found Elyra!'

'Good.' Horst turned to the tech-priest, whatever he'd been about to say forgotten in the face of this unexpected development. 'Is Danuld with Barda yet?'

'He's just arrived at the pad,' Vorn confirmed, glancing up from the array of vox equipment walling the back of the room.

'Then get them in the air at once. I want Vos back here for debriefing as soon as possible.' Horst hesitated. 'Then I suppose we ought to tell Quillem.'

'I'll do that,' Keira said, both relieved and disappointed at the interruption. But duty came first with both of them, as it always would. Her palms tingled with the phantom weight of her weapons, eager to shed heretic blood. Whatever Mordechai had been about to say could wait until a more propitious moment; right now there was the Emperor's work to do, and nothing could be more important than that.

TWENTY

The *Emperor's Justice*, Scintilla System
260.993.M41

'WELCOME ABOARD, INQUISITOR,' Quillem said, nodding respectfully to the black-clad figure striding towards him across the hangar deck of the *Emperor's Justice*, the echoes of his bootsoles ringing from the deckplates in the cavernous space. 'The others are already assembled.'

'Good. I can assure you there's no time to waste,' Karnaki said. A small constellation of servo-skulls was trailing after him from the passenger compartment of the shuttle Inquisitor Grynner had dispatched to collect him, parked neatly next to the crimson and grey Lightnings of the vessel's fighter wing, and he glanced back, as if to make sure none of the hovering servitors had got lost. 'Please direct a few of your crewmen to see to the safe stowage of my equipment.'

'Equipment?' Quillem echoed, a little taken aback. So far as he was aware, the Ordo Malleus inquisitor was simply here to exchange information.

Karnaki nodded. 'My plasma pentacle, and a few other warding devices. They may well prove necessary.'

There was no point in arguing, so Quillem simply accosted the nearest deckhand, and issued the appropriate instructions. 'And make sure accommodation is prepared for our guest,' he concluded. If Karnaki was to accompany them, subject to Inquisitor Grynner's approval of course, he'd need quarters of his own.

Part of his mind wondered if he'd agreed so readily because of the strange power of compulsion the Malleus inquisitor apparently possessed, but he dismissed the fleeting thought as fruitless paranoia; compelled or not, he'd merely done exactly what he would have in any case.

'This way.' He led their guest, and his ossiferous comet tail, to a conference suite adjoining his patron's living quarters; Jorge Grynner guarded the sanctity of his study jealously, and few of his acolytes were permitted entry, fewer still as freely as Quillem.

The metal-walled room, which could have seated a score of delegates, seemed strangely deserted with so few occupants. Grynner was at the head of the table, as befitted both his status and his position as the owner of the ship on which the meeting was taking place, the gilded aquila grasping the sigil of the Inquisition in its talons visible on the wall behind him. Horst was sitting halfway down one side of the slab of polished wood, trying to look unimpressed by his surroundings, without much success, accompanied by the tech-priest Vex. At a nod from his patron, Quillem seated himself opposite the two Angelae, while Karnaki, as the most senior guest, settled comfortably into the chair facing Grynner along the length of the table.

'Inquisitor.' Grynner inclined his head courteously. 'Thank you for concluding your researches so promptly.'

'There's little time to waste,' Karnaki said, returning the nod. 'Particularly in the light of the information supplied by the young lady who wandered into our library the other evening.' He glanced at Horst and Vex. 'Is Miss Sythree not accompanying you?'

'She's aboard,' Horst said, 'keeping an eye on our luggage.' To Quillem's amusement, the assassin had refused to be parted from a single item until it had all been safely transferred to the cabins assigned to the Angelae; it seemed the incident aboard the *Misericord* had left its mark. 'Inquisitor Grynner persuaded us that our interests coincide, at least for the moment.'

'Until your missing patron turns up again, you mean,' Karnaki said. Horst nodded, and Karnaki echoed the gesture, a trifle dismissively. 'I suppose he still might,' he conceded.

'What do you mean by that?' Horst asked, clearly nettled.

Karnaki steepled his fingers thoughtfully. 'Simply that, if I'm right in the conclusions I've drawn, he was well advised to be cautious. The entities he, and you, encountered on Sepheris Secundus are a particularly insidious threat. There's no reason to suppose that they have actually spread their influence as far as the ranks of the Ordos Calixis, but it certainly isn't beyond the bounds of possibility.'

'From which, I take it, we are to infer that you have identified them?' Inquisitor Grynner asked.

'I believe so,' Karnaki said. He turned his head to look directly at Horst, in a manner which reminded Quillem of a raptor catching sight of a small rodent in the grass that's probably not worth the effort of going after. 'Your assumption that they were daemons is quite understandable, but completely erroneous. From the visual memories I lifted from Miss Sythree's mind, and the fact that they appear to have possessed psykers, I'm quite confident that they were a species we refer to as Enslavers.'

'That's rather disturbing, if true,' Inquisitor Grynner said, absently polishing his spectacles on the end of his neck cloth.

'You're familiar with these creatures?' Karnaki asked, a faint tone of scepticism edging into his voice.

Grynner shook his head. 'I've heard the name mentioned. In connection with the Gadarine incident. But the details didn't particularly interest me at the time.' He blinked mildly at the black-clad man facing him. 'I seem to recall Exterminatus was resorted to on that occasion.'

Quillem tried to mask his shock, which he could see reflected in Horst's face opposite him. A decree of Exterminatus, eradicating every trace of life on a populated world, right down to the viral level, was the Inquisition's ultimate sanction, and only resorted to in the direst of circumstances.

'That's quite correct,' Karnaki confirmed. 'By the time the Ordo Malleus had responded, the situation had deteriorated beyond any hope of recovery. Thousands of psykers had been possessed, and billions of citizens had fallen under the influence of those creatures which had already broken through from the warp. Without swift and decisive action, the taint would have spread to the neighbouring systems.'

'You mean they can control non-psykers?' Quillem asked, and Karnaki nodded, as though at a particularly promising pupil.

'Quite so. But in order to do that, they need to be physically present in the material universe. If enough of them break through, they can seize control of a hive, even an entire world, then spread the taint to neighbouring systems. Left unchecked, a large enough outbreak could theoretically engulf an entire cluster.' He smiled bleakly. 'Which is why we're willing to take such extreme measures to keep an infestation contained.'

'Are we to understand, then, that they use psykers as a conduit to the materium?' Grynner asked.

'Exactly,' Karnaki agreed. 'As I'm sure you're aware, the souls of unprotected psykers blaze like beacons in the warp, attracting many of the predators which dwell in that realm. Among them, the Enslavers. When they find such a soul they devour it, possessing the physical body, in a manner similar to that of daemons.'

'Technomancer Tonis didn't seem possessed when we saw him at the citadel,' Vex objected. 'He seemed perfectly normal.'

'Which is precisely why possession by these creatures is so insidious,' Karnaki replied. 'The flesh of a daemonhost is twisted by the corruption within, but a victim taken by an Enslaver shows no outward sign of their true nature. They can work towards their goal of conquest, completely hidden from view, for as long as it suits them.'

'And then they burst out of the flesh containing them,' Horst said. 'Like Tonis, and the psyker in Adrin's mansion.'

'Exactly.' Karnaki nodded. 'The host body is completely destroyed, but that means nothing to the Enslaver. It's fulfilled its purpose, in allowing them to enter the physical world. Once present, it can begin to exert its malign influence over any minds in the vicinity.'

'Then why didn't the one in Adrin's mansion simply control us, instead of allowing us to kill it?' Horst asked.

'Because, according to Miss Sythree's memories, apart from your team, there was a score or so of storm troopers present. That was a lot of minds to assimilate at once. Had there only been one or two potential slaves in the room, you wouldn't have been so lucky.' Karnaki nodded thoughtfully. 'Of course, they feed on the minds they control; the more slaves they dominate, the stronger they are, and the more fresh minds they can consume. Which means they aren't vulnerable for very long. In theory, a sufficiently strong psyker, or powerfully warded individual, should be able to resist for long enough to mount a physical attack, hoping to return them to the warp as you did on Sepheris Secundus. But since such a course would also mean getting through a small army of meat puppets, that doesn't offer much of a chance.'

'I see.' Inquisitor Grynner tilted his head meditatively. 'This has been most informative. Thank you, inquisitor.'

'Perhaps I haven't made myself clear,' Karnaki said. 'We need to act now, without any further delay.' He leaned forwards a little, and Quillem could feel the force of his personality, and the passion which clearly drove him. 'Do you see? They were possessing psykers on Sepheris Secundus, and a whole group of fugitive wyrds from there have just arrived in this system. Any one of them could have been tainted, if not more.'

'Elyra,' Horst said. 'She's infiltrated the group. If he's right, she's in terrible danger.' He turned to Inquisitor Grynner. 'We have to pull her out, now.'

'If we do that,' Grynner said mildly, 'we lose our lead to the Faxlignae. And, possibly, our best chance of finding and aiding Carolus, since I'm certain he'll be continuing the investigation you started together on Sepheris Secundus.' He shook his head. 'For now, we do nothing, and simply observe.'

'You might be willing to take that risk,' Karnaki said, rising from the table, 'but I most certainly am not.' He glanced casually at Horst. 'Where are the psykers hiding?' he asked, in a conversational tone. 'Ah, I see. An abandoned agridome on the Tarsus orbital.'

Horst sat bolt upright, looking shocked and horrified. 'I'm sorry,' he blurted out, 'he just...' Words failed him.

'I'm aware of Inquisitor Karnaki's peculiar talent,' Grynner said. He blinked mildly at Horst. 'And I can assure you, you have nothing to reproach yourself for.' His attention returned to Karnaki, and his expression became a little harder. 'I had hoped you would refrain from the discourtesy of using it in so petty a fashion, however. Please resume your seat.'

'My apologies.' Karnaki inclined his head, and complied with the request. 'But my recommendation stands.'

'And will be duly considered,' Grynner assured him. 'Along with the other alternatives.'

Hive Tarsus, Scintilla
260.993.M41

'Vos!' Drake greeted his friend at the top of the boarding ramp, which was already beginning to rise. Barda had kept the engines of the sturdy little shuttle idling, and now, as he fed power to the main boosters, it began to lift in a flurry of sand. 'You're a sight for sore eyes.'

'You too, mate.' Kyrlock seemed different to the man he remembered, marked by his experiences in the long weeks since they'd parted, but then Drake supposed he was too. It was something about the eyes; he'd seen it in veteran soldiers, a wariness that never quite went away. 'What's been happening? Mordechai told me a bit about it over the vox, but he didn't want to say too much for obvious reasons.'

'Quite a bit,' Drake said, taking the holdall his friend was carrying. It was heavy, containing the shotgun, Kyrlock's furs and a few other items he'd acquired since they'd last seen one another. The chainaxe was hanging in its usual position, over Kyrlock's shoulder, and the red-headed Guardsman removed it from its sling as they passed through the narrow door to the passenger compartment.

Barda was evidently enjoying the challenge of navigating his way through the tangle of intersecting levels which made up the hive; the pad they'd landed on had been a small one, intended only for the light utility craft capable of threading their way through the tightly woven infrastructure, and even a shuttle as small as theirs had never been intended to land there. Vex had supplied the coordinates from memory, hinting that the Angelae had used it on a previous assignment, although he hadn't elaborated; Elyra had evidently shared something of the same memories with Kyrlock, as he seemed to have found his way to the rendezvous without much difficulty.

'Interesting place,' Drake commented, dropping into a nearby seat, and trying to take in the dizzying panorama of overlapping hab zones, twisted around one another like a tangle of twine. A lot of it seemed to be hurtling past at a speed and proximity he would normally have found alarming, but he'd had time to get to know Barda quite well since their arrival on Scintilla, and he had complete confidence in the young pilot's abilities. Besides, if he was wrong, at least at this speed they'd be dead before he knew anything about it.

'You could say that,' Kyrlock agreed, as Barda jinked around the last few structural members, and the shuttle broke through into clear air at last. The note of the engines increased in pitch as the pilot boosted them to full thrust, and the gallant little craft leapt forwards, like a hunting hound let off the leash. 'I'll be interested to see how Sibellus compares.'

'We're not going back to Sibellus,' Drake said. 'We're meeting a starship.' The sky outside the viewport was already beginning to darken, taking on a rich purple hue, and the first faint stars were beginning to show in the firmament, outshone for the moment by the brighter lights of the orbital docks and the swarm of vessels surrounding it.

'A starship?' Kyrlock said, without much enthusiasm. 'I've only just got off a rutting starship.'

'This one's different,' Drake said. 'It belongs to a friend of the boss's.' He took a deep breath. 'In fact, there's a lot you need to know...'

The *Emperor's Justice*, Scintilla System
260.993.M41

AFTER INQUISITOR GRYNNER'S admonishment, the conference proceeded smoothly enough, although Horst couldn't prevent himself from glancing furtively at Kar-naki every few minutes. He'd known about the man's abilities from Keira's report, but he'd still been completely unprepared for them. As soon as the black-clad inquisitor had spoken, the information had been spat out automatically by his memory, only to be skimmed from the surface of his mind like fat from a stock pot. In spite of Grynner's assurances that he had nothing to reproach himself for, he seethed with resentment, convinced now that the Ordo Malleus inquisitor was not to be trusted.

Forcing himself to concentrate on the discussion around the table, he became abruptly aware that it had moved on while he'd been brooding, and that Vex was now speaking.

'It seems clear from the files Vos obtained that the Faxlignae, if that is indeed who's behind all this, take the legend of the *Voidwraith* perfectly seriously, and are actively seeking it.' The tech-priest hesitated. '*Voidwraith* being the nearest Gothic equivalent to the eldar name for the hulk, which translates more literally as "eternally lost wanderer of the stars". Seeking the services of the Conclave of the Enlightened was quite shrewd of them, as, being endowed by wealthy patrons with little understanding of what they're buying, their libraries often include esoterica generally lost or unknown to more reputable academic institutions.'

'You mean the slate actually contains something we didn't know?' Quillem asked, leaning across the table. Knowing Vex's talent for making connections not immediately obvious to most people, Horst was far less surprised by this than their new associate.

'I suspect so,' Vex said, 'although I can't be completely certain. This is, after all, a fresh area of inquiry for me, so I'm unfamiliar with much of the extant information.' He'd been asked to assist Inquisitor Grynner's team of analysts almost as soon as they'd arrived on the *Emperor's*

Justice, although Horst had no idea why they didn't just give the job of filtering the data to one of their own tech-priests. He was certain that Grynner must have some among his acolytes. Perhaps it was just intended to make the Angelae feel valued members of the partnership; unless the opposite was true, and they were being subtly directed away from the main investigation. 'However, I'm given to understand that at least one reported sighting of the *Voidwraith* in the new material is unmatched in any of the other sources. If so, that may well be significant.'

'Significant how?' Grynner asked.

'It may complete a pattern,' Vex said. 'It's too early to be certain, but if I'm correct, it might be possible for a sufficiently skilled Navigator to narrow down its potential location significantly. If, of course, it actually exists at all.'

'I think we should assume that it does,' Inquisitor Grynner said thoughtfully, 'if only because the Faxlignae are clearly operating on that basis. And if they turn out to be right, they'll be able to recover as much wraithbone as they need.' Apparently remembering that not everyone present shared his knowledge of such esoteric matters, he added, 'It would appear to be used as a structural material aboard the eldar craftworlds.'

'Which means they could find tonnes of the stuff lying around for the taking,' Quillem said, looking visibly apprehensive. Remembering how much havoc Tonis had been able to wreak with a mere sliver of the stuff, Horst could understand his concern.

'I'll continue with the analysis,' Vex said. 'That being so, it might be prudent to arrive ahead of them, if at all possible.'

'None of which addresses the problem of the Enslavers,' Karnaki put in from the foot of the table. His servo-skulls circled warily below the ceiling, as if competing for the best view of the proceedings, and Horst became uncomfortably aware that many of them bore visible weapons.

'No, it doesn't,' Inquisitor Grynner agreed. 'So, with that in mind, I've invited another expert to join us.' He glanced expectantly at the door. A moment later, as if on cue, it opened.

Horst's first impression was that the space beyond had been blocked by a fresh bulkhead, erected while the debate had been going on, but then it moved, and he felt the breath still for a moment in his throat. Well over two metres of glossy black ceramite armour squeezed through the gap, and straightened, the shaven head surmounting it almost brushing the low ceiling typical of the corridors and chambers Horst had so far seen aboard the starship. The armour was surmounted by a surcoat, of the same sable hue, in which intertwining phrases of High Gothic had been painstakingly worked in gold thread, along with arcane sigils which meant nothing to Horst. Thin scraps of parchment, for the most part obscured by the surcoat, had been fixed to the armour with seals of wax, as red as clotting blood; with the exception of the Space Marine's left shoulder guard, which had been bordered in silver, and on which a stylised human skull had been etched in the same gleaming material, these were the only splashes of colour visible anywhere. Even his face was dark, the skin as black as Vex's, although the tech-priest's bore far fewer visible scars.

Grynner nodded affably at the towering figure, which loomed over Karnaki, leaving the Ordo Malleus inquisitor looking curiously shrunken. 'Brother Paulus,' he said. 'Good of you to join us.'

'I go where my duty demands,' the giant said, remaining where he was; which was probably just as well, Horst thought. None of the chairs looked remotely big enough to support him, let alone sufficiently robust. His voice resonated through the room, making Horst's ribs vibrate within his chest.

'Quite so.' Grynner looked at Karnaki, his head cocked quizzically to one side, assessing the other man's reaction. 'Brother Paulus is the Librarian of the Deathwatch team assigned to this vessel. Accordingly, I felt his expertise in both tactics and matters of the warp would prove helpful to us.'

'No doubt,' Karnaki said. If he was surprised at being confronted by another powerful psyker, he gave no sign of the fact. He glanced at the towering figure behind him with no more than mild curiosity. 'Are you aware of the matters being discussed here?'

'I am,' Paulus confirmed, in the tones of a small avalanche. 'My battle-brothers and I have been assessing the feasibility of an assault on the heretics' location. It would be a straightforward undertaking.'

'Then it should be done,' Karnaki urged again. 'If any of the psykers it harbours are possessed by Enslavers, this entire system is in danger.'

'I concur,' Paulus said, to the evident surprise of both inquisitors. 'The Silver Skulls took part in the initial stages of the Gadarine operation.'

Clearly noticing Horst's confusion, Quillem leaned across the table. 'His home Chapter,' he explained in an undertone. 'The Deathwatch recruits from all of them.'

'By the time it became clear that we were facing something more than a mere civil insurrection, the world was already lost,' Paulus continued, 'and many of my battle-brothers with it.' He paused, letting the magnitude of that sink in; threats potent enough to cause the loss of a significant number of Space Marines were few and far between, and not to be taken lightly. 'I do not wish to see Scintilla go the same way.'

'There, you have it,' Karnaki said, recovering his composure first. 'Your own expert confirms my assessment.'

'Which lends a great deal of weight to it,' Grynner agreed, blinking in apparent perplexity. 'I'm still concerned about losing our best lead to the Faxlignae, however.'

'You have a fresh one, in this phantom craftworld,' Karnaki pointed out. 'And your agent might well have discovered their location herself by now.'

'That's possible,' Horst agreed. 'Elyra's very resourceful.' If he was honest with himself he didn't think it all that likely, but showing his support for a raid looked like the best chance of getting her to safety. He shrugged. 'And we may find physical evidence of the next step in the chain anyway.'

'Unlikely, given how well they covered their tracks the last time we tried that,' Quillem said, an unexpected edge of bitterness in his voice, and Horst belatedly remembered what he'd read in the data-slate he'd been given. Quillem had lost most of his team in the last attempt to raid a Faxlignae facility.

'Nevertheless,' Inquisitor Grynner said, his reluctance palpable, 'given the circumstances, I don't think we have a choice. Ignoring a clear and present danger in the hope of uncovering a more deeply laid plot at a later date would hardly be prudent.'

'Then I will instruct my battle-brothers to prepare,' Paulus rumbled.

'Please do so,' Grynner agreed, and swept his gaze the length of the table. 'I suggest we follow their example. And may the Emperor watch over us all.'

I

TWENTY-ONE

Tarsus High Orbital Docks, Scintilla System
260.993.M41

ELYRA WOKE SLOWLY, and stretched. The bedroll was empty beside her, but a faint residue of warmth still lingered in the blankets, along with the rich, earthy scent of spent passion. Her ostensible celebration with Voyle had perhaps gone a little further than she'd anticipated, but she couldn't bring herself to regret it; if nothing else, sharing a bed with a geist, who could touch her in more ways than the merely physical, had been an interesting and enjoyable novelty.

On the purely practical level, it had also created a bond between them she knew she'd be able to exploit; now Voyle would be even more useful as a source of information, and a far more effective shield against the suspicions of his colleagues in the Sanctuary when they finally reached the mysterious refuge.

'You're awake then,' he said, and she opened her eyes, squinting at the sunlight beginning to filter through the fringe of vegetation above her face. They'd chosen a secluded corner of the agridome for their tryst, surrounded by vines of some kind, and the shade it created was dappled across her skin. Voyle was sitting nearby, chewing a protein bar; as she sat up, he threw another across to her.

'Thanks.' Elyra plucked it from the air, and bit into it as she began to get dressed. 'I'm ravenous.'

'Then you'd better eat while you can,' Voyle said.

She smiled flirtatiously, although she supposed they were a long way beyond mere flirtation by this time, and started lacing up her boots. 'Why? Do you think I'm going to need the energy?'

'Yes.' Voyle returned the smile for a moment, before his expression became businesslike again. 'But not for what you're thinking. I just got word, our escort's on the way to pick us up.'

'Are you sure?' Elyra said, trying to mask her dismay. She'd known this was bound to happen, but part of her had always clung to the hope that Carolus would find a way to extract her before it did. Well, that hope was now gone, and she'd just have to do whatever it took to complete her mission alone.

Voyle nodded, and tapped the comm-bead in his ear. 'Sure as the Powers protect. The shuttle's already inbound, and should be docking any time now.'

'Where?' Elyra began packing her belongings. 'The same bay we used before?' They'd ridden down to Hive Tarsus in the back of a cargo shuttle, and returned the same way, blending into the general bustle of a busy commercial hangar completely unnoticed, but she couldn't see an entire contingent of fugitive wyrds being able to pull off the same trick.

Voyle shook his head. 'Not this time,' he said. 'There's a maintenance airlock a few levels down...' Before he was able to elaborate further a streak of fire appeared in the firmament beyond the armourcrys dome, impacting against it an instant later with an explosion which shook the deck plating beneath their feet, and he broke off in surprise. 'What the hell was that?'

'Shuttle crash?' Elyra hazarded, hoping that was all it was. Carolus wouldn't have ordered a direct assault, she knew him well enough to be certain of that. But there were clearly other players in the game she was unaware of; someone must have ordered the raid on Voyle's warehouse aboard the void station. If whoever that had been was repeating the tactic here, she was in as much danger as the rest of the psykers; the raiders wouldn't know she was an Inquisition agent, and would gun her down as casually as any of the others. She drew her laspistol, and slung her pack across her shoulders.

'No.' Voyle was listening to the voices in his earpiece, his expression grave. 'It's an attack.' There could be no doubt of that now. The first explosion had been followed by a second, then a third. Directly above them, a section of the dome shuddered visibly, and began to tear free of the structural beams supporting it, the heavy girders twisting like overwarmed sugarsticks.

Elyra felt her heart stop for a moment. If that vast mass of steel and armourcrys fell, it would obliterate them all. But to her relief it turned out to be beyond the reach of the gravity generators; as she watched, in horrified fascination, it began to peel away, drifting out into the void instead.

Abruptly, a gale swept across the tangle of vegetation, ripping leaves from plants, and rippling the grass like the waters of a storm-lashed sea.

'They've breached the dome!' Elyra shouted, raising her voice above the screaming of the wind. 'We have to get back to the service ducts!'

'Yes,' Voyle agreed, surprisingly calm under the circumstances; heretic he might be, but, at least for the present, Elyra instinctively felt that she could trust his judgement. 'Got everything you need?'

'Right here.' Elyra hefted her laspistol, then, belatedly remembering to stay in character, added, 'What about my money?'

'Trust me,' Voyle said, 'if we get out of here alive, I'll make sure you get paid.'

'Good enough,' Elyra agreed. 'Can't spend it anyway if I'm dead.'

'That's my girl,' Voyle said, narrowing his eyes against the storm of dust and debris raised by the howling wind. He gestured in the direction of the service hatch, raising his voice a little to be heard above the noise. 'Ladies first: you've got the gun.'

FROM SPACE, THE rent in the dome looked like a geyser of mist, the plume of escaping atmosphere freezing instantly into crystals of ice, which slowly dissipated into the surrounding void. Barda watched the drop-pod of the Deathwatch plunge into the boiling vortex, and followed without hesitation, feeling the airframe of his own craft shudder as it entered the turbulent stream of solidifying gas.

There could be no question of taking the same route as the Astartes; their lander could tolerate stresses which would rip the vessel he piloted apart. Instead, he took a shallower angle of approach, riding the fringes of the maelstrom as he would a storm system in the atmosphere of a planet, descending in a wide, slow spiral to the surface of the dome below.

'Hang on,' he voxed, mindful that his passengers would probably appreciate a few reassuring words, 'things are going to be a little rough for the next few minutes.' Then he forgot about everything, except the business of keeping the quivering shuttle in the air.

'NO KIDDING,' DRAKE said, clutching the arms of his seat, and wishing that he'd pulled the crash webbing a little more tightly while he'd had the chance. His lasgun was braced across his knees, and he checked the charge in the powercells reflexively, murmuring the litany he'd memorised from the *Uplifting Primer*. Belatedly he wondered if he should have asked Vex to bless the weapon for him again, but it had performed well enough against the mutants aboard the *Misericord*, so he supposed it was still pretty well sanctified. Killing the Enslaver in Adrin's mansion would have left its own mark on the gun, he knew, leaving it imbued with holy purpose, and it wouldn't be prudent to meddle with that.

'Here we go again,' Kyrlock said, with heavy irony, and grinned at his friend across the narrow aisle. 'Just like outside the Citadel.'

'Except this time we're the attackers,' Drake said, with more confidence than he felt, 'and there's only a handful of wyrds down there.' Even so, the memory of the rogue psykers they'd faced in the blizzard on Sepheris Secundus, the night they'd met Inquisitor Finurbi and his agents, was strong, and filled him with a nameless dread.

'I don't care how many there are,' Kyrlock said. He patted his chainaxe as though it was a favourite pet. 'They won't be hexing anyone if they haven't got a head.'

'Quite so,' the black-garbed inquisitor said evenly, from his seat at the rear of the compartment. 'I'd recommend terminating any psykers you see on sight. If they are possessed, that will either banish the Enslaver within at once, or force it into the open.'

'Except for Elyra,' Keira said, from her seat at the front; Karnaki nodded slowly, but said nothing, his expression thoughtful.

Quillem was sitting at the front too, just across the narrow aisle from the young assassin, but had said virtually nothing since they'd left the hanger bay of the *Emperor's Justice*. Drake had found that a little strange at first, until he'd realised that the interrogator was suffering from void sickness, and suppressed a wry smile. It seemed he did have something in common with Horst after all.

That thought brought its own flare of disquiet with it. In the relatively short time he'd been a member of the Angelae, Drake had grown to trust Horst's leadership, and found it faintly unnerving to be going into action without him. Quillem could take care of himself, he had no doubt, his position as Grynner's principal aide made that more than obvious, and he'd certainly saved Vex's life; but if push came to shove, he'd follow his patron's agenda, and if that meant abandoning Elyra, he undoubtedly would. At least he didn't seem to consider her completely expendable, like the man from the Ordo Malleus plainly did.

In the end, Drake supposed, it had come down to politics, and the preservation of the fragile alliance they now found themselves a part of. Quillem was there to keep an eye on the Angelae, and probably Karnaki, at Grynner's behest, while Horst stayed behind to keep an eye on the inquisitor. He sighed, and checked the lasgun again. That, at least, was something he knew he could rely on.

The *Emperor's Justice*, Scintilla System
260.993.M41

VEX HAD NEVER seen the bridge of a starship before, and hadn't been entirely sure what to expect, but he had to admit to being quietly impressed. He'd never seen so many fine examples of the Omnissiah's bounty in one place before, outside the precincts of an Adeptus Mechanicus shrine, and would probably have allowed himself the luxury of stopping in the doorway to marvel at it had such a thing not been unseemly in the presence of an inquisitor.

'Master Castafiore,' Grynner said. 'Good of you to join us.'

Vex tore his attention away from the serried ranks of polished wooden consoles, the brass switches mounted in them burnished by the touch of generations of hands, and the glass faces of their dials dulled by a myriad of faint scratches. The vast room was dimly lit, as befitted so sanctified a space, and the glow of the instrumentation made pale wraiths of the crew members ministering to the needs of the machine-spirits, a number of them wearing the robes of his own calling. Horst was gazing at their surroundings with an expression of awestruck wonderment on his face, too distracted for the moment to even register the presence of the little man in the red satin jacket, who nodded dismissively at the inquisitor's greeting.

'It's your own time you're wasting as well as mine,' he said. Horst glanced in his direction, his attention caught by the sound of the man's voice, and the expression on his face changed to one of complete astonishment as he registered the silk bandana tied around the newcomer's forehead. An eye had been embroidered on it, right in the centre, the unmistakable badge of a member of the Navis Nobilite.

Grynner nodded, ignoring the discourtesy. 'Master Castafiore is our Navigator,' he said to Vex and Horst, as though making introductions at a social function. 'And quite exceptionally gifted, even by the standards of his peers.'

The little man preened visibly, making minute, and completely unnecessary, adjustments to the points of his waxed moustache. 'It has been said,' he agreed complacently.

Navigators were notoriously difficult to work with, Vex recalled, and clearly the key to getting this one to cooperate was copious amounts of flattery.

'Then we're most fortunate to be able to consult him,' Vex said, calculating that something of the sort was expected.

'Of course you are,' Castafiore said, looking directly at the two Angelae for the first time. 'I assume you're the Mechanicus drone who thinks we should be looking for a myth?'

'Hybris Vex.' The tech-priest inclined his head. 'And I make no such claim. I have merely been asked to analyse some data, which might provide a clue to the location of some eldar artefacts.' He paused for a moment to allow the idea to register. 'If there actually is anything there to find, it will require a Navigator of unparalleled expertise to do so. If you feel the challenge is beyond you, however...'

'Beyond me? Beyond Jaquamo Castafiore?' The little man's countenance took on something of the colouration of his coat. 'Show me this data of yours.' He nodded stiffly to Grynner. 'I will have your coordinates within the hour!'

'I don't doubt that for a moment,' Grynner replied dryly, as the Navigator bustled over to a console bristling with dials, levers and a hololithic projector, its importance clearly signalled by the number of prayer seals attached to it.

Horst lowered his voice. 'Nicely done,' he said, with a trace of admiration.

'I'm not sure that I did anything,' Vex replied. 'I merely stated the salient facts. I'm hardly responsible for the way Master Castafiore chooses to interpret them.'

'Nevertheless,' Grynner said, with a trace of amusement, 'he seems sufficiently motivated.'

'Then let's hope he can find what we're looking for,' Horst said, as they began to cross the bridge to where the Navigator was waiting impatiently to begin.

Tarsus High Orbital Docks, Scintilla System
260.993.M41

As ELYRA AND Voyle hurried through the wind-lashed overgrowth of the violated agridome, she kept her gun at the ready, prepared to fire at the first sign of a threat. Not that she'd be prepared to kill a fellow Inquisition operative, unless the alternative was her own death and the premature curtailment of her mission, but she was a good enough shot to keep their heads down, and inflict a disabling wound if that wasn't enough. Something moved in the corner of her eye, and she whirled to face it, her finger tightening on the trigger.

'Elyra!' Zusen clawed her way though a tangle of vines, her face pale, and her voice shrill with panic. 'The Inquisition's found us! They'll kill us all!'

'Not if I can help it,' Elyra said, lowering the weapon. She turned to Voyle. 'What's the quickest way to the tunnels?'

'This way,' Voyle said, his sense of direction apparently unimpeded by the vortex of dust and debris whirling around them.

'We'll suffocate before we get there,' Zusen said, although she seemed a little calmer, no doubt absorbing some of her companions' composure. 'The air's leaking out!'

'Not a problem,' Voyle said. 'It's coming in just as quickly.'

Elyra nodded, understanding what he meant. The entire habitat was vast, the size of a hive in its own right; catastrophic as it seemed this close to the rent in the outer hull, it would take days for the atmosphere it contained to leak away through so relatively small a hole. Even if the entire section was sealed off, as it undoubtedly would be before long, they'd still have plenty of time to make it to safety before the air thinned noticeably.

The deck plates shook under her feet, a solid wall of sound making her stagger, and she whirled, staring in astonishment as something which looked like a starship lifepod slammed into the surface at a velocity she was certain would have injured or killed most of its occupants. Voyle had evidently come to the same conclusion, judging by the expression of vindictive satisfaction on his face. Elyra looked at it a little more closely, before turning away hurriedly; it was matt-black, devoid of insignia, and even inert it seemed threatening. She had no idea what that meant, and she had no intention of waiting long enough to find out.

'The Black Ships,' Zusen moaned, in abject terror. 'They've found us!'

A handful of other fugitive psykers, including Ven and Trosk, had joined them by now, most of them evidently of the same opinion judging by their panicky demeanour and muttered imprecations.

With a resonant clangour of metal against metal, the lifepod suddenly unfolded like a malign flower, its four sides falling away to reveal the interior. Instead of the maimed or dead storm troopers she'd expected to see, other figures were moving in there, very much more dangerous, and very much alive: giants in ceramite armour, carrying heavy-calibre bolters a normal man would hardly have been able to lift, as casually as she hefted her laspistol. As they bounded out onto the deckplates, seeking a target, a storm bolter on a rotating mount above their heads traversed towards the group of fugitives, apparently impelled by a machine-spirit of its own.

'If you want to live, run!' she shouted, taking her own advice, heedless of whether her voice could be heard over the howling wind.

'Good advice,' Voyle agreed at her elbow, as the slowest of the group to react went down in a spray of blood and viscera, torn apart by the first few bolter shells to find their mark. Once again the paradox of her position struck her forcefully; her duty as an agent of the Inquisition was to ensure the capture or death of every single one of the fugitives she fled among, but the demands of her mission made it imperative to help them escape.

'Those are Space Marines!' Zusen shouted, in stunned disbelief. 'We can't fight them!'

'We won't have to.' Voyle tapped the comm-bead in his ear, his voice confident. 'Help's already on its way.'

'Then it better be quick,' Elyra said, flinging herself flat behind a raised bed of some kind of overgrown squash. The bloated vegetables exploded into fragments, along with the torso of the card player, but the thick bank of earth afforded her a modicum of cover. 'Or we'll never make it to the tunnels without being cut to pieces!'

THE SHUTTLE GROUNDED on the clearest space Barda could find, crushing several of the agricultural beds as it settled to the dirt-covered deck plating, and incinerating whatever they'd held in the white-hot torch of its landing thrusters. The smell of smoke, burning vegetables and charred dust punched its way in through the widening gap as the boarding ramp descended, and Keira ran lightly down the metal incline, her sword drawn, disappearing into the swirling murk almost at once.

Drake and Kyrlock followed more slowly, their guns at the ready, pausing at the base of the ramp to secure it with the smooth precision of the Guardsmen they'd both once been. Drake narrowed his eyes against the stinging dust thrown up by the screaming wind, and swung his lasgun, searching for a threat.

'Just like old times,' Kyrlock said, his voice reassuringly confident in Drake's comm-bead. Drake nodded, although he knew his comrade wouldn't see him; Kyrlock's attention would be directed outwards, as his was, searching for any sign of an external threat.

'That's what worries me,' Drake said, reminded all too vividly of the blizzard in which he and Kyrlock had first encountered Inquisitor Finurbi and his entourage. He looked back into the belly of the shuttle. 'We're secure. No sign of movement.'

'Confirm that,' Keira's voice agreed, sounding slightly disappointed. 'No heretics here.'

'Then let's go and find them,' Quillem said, jogging down the ramp, his bolt pistol at the ready. Like the two Guardsmen, he was wearing camo fatigues and body armour, and a bandolier of grenades was slung across his chest. As he came level with Drake, he hesitated, listening to something in his own earpiece, which was evidently tuned to a wider range of frequencies. 'Confirm that. Keep them contained. We want as many as possible alive for interrogation.' He smiled grimly, and glanced at Drake, his voice overlapping strangely with the echo of it in the Guardsman's comm-bead. 'The Deathwatch have made contact.'

'Is Elyra all right?' Kyrlock asked, and Quillem nodded.

'Probably. A blonde woman matching the picts Horst gave us is with them, and seems to be unscathed so far.'

'Holding back is a mistake,' Karnaki said, striding down the ramp to join them, his black robe billowing in the wind. His entourage of servo-skulls followed, bobbing uncertainly in the turbulent air as they tried to maintain formation. 'Any one of the wyrds could be harbouring an Enslaver. Perhaps all of them. Complete eradication is the only way to be sure.'

'None of the ones killed so far were possessed,' Quillem said, 'or the creatures inside them would have manifested as they died.'

'One would be more than sufficient to pose a threat,' Karnaki said, evidently disinclined to discuss the matter further. He strode off into the enveloping duststorm, his ragged tail of servo-skulls trailing after him as best they could.

Drake tapped his comm-bead. 'Keira,' he said, 'Karnaki's heading in your direction. Can you follow without him noticing?'

'Easily,' the young assassin said, her voice full of confidence. 'Do you want me to take him out?'

'No,' Quillem cut in hastily, 'just keep an eye on him.' He paused. 'At least for now.' He exchanged an uneasy look with Drake, apparently sharing at least some of the Guardsman's misgivings about the Ordo Malleus inquisitor. Then he, Drake and Kyrlock left the sanctuary of the shuttle, to face the full fury of the gale.

* * *

The *Emperor's Justice*, Scintilla System
260.993.M41

'BEHOLD!' CASTAFIORE SAID, activating the most sophisticated hololith Horst had ever seen. A starfield appeared,
wavering slightly, like the night sky seen from an agri-
world, rotating gently in the middle of the bridge. None
of the crew members looked up from their duty stations,
so he assumed they were used to this marvel; either that,
or extremely well disciplined. 'The Calixis Sector.' The
Navigator adjusted the controls a little, and the image
shrank, fresh stars appearing at the margins of the field.
'And adjacent regions.'

'These are the locations which appear to be of interest
to the Faxlignae,' Vex said, moving swiftly to the control
lectern, and making some adjustments of his own. A rash
of dots appeared, concentrated for the most part in the
Malfian Subsector, Drusus Marches, and spilling over
into the adjacent Halo Stars. 'As you can see, there seems
to be an underlying pattern, but I lack the expertise to
refine it further.'

'Of course you do,' Castafiore said, but this time his
manner was less brusque and more thoughtful. 'Are any
of these sightings dated?'

Vex nodded. 'For the most part,' he said. 'Although
many of these timings are conjectural at best, given that
the reports are fragmentary, and often filtered through
several layers of rumour and hearsay.' He adjusted the
display again, and figures appeared next to the illuminated dots. 'The most reliable ones are in red, the next
most plausible in orange, and so on through the rest of
the spectrum.' Most of the ones that Horst could see were
coloured blue or violet.

'Most intriguing,' Castafiore said, his tone even more
thoughtful. He gestured. 'That one's clearly wrong. The
warp currents in that region...' He manipulated the
hololith controls, changed the date, and looked at it,

nodding in a self-satisfied fashion which made Horst want to punch him.

Not for the first time, he wished he'd gone with the others, but he was the team leader, and the natural choice to liaise with Inquisitor Grynner's staff. If the man couldn't be trusted, leaving him unobserved would have been foolish in the extreme. He glanced at the grey-robed man beside him, and wondered what was going on inside his head.

Tarsus High Orbital Docks, Scintilla System 260.993.M41

'THEY'RE COMING!' ZUSEN said, and Elyra raised her head cautiously over the metal rampart and the bank of churned-up soil which had protected her. The storm bolter had ceased firing, but the evidence of its fury was written all around them in shredded metal and shattered vegetation. Nothing else in the vicinity could have afforded her any protection against it, and her reluctant respect for Voyle rose a little more; he'd led them unerringly to the only place they could have found safety. Temporarily, at any rate; her stomach knotted at the sight of the squad of Space Marines advancing against their position.

They were hard to focus on at first, their matt-black silhouettes seeming to fade into existence like phantoms as they emerged out of the dust storm, their bolters held casually, ready for use. They were walking with a precise economy of motion, secure in the knowledge of their invincibility, their heavy tread resonating in unison through the deck beneath her feet.

'You've got a gun!' Trosk shouted at her. 'Why don't you use it?'

Before she could reply, one of the pyrokines, goaded by panic, conjured a ball of fire into existence, and flung it at the advancing Astartes. It burst against the chest of one of them; without breaking stride, he levelled his bolter and cracked off a retaliatory round. The pyrokine's head exploded into crimson mist.

'That answer your question?' she said. Trosk nodded, once, his face set.

'Surrender, in the name of the Emperor,' the leading giant said, his voice amplified by a vox-unit set into his helmet. Even above the screaming of the wind, it was deep and resonant, as sure and unwavering as the voice of the Emperor Himself. 'Surrender or die.'

'I'll take the third option,' Voyle said, glancing upwards, and Elyra became aware of a new sound on the edge of her awareness. A dull roar, becoming audible even over the howling of the gale, it grew louder by the second. She tilted her head back, in time to see a strange, rounded vessel swooping low overhead, and a chill gripped her heart. She hadn't seen the xenos ship which had downed the Angelae's Aquila on Sepheris Secundus, but Vex had retrieved picts of it from the crippled shuttle's flight recorder, and she had no doubt at all that what she was seeing was the same craft. Everything about its smooth lines, like a deep-sea predator, seemed wrong to her, completely at odds with the reassuringly solid functionality of the Imperial vessels she was familiar with.

'Is that our pickup?' she asked, as the Astartes turned as one to engage the vessel, their bolters spitting defiance at the looming shape above them. The effort seemed futile, however, the explosive tipped bolts having no discernible effect against the drop-ship's armoured hull. 'Why aren't they firing back?'

Voyle shook his head. 'Because they'd take us out too.' He began to move off, at an oblique angle, keeping behind the banks of earth, and heading in the direction of the descending ship. 'Besides, they've got other ways of keeping the fleas off our backs.'

* * *

KYRLOCK'S FIRST IMPRESSION of the descending drop-ship was a powerful flash of *deja vu*, and he flinched in anticipation of another display of the awesome firepower he'd witnessed being unleashed against the Inquisition fortress on his home world. To his relief, though, it merely grounded, floating gently to the surface of the agridome, heedless of the buffeting winds which surrounded it.

'Is that the vessel you saw before?' Quillem asked, and Kyrlock nodded.

'Yes,' he said. 'And hoped to the Throne I never would again.'

'It's tau,' Quillem said, with a touch of awe. 'Only the Faxlignae could have obtained a prize like that, or would dare to use it.'

'Why don't they use the main weapons?' Drake asked. 'They could take out the Astartes with a single volley.'

'Along with the rest of this dome,' Quillem said. 'They didn't come all this way just to kill their own people.'

'I guess not,' Drake agreed. He pointed to a boarding ramp, which was dropping to the deck even before the strange, rounded spacecraft had fully settled. Figures were moving there, with precision and purpose, and Kyrlock gripped his shotgun with renewed determination. The mercenaries who had attacked the Citadel of the Forsaken on Sepheris Secundus were deploying in battle formation, fanning out to cover the approaches to their ship.

'And talking of killing,' Quillem said, pointing to their leader, the figure with the strange crested helmet Kyrlock had last seen directing the assault in the snowfields of Sepheris Secundus, 'that one's mine.'

'You're welcome to him,' Kyrlock said, with a sidelong glance at Quillem. He'd never met the man before today, but he could read him well enough to know that standing between him and that particular goal would be very unwise indeed.

* * *

The *Emperor's Justice*, Scintilla System
260.993.M41

'HAVE YOU REACHED a conclusion?' Inquisitor Grynner asked, as Castafiore turned away from the hololith. To his faint surprise, the Navigator's reply was almost courteous.

'Perhaps. In a moment...' He manipulated the controls once again, as he had done several times since they'd started, and a few more of the dates and times appended to the dots in the display shifted and changed. 'That pattern would seem to make sense, given what we know of the warp currents in this region of space and time.'

Vex examined the projection in the hololith appraisingly, then glanced at the data-slate in his hand, paging through it with an expression of intense concentration. At length he looked up. 'Those timings are generally within the bounds of possibility,' he agreed. 'The few instances where the matter is still debatable, or the pattern does not appear to fit, can plausibly be argued to fall within the parameters of unreliable reporting.'

Horst shrugged. 'Hardly surprising if you're chasing a myth,' he pointed out.

'Most legends have a germ of truth at their core,' Inquisitor Grynner said, allowing a faint tone of reproof to enter his voice. 'I don't believe for one moment that there's an entire craftworld drifting about the segmentum, but the story of the *Voidwraith* probably conceals something of interest. A derelict vessel, perhaps, or even a space hulk with some eldar artefacts aboard. At any event, a prize big enough to have attracted the attention of the Faxlignae.'

'And now you,' Horst said.

'Quite so,' Grynner agreed, nodding. 'Anything a heretic group wants that badly is best denied them.' He turned back to Castafiore. 'Can you plot its current location?'

'No,' the Navigator said, his tone managing to imply that only an imbecile would have asked such a question in the first place. 'But I can estimate it within a reasonable margin of error. If these revised dates are to be relied on, they chart the journey of something adrift in the warp currents, emerging periodically into the materium in the manner characteristic of such objects. That being so, I can estimate the speed and direction of the current concerned, and...' He manipulated the controls of the hololith, before indicating the image again with a theatrical flourish. 'There we have the most likely location at the present time. Assuming it's not still in the warp, of course.'

A new nebula blossomed suddenly among the Halo Stars, covering a globe of space a handful of light years in diameter.

'Thank you, Master Castafiore,' Grynner said, deciding that a further dose of flattery couldn't hurt. 'Once again, it seems, you've excelled yourself.'

Castafiore swelled visibly beneath his ornately embroidered waistcoat. 'Once again, inquisitor, you show your wisdom in engaging my services.' He adjusted his moustaches, with an air of profound satisfaction. 'How soon do we depart?'

'That rather depends on how our friends are faring aboard the orbital,' the inquisitor replied.

TWENTY-TWO

KEIRA SAW THE heretic drop-ship pass low overhead, but spared it little more than a glance. It didn't pose any immediate threat to her, and even if it did, there was nothing she could do to damage it with the weapons she had. Confident that the swirling dust storm had kept her concealed, she refocused her attention on the gaunt figure of Karnaki, who was still picking his way through the storm-lashed vegetation and the scattered detritus on the grass-choked deck plates with evident purpose.

So far he seemed unaware of her presence but, knowing his formidable psychic powers, she wasn't about to take anything for granted, and hung back, staying just within range of her crossbow; whatever Quillem might say, she neither liked nor trusted the man, and would remove him at the first sign of treachery. For a moment she found herself wondering if she was just looking for an excuse to kill him, in revenge for the way he'd got inside her mind at the Tricorn, before dismissing such speculation as fruitless. She was a weapon in the hand of the Emperor, and was certain that whatever course she took was in accordance with His divine will.

As the strange, smooth lines of the heretic shuttle disappeared into the murk overhead, Karnaki hesitated, then changed the direction he was walking in. For a moment Keira wondered if he was going to meet it, and tightened her grip on the hilt of her sword, suspecting evidence of the treachery she'd anticipated; then she relaxed again. He seemed to be heading for a point somewhere between his original destination, and the point the drop-ship was descending towards. What that portended, she had no idea, but was sure she'd find out soon enough.

ONCE THE FIRST shock of seeing the psyker who'd killed Rufio, and led the massacre of the rest of his team, had worn off, Quillem found himself thinking more rationally again. However much he might yearn for personal revenge, he could hardly fight his way through a strike force of heretical footsoldiers to take it, and challenging so powerful a wyrd would probably just mean his own death in any case. Besides, his duty was clearly to take the abomination alive for interrogation, if that was at all possible.

He glanced at Drake and Kyrlock. They were still thinking like the soldiers they used to be, making use of whatever concealment they could find, and learning all they could about the enemy before closing to contact. Ducking behind the cover afforded by a line of wind-stripped fruit trees, and ignoring the minor scratches inflicted by the flailing branches, he signalled to Drake. 'How are they deploying?'

'Standard pattern,' Drake replied. 'One team to secure the LZ, the rest moving off to the objective. Looks like a couple of full squads at least, maybe more.' After a moment Quillem was able to mentally translate 'full

squad' to ten troopers, the standard size of an Imperial
Guard unit, and nodded.

'They seem to be spreading out,' he said.

'Probably breaking down into combat squads to search
for the wyrds,' Kyrlock said, and Drake nodded.

'That's what I'd do,' he agreed.

'You're the expert,' Quillem said, recalling that Drake
had been a soldier most of his adult life. He voxed a short
situation report to Brother Paulus. 'Be advised that several are carrying xenos weapons,' he concluded. 'Eldar
and tau.'

'It makes no difference,' the Deathwatch Librarian
assured him. 'We will prevail.' His voice had the flat ring
of complete certainty, and Quillem felt his own resolve
stiffen in response.

'So what do we do now?' Drake asked. 'Just sit here,
and wait for the Astartes to take them out for us?'

'No,' Quillem said, indicating the rounded bulk of the
tau vessel, through the swirling dust clouds which surrounded it. 'We're going to take the ship.'

KEIRA AND KARNAKI became aware of the newcomers at
almost the same instant, his preternatural senses apparently detecting their presence as effectively as her
Collegium-honed ones. Figures were moving behind the
swirl of dust, and she wondered for a moment if it was
the Astartes, before the leading silhouettes became close
enough to resolve. Any doubts she might have had about
their identities were abruptly dispelled as soon as she
was able to get a good look at them; their variegated
body armour, no two sets of equipment exactly alike,
marked them out as mercenaries, and the variety of
weapons they carried was no less eclectic. Several were
armed with lasguns, like Drake's, while others favoured
simple and robust firearms. A few carried more exotic
guns, which she didn't recognise, but was prepared to
believe were of xenos manufacture; the vessel they'd

arrived in undoubtedly was, so it would hardly be surprising if some of their personal kit had come from the same source.

Karnaki came to a halt, facing them, his retinue of servo-skulls spreading out into a defensive formation. It could only be a matter of moments before the leading mercenary noticed him, Keira thought, and sheathed her sword in order to ready her crossbow. She could draw the blade quickly enough if she needed it, and it seemed more prudent now to have her ranged weapon ready for use. Much as she detested Karnaki, she couldn't just stand by and watch him get cut down if he was indeed a loyal servant of the Emperor. And if he turned out to be in league with the heretics after all, a single shot would be all she needed to reward him as he deserved.

Just as the leading mercenary drew close enough to detect them, however, his attention was diverted by the unmistakable roar of bolter fire, and several of his comrades went down, blown apart by the heavy-calibre explosive-tipped projectiles. The survivors turned, and began to shoot at something behind them; after a moment more figures could be seen, emerging from the murk, advancing unstoppably though the blizzard of fire.

Keira felt the breath stilling in her throat. No stranger to the arts of violence, she could appreciate the level of casual expertise the huge figures in their space-black armour were bringing to the combat as few other observers could have done. In its own way, she reflected, it was beautiful, a dance of life and death, enacted with the precision of a ballet and the lethal effectiveness of a knife blade.

The first volley of fire from the mercenaries ripped into the middle of the Astartes kill team, las and plasma bolts bursting against their armour, and the hissing, razor-edged discs discharged by the eldar weapons scoring deep gouges in the ceramite. No mere human warriors could have withstood so lethal a barrage, but the Death-watch simply shrugged it off, albeit at the expense of an injury or two; the one with the grey shoulder pad, marked with the snarling sigil of the Space Wolves, moved a little more awkwardly than his battle-brothers after that, favouring his left leg, but keeping pace with them nonetheless. Then the bolters spat again, in furious retribution, and the greater part of the heretic squad died where they stood. The rest turned, melting back into the shroud of dust and the shrieking wind, and the Space Marines followed, as stern and unyielding as the wrath of the Emperor.

Keira turned back to Karnaki, to find that the man from the Ordo Malleus was nowhere in sight. Berating herself for becoming distracted, if only for the handful of seconds the firefight had lasted, she began moving again, in the direction she'd last seen him, hoping to pick up his trail. A flicker of movement in the distance resolved itself into a solitary servo-skull, bouncing in the wind as it tried to keep up with its master, and she picked up her pace to follow it, closing in again on her prey.

'WHAT WAS THAT?' Trosk asked, turning his head in an attempt to distinguish the noises he wanted to hear from the constant shrieking of the wind, as the distant sounds of combat threaded themselves through the turbulent air.

Elyra shrugged. 'Gunfire,' she said. The unmistakable ripping sound of bolters was mingled with the more conventional crack of lasguns and the staccato rattling of assault rifles, which meant that the Astartes had run into some serious resistance; probably a landing party from the heretic drop-ship they'd seen.

'I can feel fear,' Zusen said, pointing into the swirling dust, and smiled wryly. 'Someone else's, I mean.'

'Blood and death, the darkness descends...' Ven babbled, his fragile mind overwhelmed once again.

'This way,' Voyle said decisively, listening to the voice in his comm-bead. 'Our escort's engaging the enemy. They'll keep us screened while we get to the ship.'

Not for long, Elyra thought. The Space Marines would cut down anyone foolish enough to stand against them in a matter of seconds, but perhaps this escort, whoever they were, would have enough sense not to attempt to engage them head-on. Judging by the distinctly sporadic firing, however, they didn't seem to have learned that lesson yet.

'Someone's coming,' Zusen said, pointing in the same direction as before, her face troubled. 'He's seems fearful, but he's not slowing down.'

'Afraid of us?' Trosk asked, and smiled, in the way Elyra remembered him doing after he'd disposed of the bandits in the hold of the *Ursus Innare.* 'Well, he should be.'

Elyra kept moving, in the direction Voyle had indicated, the entire group spreading out a little in their eagerness to reach whatever safety the ship they'd seen had to offer. The battering wind made it hard to stay orientated, and she made sure she kept Voyle in sight; every few moments he would listen to the voice in his earpiece, and change direction a little, presumably in response to reports of the whereabouts of the Astartes. The sound of gunfire had died away by now, although whether their escorts had disengaged, or simply been wiped out to a man, she couldn't have said.

'Look out!' Ven shouted, pointing into the swirling dust, either entering a lucid phase in the nick of time, or sensing the danger in his delirium. A line of servo-skulls was swooping out of the murk, heading straight for the ragged group of fugitive wyrds. 'Death among the dead!'

An instant later his words were vindicated, as a las-bolt impacted on the earth at his feet, and the wyrds scattered, seeking what cover they could. Elyra dived for the ground, and rolled under a long-abandoned water tank, which must have been a part of the old irrigation system;

as she did so, another bolt kicked up a gout of dirt where she'd been standing an instant before.

She moved the pistol in her hand, tracking one of the skulls, but it was a tricky shot; the target was small, fast-moving and jinking erratically in the crosswinds. She squeezed the trigger, and was rewarded with a puff of pulverising bone: the tiny servitor wavered uncertainly for a moment, then broke off, spiralling away as the wind took it.

'Good shot,' Voyle said, from a few metres away. 'You must have damaged the grav unit.'

'Lucky shot,' Elyra corrected, trying to find a fresh target. She couldn't tell how many of the whirling skulls there were swooping around them, but there must have been half a dozen at least. Twin laspistol barrels protruded from their eye sockets, firing continuously, and the screaming around her made it obvious that a few of the shots were finding their mark.

'Allow me,' Voyle said, and, to her astonishment, she realised that he was standing out in the open, completely unprotected. The skulls circled, and began to swoop towards him, firing as they came, but every las-bolt seemed to deviate at the last minute, expending itself harmlessly at his feet. Then he gestured dismissively, and the skulls scattered, thrown aside by the force of his will. Most simply vanished into the vortex of air, whirled away through the rent in the dome above them, but a couple shattered against stanchions and decaying agricultural equipment in shards of splintered bone and twisted metal.

'Impressive,' a new voice said, and a figure dressed entirely in black, his robes billowing around him in the wind, seemed to solidify out of the swirling dust. 'It seems we'll have to do this the hard way after all.'

CAPTURING THE HERETICS' shuttle might have sounded simple enough while Quillem was explaining his plan, but when it came to putting it into operation, the task turned out to be just as difficult and dangerous as Drake had expected. Keira would undoubtedly have been able to sneak up on the sentries at the foot of the boarding ramp undetected, and dispatch them swiftly and silently once she'd done so, but the three Inquisition operatives lacked her infiltration skills, and were forced to use more direct methods.

'In position,' Drake voxed, sighting on the nearest sentry down the length of his lasgun, and hoping that the small grove of fruit bushes he'd crawled among would be sufficient concealment. He couldn't see any sign of Kyrlock or Quillem, but then he hadn't expected to, the stinging grit clotting the air reducing visibility to no more than a few score metres. The wind-blown haze was the biggest advantage they had: the sentries seemed alert, constantly scanning their surroundings for any sign of a threat, and approaching the shuttle too closely without something to keep them hidden from view would simply draw down a barrage of suppressive fire.

'Me too,' Kyrlock said, 'and it's rutting uncomfortable. It smells like something died in here.'

Narrowing his eyes against the abrasive wind, Drake scanned the metal bin on the far side of the boarding ramp where his friend was supposed to be concealed. It was far closer to the heretic vessel than he'd dared approach himself, but Kyrlock had spent most of his life stalking game in the forests of their home world, and although his ability to move silently and undetected was far inferior to Keira's, it was still a great deal better than Drake could have managed. Just as well, too; the shotgun he carried was only effective at short range, and once the attack began, he wouldn't get a second chance to use it.

'What did you expect?' Drake asked. 'It's for storing fertiliser.'

'Well, it wouldn't be the first time I've been in the–' Kyrlock began, only to be interrupted by Quillem.

'All set. Go on my mark.'

'Confirm,' Drake said crisply, fighting down a sudden flare of nerves, the tension-relieving banter already forgotten.

'Confirm,' Kyrlock repeated, almost in the same breath.

'Three seconds,' Quillem said, and Drake counted them down under his breath. 'Go!'

As Drake squeezed the trigger, dropping the guard he'd already had in his sights, the sound of an explosion echoed in the air around them, audible even over the howling wind. The rest of the sentries turned to look towards the raised beds where Quillem had lobbed a grenade at random to distract them, and Kyrlock burst from cover, his shotgun blazing as he came. He caught one man in the hail of shot, but the mercenary's body armour absorbed most of the impact: he was already bringing his weapon round to bear when Drake fired for a second time, taking him in the head.

Belatedly becoming aware that they were under attack, the three remaining sentries rallied, aiming as one at the only target they could see: Kyrlock. Fearful for his friend, Drake fired again, but the shot was hurried, and ricocheted from the helmet of a woman carrying a lasgun like his own. She staggered from the impact, too dazed to present much of a threat for the next second or two, but he'd revealed his location now, and one of the remaining guards turned away from Kyrlock to return fire. He was carrying one of the strange, smooth-sided rifles Drake had seen the mercenaries using in the assault on the Citadel of the Forsaken, and, aware of the damage it could do, the Guardsman was already rolling desperately away as the bolt of plasma arrived.

He only just made it, the acrid scent of baking earth sour in his nostrils, dazzled by the glare and scorched by the heat of the detonation. Coughing, he scrabbled away from the burning bushes, and tried to make out what was happening through the strobing after-images clogging his vision.

Quillem had joined the fight for the boarding ramp too by now, taking down one of the guards threatening Kyrlock with a round from his bolt pistol as he charged forwards. Suddenly presented with two targets, the other man hesitated, the muzzle of his weapon wavering between them, until Kyrlock pulled the trigger of his shotgun again; at so close a range the hail of shot was devastating, reducing the fellow's arm to a bloody ruin, and making him lose his grip on the strange, bulbous rifle. As it fell to the deck plating, Kyrlock reversed the shotgun, smashing the butt into the mercenary's face, and he fell heavily to the deck.

Orientated again, Drake began to run towards the drop-ship, as Quillem and Kyrlock began advancing up the ramp towards the sole surviving sentry, the woman he'd stunned with his third las-bolt. Backing away, she dropped her weapon, and raised her hands.

'Enough!' she shouted, an edge of panic in her voice. 'I give up!'

'Smart choice,' Quillem said, pulling a loop of plastek from his belt pouch, and securing her wrists with a quick tug. He glanced up as Drake reached the foot of the incline. 'What kept you?'

'A quick smoke,' Drake said, indicating the burning fruit bushes he'd been hiding behind. He hadn't thought Quillem was capable of cracking a joke at a time like this, and was agreeably surprised by the fleeting smile he received in response to his own. Perhaps the man was all right after all.

'This one'll live,' Kyrlock said, stooping briefly to check on the man he'd knocked unconscious.

'Good.' Quillem nodded, glancing at their prisoner like a canid getting wind of fresh meat. 'That's two to interrogate at least.'

'Tusdaie, Rubi, Free Company Trooper, contract number seven three double six–' the woman began, and Quillem backhanded her casually across the face.

'When I want to hear anything from a heretic bitch, I'll beat it out of you,' he said. To his evident surprise, instead of being cowed, Rubi stared back at him scornfully.

'You have no idea who you're dealing with, do you?' she said.

'We'll find out,' Quillem assured her. 'Believe me. And if you're so keen to enlighten us, you can be first in the queue when we get back to the Tricorn.'

'The Tricorn?' To Drake's surprise, the woman seemed puzzled rather than terrified, as he would have expected. 'You're Inquisition?' She shook her head. 'There's been a major screw-up somewhere...'

'Damn right. And you just made it,' Quillem said, shoving her ahead of him up the ramp. 'Ladies first. In case your friends inside have got any ideas about jumping us.'

'Works for me,' Kyrlock agreed. 'Let's get this barge secured, so Hybris can start going though the cogitator banks.'

'Easier said than done,' a new voice cut in, and Drake brought his lasgun up, a chill of pure dread knotting his stomach. The psyker in the strange, crested helmet he'd seen leading the assault on the Inquisition fortress on Sepheris Secundus was standing at the top of the ramp. He tried to pull the trigger, but before he could complete the motion, something picked him up and threw him aside, like the toy of a petulant child.

He hit the ground hard, the wind driven from his chest, and tried to claw some of the screaming air into his lungs. As he staggered to his feet he saw Kyrlock swatted aside too, and prayed to the Emperor that he'd be equally lucky.

'You bastard, you killed my people!' Quillem brought the bolt pistol round on aim, but fared no better than Drake had done; a second later he smacked into the deck plates next to the Guardsman, and lay still.

'Not thoroughly enough, it seems.' The man in the crested helmet sounded amused, Drake thought, looking around frantically for his lasgun. There was no sign of it, and he reached for the Scalptaker in its shoulder rig instead. 'But I can soon remedy that.'

FROM HER VANTAGE point in the lee of a cracked and corroding atmospheric condenser, Keira watched the confrontation between Karnaki and the leader of the psykers. The man simply stood there as the inquisitor raised his bolt pistol, and with a thrill of horror she recalled her own paralysis in the face of Karnaki's power of compulsion. For a moment she hesitated, the crossbow a reassuring weight in her hand, and wondered whether she ought to intervene; but the man was a wyrd, and a heretic, and more than deserving of the Emperor's judgement. Her assignment, like the rest of the Angelae, was to extract Elyra if possible, and determine the final destination of the fleeing psykers. So far, Karnaki didn't seem to be hindering that; quite the opposite, in fact, if he reduced the number of wyrds standing between her and her friend.

An instant before the black-garbed inquisitor could fire, Elyra's laspistol cracked, and Karnaki staggered, the ugly bloom of a las-bolt hit cratering his shoulder. The bolt pistol dropped from his hand, and the psyker suddenly moved, closing in on his antagonist with astonishing speed.

Interesting, Keira mused to herself. It seemed that Karnaki needed to concentrate in order to control people, and if he was surprised, or hurt, his influence was broken. That could be a significant weakness, and she determined to tell the others as soon as possible. Her hand rose to the comm-bead in her ear, then fell away again. It was possible the Ordo Malleus inquisitor was monitoring the frequency they used; better to wait until she was able to tell them face to face.

The psyker lashed out, apparently channelling his energy through his own body, striking Karnaki hard enough to send the inquisitor reeling back, before falling heavily to the ground. Keira tensed, levelling the crossbow, intending to kill the wyrd when he moved in to finish the inquisitor off, but instead he turned away, gesturing to the little knot of cowering wyrds to follow him.

'Hurry!' he called, his voice attenuated by the gale. 'The ship's under attack: they won't wait for much longer!'

Elyra jogged over to join the man, with a convincing display of concern for him, and they exchanged a few words which Keira couldn't hear over the screaming of the wind. Then both of them, and their companions, passed out of sight.

Folding the crossbow, and stowing it on her thigh, Keira trotted over to where Karnaki had fallen. He was still alive, trying to drag himself to his feet, and looked up with an expression of relief as he registered her approach.

'Miss Sythree,' he said. 'Thank the Throne. Go after them, and kill them all...'

Keira nodded. It was the only way to be sure. Even Elyra was a potential danger to the whole system. As she turned away, her hand falling to the hilt of her sword, an idea struck her, and she kicked down hard, grinding the heel of her boot into the wound on the inquisitor's shoulder. His breath hissed through his teeth, and Keira found the idea of killing Elyra didn't seem so inescapable after all. She drew her blade, and rested it against Karnaki's neck.

'I decide who I'm going to kill,' she said. 'Not you. And if you ever try to swive with my head again, you're going to the top of the list. Are we both clear about that?'

'We are indeed,' Karnaki said, a hint of something she couldn't read flickering behind his eyes.

'Good.' She turned away, in the direction the wyrds had taken. Emperor willing, she might still be in time to rescue Elyra.

* * *

'DANULD?' KYRLOCK VOXED. He'd landed hard, but one of the agribeds had broken his fall, some pulpy red vegetables he didn't recognise smearing his face and body armour. Somewhere along the parabola he'd described through the air, he'd become detached from his shotgun, but his chainaxe was still slung across his shoulders, a reassuring presence. He rolled to his feet, drawing it, and activating the device. The teeth whined into motion, and he began moving towards the alien ship again.

'Still here,' Drake said, to his intense relief. 'Quillem's down, unconscious. Looks like it's up to us.'

'Wonderful,' Kyrlock said. 'Any ideas?' He looked around, trying to catch sight of his friend through the windblown debris; after a moment he saw Drake moving forwards, crouching to take advantage of what cover he could, his revolver in his hand. Another squad of the heretic troopers was forming up behind their leader, weapons at the ready, and he sighed ruefully. As if the odds against them weren't great enough as they were.

'What I said before,' Drake replied. 'Let the Astartes deal with them. They're on their way.'

Kyrlock felt a sudden flare of hope. 'How do you know?' he asked.

'I borrowed Quillem's comm-bead. He wasn't using it.' Drake flattened himself against the side of a storage bin. 'Once they arrive, we go for the psyker. Maybe he'll be too distracted to hex us again.'

'And maybe he won't,' Kyrlock grumbled. 'That's a hell of a plan.'

'Best I've got,' Drake said. 'Can you think of a better one?'

'Run like rut,' Kyrlock said, thinking of their flight from the army of witches on Sepheris Secundus. But neither of them would, he knew; their service with the Inquisition had changed them both.

Then there was no time for further reflection, as the howling air was ripped by a volley of bolter fire: fixing his eyes on the psyker, he charged forwards, his chainaxe screaming almost as loudly as he was.

'WHAT'S THAT?' ZUSEN asked, as a renewed burst of firing echoed through the shrieking air.

Voyle listened to the voice in his comm-bead for a moment, his face grave. 'Trouble,' he said, picking up his pace, and moving off to the left.

'I thought the ship was that way,' Elyra said, pointing in the direction they'd been moving.

'It is,' Voyle replied shortly. 'But we need to circle round. Otherwise we'll get cut to pieces before we get a chance to board.' He glanced at her as he spoke, and his voice softened. 'Thanks for what you did back there. The bastard had me. I've never met such a powerful 'path.'

Elyra shrugged. It had been necessary to preserve her cover, and continue with the mission; without Voyle, she'd never be able to discover where the wyrds were going. 'You think I'd let anything happen to you while you still owe me money?' she said, allowing her voice to hint that she might have had less mercenary reasons for saving his life, but wasn't about to admit it.

'Not for a second,' Voyle said, picking up on the unspoken subtext.

'What the hell's happening?' Trosk asked, as they came in sight of the lander at last. Soldiers were deployed around the boarding ramp, firing desperately at the black-armoured Astartes, who were picking them off with almost contemptuous ease. They were led by a man in a strange, crested helmet, and even from this distance Elyra could feel the strength of the power he wielded; it was clear that without his warp-spawned talents, the fight would have been over by now.

'People are dying to save your neck,' Elyra snapped. 'So get aboard while there still a few left.' Keeping low, she began to run for the boarding ramp, Voyle at her side, and the others straggling out behind.

She glanced at the progress of the battle, and, with a sudden jolt of shock, recognised Kyrlock breaking cover to charge forwards brandishing his chainaxe. Drake was there too, running in from another direction to join the Astartes, although what assistance he thought he might be able to render was beyond her.

The psyker in the helmet gestured towards the attackers, knocking one of the Space Marines to the ground for a moment, and as the sable giant rose, bringing his bolter to bear once again, her feet rang on metal. Suddenly aware that she was aboard the strange craft at last she turned, cut off from the view outside, and saw no more of the fight.

DRAKE RAISED HIS pistol, taking aim at the man in the helmet, heedless of the las-bolts and more exotic forms of death bursting around him. Kyrlock was on the move too, and if he could just distract the man for a crucial few seconds, his friend would be within reach of his target. In the corner of his eye he could see movement on the ramp of the drop-ship, the troopers guarding it apparently pulling back aboard, but he had no time to think about that; it just meant that the psyker would be joining them, and out of reach of the vengeance he hoped to wreak, within a matter of moments.

Something huge and black blocked his sight line for a second, a downed Space Marine regaining his feet after being knocked back by a bolt of psychokinetic force, and he chafed at the delay.

'Enough!' the Astartes with the intricate robe over his armour said, advancing on the psyker. The wyrd gestured again, apparently intending to unleash another demonstration of his power, and faltered, as the physical world unaccountably failed to obey his will. Drake felt a sudden surge of hope; it seemed the Space Marine could somehow nullify the man's arcane abilities.

The psyker had evidently come to the same conclusion, turning and running for the boarding ramp, which was now clear; a few troopers were crouched at the top of it, seeking protection from the rain of bolter fire behind the impenetrable armour plate of the vessel's hull, and keeping up sporadic covering fire in an attempt to allow their leader to reach safety.

He never made it. Kyrlock lunged forwards, his chainaxe screaming, and struck, the spinning adamantium teeth gouging deep into the xenos armour he wore. The psyker turned, seizing the shaft of the polearm, and grappling with the Guardsman for possession of it.

Drake hesitated, the Scalptaker aimed at the middle of the melee, unwilling to fire for fear of hitting his friend. The Astartes evidently felt the same way, preferring to keep up their barrage against the ship, preventing any of the troopers aboard from attempting to rescue their leader.

Suddenly the psyker fell backwards, the shaft of a crossbow bolt protruding from the neck joint of his armour, where the helmet met the breastplate, and Drake turned, to see Keira jogging towards them.

'Is Elyra here?' she called, and Drake shook his head. 'I was following the group she's with.'

'They're already aboard,' Drake said, suddenly realising what the movement on the ramp he'd taken so little notice of must have meant, and Kyrlock nodded in confirmation.

'I saw her. She's still with Voyle.'

'Then she's out of our reach,' Keira said flatly, turning to look at the drop-ship. The ramp was retracting, and the pitch of the engines was rising; then the duststorm enveloping them grew more dense, as it lifted from the ground.

'We've still got this one,' Drake said, turning to the fallen psyker. 'Perhaps he can tell us where they've gone.'

'He won't be telling us anything,' Kyrlock said, pulling the man's helmet off. His head lolled slackly, the eyes blank, and a gush of blood spattered the dirt, released from the wound in his neck as the helmet came free.

'What's that?' Keira asked, bending down to the corpse. A thin chain was round the man's neck, and she pulled it over his head, releasing a small gold medallion from inside his chest armour. 'Sinning hell!'

'Oh rut,' Drake said, as she held it up. It bore a stylised letter I, inset with a skull; a sigil they all knew intimately. 'I think we just killed an inquisitor.'

EPILOGUE

The *Emperor's Justice*, Scintilla System
260.993.M41

THE GATHERING WHICH took place in the conference suite aboard Inquisitor Grynner's starship in the wake of the attack was a subdued one. Horst met Keira and the other Angelae in the hangar bay, his mood as sombre as theirs clearly was.

'I'm glad you made it back,' he said to her, as they took the short journey through the intervening corridors together, conscious that there was still a great deal left unresolved between them.

She nodded. 'Thanks. But Elyra didn't.'

'We'll find her,' Horst said, grimly determined, as they took their seats at the table. The Angelae looked after their own. Any other outcome was unthinkable.

Vex, who was already seated, nodded his agreement. 'The coordinates we deduced are quite promising,' he said.

Inquisitor Grynner coughed, attracting everyone's attention, and toyed briefly with the medallion Keira had recovered, before speaking. 'It seems,' he said dryly, 'that

413

Carolus was right to invoke Special Circumstances. This changes everything.'

'With respect, inquisitor,' Quillem put in from the opposite side of the table, 'I don't see that it does. We already knew he didn't trust anyone in the Calixis Conclave.' Almost everyone present glanced involuntarily at Karnaki, who had resumed his former seat at the opposite end of the table from Grynner, his shoulder stiff where Elyra's lasbolt had struck him. He seemed a little less imposing without his retinue of servo-skulls, but judging by his demeanour, his self-confidence remained undiminished.

'True,' Grynner said. 'But now we have proof of a long-standing rumour which I've always been reluctant to believe.'

'And that would be?' Karnaki asked dryly.

Grynner adjusted his spectacles. 'That the Faxlignae was originally founded by Radical members of my own ordo,' he said flatly, 'and might still be controlled by them.'

'Whether or not that's true,' Horst said, trying to absorb the implications of this revelation, 'it doesn't change our duty. We have to find out what they're planning, and stop it.'

'Quite so,' Grynner said, and looked around the table. 'Master Castafiore is plotting a course to the region of the Halo Stars we believe to be of interest to the heretics. But it's Astra Incognita, beyond the bounds of the Imperium. Throne alone knows what we'll find when we get there.'

'It doesn't matter,' Keira said, speaking for the first time, and eliciting nods of agreement from around the table. 'The Emperor remains our strongest shield.'

'Then it appears we must rely on His protection,' Grynner said, 'no less than your colleague, and Inquisitor Finurbi.'

Horst nodded again, seeing his own thought reflected in Keira's eyes.

Wherever they are.

ABOUT THE AUTHOR

Sandy Mitchell is a pseudonym of Alex Stewart, who has been working as a freelance writer for the last couple of decades. He has written science fiction and fantasy in both personae, as well as television scripts, magazine articles, comics, and gaming material. Apart from both miniatures and roleplaying gaming his hobbies include the martial arts of Aikido and Iaido, and pottering around on the family allotment.